Abou

Laura Martin write
adventurous undercu
spends her time worki
where she lives with he
Laura loves to lose herself in a book, and has been
known to read from cover to cover in a single day when
the story is particularly gripping. She also loves to
travel—especially to visit historical sites and far-flung
shores.

Regency Rogues

Regency Rogues:

Wives Wanted

LAURA MARTIN

MILLS & BOON

First Published in Great Britain 2020
By Mills & Boon, an imprint of HarperCollins*Publishers*
1 London Bridge Street, London, SE1 9GF

REGENCY ROGUES: WIVES WANTED © 2020 Harlequin Books S.A.

An Earl in Want of a Wife © 2016 Laura Martin
Heiress on the Run © 2017 Laura Martin

ISBN: 978-0-263-27952-8

0420

MIX
Paper from
responsible sources
FSC™ C007454

This book is produced from independently certified FSC™ paper to ensure responsible forest management.

For more information visit: www.harpercollins.co.uk/green

Printed and bound in Spain
by CPI, Barcelona

AN EARL IN WANT OF A WIFE

For Jack, my constant companion,
your smile melts my heart.

And for Luke, every day with you is
even better than the last.

Chapter One

Lizzie peered out of the carriage window and tried to calm her racing pulse. Never before in her life had she felt so alone. Before boarding the boat bound for London she'd heard so much about the city, but now she was here she couldn't quite believe how busy and crowded it was. Momentarily she longed for the rolling hills just outside Bombay, but then silently reprimanded herself. She hadn't been happy there, not truly. This was the opportunity she'd been waiting for her entire life.

As the carriage slowed Lizzie let the curtain fall back into place and tried to put herself into the role she was to play for the next few weeks. For at least a fortnight she was no longer to be Miss Elizabeth Eastway, orphaned daughter of a penniless second son. Instead she would play the role of Miss Amelia Eastway, cherished only child and heiress to a substantial fortune. She found herself smiling ruefully, knowing Amelia was the only person in the world who could have persuaded her to go along with such a ruse. If anyone else had asked, she would have laughed and shook her head, then proceeded to bury it in whatever book it was she was reading, but Amelia was different. Amelia was the sister she'd never had, her only champion and friend in a world that did not favour penniless orphans. Lizzie knew she would jump in the path of a crazed horse to save Amelia, so when her cousin had asked her to swap identities for a couple of weeks she could hardly say no.

Of course, Amelia hadn't thought the whole thing through. Lizzie knew by agreeing to swap identities with her cousin it would be she who suffered in the long-term. She didn't have a large dowry or a substantial inheritance; people would forgive Amelia, but penniless Lizzie would be ruined. If her cousin had realised that, Lizzie knew she wouldn't have asked, but as always Amelia hadn't even stopped to consider the consequences. In Lizzie's mind she didn't have much to lose, so when Amelia asked, she agreed. It wasn't as though she ever expected to make a good marriage or start a family, so Lizzie kept telling herself she wasn't sacrificing that much for her beloved cousin.

The carriage rolled to a stop and Lizzie took a second to compose herself, trying to mimic the sunny smile that came so easily to Amelia's face. She had to be cheerful and outgoing these next few weeks; there was no one to hide behind, no one to take the focus off her. All her life Lizzie had been kept in the shadows and she'd rather got used to it there. Now she was being pushed into the light and she just hoped she didn't let her cousin down.

A footman opened her door and Lizzie allowed him to help her down. She stared up in awe of the mansion they'd stopped across the street from and had to remind herself not to gawp.

'If you'd just follow me, miss,' the footman said, indicating they were to cross the road and ascend the steps to the very house she was in awe of.

Lizzie nodded, stepping out on to the street.

Immediately she heard a man shout and a horse let out a snort. Spinning to her left, Lizzie cowered backwards. The beast was almost upon her, rearing up, hooves flying through the air towards her face. Lizzie stumbled and lost her balance, landing with a jarring thud on the dusty street. She wished she could close her eyes, wished she could look away, but it was as though she were entranced. As if in slow motion she saw the rider pull on the reins, trying desperately to bring the beast under control, but Lizzie knew it was too late. The horse would trample her and there was nothing she or the rider could do about it.

With an almighty shout the rider threw himself off the horse and used the momentum to push the beast to one side. The horse's hooves met the ground just inches from Lizzie's head and she shuddered at the sound of the impact.

For a long few seconds the entire street was silent, as if digesting the near tragedy. Then the horse whinnied and the spell was broken. Half a dozen people rushed towards her and the rider, but he motioned for them to stay back. Slowly he rose from the ground, limping slightly from where he had landed on one leg, and approached his horse. Lizzie watched as he soothed the beast, stroking its mane and speaking quietly in a gentle tone. After handing the reins to a young lad he turned back to Lizzie.

Lizzie swallowed and tried to meet his stare, but she could tell he was furious. Slowly he walked towards her and she felt at a distinct disadvantage sitting on the dusty ground, her skirts tangled between her legs and her body still shaking from fear.

He stopped when he was almost directly above her, his body blocking out the sun. Lizzie swallowed and offered a weak smile.

'What were you thinking?' he asked in clipped tones.

Lizzie opened her mouth to answer but found no sound would come out. She motioned vaguely with one hand.

The rider stared at her for what felt like an eternity, then offered his hand.

Lizzie reached up and took it, and allowed him to effort-lessly pull her to her feet.

Now she was standing Lizzie felt a little more at ease, but only a little. He still held her hand in his own, so their bodies were quite close together and for the first time Lizzie was able to make out his features. She gulped. Trust her to be almost trampled to death by the most handsome man in London.

As she studied him Lizzie felt his eyes roaming over her features. Immediately she stiffened. Lizzie knew she wasn't a hideous crone, but she also knew she wasn't what society deemed to be attractive. Her hair was just a little too brown, her skin had a few too many freckles, and where men seemed to admire petite women Lizzie could look most men in the eye without straining. Many she even had a good view of their bald spots.

It had happened so many times that she could see this man's thoughts as he looked her over. Within two seconds he had dismissed her.

'Be more careful in future,' he said with authority.

Lizzie found herself nodding despite his imperious tone. She wished she had mastered Amelia's haughty look. Her cousin could slay a man merely by raising an eyebrow. Lizzie supposed it came with confidence and probably being a stunning petite blonde didn't hurt, either.

She watched as he strode back to his horse, athletically mounted the beast and moved off. Their whole encounter couldn't have lasted for more than a minute, but it had been enough to crush any confidence Lizzie had summoned to face the world as Miss Amelia Eastway.

The footman appeared back at her side.

'Are you harmed, miss?' he asked, his face ashen.

Lizzie smiled at him kindly, knowing he would likely get the blame for her clumsiness.

'Not at all,' she said with a false bravado. 'Just a little shaken.'

Carefully they crossed the road and ascended the steps. As they reached the top the front door opened and Lizzie was ushered inside.

'My dear Amelia, what on earth happened?' A woman in her midforties rushed forward to greet her.

Lizzie supposed this was Amelia's aunt Mathilda. And the young woman standing in the corner with a smug grin on her face was probably her odious cousin Harriet.

Lizzie felt the colour start to rise in her cheeks as she began to mumble something about falling over, then she realised this would never do. She was meant to be Miss Amelia Eastway, the sort of young woman other people admired. She needed to start acting the part.

'It was most harrowing,' she said, pressing her fingers to her temple. 'I was crossing the street and I was almost trampled by a careless rider.'

Aunt Mathilda rushed to her side and took her hand.

'What an awful ordeal for you, my dear, why don't you come and sit down?'

Lizzie allowed the older woman to lead her into a drawing room, but as she left the hall she caught a glimpse of the expression on Harriet's face. Lizzie knew then that Harriet had seen the whole episode and knew that Lizzie's carelessness was to blame.

'You must be exhausted after such a long journey.'

'It was only an hour from the dock.'

'Mother meant from India,' Harriet said as she followed them into the room.

'Oh, of course,' Lizzie mumbled.

'Although I never understand why people insist that travelling wearies them. It's not as though you have to sail the ship yourself.'

Lizzie thought of the endless days of nausea and disequilibrium, the nights she'd spent staring at the rocking ceiling and wishing it were all over. Even now, hours after disembarking, she still felt a little wobbly.

'Have you ever been on a long sea voyage?' she asked sweetly.

Harriet shook her head.

'No, I didn't think so.'

Lizzie perched on the edge of an uncomfortable armchair and watched as the young woman's eyes narrowed to slits, and realised she'd just made a big mistake. Her life for the next couple of weeks would be hard enough without making an enemy in the place that was supposed to be her sanctuary.

Either Aunt Mathilda didn't notice the animosity between the two girls, or she deliberately ignored it.

'I can't believe my dear little niece Amelia is here sitting in my drawing room,' Aunt Mathilda said. 'The last time I saw you, you were a lovely little thing with pigtails and a gap between your front teeth.'

Lizzie smiled serenely, trying to quell the sickness in her stomach. No doubt Aunt Mathilda was remembering the sweet little blonde-haired girl and wondering when she had turned into this tall brunette. Luckily Amelia's father had settled in India fourteen years ago and Amelia hadn't seen her aunt since. Hopefully the older woman would just assume time had changed her sister's daughter beyond recognition.

'We've got such a busy week planned, my dear,' Aunt Mathilda said as she rang the bell for a maid. 'We've got dress fittings and shopping trips galore, and at the end of the week you shall make your début.'

Lizzie's eyes widened.

'So soon?' she managed to ask, her voice breaking a

little with the surprise. Amelia had assured her it would be weeks before she was meant to make her début. The plan had always been for Lizzie to step into her shoes for a fortnight at the most, and that fortnight would be spent settling into London life, going shopping and strolling round the parks. Neither of them had ever expected Lizzie would actually have to go out in public as Miss Amelia Eastway.

'Your father was quite insistent,' Aunt Mathilda said softly. 'He instructed that you make your début as soon as possible.'

Of course it was all Uncle Robert's doing. Even Lizzie had to admit Amelia had become a handful in the past few months, although she, of course, knew the reason behind this rebellion. Amelia's father had sent his daughter to London so she would find a husband and settle down, and by extension not be his problem any longer. It made sense that he had wanted Amelia to be out husband-hunting as soon as possible—it meant less time for her to cause mischief.

Lizzie knew she couldn't be introduced to London society as Amelia, but right now she couldn't think of a good reason to give Aunt Mathilda, so instead she just smiled and nodded. She would have to feign an illness, or invent some family tragedy that required a period of mourning. Anything that would push back the début until Amelia returned. Her cousin had promised she would not leave Lizzie alone in London for more than a week, two at the most, and flighty though Amelia was she normally kept her promises. Amelia simply wanted to have a few days of freedom to find the young officer she was enamoured with before being introduced to society. Lizzie had no doubt they would both get into trouble for this ruse, but she was certain Aunt Mathilda would want to keep any hint of the scandal quiet and that would only be possible if she hadn't been presented to London as the season's most eligible heiress.

'But let's not get ahead of ourselves,' Aunt Mathilda said. 'You've had a long and tiring journey and I'm sure you just want to settle in and rest. I will have one of the maids bring some light refreshments to your room.'

'Thank you,' Lizzie said and stood. She smiled at her aunt and cousin and exited, but instinct made her pause outside the door, just out of sight.

'It's a good job she's rich,' Harriet said quietly.

Lizzie heard Aunt Mathilda tut at her daughter, but no reprimand was forthcoming.

'Don't tell me you're not thinking the same, Mother. She's hardly beautiful and she's one of the most awkward people I've ever seen.'

'Don't complain, Harriet, you'll have enough to contend with when the gentlemen hear how much her dowry is. We want you to make a good match as well, remember.'

'It's so unfair,' the younger woman said. 'She'll get to marry someone titled and be a great lady, all because her father has made money in trade. She doesn't deserve it. Not after what her father did to us.'

Lizzie realised she didn't want to hear any more. Quietly she slipped away, following a maid upstairs and trying to fight the tears that were forming in her eyes.

Chapter Two

Daniel was in a foul mood and he knew he only had himself to blame. He was standing on the perimeter of the Prestons' ballroom trying to look inconspicuous. And failing quite spectacularly. Already the eligible young women were beginning to flutter their eyelashes in his direction and, even worse, their mothers were looking at him with undisguised interest. He hadn't attended a society event like this in years; in fact, he could count the number he'd shown his face at on one hand.

Which meant all the young ladies of marriageable age were immediately intrigued, and convinced he must be there to search for a wife.

Daniel groaned. He was there to look for a wife. As little as he wanted his current lifestyle to change, a visit to his accountant that afternoon had put things into perspective. He needed money, and he needed it soon. Hence his presence at the Prestons' ball this evening, and his need to be sociable and personable.

'What on earth brings you here, Blackburn?' A familiar voice broke into Daniel's thoughts.

Daniel turned and smiled his first genuine smile all evening. The night wouldn't be such a disaster with Fletcher by his side.

'I'd have thought that was obvious,' Daniel said, keeping his expression impassive. 'I'm here for the scintillating company.'

Fletcher moved to Daniel's side and perused the ballroom.

'You're creating quite the stir. I've heard the name Lord Burwell mentioned at least a dozen times and I've only been here five minutes.'

Daniel knew he should be pleased, he should want every eligible young woman with a good dowry thrown at him that evening, but he couldn't quite conjure up the enthusiasm.

Fletcher looked at him appraisingly. 'You're looking for a wife,' he said in a matter-of-fact tone after a few seconds.

'Good God, is it that obvious?' Daniel asked, hoping he wasn't coming off as desperate.

'There are only three reasons a man comes to these events,' Fletcher explained. 'And seeing as you don't have any female relatives to escort and you don't need to do any social climbing, it must be to look for a wife.'

Daniel nodded glumly. Fletcher was right, of course, he was there to look for a wife and he felt rather shocked by the fact. Just yesterday he had been a bachelor, firm in his conviction that he would never marry, happy to flirt with any woman who crossed his path, but unwilling to settle down. The problem was now he had no choice—he had to marry. The idea of finding a young woman with a good fortune and marrying her to acquire that fortune didn't sit well with him. In fact, he felt rather disgusted with himself that he was about to become one of the fortune hunters he so despised in society, but he really had no other option. He kept telling himself his future wife would be well-treated, she'd gain a title and an old family name, but he felt bad that she wouldn't be loved. For one thing Daniel was sure of was that he was never going to risk his heart again. He'd loved once and the experience had left him emotionally battered. He wouldn't allow that to happen a second time.

'There's no need to look so down, old chap. We'll have you dancing with the most interesting and beautiful before the evening's out.'

Daniel found himself scowling. He didn't want a beautiful wife, or one that was particularly interesting. He wanted someone kind and quiet, who would let him continue with his current lifestyle and not interfere. Plus, of course, she needed to be wealthy. He found himself wondering when he had become so cynical, but deep down he knew. You couldn't have your heart broken and come out unscathed, and Daniel had certainly had his heart trampled on.

'I need someone rich,' he said bluntly.

Fletcher looked at him appraisingly but didn't comment.

'Then we have a shortlist. There are three very wealthy young women in attendance tonight.'

'How do you know all this?' Daniel asked.

'When you have four sisters out in society it's hard not to know everything about their competition. Including the size of their dowries.'

'Who are the three?' Daniel asked, hating having to be so direct, but knowing it would be better to get directly down to business. Then he wouldn't have to attend so many of these events.

'First up is Miss Priscilla Dethridge, daughter to the very successful banker Mr James Dethridge.' Fletcher motioned discreetly to a young woman in her early twenties. She was pretty enough and seemed to be having a lovely time on the arm of a young gentleman Daniel didn't know.

'Then there's Miss Trumping. No one knows how her father made his money, probably wasn't strictly legal, but she does have the advantage of being very attractive.'

Daniel looked over at the stunning young woman Fletcher was indicating. She was beautiful, there was no denying it, and she was surrounded by far too many men.

'And the last?' Daniel asked.

'Miss Amelia Eastway.' Fletcher was scanning the room looking for the young lady in question. 'Father is Colonel Eastway, an army man settled in India, very successful trading business. She'll be an extremely rich young woman when he meets his maker.'

Daniel waited patiently for Fletcher to locate her and perhaps even introduce him.

'I can't seem to see her.' Fletcher shrugged. 'She is quite an unassuming young thing. Not unattractive exactly, just rather normal.'

Daniel smiled. She sounded perfect. Or at least perfect for him. Wealthy, available and not someone he was going to lose his head over. Although all three qualities were necessary, he rather thought the last was the most important. Daniel was certain he never wanted to lose control like that again and Miss Amelia Eastway sounded like the perfect young woman to save him financially and allow him to carry on with life as normal.

'And now I need to go and do my duty,' Fletcher said with a sigh that Daniel didn't quite believe. His friend was quite dedicated to his family, whatever he'd have the world think.

Once again Daniel was left alone on the perimeter of the ballroom. He could sense the curiosity of the female guests almost reaching a peak and knew if he wasn't careful he would find himself trapped into dancing with some young woman or another. He grimaced. All he wanted was an introduction to the eligible Miss Eastway, to murmur something charming as he kissed her hand and to make his escape. Desperate though he might be, Daniel was sensible enough to know he would not make much more progress than that tonight, but he at least wanted to make the acquaintance of the woman he was going to marry.

He scanned the ballroom for someone who met Fletcher's description of Miss Eastway with little success. There were no plain-looking women surrounded by fortune hunters that he could see. He felt a stab of panic as he wondered whether she had already been claimed and let his eyes wander to the open doors leading to the terrace. Surely even a naïve young woman new to London society wouldn't allow herself to be led outside by an unscrupulous suitor.

Telling himself he was just being a gentleman, checking on a lady's safety, he strode across the ballroom, resolutely not looking at anyone in his path. In truth, he felt a bubble of irritation. If the innocent Miss Eastway had gone and got herself compromised, it would ruin all his plans.

He stopped short as a young woman stepped into his path.

'Lord Burwell,' she purred, dipping into a curtsy and looking up at him with a coquettish smile.

'Mrs Winter.' Daniel took her hand and brought it to his lips.

'It has been far too long,' the widow said.

Daniel couldn't help but smile. He and the charming Mrs Winter had been bumping into each other for six months now. Each time they shared a drink and a few words and then moved on, but there was a certain spark in her eyes that told Daniel he wouldn't need to do much more than smile and she would come to him willingly.

'I've missed our scintillating chats,' Mrs Winter said, her hand curling around Daniel's upper arm possessively.

They walked a few steps together, Daniel always keeping one eye on the door to the terrace in case someone matching Amelia Eastway's description came through the opening.

'I heard the most scandalous rumour about you,' she said, dropping her voice to a loud whisper.

'I'm sure it's not true.'

'It was involving you and a pretty little actress called Victoria.'

Daniel felt a grin tugging at the corners of his lips. Victoria was a sweet little thing who just seemed to enjoy Daniel's company and demanded nothing more.

'And my dear friend Mrs Highton has been dropping the most obvious of hints. I do hope you don't favour her over me.'

Daniel grimaced. This was why nothing had happened between him and Mrs Winter; he got the impression that she could become rather possessive. Daniel had never wanted a long-term mistress, instead preferring short liaisons with women who did not make a fuss if he called things off.

'How could I prefer anyone to you?' Daniel asked, turning towards the young widow with his most dazzling smile.

That seemed to placate her a little and Daniel took the opportunity to escape. He wasn't in the mood for flirtation tonight. His decision to marry was sitting heavily on him and he wanted to find his possible future wife, introduce himself and return home before he could talk himself out of it.

He reached the terrace doors in less than a minute and slipped out into the cool summer's night. The outdoor space was illuminated by candles dotted along the stone balustrade, but there were plenty of dark corners a young woman with little experience could find herself lured to by a man with less than noble intentions. Daniel wondered what to do next—he'd expected to come outside to find someone who fitted Miss Eastway's description and had planned to whisk her gallantly away from danger. Now he was here even he knew that plan was foolish. Firstly, the people who slipped outside normally didn't want to be disturbed, and secondly, he couldn't very well rescue a damsel in distress if he couldn't see her.

Daniel almost gave up and returned to the ballroom, but compared to the cramped, stifling atmosphere inside, the summer's evening was lovely and cool. He thought he might sit for a moment or two before returning to find the woman he was going to marry.

Quietly he slipped down the stone stairs into the garden proper and seated himself on a little bench looking out into the garden. Not for the first time he wished he was back on his estate in Cambridgeshire, strolling about his own garden with a glass of whisky in his hand. Or even at his club in London, sitting quietly with a newspaper or discussing the day's events with his friends. Balls and ballrooms didn't suit him. He wondered not for the first time if there shouldn't be an easier, more pleasurable way of finding oneself a spouse, but knew in today's society things were unlikely to change any time soon.

Daniel was just about to get up from his bench when he heard the doors to the ballroom open on the terrace above him. For a few seconds the music swelled and pulsed, then it was quiet as whoever had slipped outside closed the door. Daniel waited for the whispers of two illicit lovers and wondered if he should clear his throat to let them know they were not alone.

No whispers came, just the unmistakable swish of silk as someone started to descend the stairs towards him.

Daniel didn't want to startle the woman, but equally he didn't want to be caught in a deserted garden with some empty-headed young thing. He stood, coughed quietly, then approached the steps.

In the darkness Daniel heard a cry of surprise before he saw something moving towards him at great speed. He tried to jump backwards, out of the way of the careening object, but his reflexes weren't quite quick enough. Something warm and soft crashed into him and knocked the breath from his lungs. Unable to keep his balance Daniel toppled backwards, taking whatever it was with him. They landed together with a quiet groan.

For a few seconds Daniel was too stunned to move. It was obvious now the object that had come hurtling down the stairs towards him was a woman. A rather stunned young woman if her silence was anything to go by.

Slowly he became aware of her body pressed up against his. One of her legs was nestled between his thighs and her chest was pressed closely to his. Her face must have been cradled into his neck as he could feel her soft breath tickling his skin. She was trembling, he realised, and too shocked to move.

Gently he rolled her over and sat up, being careful not to move suddenly.

'Are you hurt?' he asked, thinking himself rather foolish. After all, who could fall down quite so many steps and not be hurt?

'Erm…yes…no. I don't know.'

Daniel found himself smiling. She was conscious at least and sounded rather charmingly befuddled.

'Let me check you over,' he said, in a voice that invited no argument.

It was dark outside, too dark to make out much of the young woman's features, but Daniel's eyes had become accustomed to the blackness and he could at least see her outline. Gently he reached over and took one hand in his.

He heard a sharp intake of breath as he traced the lines of her arms with his fingers, checking for any broken bones. He did the same with her legs, but when he was just reaching her knees it seemed she had regained at least some of her wits and pulled sharply away. Daniel sighed—he was just starting to enjoy himself.

'I'm sure I'm fine,' the young woman said in a voice that wasn't in the least bit convincing. 'What about you?'

'Me?' Daniel asked. 'Oh, I'm used to cushioning the falls of fair maidens,' he said with a grin. 'But that was certainly the most pleasant introduction I've had all evening.' Daniel pictured the young woman's cheeks turning pink and silently reprimanded himself; sometimes he couldn't help his flirtatious side. 'There's a bench just over here. Let's see if you can make it over.'

Daniel thought he saw her nod her head in the darkness and stood, leaning down to assist her up. He felt her totter a little and slipped an arm around her waist to steady her. She was slender, but Daniel could feel the flare of her hips beneath her dress and felt the first stirrings of desire. Reluctantly he pushed them away. This was most likely a well-bred young lady who he couldn't dally with. And, he reminded himself sternly, he was here for one purpose only: to find a wealthy wife, no matter how much the idea galled him.

Together they hobbled over to the bench and sat down.

'What happened?' he asked gently, not letting go of the woman's hand.

She sighed. 'You'll think me foolish.' There was a modicum of humour in her voice and Daniel found himself smiling. The whole situation was farcical really, and most young women would be in hysterics, but this one was taking it all in her stride.

'I wanted to escape…' She paused, then corrected herself. 'No, I needed to escape. If I spent one more second in that ballroom, I would have screamed.'

'Surely it wasn't so bad that you had to throw yourself down the steps?'

Although he couldn't see her expression Daniel rather thought she'd smiled.

'Almost.' She sighed. 'I'm sorry, I'm sure I've ruined your...' Instead of finishing the sentence she waved a hand in his general direction. 'Whatever it is men wear to these balls.'

Daniel found himself leaning in a little closer, trying to make out what his mystery woman looked like. He knew she was tall, with a slender waist and delightfully curvy hips, but he wished he could catch a glimpse of her facial features.

'I just wanted some peace and quiet, just for a few minutes. When you coughed you startled me and I tripped.'

'I wanted you to know you weren't alone.'

Daniel felt himself drawn to this woman and started to gently trace his thumb backwards and forwards across her hand. He knew it was wrong and he knew he should send her back inside immediately. If they were found in this position, outside and alone together, there would be a terrible scandal, but he couldn't quite bring himself to send her on her way just yet.

'Why did you want to escape the ball so much?' Daniel asked. 'A lovely young woman like you must be the centre of attention.'

He could tell she grimaced even in the darkness. 'I feel like an antique up for auction.'

Daniel laughed, he couldn't help himself.

'Not that I think I'm any kind of prize, quite the opposite,' she rushed to reassure him. 'It's just when you know people are only interested because of money...' She let her sentence trail off.

Daniel suddenly felt a little guilty. All evening he hadn't

thought of anything but securing himself a wealthy wife. He hadn't considered what his potential spouse's feelings would be on the matter, hadn't even thought of her as a real person. That must be what this young lady felt like, an object up for auction. Daniel pushed his qualms aside. He would treat his wife well, give her anything she asked for, and all he needed in return was for her to save him financially. It wasn't even as though he'd squander all her money gambling like most husbands; her fortune would be going to a good cause.

'We should get you back inside before you're missed,' Daniel said reluctantly. He didn't know why he was so loath to let her go, he was certainly enjoying himself more than he'd expected to at a ball, but he knew she had to return to the ballroom before someone noticed she was gone.

'I am sorry I fell on you,' the woman repeated.

Daniel stood and offered her his arm. She stood up rather too abruptly and he found himself face-to-face with her. Even in the darkness Daniel could make out the curve of her lips and suddenly he had an overwhelming urge to kiss her.

Without thinking of the consequences Daniel lowered his lips to hers, feeling the sharp intake of breath as she realised what he was about to do. He half expected her to push him away and storm off, but for a few seconds she stood frozen, as if too stunned to react. Then he felt her body melt into his.

It was the first time she'd been kissed, Daniel was sure of it, but her lips were full and inviting and Daniel knew he wouldn't be able to pull away. He breathed in her scent and pulled her closer to him, revelling in the small moan that escaped from her lips as they kissed.

Suddenly she stiffened and Daniel knew the moment was over. Even though he'd met this woman only a few minutes previously he knew she wouldn't become hysterical, just that she'd come to her senses. Slowly he pulled away, keeping one hand resting gently on her waist.

'That... I mean... Well.'

Normally Daniel would have prided himself at rendering a woman speechless, but already he was beginning to feel like a churl. He'd just seduced an innocent young woman he had no intention of marrying. It went against everything he believed in, every code of honour he lived his life by.

'That was unforgivable of me,' he said softly. 'I just couldn't help myself. I wouldn't have been able to resist kissing you even if there was a sword to my heart.'

'I should go,' she said, pulling away. Almost immediately she stumbled and Daniel sprang forward, steadying her so she didn't lose her feet.

'Can I at least know your name?' he asked quietly.

It seemed like an eternity before she answered and Daniel had the absurd feeling that she might give him a false name.

'Amelia,' she said eventually. 'Amelia Eastway.'

Daniel felt the bottom drop out of his world as Amelia slipped from his grasp and started to ascend the steps back to the terrace.

'May I call on you tomorrow?' he called after her.

He wasn't entirely sure, but he thought he saw her nod her head before she disappeared into the darkness completely.

Chapter Three

Lizzie was a bundle of nerves. It didn't help that she hadn't slept much at all. Every time she'd closed her eyes she'd been back in the Prestons' garden being seduced by a mystery man. She didn't even know his name. Even now she could feel the faint tingle of desire as she remembered his hands on her waist and his lips brushing her own.

She wondered if he would call on her, as he'd said he would. She didn't know if she even wanted him to. She was torn. Half of her wanted to meet this man who had kissed her so passionately the night before, but the other half wanted to hold on to the dream. If he saw her in the light of day, Lizzie knew he'd realise he'd made a mistake. Perhaps it would be better if their dalliance was kept as something magical, something Lizzie could hold on to for the rest of her life. It wasn't as though he would desire her once he actually met her properly and maybe it would be better if she didn't actually see the disappointment in his face as he looked at her in the daylight.

'Look, Amelia,' Aunt Mathilda said as she entered the room, 'these have just arrived for you.'

She was carrying a beautiful bouquet of flowers, tied with a red ribbon. Lizzie found herself smiling, wondering if they were from her mystery gentleman the night before. She hadn't even found out his name, she realised.

She took the card from Aunt Mathilda and felt her smile falter slightly as she read it. No, these certainly weren't from her mystery gentleman. The card was signed Mr Anthony Green and Lizzie found it hard not to shudder as she remembered their encounter the night before. She'd been introduced to many eligible gentlemen, both young and old. Most had been pleasant, although she suspected had been more interested in putting a face to the dowry than actually making her acquaintance. Mr Anthony Green had been repulsive. Not in looks—in fact, he was quite a handsome man in his early thirties—but in manner. He'd lingered over her hand just a little too long and gone out of his way to touch her upper arm at any opportunity. That in itself, of course, didn't make him repulsive, but she'd found that he had spent more time ogling the fine jewels that hung around her neck than actually looking at her. And he'd spoken of her fortune and her dowry to her face. It might have been Lizzie's first night out in society, but even she knew dowries were something that were whispered about behind closed doors. Mr Green had made it perfectly clear that all he was interested in was her money, and that he didn't even think it was worth trying to disguise the fact.

Aunt Mathilda arranged the flowers on the windowsill and looked at them approvingly.

'I'm sure you'll be receiving many more bouquets, my dear, and hopefully a few gentlemen callers this afternoon.'

Lizzie saw Harriet's eyes narrow at the idea of her receiving a call from an eligible gentleman, but Lizzie tried to ignore it. She wasn't sure why Harriet disliked her so much on first sight, but she wasn't going to provoke the situation.

'I'm sure you're glad you were sufficiently recovered

from your illness to make your début now,' Harriet said snidely.

Lizzie had tried to feign an illness to delay her coming out, hoping that Aunt Mathilda might let her stay hidden in her house until Amelia returned. She'd complained of a headache, fever and light-headedness, and had even gone as far as to hold the teapot to her cheeks before Aunt Mathilda came to check on her, but the older woman had sat down beside her, taken her hand and told her not to worry. She had seen through Lizzie's ruse and put it down to Lizzie feeling nervous about making her début, so Lizzie had found herself hustled into her beautiful dress and into the carriage before she could even begin to think of another excuse to delay.

The door to the drawing room opened quietly and the butler, an elderly man with an unflappable demeanour, stepped inside.

'The Earl of Burwell to see Miss Amelia Eastway,' Tippings announced.

Immediately all three women stiffened. Certainly they had been expecting calls from gentlemen of the *ton*, but an earl was in quite another league.

Aunt Mathilda quickly crossed the room to Lizzie's side.

'You know the Earl of Burwell?' she asked, her face drained of colour.

Even Harriet looked a little impressed.

Lizzie couldn't answer. Had she met the Earl of Burwell? If so, he hadn't stuck in her mind and she rather thought an earl should do.

Unless, of course, he was her mystery gentleman. Lizzie suddenly felt sick. Had she been kissed by an earl in the Prestons' garden? Surely not. Surely that was something a girl would know. He'd seemed so nice, so normal, not earl-like at all. She felt her face flush at the idea of him seeing her in the light of day and wondered if she had time to escape. Maybe feign a swoon.

The door opened once again and a man stepped inside. Out of habit Lizzie found herself standing and dropping into a little bob of a curtsy as a greeting. Only then did she have the courage to raise up her eyes and look at the man she might or might not have kissed the night before.

Her mouth fell open and her eyes widened. Whomever she had expected to be standing in front of her it wasn't this man.

'You,' she said before she could stop her mouth forming the words.

Lizzie could see this man was equally as surprised.

A thousand thoughts ran through Lizzie's mind at once, not a single one coherent or helpful. Aunt Mathilda looked between Lizzie and the earl, but ever the polite hostess she invited him to sit without any further enquiry.

'It is delightful to see you again, Miss Eastway,' the earl said, sounding rather too composed for Lizzie's liking.

The pieces started to fall into place and Lizzie wondered how she had not recognised his voice the night before. The Earl of Burwell was certainly her mystery gentleman, but it was not the first time they'd met. He was also the gentleman who had saved Lizzie from nearly being trampled to death by his horse, the man who had dismissed her with a single glance.

Lizzie wanted to curl up and disappear. She wondered how disappointed he was when he saw her, when he realised last night was not the first time they'd set eyes on each other.

'It's a beautiful afternoon,' Aunt Mathilda said, trying to break some of the tension in the room.

'It is indeed,' the earl said.

'How did you and Miss Eastway meet?' Harriet asked

and Lizzie remembered the smirk on her cousin's face as she had witnessed Lizzie's humiliation on her arrival to London.

The Earl of Burwell turned to face Harriet and looked at her appraisingly. His gaze was superior and a little haughty, and Lizzie was surprised Harriet didn't squirm under the intensity of it.

'We were formally introduced last night,' he said eventually. 'And I enjoyed our conversation so much I decided I wanted to see Miss Eastway again today.'

Although Lizzie knew that wasn't quite the whole truth she was glad he'd silenced Harriet's mocking before it had started.

'How absolutely delightful,' Aunt Mathilda said. 'Now, Harriet, why don't I show you that thing I was talking about earlier?'

Harriet looked blank but allowed her mother to usher her out of the room. Aunt Mathilda pulled the door behind her but left a chink between the wood and the frame for propriety's sake.

Lizzie knew she would have to turn and face the earl, but she was finding it hard to summon the courage. She didn't want to see the disappointment on his face, she didn't want to hear him utter some made-up excuse to escape as soon as possible. For she knew he would be disappointed. Last night he hadn't known who she was, she was sure of that. He hadn't realised she was the woman who had caused so much havoc in the street just a week before. That woman he had dismissed without a second look, but last night he had treated her as though she were the most desirable woman on earth.

Lizzie's heart started to sink. Maybe it had all been engineered, maybe her perfect fairy-tale moment had actually been nothing more than a fortune hunter making a naïve young girl feel attractive. She glanced briefly at the earl. He didn't look like a fortune hunter, but she knew they came in all shapes and sizes.

'I should apologise for last night,' he said as he caught Lizzie's eye.

She waited for him to actually apologise, but he was not forthcoming.

'But I find myself unable to regret my actions.'

'Why?' The word was out before Lizzie could stop it. She berated herself immediately. She needed to get control of her tongue.

'Why?' he asked, raising an eyebrow.

'Why did you kiss me?' she whispered.

He regarded her silently for a minute, then looked away. She wondered if he were concocting a lie, trying to find something flattering to say.

'It was rather magical last night, wasn't it?' he said eventually. 'The warm summer's evening, the faint echo of the music from the ballroom. Then a charming young woman comes and crashes into me and I just couldn't resist.'

Lizzie found herself nodding. It had been rather magical. Not the part where she'd fallen down the stairs, or winded him so badly he hadn't been able to breathe for a few moments, but afterwards. The caring way he'd helped her up, the feel of his touch on her skin and the moments they'd spent sitting on the bench side by side.

Then they'd stood up and Lizzie had felt him move towards her and she'd known she was about to be kissed.

'It was not gentlemanly,' he said seriously, but then broke out into a smile. 'But I don't regret it.'

She tried to believe him, tried to believe that sitting here he was not regretting the moment from the night before, but she wasn't sure she could. Self-consciously Lizzie brushed a strand of hair away from her face. Ordinary brown hair, framing an ordinary face with just a few too many freckles.

With a glance at the door the earl stood and moved towards Lizzie. She found herself staring up at him, trying to control her breathing.

'I really did enjoy our time together last night,' he said, sitting himself down beside her.

Lizzie found herself nodding again. She'd enjoyed it, too.

'And I really would like to get to know you a little more.' His voice was low and a little seductive and Lizzie knew hundreds of women had fallen prey to him before.

She wanted to ask him why, wanted him to confess he was only interested in her for her supposed dowry, but she found her words had deserted her. His body was just that little bit too close, his thigh pressing against hers, and Lizzie knew she wouldn't be able to construct a coherent sentence.

'I think last night might have been the start of something special,' he said.

Lizzie made a small murmur of agreement, even though she wasn't sure she agreed. She felt mesmerised by him, completely under his spell, and even though her mind was screaming out that it wasn't her that he wanted, it was Amelia, Lizzie found at this moment she didn't really care.

She felt him studying her, his eyes flicking from her mouth to her cheeks to her hair, but always back to her mouth. Involuntarily she felt her lips part ever so slightly and she realised she wanted him to kiss her. Right then it didn't matter why he was doing it, just that she wanted him to. She wanted to be lost once again in the oblivion of a kiss, wanted to feel the explosions within her body as his lips met hers.

Slowly, as if building the anticipation, the earl lowered

his lips to hers. He started out gently, barely touching her. Lizzie felt the tension mounting and a soft moan escape her lips. She wanted more, needed more.

As if responding to her innermost thoughts he pressed his lips more firmly on to hers and deftly flicked his tongue inside her mouth. Lizzie's eyes closed and she was lost. She didn't care why he was kissing her; all she wanted was for it not to end.

She felt her body melting into his and relished his touch as he looped an arm around the back of her head, pulling her closer towards him. She wanted his hands all over her body, wanted him to touch her in places no one else had ever even seen.

Just as she felt the kiss couldn't get any better suddenly the earl pulled away. He was smiling, but Lizzie could tell something was wrong. She wondered if she'd inadvertently done something terrible, something that would make him want to run from the room.

Suddenly Lizzie felt very self-conscious and raised a hand to cover the lips he had been so thoroughly kissing just moments before.

'I'm sorry,' he murmured. 'I just couldn't seem to help myself.' He sounded a little puzzled and Lizzie could see a flicker of confusion in his eyes.

'You are just so tempting,' he said, tracing a pattern on the back of her hand.

Immediately Lizzie crashed back to reality. She knew that was a lie. She straightened up, pulling away, and gave him a forced little smile.

'I'm sure my aunt will be back in a few minutes,' she said pointedly.

The earl looked confused, as if no one had ever rejected him before, but took the hint and moved back across the room to the chair he'd been sitting in before. An uncomfortable silence followed and Lizzie found herself blinking the tears away from her eyes. This was cruel and unnecessary. Up until very recently she'd been quite content with her lot. She'd known she wasn't a great beauty. Combining that with her lack of fortune, she'd never expected to make a good marital match. In fact, she'd been quite convinced she would never be a wife, just a spinster all her life. Now here she was being utterly seduced by a handsome and charming man, knowing all along it wasn't her that he wanted at all.

Chapter Four

Daniel wasn't quite sure what had just happened. He *knew* he'd just kissed the young woman sitting across the room from him. He just didn't know how to classify his reaction.

He'd been thrown when he realised he'd met Miss Amelia Eastway before last night. He'd hardly taken any notice of the unassuming young woman who had stepped in front of his horse. She'd seemed so ordinary, so normal. Not like the woman in the garden. She had been intriguing and almost mystical. Daniel had found himself drawn to her, attracted and aroused despite his years of experience.

Then when he'd found out the woman who he'd kissed was the very one he was meant to be pursuing, his world had almost fallen apart. He didn't want to desire his future wife. Desire complicated everything. Desire made a man lose all sense of reason and preceded bad decisions. Over the past four years Daniel had become a master at keeping his desire in check. That wasn't to say he'd been celibate, just that he hadn't let his desire overshadow his common sense.

It was the shock, he realised. He hadn't expected to recognise his mystery woman in the daylight, he hadn't even considered that they might have met before. He'd looked her over appraisingly and found rather an ordinary young woman sitting in front of him. Not someone who made his pulse race and his temperature rise. He'd felt comfortable, reassured. She wasn't the irresistible vixen he'd thought the night before, she was just an average young woman with no particular distinguishing features.

He'd planned to kiss her, of course. He needed to marry her and he needed to do it soon. After their kiss the night before Daniel knew she was an innocent and he knew that his charm was legendary with women all over London. He was hopeful that Amelia would enjoy his attention and flirtation.

And then it had happened. He'd moved closer, leant in to begin his seduction, and he felt as though he'd been punched in the gut. He couldn't quite put his finger on why he felt this way, just that he needed to kiss Amelia Eastway, not so she would have to become his wife and save him from financial ruin, but because it was the only thing that would keep him going.

He wasn't sure if it was the delicate curve of her lips or the charming set of freckles that covered her nose, he just knew he had to kiss her. And far from being completely in control, as he had planned, Daniel had felt rather wonderfully at sea. He'd kissed her as though he hadn't kissed a woman in years, allowing himself to pull her body towards him, run his hands over her skin. He'd lost himself in that kiss and that was worrying him.

He glanced back across at Amelia and wondered if she had somehow sensed all of this. She'd wanted him, Daniel was experienced enough to recognise the signs: her pupils had dilated, her breathing had become just a little shallow and her lips had parted. She'd kissed him as passionately as the night before, but now she was regretting it. Something had changed. It was as though a shutter had come down over her face and now they were sitting apart like complete strangers, not a couple who had kissed twice in the space of twenty-four hours.

Daniel knew he had to do something to salvage the situation. Whatever his current internal conflict Miss Amelia Eastway was still the solution to all his problems. He needed to court her and marry her before the month was out. He would have to push aside any doubts he had. When he looked at her objectively he knew he should be able to resist her. He would just have to learn to control his urges and no doubt soon enough their relationship would slip into easy companionship rather than one fuelled with desire.

'Would you care to join me for a stroll in the park?' Daniel asked.

Amelia looked at him as though he had grown two heads. He wondered if he had uttered the sentence in Latin or some other foreign tongue.

Eventually she sighed and nodded her head. 'That would be most delightful,' she said, sounding anything but delighted.

Daniel felt himself bristle. Again he wondered what had happened to bring about this change in her feelings for him so abruptly. One minute she'd been melting in his arms, responding to his kiss, the next she was forcing herself to take a stroll with him.

'Maybe your aunt would be so kind as to find a chaperon?' he enquired. 'Although I'd much rather be alone together. Such wonderful things happen when we're alone,' he murmured.

Amelia seemed to soften towards him slightly.

'I'm sure she will.'

She made no effort to go and sort this out and Daniel felt his mood darken further. Most young women would be swooning at the thought of strolling through the park on the arm of an earl for all society to see.

'Would you like to go and ask her?' he suggested.

'Of course, my lord.'

'Daniel, please,' he said, thinking it was ridiculous having her call him by his title when already they were quite intimate. 'Since we already know each other so well.'

He watched as she rose and walked out of the room. Despite having fallen down stairs into him, and nearly having been trampled by his horse, Miss Eastway seemed to move with a fluid kind of grace when she was on her feet. He found himself watching the soft sway of her hips as she left the room and once again felt the first stirrings of desire deep within his body.

Daniel took a deep breath and closed his eyes. He would not desire Amelia Eastway. Although deep down he knew desire wasn't something you could easily keep in check, equally he knew he was a man of the world, not some green boy of twenty. He had control over his emotions and he would not lose his head over a woman even if she had charmingly kissable lips.

He'd have to kiss her again, of course, but next time he would be completely in control.

He rose as Amelia re-entered the room and saw with dismay that she was accompanied by her cousin. Daniel had spent less than five minutes in the young girl's company, but he knew she was spiteful and jealous.

'Harriet would like to accompany us,' Amelia said, her lack of enthusiasm obvious in her tone.

'That would be delightful,' Daniel said. 'I just hope our discussion on ancient literature does not bore you too much.'

Daniel saw the flicker of a smile cross Amelia's lips. Harriet's eyes narrowed as she tried to work out if Daniel was being serious. He kept a neutral expression on his face, hoping all the time she would change her mind and stay at home. He wasn't likely going to make much progress with Amelia if her cousin was present and annoying her.

'Harriet, I need your help this afternoon,' Aunt Mathilda said as she glided back into the room. 'I'll send one of the maids out to chaperon you, Amelia.'

Daniel wondered if Harriet would argue, she looked as though she wanted to, but in the end she kept her mouth shut.

Within minutes Daniel was strolling towards Hyde Park with Amelia on his arm. He realised she felt right beside him, her strides matched his own and the weight of her hand resting on his arm was comforting. He felt quite comfortable with her, despite the odd moment of madness where he seemed to want to ravish her. If he could only overcome those, he thought Amelia would make a very good wife. She was quiet and unassuming and he didn't think she'd protest too much when he continued with his current lifestyle.

'I understand you've only recently arrived in London,' he said, thinking a little bit of small talk would help break down the barrier between them.

She looked wistfully into the distance for a moment before replying. 'I've lived in India all my life, or at least for as long as I can remember.'

'Do you miss it?'

She nodded. 'When I was there all I could think about was getting away, coming to London, but now I've left it behind I miss the rolling green hills and the days filled with sunshine.'

Daniel wondered what her upbringing had been like. From his subtle enquiries he'd found out she'd been raised the only child of the very wealthy Colonel Eastway. She'd always been destined to marry well, but to look at her you wouldn't believe it. She seemed rather overwhelmed by the sudden attention and he had the impression that she hadn't expected to be courted this soon.

'Do you wish you were back there?' he asked softly.

She considered for a moment, then turned to him with a smile. 'No. As much as I like to reminisce, it was time for me to leave, time for me to start the next chapter of my life.'

'As a débutante in London.'

He saw her grimace out of the corner of his eye.

'Something like that,' she said vaguely.

They'd reached the entrance to the park and walked in through the archway. Daniel found he was enjoying himself more than he'd imagined. When he'd realised he was going to have to marry he'd been a little disgruntled to say the least. He didn't want his life to change, he was quite content running his estates, spending time in London and making sure he didn't make any lasting connections. The idea of having to marry was bad enough, although Daniel was a pragmatist and knew where his priorities lay, but he'd dreaded having to find and court a wife. He'd imagined some air-headed young miss that he'd have to listen ramble on about nothing. Amelia Eastway was not like that at all. In fact, he was rather enjoying himself.

Chapter Five

Lizzie slowly felt herself relaxing. She didn't know what game Daniel was playing, but she'd decided she was having none of it. She was going to be courteous and polite, but she would not allow him to kiss her again. That would be madness.

Walking along, her hand in the crook of his arm, Lizzie felt almost content. He was attentive and seemed to want to listen to what she had to say. Lizzie could almost convince herself she was having a good time. Just as long as he didn't look at her intensely with his piercing blue eyes and shift towards her, Lizzie knew she could keep up a mundane conversation. She tried not to think what would happen if he attempted to kiss her again. She liked to think she was a strong young woman who knew her own mind, but twice she'd been utterly seduced by his kiss and she wasn't sure how she would resist if he turned to her again.

Luckily they were out in public, in full view of the world. He wouldn't try anything whilst they were strolling through the park. Then Lizzie wondered if she could rely on that. For some reason he had decided to court her and she doubted it was because he found her wildly irresistible. Even if their meeting the night before hadn't been engineered, Lizzie thought there was something driving Daniel today and her first guess was her dowry. Or at least

Amelia's dowry. She sighed. This was all getting to be a bit of a mess and she'd only been out in society for one day. She wished Amelia would return and sort it all out, but she hadn't heard from her cousin since they'd disembarked the ship from India together, her cousin hopping into the first carriage she'd seen on the London dockside, and she doubted Amelia would make an appearance anytime soon. She would just have to deal with this debacle herself.

She felt a bit sorry for the earl. Not that he was the sort of man who invited pity, but he was thinking he was courting an heiress with a substantial dowry, where instead he was wasting his time on a penniless orphan. She wondered whether he would switch his affections to Amelia when she returned, and found herself feeling more than a little put out at the thought.

They stopped walking as they reached the Serpentine and Daniel led her over to a bench.

'Sometimes I come here to think,' Daniel said quietly.

Lizzie regarded their surroundings with surprise. There was no denying Hyde Park was beautiful with its myriad of waterways and copses of trees, but Daniel hadn't exactly picked the most secluded spot for his contemplations. They were sitting on a bench right next to the Serpentine, in a place where all the children gathered to feed the ducks. In the early-afternoon sunshine the children were whooping and shouting in delight as they threw bread to the obliging creatures.

She glanced sideways and saw him looking wistfully at a group of small boys out with their nanny. One of the boys was only about three or four years old and tottered after his older siblings, trying to keep up with their games.

Lizzie wondered momentarily whether this was all part of his plan, to bring her to Hyde Park and let her see how much he liked children, but then she dismissed the idea.

She could tell this wasn't all engineered. This truly was where he came to sit and think about the world.

'I guess it's because I miss the countryside when I'm in London,' Daniel said with a shrug.

'Do you spend much time here?'

He shook his head. 'I prefer the country to be honest, but I find myself in London more and more.'

Lizzie wondered what his country estate was like. She'd left England before her third birthday and hadn't been back since. Her home was the dry heat and lush green valleys near Bombay, but she doubted the English countryside was anything like that.

'But enough about me,' Daniel said with a grin, 'I want to know more about you.'

Lizzie shrugged and looked down at her hands. 'I'm sure you know the basics.'

'I don't want to know the basics,' Daniel said, leaning in closer, 'I want to know something the rest of society doesn't. Something that the masses will never know when they talk about you.'

His smile was infectious and Lizzie felt herself beginning to properly enjoy herself. She rather suspected the earl was known to be flirtatious in nature, but right now she didn't care. She was sitting on a bench with a handsome man, enjoying herself.

Lizzie thought for a moment, wanting to select something suitably vague for the earl so there was no chance he would work out she wasn't who she claimed to be.

'When I was twelve I was bitten by a crocodile.'

Daniel burst out laughing. 'You're joking?'

Lizzie shook her head.

'Well, you must be the only débutante that can make that claim. Truly unique. Now you have to tell me more, I'm intrigued.'

'I was walking down by the river near our home. As usual, I had my head in a book and wasn't really looking where I was going.' Lizzie shuddered as she remembered the moment she'd realised she had stumbled into the path of a rather large crocodile. 'For about thirty seconds it just looked at me with those terrifying little eyes and then it lunged.'

She had thought she was about to die.

'Luckily it was just a warning shot, a quick nip and then the crocodile backed off. I had some pretty deep teeth marks, but I didn't lose my foot as many do.'

'Even without an entire leg you would still light up any ballroom. In fact...' Daniel paused, raised his hand close to his eye and positioned it so it obscured one leg from his view '...being the first one-legged débutante would probably make you the most interesting person to have graced society for decades.'

'Your turn,' Lizzie said. She was really beginning to warm to Daniel. She knew she shouldn't allow him to flirt with her quite so openly, but it was nice being the centre of someone's attention.

'An interesting fact about me,' Daniel mused.

'Something hardly anyone else knows.'

'I've been shot.'

Lizzie's eyes widened and she quickly glanced over his body, wondering where exactly he had been shot. She felt a little distracted by his broad shoulders and muscular arms, but quickly pulled herself together.

'You have to tell me more,' she said.

'It was a duel. I was second for a good friend of mine. We were young and foolish at the time.'

'And someone shot you?' Lizzie asked, thoroughly intrigued.

'It's nowhere near as glamorous as it sounds.' Daniel

leaned in closer and dropped his voice. 'In fact, it's really rather painful.'

Daniel edged closer to her and Lizzie didn't protest. Sitting here by the Serpentine with Daniel felt right somehow, as if this was what her entire life had been leading up to.

'The man who was aiming at my friend had terrible eyesight, he might as well have closed his eyes and fired. The shot missed its intended target and clipped me instead.'

Daniel must have seen how Lizzie's eyes were roving over his body, trying to figure out where he had been hit.

'When we're somewhere less public I'll show you the scar.'

Lizzie's eyes widened and for a moment she hoped it was somewhere on his chest or abdomen. She desperately wanted to peel back his crisp white shirt and run her fingers over the muscles beneath. At the thought of doing something so intimate she felt the blood rush to her cheeks and she coughed to try to cover her embarrassment.

'Now it's your turn again,' Daniel said with a smile that Lizzie knew would set any woman's heart racing.

Suddenly there was a shout and a commotion over by the Serpentine. Immediately Daniel was on his feet, rushing towards the water, with Lizzie following quickly behind.

The small boy they'd been watching only minutes before had tumbled into the murky waters and was now thrashing about. It was obvious he couldn't swim and it was too deep for him to touch the bottom. His petrified nanny was trying to reach him from the bank, but his thrashing was just causing him to get further and further away.

Lizzie watched as Daniel shrugged off his jacket, kicked off his boots and jumped into the dirty water. He touched the bottom easily, the water coming up to his waist, and he quickly waded out to where the boy was thrashing. Firmly he grabbed him and lifted him clear of the water, saying something soothing that Lizzie couldn't quite hear. She was reminded of their first meeting when she had almost been trampled by his horse and the way he'd soothed the petrified beast then.

Daniel's words must have done the trick as the boy calmed down and allowed himself to be carried to the bank and back into his nanny's arms.

Lizzie could only look on as Daniel pulled himself out of the water, clothes stuck to his muscular legs and torso. His shirt was almost see-through and it outlined the contours of his chest and abdomen in quite a scandalous way. Lizzie felt the heat rising in her body and forced herself to look away, worried that otherwise she would become mesmerised. He smiled at her and shrugged, as if this kind of thing happened every day, then turned his attention back to the boy. Quickly he checked he wasn't injured and then left him to be hustled home by his nanny.

'That was remarkable,' Lizzie said as Daniel made his way back towards her.

'I couldn't just sit by and let him drown.'

Lizzie shook her head in agreement but knew that not many gentlemen would actually jump into the Serpentine to rescue a strange boy.

'You must be frozen.'

Daniel shrugged again, but Lizzie could tell the wet clothes were making him uncomfortable already.

'Perhaps we could begin to head back,' he suggested.

Lizzie nodded, motioned to the maid who was sitting a couple of benches away, and they started to walk back through the park.

'I won't take your arm,' Daniel said with a smile.

Lizzie found herself smiling back. There was something quite irresistible about the man walking next to her. He might have an agenda and he might be pursuing her for all the wrong reasons, but she couldn't quite find it in herself to dislike him.

They walked in a companionable silence back through the park for a few minutes, gaining odd looks from other members of society who were out taking their afternoon strolls. Daniel nodded in greeting to many but didn't stop to engage them in conversation. Lizzie supposed he must be feeling rather cold now. Even in the pleasant afternoon sunshine walking around dripping wet couldn't be very good for your health.

'I'm sorry we've had to cut our outing short,' Daniel said, looking down at Lizzie with a smile.

Despite all her reservations Lizzie was sorry, too. She'd been enjoying herself. She'd almost been able to forget it wasn't she that Daniel was really courting, but Amelia. She'd enjoyed his lively conversation and she'd enjoyed the small insights he'd given her into his life.

'Maybe we could do this again sometime soon,' he suggested.

Lizzie found herself nodding, even though she knew she shouldn't encourage him. It would be so much easier if she never saw him again, if he disappeared from her life and she never had to reveal that she wasn't Amelia Eastway, but her penniless cousin. Even though she knew this Lizzie found herself agreeing with him.

'That would be lovely.'

She glanced up at his face and found him smiling at her, and just for a second she thought she saw a flicker of desire. She almost laughed. No matter what had happened in the Prestons' garden she knew Daniel didn't really desire her. She'd seen the quick way he'd dismissed her on their first meeting and she knew she wasn't the sort of woman men fantasised about.

'Please don't feel you have to escort me home,' Lizzie

said as they neared the edge of the park. 'You must get back to your house and get out of those wet things.'

Daniel considered a moment, as if weighing up his gentlemanly duty against his discomfort.

'Only if you promise to let me call on you again tomorrow,' he said with a devilish smile.

'People will talk,' Lizzie warned him.

'People will always talk. By this evening there'll be ten different versions of what happened down by the Serpentine, each more ludicrous than the last.'

Lizzie knew it was true. Already half of society would know that she had spent the afternoon with the Earl of Burwell. She cringed a little. This would make it all that much worse when she had to reveal her true identity to the world.

'Either you agree to my calling on you tomorrow, or I'll insist on walking you home now. You'll be responsible if I catch a fever and spend weeks delirious and at death's door.' He said it with a grin on his face and Lizzie knew she wasn't going to be able to resist.

'I would very much welcome you calling on me tomorrow, my lord.'

'I told you to call me Daniel.'

'Daniel.' Lizzie uttered his name quietly, nothing more than a whisper between her lips. It seemed too intimate, too informal, but she felt a wicked little chill down her spine as she said it.

'And I shall call you Amelia,' he murmured in her ear.

It was enough to force Lizzie back to reality. For a moment she'd allowed herself to live the fantasy, to believe that it was her Daniel wanted, but just the mention of Amelia's name made all those dreams come crashing down.

She pulled away slightly but forced herself to smile, even though she feared it would look like a grimace on her face.

Daniel looked at her intently for a few seconds, then turned away, as if he sensed she needed a moment of privacy to compose herself.

'Lord Burwell, whatever has happened to you?'

Lizzie turned to see an attractive young woman gliding towards them. The newcomer looked Lizzie up and down and then turned her full attention to Daniel.

'Mrs Winter,' Daniel said. 'I took a little dip in the Serpentine.'

Lizzie recognised the woman and realised she must have been at the Prestons' ball the night before.

'You must look after yourself, Lord Burwell, you would be sorely missed if anything were to happen to you.'

Lizzie didn't miss the suggestion that Mrs Winter would be the one missing him.

'Please excuse us, Mrs Winter, Lord Burwell needs to get out of these wet clothes,' Lizzie said. Immediately she knew she had made a mistake. The older woman turned to her and gave her an icy glare, before catching herself and replacing the expression with a sweet smile.

'Of course. Take care, my lord. And if you catch a cold and need someone to nurse you back to health, don't hesitate to ask.'

Daniel said farewell and they continued on, Lizzie feeling rather inferior to the attractive Mrs Winter. They were just nearing the entrance of the park when Lizzie noticed Daniel freeze beside her. One moment he was walking along, seeming like the carefree peer of the realm he'd been all morning, the next he was just frozen. She stopped beside him and waited for him to move. Five seconds passed, then ten. She followed his gaze, trying to figure out what was going on.

His eyes were fixed on a young woman and a small boy about thirty feet away. The woman was pulling the boy along behind her impatiently and the boy was dragging his feet.

'Daniel?' Lizzie asked, wondering what exactly about the scene had caused him to turn so white.

He didn't answer, didn't even acknowledge that she'd spoken. To Lizzie it seemed as though he was so lost in his own world that he hadn't even heard her.

The woman and boy were drawing closer and Lizzie wondered whether there would be some sort of confrontation.

Lizzie knew the exact moment the woman noticed them. Daniel stiffened beside her, his eyes met this woman's and his expression deepened into a frown. The woman stopped in her tracks and looked at them for a few seconds, before smiling sweetly and continuing on her way. Daniel followed them with his eyes for a long minute until they disappeared out of view.

No one had uttered a single word during the confrontation, but Lizzie felt as though she'd just witnessed something monumental.

'Daniel?' she repeated.

This time she got a response. Daniel took her elbow in his hand and guided her quickly from the park. He didn't say a single word to her and Lizzie felt too stunned by this sudden change in character that she didn't know what to say herself.

They exited the park and walked briskly down the street, Lizzie having to stumble to keep up with Daniel in his frenzied state.

'Who was that?' she managed to ask as they reached the corner.

He didn't answer her, didn't even acknowledge that she'd asked him a question.

'Daniel?'

'Will you be able to find your way home from here?' he asked stiffly.

Lizzie nodded, stunned at the change in the man who could laugh off ruining his clothes jumping into the Serpentine, but would not even look at her after this latest confrontation.

'I will call on you tomorrow.'

Again Lizzie nodded, unsure what else she could say. Open-mouthed, she watched as he hailed a passing hackney carriage and jumped in. He didn't even look at her as it pulled away, let alone bid her goodbye. She stood there motionless for a good minute after the carriage had pulled away, unsure what had just happened. Daniel had changed completely and it had been just as he'd seen that woman.

Shaken and confused Lizzie roused herself and began the walk home, wondering whether tomorrow she would get any answers from him.

Chapter Six

Daniel felt sick. No, he felt more than sick. He felt as though his whole world had collapsed. Up until that point the whole afternoon had been a success. Amelia seemed receptive to his advances, and even if she withdrew every so often, that was something that could be easily overcome.

He'd found her a pleasant companion, they'd talked easily during their walk around the park and he'd managed to convince himself that the desire he'd felt the evening before and when he'd kissed her in the drawing room had been anomalies. When he looked at her in the light of day he could see she wasn't a seasoned temptress. She was just a normal young woman who shouldn't drive him mad with desire. And if his pulse raced a little when he glanced at her lips, then he could put it down to the memory of their kiss and nothing more.

He'd even not minded his little dip in the Serpentine. Of course, he'd had no choice, he couldn't have let the young boy drown, but he knew Amelia had seen his act as heroic and that could never hurt a man's chances.

Everything had been going swimmingly well…until he'd seen them.

Daniel ran a hand through his hair and tried to focus on something other than his rage. At this moment he was close to losing control and he hated not being in control.

He breathed in deeply through his nose and watched the world pass by as the hackney carriage weaved through the busy streets.

He'd last seen his son four months ago when Annabelle had shown up at his estate, demanding more money. He'd been heartbroken. Already the boy was growing up so fast he barely looked like the young lad he'd seen six months earlier. Daniel knew he'd missed his son's first steps, his first words, and he would miss a whole world of firsts as time went on. The knowledge that he wasn't the one there, watching his son grow up, broke his heart.

If only there was another way, but he knew there wasn't.

Then today, in the park, Daniel knew that Annabelle had engineered that little meeting. She'd done it to let him know she was in town, to remind him of his promise and let him know she wasn't afraid of the consequences if he didn't pay up.

Daniel closed his eyes and pictured the little boy she'd been dragging behind her. His son, Edward. He had beautiful dark hair and piercing blue eyes, skin like porcelain and full lips. And he hadn't even once glanced at Daniel. That was what hurt the most. Throughout the whole encounter Edward had been looking around at the park. He hadn't taken one little bit of notice of the man whose heart was breaking just watching him.

Daniel ran a hand through his hair and made himself relax back into the seat of the carriage. There was nothing to be done about it. He'd made his bed four years ago when he'd invited Annabelle into his life. He'd been convinced she was the woman of his dreams, convinced that she loved him the way he'd loved her. It hadn't been long before he'd found out differently, that he'd found out that he was just the latest in a long line of conquests for Annabelle. She'd swept into his life when he was grief-stricken and vulnerable, and then like a seasoned con artist she had become his entire world, slowly cutting him off from his old friends, his old life. When he had found out the truth about Annabelle, the fact that she was already married, he had been devastated. His pride had been irreversibly damaged when he'd realised he'd been tricked into loving her, and his heart broken, but he'd known he would recover eventually. He was a young man with a full life ahead of him, he would get over the betrayal once she was out of his life.

The problem was she hadn't left his life, not really. A year after he'd thrown her out she'd turned back up with a baby in tow. Daniel had laughed at first, telling her he wouldn't believe a word she said and that there was no way this baby was his. Although from her very first words Daniel had begun to doubt himself. When they had been together Annabelle had told him she couldn't get pregnant, couldn't have children, so he had never insisted that they use protection.

Then he'd looked down at the baby and he'd known the truth. Just one glance and he'd known irrefutably that the child was his. The bond was immediate and unbreakable, and Annabelle had looked on with glee.

His world had crumbled. Of all the things that could have happened to him this was the very worst. He didn't care that Annabelle had tricked him into loving her. He didn't care that he was now much more jaded and untrusting. But he did care that he had fathered an illegitimate child.

His whole world had come crashing down. He knew first-hand what tragedy haunted illegitimate children. He'd seen the suffering and the contempt and he knew it was the very last thing he would wish upon anyone, let alone his own son.

He'd tried to take the child, but Annabelle had refused. And then the blackmail had started.

Daniel watched as the carriage pulled up outside his town house. In a daze he stumbled out on to the pavement, paid the driver and made his way up the steps. Once safely ensconced in his study, he reached for the whisky and started to drink. He wanted to drink to forget and he wanted to drink to numb the pain.

After two glasses of whisky Daniel started to feel a little more in control. He poured one final glass, then set down the decanter and regarded it for a second. Later he could get drunk, later he could lose himself in the oblivion of alcohol, but right now he needed his wits about him.

Annabelle was only here for one reason. Despite all his pleas and his following of her terms she never let him see his son other than when she wanted something. Then it was just a brief encounter like today in the park. Daniel longed to sit the boy on his knee, to read him a story, or perhaps take him for his first riding lesson, but he knew all of that was impossible. He was destined to be in the background for ever, never knowing his son's personality, his likes and dislikes, never knowing what made him laugh and what made him cry.

Annabelle was here for money. Again. Every few months she turned up and demanded even more. Sometimes she came alone, sometimes she brought Edward with her, allowing Daniel just a fleeting glimpse of his son, but always the demand was the same. Pay up or the whole world gets to know Edward is illegitimate. Including Edward himself. Daniel knew he couldn't have that on his conscience. He needed the boy to grow up happy, to grow up thinking he had lost his father in the war. Better to have a hero for a father than to be illegitimate. Daniel couldn't bear his son's heart breaking as other children tormented him for that. He knew what the consequences could be and he wasn't about to risk that with his own son.

The problem was he didn't have any money. Annabelle had bled him dry over the past few years, demanding more and more. He knew it would never stop, but he couldn't see any other way out. Hence his need for a wealthy wife. A good-sized dowry would keep Annabelle at bay for years to come and when that ran out, well, maybe then his son would be old enough and strong enough to learn the truth, to be able to withstand the jibes from society and still hold his head up high.

Taking a gulp of the whisky, Daniel relished the burning sensation in his throat and wondered how long it would take Amelia to agree to marry him. Maybe a couple of weeks if he worked fast, but then it would still be even longer until the wedding. He could apply for a special licence, but doing so would raise suspicion. He sighed. One thing Annabelle wasn't was patient. Now she had turned up in London he expected to hear her demands within the next day or two, then he would have a matter of weeks to raise the money. If he didn't, then she would threaten to reveal the truth to Edward and to the world.

Daniel really needed Amelia's dowry. He grimaced and wondered when he had become quite so cynical. When he had been a young lad setting off for Cambridge he'd felt as though the whole world was at his feet. He was heir to an earldom, about to commence on a great life adventure and was surrounded by friends. He'd been convinced one day he'd fall in love with a beautiful woman and have a lovely family. Never did he think he'd have to marry for money. How different life had turned out to be.

He hated the fact that he was going to have to marry Amelia under false pretences. Whatever his faults he had always prided himself on never deceiving women. Over the years he had enjoyed many short liaisons, but he had always made it clear from the start these encounters were not going to be lasting relationships. Already he was deceiving Amelia, courting her with the express intention of getting her to marry him. He hated the idea that he was going to have to marry and give up his old lifestyle, but he hated the idea of not being entirely truthful about his motivations to Amelia more. He was turning into one of the fortune hunters he'd always despised.

Refusing to let himself become too melancholy, Daniel tossed back the rest of the glass of whisky and firmly set the decanter down on the table beside him. He needed a plan. In fact, he needed two plans. He needed a plan to make Amelia agree to marry him in record time and he needed a plan to raise a little bit of money to keep Annabelle at bay in the meantime.

He grimaced. He knew exactly where he could raise a little bit of money, but it meant renewing an acquaintance with a man he'd hoped never to see again. He wondered whether the man would agree to see him—they'd not parted well all those years ago. Daniel distinctly remembered telling Ernest Hathaway never to speak to him again.

He doubted Hathaway would agree to meet him, so he'd have to be far more underhand. Maybe if he recruited his old friend Fletcher to his cause he could help. Fletcher wouldn't have to know all the details, all the sordid ins and outs, but he would be able to persuade Hathaway to be at a particular place at a particular time and to hear what Daniel had to say. If nothing else Fletcher was a persuasive man.

Daniel allowed himself to relax a little. Maybe things would work out all right in the end. He would continue his pursuit of Amelia tomorrow and he would sort out some money to keep Annabelle at bay in the meantime.

His thoughts went back to Amelia and he wondered if he'd ruined his chances with her by acting so strangely. He'd have to come up with some sort of story to satisfy her curiosity. Amelia might be a quiet wallflower, but she wasn't stupid. Her eyes shone with intelligence when they conversed and she had noticed something was wrong from the very start.

Maybe he could make her forget with a few illicit kisses. He knew she responded to his touch and his kiss, and if he was honest with himself he enjoyed kissing Amelia more than he'd enjoyed anything in years.

At the thought of kissing her Daniel felt the first stirrings of desire and frowned with agitation. He didn't want to desire his future wife. He'd desired one woman, let his heart rule over his head, and look where that had got him. Amelia was perfect for him because she wasn't head-spinningly beautiful. She was just nice and average.

He thought of the little freckles across her nose and the curve of her lip when she smiled and repeated to himself that he would not be attracted to her. He refused to desire his future wife. They would have a comfortable companionship and nothing more.

Standing, Daniel repeated to himself that he didn't desire Amelia. He was far too in control for any nonsense like that.

Chapter Seven

Lizzie forced herself to step away from the window and sit back down in her chair.

'No sign of the earl today, then?' Harriet asked mildly.

Lizzie forced a smile on to her face. 'He said he would call today. I'm sure he'll be here later.' She was sure of no such thing after their parting yesterday. She'd never seen a man change in character so quickly.

'I'm surprised he didn't walk you home yesterday afternoon,' Harriet said.

'He had some business to attend to.'

'Still…' She let the word hang in the air.

Lizzie picked up a piece of embroidery she was meant to be working on and started stabbing at it with the needle. She had never been very good at sewing or embroidery, she much preferred to be out and about in the fresh air, but it gave her hands something to do and stopped her reaching across the room and strangling Harriet.

Lizzie had spent half the night tossing and turning in bed, trying to work out why Daniel had become so agitated in the park. She wondered if the woman was one of his former mistresses, someone he had used for pleasure, then abandoned when he had grown tired.

'The earl has quite a reputation, you know,' Harriet said after a couple of minutes.

Lizzie knew she shouldn't rise to the bait, but she desperately wanted to know more about Daniel. She wanted to know what motivated him and what secrets lay buried in his past.

'Oh?' she said, trying not to sound too interested.

Harriet glanced over her shoulder to check her mother wasn't about to enter the room before continuing.

'He's quite the rake. Rumour has it that once he had four mistresses at one time. And he's dated an opera singer.'

Lizzie smiled serenely. 'Well, I suppose everyone has to have a past.'

Maybe that woman was the opera singer. The quick look Lizzie had got of her had shown her to be very pretty, but seeing a former mistress didn't explain why Daniel had become quite so withdrawn.

'He's known to be very selective in his choice of woman, apparently only the most beautiful will do.'

Lizzie felt her heart starting to sink. She couldn't help but picture the beautiful Mrs Winter they had met in the park and realised she was probably more Daniel's normal type of woman.

'He'd never shown any interest in settling down before,' Harriet continued, 'but I suppose even earls can become short of funds.'

Lizzie couldn't even bring herself to answer. She knew Harriet was just saying these things to be cruel, but whatever her motivation there was certainly some truth in her words. Why else would Daniel be interested in a nobody like her? He was titled, handsome and charming. He could have his pick of fawning young ladies, or he could just as easily continue having illicit affairs with more experienced women. The only reason he'd ever be interested in her was her dowry. Or at least Amelia's dowry.

She stabbed her needle once again into the piece of

fabric and watched as the colours blurred before her eyes as the tears started to form. Just once she wanted something of her own. She wanted someone to be interested in her, not just pretending so they could get closer to Amelia. All her life she had been second best, often ignored completely when her cousin was around. From a young age her uncle had made it clear she was nothing more than a burden, someone no man would want to marry. For a few moments Lizzie had indulged in a sweet dream that Daniel might like her for who she was, but deep down Lizzie knew it wouldn't be so.

Blinking away the tears, Lizzie looked up as the butler entered the room.

'The Earl of Burwell,' he announced.

Daniel strode in, looking his normal composed self. There was no trace of the haunted and shaken man she'd glimpsed yesterday.

'Miss Hunter,' Daniel said, addressing Harriet, but not really looking at her. 'And, Amelia, it's lovely to see you again.'

Lizzie suppressed a smile as Harriet's eyes narrowed at the familiarity.

'Thank you for calling on me again.'

'I can't think of anywhere I'd rather be.'

Lizzie didn't bother pointing out he hadn't been able to get away from her fast enough yesterday afternoon. She smiled serenely at the compliment and wondered how they could get rid of Harriet so she could find out what had upset him so much. The idea of being alone with him sent a shiver down her spine. She told herself she was just curious, she just wanted to know what about the woman and small boy had spooked him, but if she examined her feelings hard enough there was also a desire to see if he would kiss her again. Although she knew their liaison was built on lies and it wasn't really her that he wanted, Lizzie couldn't help but want Daniel to kiss her one last time. For his lips to meet hers and for her to feel that tightening of desire deep inside her. To forget that she was plain old Lizzie Eastway and become a woman a man like Daniel could want.

'I'm afraid I've been a little presumptuous,' Daniel said with a wide smile.

Lizzie marvelled at how relaxed he seemed—there was no trace of the harrowed man she'd seen yesterday.

'I thought it would be the perfect afternoon to go for a ride.'

Lizzie found herself nodding. She missed the freedom of racing along the mud tracks surrounding her uncle's home just outside Bombay, she missed feeling the warm breeze on her face and seeing the scenery whip by. She'd always much preferred being outside to indoors. Back home her perfect afternoon had been trotting off on her own on horseback with a book tucked under her arm. She'd ride for a while, then find a spot to sit and read for hours on end until the light was fading. Amelia never had understood how Lizzie could spend so long in her own company, but for Lizzie it had been a welcome escape from a home where she didn't really belong.

'I've instructed my groom to be waiting in Hyde Park with two horses. If you would like, we can spend the afternoon on horseback.'

Lizzie stood and smoothed down her skirt. It sounded like a wonderful way to spend the afternoon and if they were riding they would be alone, which gave her the opportunity to find out exactly what secrets Daniel was hiding.

'I'll go and change,' she said, hurrying from the room.

* * *

Twenty minutes later they were strolling through one of the entrances to Hyde Park. Lizzie noted that Daniel was careful enough to avoid the spot where they'd seen the woman and small boy the day before, as if by not reminding Lizzie of it he could pretend the encounter hadn't happened.

'What beautiful horses,' Lizzie said as they approached Daniel's groom.

One was the huge black beast that had nearly trampled Lizzie the week before. The other was a slightly more docile-looking chestnut mare.

'Will you let me assist you up?' Daniel asked.

Lizzie nodded, feeling her heart start to race as he moved behind her. She positioned herself to mount the chestnut mare and glanced back over her shoulder. Daniel was close, almost as close as he'd been during their encounter in the Prestons' garden. She could feel his breath on the nape of her neck and it sent delicious shivers down her spine. She could imagine him wrapping his arms around her waist, pulling her back against his body and lowering his lips to her skin.

Lizzie swallowed and tried to regain control. She wasn't even sure if she liked him and here she was fantasising about him being entirely inappropriate in a public park.

'Are you ready?' His voice was low and seductive in her ear.

She managed to nod before she started to pull herself up on to the horse. His hands looped under her leg and boosted her the rest of the way, lifting her as effortlessly as if she were a rag doll.

Seated on the horse, Lizzie took a moment to regain control. Now Daniel wasn't quite so close she felt as though she were in charge of her brain once again.

'Shall we set off?' Daniel asked as he pulled himself up on to his horse.

Lizzie nodded and nudged her horse forward, concentrating on finding her equilibrium for a few seconds before falling into step beside Daniel.

They rode slowly at first. This part of the park was busy and Daniel had to greet most of the people they passed. It gave Lizzie the opportunity to watch him and try to figure him out. Daniel was still very much a mystery to her. She'd seen so many sides to him she didn't feel as though she knew the real man.

After about ten minutes the crowds started to thin out. Lizzie knew now was her opportunity to ask him what had upset him so much the previous day. If she left it much longer, it would be difficult to bring up.

'Daniel,' she said, still wondering how to phrase her question.

He turned to her with a lazy smile and for a few seconds Lizzie forgot entirely what she was meant to be saying.

'Yesterday, just before we left the park, something upset you.'

Daniel nodded, the smile remaining on his face, but Lizzie could tell underneath he was frozen.

'What happened?'

There was silence for well over a minute and Lizzie had almost convinced herself that he wasn't going to answer her question.

'I am sorry about how I left you yesterday,' Daniel said. 'It was rude and ungentlemanly. I hope you can forgive me.'

Lizzie nodded, she'd forgiven him already, but it wasn't his apology she wanted, it was an explanation.

'Something upset you. Was it that woman who walked past?'

His whole body stiffened and Lizzie knew she was right. He'd known the woman who'd not even stopped to speak to him. She wondered again if it was an old lover and felt an immediate pang of jealousy. Lizzie tried to shake it away, Daniel wasn't hers to be jealous over.

'It was nothing,' he said eventually. 'A case of mistaken identity. I thought she was someone I once knew. I was wrong.' It was said with such finality that Lizzie knew he would say no more on the matter.

They lapsed into silence. Daniel's evasive answer had reminded Lizzie that she didn't really know anything about the earl. He was charming and attentive towards her, but she had to keep telling herself it was because he thought she was someone else. In reality she didn't know this man at all. It might feel as though she'd known him for ever when he covered her lips with his own, but for him that was probably just another part of this charade.

It was clear Daniel was not going to tell her who his mystery woman was, and for a moment Lizzie wondered if he might still be seeing her. Surely he wouldn't be courting her and carrying on with a mistress at the same time. Lizzie knew a lot of married men kept mistresses, but she didn't want to believe Daniel would be kissing her by day and sleeping with another woman at night. With a shake of her head Lizzie dismissed the thought. She might not know the earl well, but she was almost certain that he wouldn't be so cold and disrespectful. Which still left the question of who the woman was.

'I wanted to ask you a favour,' Daniel said as they rode, his expression serious. 'I want you to educate me about India. I find I'm most ignorant on the subject. Did you know before yesterday I didn't even know they had crocodiles in that part of the world?'

Daniel grinned and Lizzie couldn't help but smile. His

good mood was infectious and very effective at distracting
her from thinking about his potential mistresses.

'What do you want to know?'

'All the interesting stuff,' he said. 'I'm your avid pupil.'

Lizzie thought a moment before saying anything more.

'The cow is the sacred animal of India, at least to the
millions of Hindu people who live there.'

'The cow? Really?'

'Trust me, we found out the hard way just how sacred
they are.'

'You have to explain.'

'My cousin was very popular with the army officers,'
Lizzie said, knowing that was a bit of an understatement.
'She happened to mention one day that she was fed up of
eating curry and wished she could have a lovely meal of
roast beef and potatoes.'

'Ah.'

'Some of the more eager young officers took it on themselves to provide the freshest beef possible, enraging the
locals. There was nearly a rebellion.'

Daniel turned to her with a smile. 'At least she didn't
say she wanted an elephant steak for lunch.'

Lizzie felt herself smiling, too. There was something
about Daniel's easygoing manner that made her relax. She
knew she shouldn't encourage him, but he made their time
together so enjoyable. Lizzie couldn't remember the last
time anyone had wanted to know anything about her life
and Daniel's attention and good-humoured observations
meant she was having a lovely time on their outing.

'I took the liberty of laying out a picnic,' Daniel said
after a few minutes of riding in silence. They were just
reaching the top of a small hill and there were wonderful
views over the rest of the park. Lizzie could see a blanket
and a hamper on the grass ahead of them. She glanced

around, knowing he must have had a member of his staff set out the picnic, but not able to see anyone in the vicinity.

'We should be quite alone for a while, not many people venture this far into the park,' he said. He gave her a salacious wink that was so over the top Lizzie couldn't help but laugh. Daniel might have a reputation as being a flirt, but he also knew how to poke fun at that reputation and laugh at himself. It was rather an attractive quality.

They stopped beside the blanket and Daniel quickly dismounted. Before Lizzie could even begin to get off her horse she felt his strong hands around her waist, lifting her to the ground. Even though there were at least three layers between his skin and hers Lizzie felt the heat from his hands as if he were touching her bare skin. They were close, almost chest to chest, and Lizzie knew if she tilted her head back she would see that smouldering look in his eyes. Then she'd be lost, unable to control what happened next.

Slowly she tilted her chin back. Daniel's eyes met hers and there was an intensity there that Lizzie had never seen before. One of his hands moved from her waist to her face, tracing the soft skin of her cheek with his fingers. The other hand stayed possessively on her waist.

Lizzie knew there was nothing she could do to stop him. She wanted this so much. Even though she knew their whole brief relationship was built upon lies, she didn't care. She wanted him to kiss her, she wanted him to lay her down and cover her body with his own. She wanted to feel desired and to know she was the one who drove him crazy.

Her heart was pounding in her chest as he continued to trace the contours of her face with his fingers. She felt herself stepping even closer, wanting to feel his body pressed up against hers. Lizzie didn't know why he wasn't kissing her, the anticipation was driving her crazy.

With a deep groan he dipped his head and covered her lips with his. Lizzie felt her body relaxing into his and for the first time she let her instincts take over. Her hands came up and laced through his hair, pulling him closer to her. She trailed her fingers down his neck and felt him shiver as she traced circles on his skin.

Gently Daniel dropped a hand to her shoulder. Lizzie felt her breath catch in her throat as she anticipated his next move. Slowly, so slowly Lizzie thought she might scream from frustration, Daniel ran his fingers along the neckline of her dress. He paused just for a second, then dipped his fingers inside the thin material. Lizzie felt the coil of desire deep inside her and silently begged Daniel to continue. His fingers were inching over her breast and she knew she'd scream if he didn't delve even deeper. Lizzie knew what they were doing was wrong, but she also knew if Daniel stopped she would shatter from pure frustration.

Daniel stopped. Lizzie moaned, trying to pull him closer again, not caring if she was behaving like a common streetwalker. She wanted Daniel, her body was screaming out in need of him.

She looked up at him with unfocused eyes and saw the confusion on his face. Of everything she'd expected to see there confusion wasn't part of it.

Daniel grasped her by the upper arms and studied her face, as if trying to work out who she was.

Lizzie looked back, wondering once again what he saw when he looked at her. She knew he couldn't truly be attracted to her, but when he kissed her it seemed so real, so passionate, she couldn't believe he didn't feel some spark of desire. Surely even the most consummate of actors couldn't fake what they had just shared.

She had nearly summoned the courage to ask him when Daniel quickly dropped his hands and stepped back. Lizzie followed his gaze and saw they had company. She felt the colour rise in her cheeks as she wondered how much the man had seen. Trying to act as though nothing had just happened, Lizzie turned to face the newcomer. As she turned she noticed the dark expression on Daniel's face and wondered what side of the earl she was about to witness next.

Chapter Eight

He must be sick, it was the only explanation. Daniel had always planned on kissing Amelia again, but in his imagination he'd been cool and in control, not breathless with anticipation like a green boy.

He shook his head. Something was wrong with him, that was for sure, but now wasn't the right time to figure out what. Later in the privacy of his study he could analyse what exactly was going on, but right now they had company. Decidedly unfriendly company.

Daniel forced a smile on his face as the newcomer stopped his horse in front of them. He wondered how much this man had seen and cursed himself for not choosing somewhere more private for his and Amelia's liaison. He'd thought the park would seem romantic to her, with the views across London, but he'd known there was a risk of passers-by happening upon them. Not that this man was a simple passer-by. Daniel groaned quietly as the man slowed his horse, and wondered how the newcomer had found them, for it could not be mere coincidence that Ernest Hathaway had come upon them.

'Burwell,' Hathaway said, looking down at Daniel.

'Hathaway,' Daniel greeted him in clipped tones.

'Won't you introduce me to your lovely companion?'

Daniel gritted his teeth. He didn't want Amelia to be

introduced to this man. Hathaway was untrustworthy and selfish and looked out only for himself.

'Miss Amelia Eastway, this is Mr Ernest Hathaway.'

Amelia inclined her head in greeting. Her eyes were wide with curiosity and silently Daniel cursed. This was going to be something else he had to explain his way out of.

'Ah, the famous Miss Eastway. Your arrival in London has caused quite a stir.'

Amelia's eyes narrowed. 'I'm sure you must be exaggerating,' she said mildly.

Despite most of his mind being focused on Hathaway, Daniel felt a bubble of annoyance at her words. Although he'd known her only a short while Daniel knew Amelia sold herself short. Indeed, she might not be what society classically thought of as stunning, but his own reaction to her was enough for him to know she was attractive in her own way. Shaking his head, he turned back to Hathaway.

'Not at all, all of society can't help but talk about London's most eligible *heiress*,' said Hathaway. The emphasis was entirely on the word *heiress*, making it clear this was the only reason the *ton* thought Amelia gossip-worthy. Daniel glanced sideways and saw two faint spots of colour appear on Amelia's cheeks; she'd understood Hathaway's message and the implied insult. He almost reached up to pluck Hathaway from his horse and punch him, but managed to keep his temper in check. He needed the man and punching him, no matter how tempting, would not help his cause.

'Can we help you at all?' Daniel said, trying to make his voice as polite as possible. 'We were just about to sit down for some refreshments.' Daniel motioned to the blanket and the hamper, hoping Hathaway would take the hint and leave them alone. He might need to speak to the man, but there was no way he was going to do it in front of Amelia.

'That's a most gracious offer,' Hathaway said, swinging himself to the ground and walking towards the small picnic that was laid out.

Daniel's eyes narrowed. He knew Hathaway had deliberately misconstrued his meaning. There was no way he'd ever invite the slimy man to sit with them. Over the years Daniel's and Hathaway's paths had crossed numerous times and each encounter had left the two men disliking each other more than the last.

'I spoke to Fletcher,' Hathaway said casually. 'He said you wanted to discuss some business.'

Daniel felt like punching Hathaway. He had asked Fletcher to set up the meeting, not really expecting Hathaway to agree to it. What he certainly hadn't been expecting was an ambush like this whilst he was out with Amelia. He cast a glance sideways at Amelia and wondered how he was going to get out of this situation. The last thing he needed to do was discuss his business with Hathaway in front of the woman he was meant to be courting.

Hathaway waited until Amelia had sat down on one edge of the blanket, then proceeded to sit himself. Knowing Hathaway had trapped him in a very awkward situation, Daniel sat and waited for the disaster to begin.

'I'd heard rumours Burwell was courting you, Miss Eastway. How delighted I am to find out it is true.'

Daniel knew Hathaway was anything but delighted.

'You have known the earl a long time?' Amelia asked.

'Oh, we go back years. We were at school together.'

Amelia smiled, but Daniel noticed it didn't quite meet her eyes. She was astute, he realised, and hardly missed a thing. She had definitely picked up on the fact that Daniel and Hathaway were not friends, despite their long acquaintance.

'How lovely,' Amelia murmured.

'Although of course I was closer to Burwell's brother at the time.'

Daniel froze. He felt the blood drain from his face and for a moment the world around him seemed to stop.

'I didn't know you have a brother,' Amelia was saying as everything came back into focus.

'I don't,' Daniel said curtly. 'He died.'

He could see the shock on Amelia's face, but he didn't have it in him to sugar-coat the words. Rupert's death had torn him apart and still, over a decade on, he hadn't forgiven himself for what had happened.

'So tragic, to die so young,' Hathaway said, his voice laced with sympathy.

Daniel suppressed the urge to strangle the man. Hathaway wasn't responsible for his brother's death, but he certainly hadn't helped to prevent it.

'Such a shame nothing could be done to prevent it,' the man continued.

Daniel felt burning fury rise up inside him. He would have done anything to change what had happened to his brother, he'd have moved heaven and earth to stop his tragic death, but the truth of the matter was Rupert was dead. He had died years ago and every day since Daniel had regretted not having done more to keep him alive. Hathaway knew this and was trying to stir up the guilt and regret Daniel still felt so keenly.

'I'm so sorry,' Amelia said, reaching and covering his hand with her own.

Daniel barely felt her touch. His mind was back in his childhood, in his teenage years—the years when he could have helped Rupert. If only his father had accepted Rupert as a true son, or his mother had allowed him to even occasionally set foot in the house. For years he had resented his parents for the part they played in rejecting

Rupert, but there was no one he blamed more than himself. He'd been there at school, term after term, as Rupert had shrunk into himself. No amount of blaming his cold, unfeeling mother or his father, who was trying to please everyone, would change the fact that Daniel himself could have made a difference.

'It must be awful to lose a brother,' Amelia said quietly.

Daniel pulled himself back to the present and focused on Amelia, trying to block out Hathaway's presence altogether.

'It is,' Daniel said simply.

'Especially if you're close,' Hathaway supplied.

Daniel ignored the comment. He and Rupert hadn't been close, despite being less than a year apart in age. They'd shared classes at school and had even started at Cambridge together. They should have been inseparable. And maybe if Daniel had spent a little more time with the boy who had shared his blood he would have been alive today. Daniel knew this and wished every day that the outcome had been different.

'I know I'm affected by the loss of my parents still,' Amelia said quietly. Daniel glanced at her quickly and saw her eyes widen as if she'd said something she shouldn't. 'The loss of my mother,' Amelia said quickly. 'My mother died many years ago now.'

Daniel knew she was reaching out to him, sympathising, but he couldn't deal with her sympathy right now. He wished they would change the subject, wished they would talk about almost anything else, but he knew even if the topic of conversation did change he'd still never be able to outrun his guilt.

'What happened?' Amelia asked gently.

Daniel froze. He didn't know how to answer the question. It wasn't that he was ashamed of the way his brother had died, but more that he was ashamed he hadn't done anything to stop it.

Hathaway was looking at him with barely concealed amusement in his eyes. He was enjoying Daniel's torment.

'My brother was very unhappy. He took his own life.'

To Amelia's credit she did not gasp or twitter on incessantly as most people did. Some of the colour drained from her face, but otherwise outwardly she did not react to his statement.

'I'm sorry,' she said simply and reached out and took his hand in hers.

Daniel felt oddly comforted by the gesture. Normally he hated sympathy from people on the subject of his brother's death, but he didn't feel as though Amelia was judging him. In fact, the frown she directed towards Hathaway showed she'd picked up on his character flaws pretty quickly.

'Mr Hathaway,' she said sweetly, 'was there something you wanted to discuss with the earl?'

Hathaway looked a little surprised to be addressed so directly.

'Of course,' Hathaway said with a predator's smile. 'I think *you* wished to discuss a loan, Burwell.'

Daniel groaned inwardly. Amelia was learning so many of his secrets this afternoon. He wouldn't be surprised if she ran for the hills immediately.

'We could discuss the matter later, maybe at the club.' Both Daniel and Hathaway frequented the same gentlemen's club, although normally Daniel made a point to avoid Hathaway at all costs.

'I'm not sure when I'll be free again,' Hathaway said, examining his fingernails nonchalantly. 'If you want the loan, we'd better discuss it now.'

Daniel glanced at Amelia, who was looking resolutely down at the blanket. He knew the implied conclusion of this discussion wasn't lost on her. He needed money and he needed it so desperately that he would borrow it off a man he despised. Amelia would, of course, assume that he was pursuing her for the same reason.

She was a sensible young woman and Daniel knew that deep down she was aware that many of her suitors' interest in her was because of her dowry. However, most people did not come out and say it directly.

'I'm willing to loan you up to two hundred pounds at a good rate of interest—what are friends for after all?'

'And the rate?' Daniel ground out.

'Twenty per cent.'

It wasn't as extortionate as Daniel had expected. He supposed Hathaway's humiliation of him in front of Amelia was payment enough.

'How long for?'

Hathaway eyed Amelia for a couple of seconds.

'Two months should be long enough for you to get your affairs in order.'

Amelia recoiled involuntarily as if she'd been slapped in the face. The implication couldn't have been more clear: it should take Daniel only two months to finalise his marriage to Amelia and be in possession of her dowry.

Seeing he had caused the desired effect, Hathaway stood.

'Think on it, Burwell, send word to me if you decide to accept my offer and I'll get you the funds within the week.'

Daniel wished he could punch the man. Amelia looked devastated and all he could do was sit by and watch.

'It was delightful to make your acquaintance, Miss Eastway, especially after I've heard so much about you.'

Amelia managed a short nod of acknowledgement.

Hathaway mounted his horse and rode off without another word. Daniel and Amelia sat in silence for a whole minute, the gap between them seeming to widen with every passing second. Daniel wished he could reach out and take her hand, whisper something in her ear that would bring back the closeness they'd shared just moments before Hathaway had arrived. He hated the desolate look in Amelia's eyes. Although it was true he was pursuing Amelia for her dowry and the fortune she would bring to the marriage, he hadn't wanted her to end up feeling so unwanted and unattractive. He liked her, probably more than he should, and the last thing he wanted was for her to be hurt.

'Thank you for this afternoon,' Amelia said abruptly, standing before Daniel even realised what was happening. 'But I think I will return home now.'

He watched open-mouthed as she strode across to her horse and mounted easily without any help.

'Amelia,' he called after her, knowing he had to stop her or everything was lost.

She ignored him and spurred her horse forward into a canter. He cursed loudly before jogging over to his horse and swinging up on to his back. He needed to catch her, to try to smooth over the mess Hathaway had caused, otherwise he would lose her and Annabelle would ruin his son's future.

Chapter Nine

Lizzie felt the tears stinging her eyes as she galloped through the park. She couldn't believe she'd allowed herself to get hurt. She'd let Daniel draw her in and convince her that maybe he was just a little attracted to her. How could a man kiss a woman the way he had kissed her and not be even a little attracted to her? She thought back to Harriet's words earlier that afternoon and realised Amelia's cousin was telling the truth. Daniel was a rake, a man so practised in the art of seduction he could make any woman fall for him with a single kiss whilst not feeling a thing himself. He could even make the most unattractive woman feel beautiful and desired.

She raised a hand and swiped the tears that fell down her cheeks. She would not cry over him. Lizzie had known deep down that the only reason Daniel was courting her was because of Amelia's dowry. She'd repeated it to herself several times each hour, but still a small part of her had hoped. It wasn't as though they could ever be together anyway—after her lies about who she was Lizzie knew she'd be hounded out of London society, but for a moment it had felt wonderful to feel desired. Then to have that man come and reveal Daniel's crippling debts—and they must be crippling if he was willing to turn to someone like that for money—had been humiliating for both of them. Hathaway had even gone so far as to calculate when Amelia's dowry would be available if Lizzie and Daniel married. That had been the final blow.

Lizzie shook her head and tried to regain control of her emotions. Normally she was good at hiding when she was upset. For years in India she had been a burden to her uncle and he had let her know at every opportunity. There was one memory that was seared in Lizzie's mind so clearly it never really left her. A dressmaker had come to the house to measure her and Amelia for a new dress and she'd brought some samples with her. Both Lizzie and Amelia had been very excited teenagers, trying on the dresses and parading round. Amelia, of course, told her she looked stunning. Lizzie could always rely on her cousin for a compliment even if no one else ever thought to give her one. Her uncle had entered the room, in a foul mood for some reason, and on seeing Lizzie he had snorted. He'd instructed the dressmaker not to bother with a new dress for Lizzie as nothing was going to improve the disaster that she was becoming. Lizzie had swallowed back her tears and smiled when Amelia had later said she would help alter one of her new dresses for Lizzie.

So if she could hold her head up high to her uncle back then, why was she blubbering like a fool now?

'Amelia.' The shout came from some distance away and Lizzie turned to look behind her.

Daniel was gaining on her, riding like a man possessed. Lizzie rolled her eyes. He was no doubt wanting to ensure nothing was going to get in the way of him getting his hands on her precious dowry. She urged her horse to travel faster. Trees whipped past on her right and Lizzie knew it wouldn't be long before they were back in the more popular part of Hyde Park. If she could just reach there before Daniel caught up with her, she would be saved having to talk to him. She didn't want to exchange another word with him ever again and she certainly didn't want to listen to his lies about how he found her attractive. His silence when Hathaway had insulted her had been confirmation enough of his views.

Lizzie glanced back over her shoulder once again, wanting to see if Daniel had gained on her. Just as she was turning back to face forward a branch from a tree came out of nowhere. Lizzie ducked instinctively and managed to avoid the branch, but the sudden movement put her off balance. She pulled desperately on the horse's reins, trying to slow down as she felt herself lose her seat and start to topple. Arms flailing, Lizzie knew falling was inevitable and forced her body to go limp as she toppled from the horse. She rolled as she hit the ground, the breath forced from her lungs, and when she finally stopped moving she stayed curled in a ball, too frightened to move.

'Amelia!' Lizzie heard Daniel shout as he raced towards her. She didn't look up, instead concentrating on trying to breathe.

'Dear God,' he exhaled as he pulled his horse up beside her.

Lizzie heard him dismount and immediately felt his arms embracing her. Momentarily she forgot she was angry with this man and she allowed herself to melt into his body.

'Amelia, can you hear me?' he asked, his voice panicked.

Lizzie managed to nod, not having found her voice yet.

'What hurts?'

Everything hurt. Everything from the top of her head down to the bottom of her feet hurt and she felt bloodied and bruised.

'Everything,' she managed to mutter after a few seconds.

Lizzie felt Daniel slowly sit her up and rest her body against his.

'Do you know who I am?' he asked slowly.

Lizzie nodded. 'The earl,' she said, not wanting to use his given name.

Daniel didn't seem to notice, instead he just seemed pleased she was at least a little orientated.

Slowly he moved round so he was facing Lizzie. They were both still sitting on the ground, but now Daniel was holding her round the waist whilst looking at her face.

Lizzie allowed her eyes to flutter open and raised a hand to her head. It didn't seem to have any large dents in it.

'Keep still,' Daniel instructed. Lizzie felt a pang of annoyance that he was telling her what to do, but had to concede it was good advice.

Slowly she watched as he raised his hands to her head and started to run his fingers over her scalp. His touch was gentle and Lizzie felt herself relaxing a little.

'Ouch,' she muttered as he found a sensitive spot.

'You've got quite a bump.'

Lizzie raised her own hand and traced the egg-sized bump that was forming on the back of her head. She would likely have a headache for days.

Daniel moved on, inspecting each part of her body much the way he had in the Prestons' garden when she had hurtled down the steps and landed on top of him. Gently he ran his fingers over her arms, satisfying himself there weren't any breaks, then he moved on to her body. He grasped her around the waist and slowly moved his hands upwards, squeezing as he went as if checking for broken ribs. Lizzie felt bruised and tender, but there was no sharp stab of pain.

As his hands moved higher Lizzie felt her breathing getting shallower. She hated him, hated him so much she never wanted to see him again, but she still couldn't stop her body responding to his touch. With each stroke of his fingers or squeeze of his hand she felt every nerve ending in her body come alive and begin firing. She yearned for his touch and at the same time wanted to push him away for ever.

Daniel's hands lingered on her waist for a few seconds and Lizzie knew he was trying to meet her gaze. She looked resolutely off into the distance, refusing to be sucked in by him.

'I need to check your legs,' Daniel said quietly.

Lizzie's eyes snapped upwards and met his. Already he was moving away from her and taking her left ankle in his hand. Carefully he encircled her lower leg with his hands and started to move his touch upwards. Lizzie didn't think anyone had ever touched her legs before him. It was intimate, maybe even more intimate than when his hand had dipped into the neckline of her dress earlier, and she knew she should pull away.

This was the man who had kissed her as though she were the most attractive woman on earth, then let his acquaintance insult her so openly. He'd not denied it was her supposed fortune he was after and Lizzie had to keep reminding herself he was a seasoned seducer.

Daniel moved his hands to her right ankle and immediately Lizzie let out a strangled cry.

'Does that hurt?'

She nodded, biting back a sarcastic comment.

He examined her carefully, probing gently with his fingers and stroking the length of her calf with his hand.

'I don't think it's broken,' he said eventually. 'Probably just sprained.'

Lizzie nodded, wondering if a sprain could be this painful.

'We should get you home.'

'If you would be so kind as to assist me on to my horse, I'm sure I can find my own way back,' Lizzie said, her words stilted and her tone formal.

Daniel looked at her as though she were crazy.

'You want me to abandon an injured lady in the middle of Hyde Park?'

Lizzie nodded.

'Amelia,' he said, his voice strained with emotion. 'What happened—'

'Don't,' Lizzie interrupted him. 'Please don't say anything.'

He looked as though he was going to protest, he even opened his mouth to start his explanation, but must have thought better of it.

'I will not let you ride home alone,' he said eventually.

He rose to his feet and offered her his hand. Reluctantly Lizzie took it. Always the pragmatist, she knew realistically she wasn't going to be able to mount a horse without his help.

As she stood Lizzie felt a bolt of pain shoot through her ankle and she bit back a scream. Daniel must have seen the pained expression on her face and heard the sharp intake of breath for as soon as she was upright he swept her into his arms.

Lizzie started to protest but was silenced with a single look from Daniel.

Silently he walked over to his horse and carefully set her down.

'Stay here.' It was an order and, given his tone of voice, one Lizzie didn't dare disobey. She stood where he'd set her, balancing on her one good foot whilst she watched him fetch the horse she'd been riding and carefully tie its reins to his own. Then he pulled himself up on to his horse's back and effortlessly swung her up in front of him. It had all happened so quickly Lizzie didn't have time to protest. One moment she was standing on one foot, the next she was nestled between his thighs with his arm wrapped round her waist.

'I'm perfectly capable of riding,' she mumbled, knowing it was pointless to argue. Daniel had a determined look about him and she doubted anything less than divine intervention would convince him to let her ride on her own.

He urged his horse forward into a comfortable walk and despite herself Lizzie felt herself relaxing back into his chest.

'Amelia,' Daniel said once they had started to move, 'I need to apologise.'

Lizzie didn't disagree, but she didn't want to hear it. Either he was going to admit he was just courting her for a dowry she didn't even possess, or he was going to lie to her. She didn't want to hear what he had to say in either scenario.

'Hathaway was inexcusably rude and I'm afraid I wasn't much better. I shouldn't have allowed him to speak to you like that.'

Lizzie held herself completely still, wondering what his next words would be.

'I was shaken by having the memory of my brother's death raked up, but that is no excuse.'

He sighed and not for the first time Lizzie sensed Daniel was a troubled man. He put on a good show, but underneath the smiles and easy conversation there was so much more going on.

'I only hope you give me the chance to make it up to you.'

Lizzie wanted to shout at him, force him to admit why he was really courting her. She wished the truth was out in the open, that he would tell her he was only interested in her for her dowry, then she would be able to start putting him out of her mind. It would be better all round than continuing this charade, and she would be able to go back to being plain old Lizzie Eastway, the girl who was always second best.

Chapter Ten

Daniel knew he'd made a mess of things. Actually that was an understatement; courting Amelia had turned into a complete disaster. For years he had prided himself on his ability to seduce a woman with a single look, a single compliment, and now it really mattered that not only had he not complimented Amelia, he'd allowed her to be most grievously insulted while he stood by, mute.

He'd been completely thrown by Hathaway's presence, but that wasn't any kind of excuse. In truth, he'd been thrown before the man had even turned up. It had all started with that damn kiss. Once again Daniel had planned to further his courtship of Amelia with a kiss. In his mind it was to be something of passion and romance, something she could not help but fall for. She'd responded to him, there was no denying it, but once again he'd also lost control. Far from being rational and clear-headed, he'd felt the heat rise up inside him and his desire had taken over.

After Annabelle he had sworn never to let a woman get under his skin. But there was something about Amelia, something that reared its head whenever he kissed her—hell, whenever he got close to her—that made him lose control.

Daniel was brought out of his musings by a sharp knock

on the door. Seconds later his butler was easing himself into the room.

'You have a visitor, sir.'

Daniel frowned. He wasn't expecting anyone. Maybe it would be Hathaway, come to rescind his offer of a loan from earlier. Daniel hadn't exactly jumped at the man's offer, even though he needed the money badly.

'A lady.'

Ah. Annabelle. Of course. Daniel should have known it wouldn't be long before she was knocking at his door, demanding money for her silence.

'Show her in.'

The last person he wanted to see right now was his ex-lover, but he knew if he made some excuse Annabelle would only make him suffer for it. She'd turned up at his club once before and at the house of one of his mistresses another time. Knowing his luck, Daniel thought this time she would choose Amelia as her target. It would be better all round if he just gritted his teeth and dealt with her now.

'So lovely to see you yesterday, Daniel,' Annabelle said as she sailed into the room and delicately perched on the edge of a chair. She was a beautiful woman, but she was always arranging herself to show off her best side, fussing and preening, which Daniel now saw detracted from her beauty.

'Where's Edward?'

'Our son is safe, he's with a friend of mine.'

Daniel tried not to let his disappointment show. Annabelle hardly ever actually let him see his son, just catch glimpses of him as he had done the day before.

'Bringing up a child is a very expensive business,' Annabelle said, smoothing down her skirt, then looking up at Daniel and fluttering her eyelashes.

Daniel couldn't believe he had once been in love with

this woman. She was cruel and manipulative, and he'd been completely besotted.

'You want more money.'

'For our son, of course. Otherwise I might let it slip that his father wasn't a war hero, now sadly deceased.'

Daniel grimaced. No matter how much he despised Annabelle he couldn't let her reveal the truth to his son. He couldn't let Edward grow up to be an outcast like Rupert had been, teased because he was the illegitimate son of an earl.

'How much?' Daniel asked, knowing there was no point quibbling.

'Just the usual amount. Twenty pounds a month, so two hundred and forty pounds for the year.'

It was extortionate, more than most titled gentlemen had as their yearly income. Annabelle had bled him dry over the years, but Daniel knew he would continue to pay.

'I want to see Edward.'

'I don't think that's wise. He might start asking who this strange man is.'

Daniel hated the thought that he was a stranger to his son.

'You've got a week to raise the money. I'll come back to collect it. Just remember what will happen if you don't pay.'

Annabelle stood and walked round the desk, leant over and gave Daniel a peck on the cheek.

'We could have been so happy,' she whispered in his ear.

'I think I owe you an apology.' Daniel raised his head to see Fletcher approaching his table.

Daniel had been sitting in his club for the best part of an hour nursing a whisky. His frown had stopped any passing acquaintances from approaching him, but it did not deter Fletcher.

'I asked Hathaway to meet with you. I didn't realise he would actively seek you out.'

Daniel nodded, grimacing as he remembered the expression on Amelia's face as Hathaway had insulted her.

'I take it Miss Eastway was present.'

'She was.'

'Did Hathaway actually bring up business whilst she was there?'

Daniel raked a hand through his hair. 'He brought up the subject of a loan, after telling Miss Eastway about my brother and insinuating I was only interested in her for her money.'

Even easygoing Fletcher couldn't find anything to say for a moment or two. Instead he motioned for another glass of whisky for them both.

'What happened?' he asked eventually.

Daniel didn't say anything about his brother. Fletcher had been his friend since school, so he knew most of the sordid details. He knew the guilt Daniel carried around over Rupert's death and in part he shared some of that guilt.

They'd all been at Eton together. Daniel and Fletcher had hit it off immediately, been friends from the very first day. Hathaway was already a slimy little toad and the two boys had gone out of their way to avoid him. Rupert had begun the term late, only two weeks, but it was enough to make him noticeable. Boys were notoriously unforgiving at that age and immediately they wanted to find out what had caused the delay.

When Rupert had arrived Daniel hadn't known how to act. It wasn't the first time he'd laid eyes on his illegitimate half-brother, but it was the first time they'd ever been close enough to interact. They had circled each other warily for a few days, neither wanting to be the one to make the first move.

And then everything had changed. Somehow Hathaway had found out that Rupert was illegitimate. Boys whispered about him as he walked from class to class, the few friends he had managed to distance themselves. It didn't matter that his father was bothering to send him to Eton despite being illegitimate. He was ostracised, made an outcast. Daniel could have done something. If he'd extended the hand of friendship, then others would have followed, but he'd been too wrapped up in his own life to even notice.

By the time they left Eton and started at Cambridge Rupert had turned into a recluse, leaving his lodgings only to attend lectures. Older, slightly wiser and certainly more aware of his half-brother's misery, Daniel had tried to reach out a few times, but when Rupert rejected him he all too easily gave up.

Then Rupert had killed himself. On the last day of the winter term he'd been found hanging in his room. He'd left a note, but even without it Daniel didn't need a dead man's accusations to know the truth: he could have prevented his brother's death. If he'd persevered, if he'd tried just a little harder to reach out to him, maybe Rupert would still be alive.

'It wasn't your fault,' Fletcher said softly after a couple of minutes, knowing his friend was thinking of his brother.

Daniel shook his head and took a gulp of whisky. He knew his guilt would never ease.

'Hathaway agreed to lend me the money, but he all but said the only reason I'm pursuing Miss Eastway is because of her fortune.'

Fletcher shrugged. 'Well, it is, isn't it?'

Daniel considered. When he'd asked Fletcher to point out Amelia in the Prestons' ballroom all he could think about was her dowry and the means to pay Annabelle to shield his son against the truth of his birth. Then he'd encountered her in the garden and he'd felt the stab of desire he hadn't felt in years. At each subsequent meeting he'd realised that he actually liked Amelia. She was quiet and thoughtful, but a sharp intelligence hid behind her unassuming manner. He found he enjoyed talking to her and the hours they spent together passed quite pleasurably.

He actually enjoyed the company of the woman he was hoping to marry, which would be fantastic if he didn't desire her so damn much.

Most of the time he could think rationally. When they were walking in the park or riding side by side he could look at her and see the modest, gentle woman the rest of the world saw. There was just that small percentage of the time, normally when Amelia was standing close to him, when his heart started pounding in his chest and he knew he had to have her. He wanted to run his hands over her entire body, kiss her in all her most intimate places and make her his. He wanted to lay her down and make love to her until neither of them knew where one body stopped and the next began.

'Ah,' Fletcher said, 'I see.'

Daniel knew he hadn't said a word, but with four sisters Fletcher was unusually sensitive and astute.

'What?' Daniel asked.

'You feel something for her.'

Daniel didn't bother to deny it. He did feel something for Amelia. He wasn't going to claim it was love or anything as noble. He liked the girl, but more than that he desired her.

'Most people would be happy to feel something for their future spouse.'

Daniel knew it was true. Most *ton* marriages were marriages of convenience, much like the one he'd planned to have. The match was made either for money or for a title and an alliance. Many married couples thought themselves lucky if they didn't completely despise each other.

'It complicates things,' Daniel said.

Fletcher regarded him for a few moments and Daniel knew his friend was considering whether to say anything more.

'We've all had women who have got under our skin,' he said eventually. 'The trick is not to let them control the rest of your life.' With that his friend stood, clapped him on the shoulder and walked away. Unfortunately a much-less-welcome companion soon approached his table.

'Burwell, twice in one day. What an unexpected pleasure.'

Daniel took a few seconds to compose himself before raising his head to look at Hathaway. The man irritated him and had been unforgivably rude to Amelia, but Daniel knew he needed his old acquaintance to lend him the money to get Annabelle off his back.

'Hathaway,' Daniel said, his voice low and not much more than a growl.

'So delightful to meet the future Lady Burwell earlier. Isn't she a quiet little thing?'

'Miss Eastway is a charming young woman.'

'With a charmingly large dowry.'

Daniel felt the muscles in his hand clench as he formed a fist, but forced himself to relax. He hadn't let Hathaway goad him when they had been at school or university together and he wasn't going to start now.

'Thank you for the offer of a loan. I will send a man to collect it in a few days.'

For a moment Daniel thought Hathaway might stay, that he might want to bait Daniel further, but luckily his old acquaintance didn't seem in the mood for taunting him tonight. After a few seconds of being ignored by Daniel, Hathaway picked up his drink and moved on.

Daniel nursed his whisky for a few more minutes before gulping down the last of it and standing to leave. He needed some fresh air and he needed to clear his head.

Daniel thought back to the conversation he'd had with Fletcher earlier in the evening. He knew his old friend was right; most men would be ecstatic to desire the woman they were courting, but Daniel wished he felt nothing beyond mild affection for Amelia. He had experienced gut-wrenching passion before, he'd let it cloud his judgement and overtake his life, and now he wasn't the only one paying for it. It was because of desire that he could never truly know his son and it was because of desire that one day that boy he loved so much would probably find out he was illegitimate and have his world shattered.

The past few years had forced Daniel to become a pragmatist, and as he walked he strived to take his emotions out of the equation. The facts remained: he was broke, he needed money to pay off Annabelle.

There were really only two problems. The first was the way Daniel seemed to lose his head whenever Amelia's body brushed up against his and the second was the fact that after this afternoon she probably never wanted to see him ever again.

Daniel had been walking absentmindedly for about half an hour when he realised his subconscious had brought him to the house Amelia was staying in with her aunt. He glanced up at the windows, wondering which of them belonged to Amelia's room. It was far too late to call on her, despite Daniel wanting to try to move on from their disastrous afternoon out in the park. He was just about to turn away when he saw a flicker of orange in one of the windows. Frowning, he stared for a minute before realising what it was.

Chapter Eleven

After her disastrous afternoon Lizzie had fled straight to her room on arriving home. She hadn't wanted to answer Aunt Mathilda's questions on how things were going with *the dear earl* and she hadn't wanted to endure Harriet's snide comments. All she did want to do was bury her face in her pillow and cry.

On reaching her room Lizzie allowed herself to sob for five minutes before sitting up and wiping her eyes. Whilst she was growing up there had been hundreds of occasions that had made Lizzie want to shut herself away from the rest of the world and cry until she had no more tears, but she'd learnt to control her sadness. No one comforted her then and no one was going to comfort her now.

As she had many times Lizzie wondered how different things would have been if her parents were still alive. They had died in a coach accident when Lizzie had been very young—all she could really remember was her mother's warm smile and her father's hearty laugh. She couldn't imagine having a mother, someone who would love her unconditionally, who would wipe away her tears and tell her she was worth so much more. Lizzie could never imagine being the centre of someone's world.

She shook her head. She probably wouldn't ever be the centre of someone's world. For odd moments she had fooled herself about Daniel when he looked at her with his wolfish eyes and claimed her with a kiss that was so searing and possessive she had dared to hope he might want her as he wanted no other. She had dared to hope he might be the one who could love her unconditionally.

It had all been nothing more than an illusion. What made it hurt even more was the attraction Lizzie felt for Daniel. She knew nothing could come of their liaison, she knew that once her identity was revealed she would be hounded from London society, but that didn't stop her heart racing whenever he smiled at her or her skin tingling when he touched her. He was a good-looking man and a seasoned charmer, but it was something more than that. When he touched her it was as if all the jumbled pieces of Lizzie's life fell into place.

She'd been fooling herself, wanting something that was so far out of her reach, and now it was time to accept reality and move on. When Amelia returned and revealed her identity, Lizzie would have to disappear. Her cousin would beg her to stay, of course, and normally Lizzie would do anything for Amelia, but this time she had tasted how her life could have been if she had been born Amelia's sister rather than her penniless cousin. She couldn't go back to being poor, insignificant Lizzie who no one took any notice of. She would leave London, leave the country and seek out a life for herself elsewhere.

Deep down Lizzie knew in reality it wouldn't be the *ton* in general she would be running from, but rather a very specific dashing earl with smouldering eyes.

A knock at her door gave her a moment's panic, but she took a moment to straighten her dress and wipe her eyes before answering.

'Come in.'

Rosie, a young maid who had been assigned to help Lizzie dress and do her hair whilst she was living with

Aunt Mathilda, opened the door and dropped into a little neat curtsy.

'Begging your pardon for disturbing you, miss, but a letter came for you when you were out.'

Lizzie's eyes widened with anticipation. It would be from Amelia surely. Lizzie still hadn't heard a thing from her cousin since they had parted at the dock. She was becoming increasingly worried about Amelia. In the time they had spent together on their voyage Lizzie had tried to talk her cousin out of her foolish plan so many times. She'd tried to explain the scandal that would ensue if anyone found out Amelia had run off to meet a man, but as usual her cousin had just laughed off her concerns.

Lizzie was beginning to wish she had made Amelia realise that it wasn't only her reputation she was risking, but Lizzie's, too. At the time she had agreed to Amelia's reckless plan because she never expected to want to marry, never expected to find someone who wanted to marry her. Now she was getting so worried about her cousin she would use any tactic, including guilt over ruining Lizzie's reputation, to keep her cousin from disappearing.

'I'm sure it could have waited until morning, miss, it was just…' The young maid tailed off.

'Yes?' Lizzie asked kindly.

'It was just that Miss Harriet was poking around it and I was afraid she might read something she shouldn't,' Rosie said, dropping her voice.

'Thank you, Rosie, you are very astute.'

The maid looked confused at the compliment but curtsied again, handed over the letter and backed out of the room.

Lizzie turned the envelope over in her hands and immediately felt disappointment. The handwriting was nothing like her cousin's. The two girls had taken all their lessons together, so Lizzie could recognise Amelia's hurried scrawl easily.

Instead the letters were neat and carefully spaced; it was her uncle's handwriting.

Although the letter was addressed to Amelia, Lizzie slid her finger under the seal and opened it. She needed to know what was so important he'd sent a letter so soon after their departure. For this to have got to London so quickly he must have sent it mere days after they had left India.

Sinking down on her bed to read it, Lizzie felt her eyes widen with shock and her skin start to prickle with dread.

Dear Amelia,
I hope this letter finds you well and that you are closer to securing a suitable husband.

Her uncle, the colonel, always did get straight to the point.

I will not waste time with pleasantries, instead I send instructions.

The colonel didn't waste time with pleasantries in person, so Lizzie wasn't surprised he was as direct in his correspondence.

I trust as instructed you will focus on finding a husband with all possible haste. I sent your cousin Elizabeth with you so you would have company on the voyage and for your arrival in London. However, her place is not in London society with you.

At the mention of her name Lizzie sat up straighter and started to read faster.

I have often despaired of what to do with your cousin once you are married, but now I have found a pleasing solution and would like her to return to India as soon as possible.

Lizzie closed her eyes and took a moment to steady herself before she found out what fate her uncle had in store for her.

I had assumed Elizabeth would remain a spinster. She is a plain girl who lacks the necessary attributes to marry well, but I have found a man willing to be her husband.

She gasped in shock. Not at her uncle calling her plain—he'd always made it clear she was much inferior to Amelia or any other girl of the same age—but at the idea of him wanting to marry her off. She'd always assumed Amelia would marry someone rich and she'd become her cousin's companion.

Taking a deep breath, Lizzie steeled herself to finish the letter.

Colonel Rocher is in need of a wife and is willing to take Elizabeth on. He is eager that the formalities should be taken care of as soon as possible. Please instruct your cousin Elizabeth to arrange passage back to India with all possible haste.
Your Father

Lizzie sat in shock for five whole minutes, reading and rereading the last section of the letter. She couldn't quite believe her life had changed so much in mere minutes.
She couldn't marry Colonel Rocher. Of all the men in

India he was the very last she would ever want to marry. It wasn't because he was at least double her age, or that physically he was repulsive. Lizzie wasn't so naïve to have ever expected an attractive husband and she would certainly not turn down a man just because he didn't have rippling muscles or a winning smile. It wasn't even that he leered at every woman under the age of sixty and had wandering hands that were the stuff of legend. All that Lizzie could forgive—after all, it wasn't as though she was a prize. No, the reason she just couldn't marry Colonel Rocher was because she knew he would beat her. He had beaten his first wife and he had beaten his second. Both had often been seen sporting bruises or injuries and, far from denying hurting either of the women, he had often boasted about keeping them in line.

She'd always known she was a burden to her uncle, he'd told her often enough, but she'd always hoped that deep down he loved her just a little. Or at least cared enough that he would not send her to endure a lifetime of humiliation and pain.

Lizzie couldn't stop the image of Daniel flashing before her eyes. He was everything Colonel Rocher was not—young, attractive—and Lizzie knew instinctively he would never beat his wife. However, the main difference, the most heartbreaking difference, was that once Daniel knew her true identity he would never want her as his wife.

She refused to cry any more. This interlude with Daniel had been nothing more than a fantasy. She'd allowed herself to get swept away with it, but now her head had cleared and she saw his attention for what it really was. Lizzie knew she had to stop obsessing about the earl and instead work out what she was going to do about her future.

Of course, she would have to wait until Amelia returned, which should be any day now, but then she had to decide whether to obey her uncle and return to India or whether she was brave enough to try to survive on her own.

Lizzie knew she was far too shocked to make a rational decision, so instead she busied herself getting ready for bed, placed the letter on her bedside table and blew out her candle.

It was unbearably hot. Lizzie tossed and turned in her bed, throwing off her covers as she transitioned from a deep sleep to a light state of drowsiness. Her eyes slowly opened and at first she couldn't quite make sense of what she was seeing. There was light in the room, not the piercing clarity of sunlight, but a dull flickering. She was covered in sweat and she could feel beads of water running between her shoulder blades.

Groggily Lizzie pushed herself up into a sitting position and forced her brain to engage with her surroundings.

She tried not to scream, knowing panicking would only make things worse. The room was on fire. The curtains had already been consumed by flames and every second that passed the fire was creeping closer to her bed. Black smoke billowed as furniture caught light and the room became a blazing inferno.

For a second Lizzie was paralysed with fear, then her survival instincts kicked in. She jumped from the bed, knowing if she didn't get out of this room in the next thirty seconds she would die in it. In her haste her feet caught in her nightgown and she felt herself falling to the floor. She cursed her clumsiness but caught herself on her hands and knees and pushed back up to her feet. The pain from her injured ankle shot up her leg as she stood, but she managed to stumble on. Coughing as the smoke irritated her lungs, Lizzie felt her eyes also begin to water and the outline of the door, just a few feet away, became hazy.

She staggered forward, clutching at pieces of furniture that weren't alight to try to guide herself out of the room. It was almost impossible to see anything now and as her breathing became more and more laboured Lizzie began to feel the darkness descend. She struggled on for a few more steps, dragging red-hot air into her burning lungs. Her vision, previously obscured by smoke, now was hazy from lack of oxygen and she knew she was never going to find her way to the door.

Refusing to give up, Lizzie collapsed to her knees and dragged herself a few more paces before her strength deserted her. Just before she slipped from consciousness Daniel's face flashed before her eyes and his strong, confident voice sounded in her ears. Lizzie felt herself smile; at least she'd experienced a divinely pleasurable kiss before she'd died.

Chapter Twelve

She was smiling. The crazy woman was smiling. She was seconds from death and there was no mistaking the smile that danced over her lips as she collapsed on to her front.

Daniel surged into the room, trying to ignore the fiery heat and the black clouds of smoke that obscured almost everything. Three short strides took him to Amelia's side and without pausing he scooped her up into his arms and retreated from the room.

Even though he'd only been in the burning room for seconds he felt the strain from the smoke on his chest and his skin still prickled as if the flames were licking at it. The hallway, which had been relatively clear when he'd bounded into the house, was now filled with smoke and Daniel knew it was only a matter of minutes before the whole house was consumed by flames.

As he raced through the house he glanced down at Amelia. She was a dead weight in his arms, completely unconscious. There had been no flicker of recognition as he'd picked her up, nor any stirring since. Her face was blackened with soot and her nightgown, which he assumed was normally a standard white, was singed at the edges and grey all over. He couldn't see any obvious burns on her body, but he doubted she had escaped unscathed; no one could last more than a minute in a room that was burning at that intensity and not suffer from any permanent injury.

The thought of a burn on her lovely flawless skin made Daniel feel angry at whoever had been careless enough to allow the fire to start. No doubt a candle had been left burning or a fire left smouldering when it should have been put out. Fires didn't occur spontaneously.

Daniel reached the stairs and descended quickly. As he reached the ground floor the air was a little clearer and he felt the smoke begin to leave his lungs. He resisted the almost overwhelming urge to cough and instead pressed on towards the door.

It was less than a minute after Daniel had swept Amelia into his arms that he burst through the open door and into the night. He didn't stop walking until he was a good fifty feet from the house, well clear from the billowing black smoke that was now coming from every window. When he reached the crowd of assembled family, staff and curious onlookers he sank to his knees and placed Amelia gently on the ground.

'Amelia, Amelia!' Immediately Amelia's aunt Mathilda was at their side.

Daniel ignored the frantic older woman and quickly inspected the woman lying unconscious in front of him. The first thing he noticed with relief was that her chest was rising and falling regularly; whatever other damage she had sustained at least she was still breathing.

As he bent lower to wipe some of the grime from her face he tried to block out the crowd of curious onlookers who were surging closer. He needed to focus on Amelia. He had no idea how long she had been in the room with the fire burning around her, but he was sure she needed space and a doctor.

Decisively he stood.

'Move back,' he shouted, his voice commanding despite the croak from the smoke inhalation.

The crowd obeyed.

'I need a carriage.'

A smartly dressed man caught Daniel's eye and nodded, before disappearing at speed to find one.

'And I need someone to fetch a doctor.'

A young lad who Daniel had seen emerge from a neighbouring house stepped up.

'I'll fetch a doctor for you, sir,' he said.

Daniel reckoned this boy was a servant or stable boy for Amelia's aunt's neighbours and was grateful for his volunteering.

'Send him to Twenty-Three Burton Street.'

The boy scampered off, no doubt to find the doctor his employers used whenever they were unwell.

'I'm taking Amelia to my house to be seen to,' Daniel said, turning to Aunt Mathilda.

She nodded, not really taking in what Daniel was saying. He supposed there wasn't much more distracting than watching your family home burn to the ground.

'Is anyone else still unaccounted for?'

Aunt Mathilda looked around desperately as if she hadn't considered anyone else might be left in the house.

'Everyone is here,' the butler said, stepping forward.

Daniel appraised him and saw he was shaken but able to take charge of this crisis.

'Arrange for Mrs Hunter and Miss Hunter to follow me to my town house,' he said. 'If any of the servants are injured or suffering from the smoke, send them quickly, too. After Miss Eastway has been seen to the doctor can check them over.'

The butler nodded. 'I'll keep any healthy, uninjured men with me here to supervise things and help fight the fire.'

Already the street was alive with people hauling buckets of water ready to fight the fire. Luckily the Hunters' house was detached and had a little land surrounding it, but it took only a gentle breeze to lift some embers and the whole street could be ablaze.

Satisfied things were under control, Daniel turned his attention back to Amelia. She was still unconscious—in fact, she hadn't once even stirred—and the depth of her insensibility worried Daniel.

At that moment a carriage clattered round the corner and the crowd parted obligingly. Daniel quickly gave his address to the driver, impressed on the man how important it was that they got there with all possible haste and swept Amelia back into his arms. Carefully he stepped up into the carriage and held her tightly across his lap as they set off through the streets of London.

He only lived a ten-minute carriage ride away, but those ten minutes seemed the longest of Daniel's life. In the darkness he couldn't see Amelia and he kept laying a hand on her chest to check she was still breathing. As London sped by outside the carriage window Daniel knew there was a very real chance Amelia wouldn't make it to his house alive. He choked back the emotion that overcame him, not wanting to examine his feelings as well as cope with everything else that was occurring.

Eventually the carriage slowed to a stop and Daniel hurriedly jumped down. As he strode towards his front door he called back to the carriage driver telling him someone would come out and pay him in a few minutes.

Daniel's front door opened as he reached the top of the steps and the face of his worried, elderly butler looked at him with amazement.

'Wake the household,' Daniel instructed. 'Miss Eastway has been in a fire and is gravely injured. A doctor will be arriving shortly but I need plenty of clean water and send Mrs Greystone to my room.'

Daniel hurried up the stairs and into his bedroom, placing Amelia down on top of his four-poster bed. He'd just straightened and was about to start checking Amelia over for external injuries when he heard his very capable housekeeper bustle into the room.

'Dearie me,' she said. 'What on earth happened to this poor lamb?'

Mrs Greystone took one look at Amelia and immediately began issuing orders to the two maids who trailed behind her.

'You look a state,' she said, appraising Daniel.

He grinned for the first time that evening. Mrs Greystone had known him since he was a baby and the older woman never minced her words around her young master. In a world where most servants were too respectful to meet their employers' eye as they went about their daily chores, it was refreshing to have someone like Mrs Greystone around.

'I should send you out, but I'm guessing nothing will make you leave the room until you know this lass is all right, so go and sit down in that chair and keep out of the way.'

Daniel knew it was pointless arguing with his housekeeper. He crossed the room and sank into a high-backed chair. Immediately he felt exhausted. For the past hour his body had been filled with energy as he'd rushed to rescue Amelia and then hurry her to a place where she could be best looked after. Now he'd stopped moving he felt physically drained and mentally fatigued. All he could think about was Amelia, lying on the floor of her bedroom, the life slowly draining from her body.

He watched as Mrs Greystone supervised the maids who were bringing bowls of warmed water and towels. Gently they dabbed the soot from Amelia's face before turning to the rest of her body.

Daniel knew the curves of her body, he knew them more than he should. From that first time he'd skimmed his hands over her hips and encircled her waist with his arm Daniel had memorised her contours. As she lay on the bed, draped in the shapeless soot-stained nightgown, Daniel wanted to run his hands over her body again. He wanted to assure himself no inch of her body went unchecked, that there were no hidden wounds and every single bit of skin was intact.

Instead Mrs Greystone turned to him and raised an eyebrow.

At first he didn't move, wondering if he could insist on staying and supervising, but even though this was his house and the women in the room were his staff, he knew they would band together to protect Amelia's virtue and privacy, despite never having met her before.

Wearily Daniel rose from the chair, pleased to hear a male voice in the hallway. The doctor must have arrived.

'Go and rest, Master Daniel,' Mrs Greystone said kindly. 'I'll send the doctor to see to your wounds once he's finished with this poor lass.'

Daniel nodded and left the room, knowing he would not be able to rest whilst Amelia lay unconscious. He passed the doctor in the doorway, who looked him up and down.

'You need to get that arm cleaned up,' the medical man said without any preamble.

Daniel glanced down at his arm, confused. Sure enough his jacket and shirtsleeve had been almost completely destroyed on the right side and a raw-looking wound was starting to blister on the skin. Daniel grimaced. Now he had noticed the burn it started to throb and hurt. Up until this point he'd been so focused on Amelia he hadn't even realised he'd been burnt.

Quickly he returned downstairs to his study and asked

the butler to organise some clean water to be put in the guest room next to his own. He also informed the elderly man they were likely to have an influx of guests arriving soon, many shaken and scared by the night's events.

The butler took it all in his stride. Daniel knew the older man had served in the army for years and had never encountered a situation that fazed him.

Wearily Daniel returned upstairs, eager to be close to Amelia should he be needed. As he waited for the water to clean his wound his valet quietly entered the room with a change of clothes.

Daniel sank on to the bed. He realised his hands were shaking and his heart had started to race in his chest. Throughout the entire ordeal his head had remained clear and his body in control, but now he had rested and he knew there was nothing more he could do, his body was reacting to the shock of the evening.

He tried not to imagine what was happening in the room next door. He knew Amelia would not come through this unscathed and he only hoped her injuries were superficial ones. He didn't want to examine the steely grip of panic around his heart or what it meant. He just knew his life would never be the same if Amelia didn't make it through the next few hours.

Chapter Thirteen

Lizzie struggled to open her eyes. It was as though her eyelids were made of a heavy metal and her brain was refusing to cooperate with the rest of her body. Eventually her eyes flickered open and she frowned as she tried to take in her surroundings. Everything was blurry for a couple of seconds and her eyes stung as if she'd washed them with soap.

She let out a small groan as she remembered the fire. That was why her eyes were stinging so much and why her chest hurt with every laboured breath she took. Slowly the room came into focus and she realised she didn't recognise her surroundings at all.

It was clear she was in a man's bedroom. The muted colours and functionality hinted at good taste without being over the top. Lizzie struggled to remember arriving here, wherever here was.

The last thing she remembered was falling to her knees as she rushed to get out of her burning bedroom. Her feet had caught in her nightgown and she'd stumbled. Had she ever managed to get up again?

She wondered how she had escaped from the fiery inferno, looking around all the time for clues.

When the door opened Lizzie was fully awake and she turned her head towards it to see who entered. Even that little movement sent spasms through her chest and she began coughing, the irritation spreading from her throat to her chest in no time and causing her to wince with pain.

Daniel. Of course it would be Daniel.

He walked into the room, leaving the door ajar for propriety's sake, and frowned at her. Quickly he poured her a glass of water and held it to her lips, allowing her small sips at a time. The cool liquid soothed Lizzie's throat, but did nothing for the heaviness in her chest. It was a few minutes before the coughs subsided and she felt able to speak.

'What happened?' she asked, her voice unnaturally croaky.

Daniel didn't answer for a few seconds and Lizzie took the opportunity to look him over. He appeared tired, as if he hadn't slept at all. He was neatly turned out, but not dressed for the outside world. It must be his house they were in. She glanced down at his arm and grimaced when she saw the bandage. He was holding his injured arm across his chest, as if it pained him, but she saw no evidence of it in his face.

'What do you remember?' Daniel asked.

Lizzie closed her eyes and tried to think back, past the billowing black smoke and inferno of flames, past the panic and the feeling of certainty she'd had that she was going to die.

'I remember going to bed,' she said. She'd been reading her uncle's letter over and over again, but eventually she'd decided to sleep. She had placed the letter down on her bedside table and blown out her candle. 'Then I awoke and the room was boiling hot and filled with smoke. The curtains were on fire and it spread so quickly. I couldn't breathe.'

Lizzie tried to block out the panic that was rising with the memory. She felt Daniel's hand cover her own and immediately her racing heart started to slow and her mind cleared.

'I tried to escape, but I tripped,' she said with a shake of her head. 'I thought I was going to die.'

Lizzie glanced at Daniel again, taking in his bandaged arm and concerned expression, and realised the truth. He'd saved her. Somehow he'd battled the flames and the smoke and he'd saved her.

'You found me?' Lizzie asked quietly.

He nodded. 'I was passing the house when I saw the fire. When you didn't emerge I went in and got you out.'

Lizzie knew there must have been much more to it than that. He would have had to push past everyone fleeing the burning house, going against every survival instinct that was screaming for him to stay well away from the fire. Then he would have had to brave the smoke and the flames and search the burning building before he came across her unconscious body. Once he'd found her, he would have had to carry her all the way outside even though the flames would have been licking at his heels and the smoke filling his lungs.

'Thank you,' Lizzie said sincerely, holding his eye. She knew what he had done deserved so much more than a 'thank you', but she also knew he was not the sort of man to seek out praise. It was enough that he had saved her. 'Did everyone...?' She trailed off, not knowing how to ask the question.

'Everyone got out alive. Some of the staff have minor injuries and smoke inhalation, but nothing that time won't heal.'

Lizzie nodded, the movement setting off another bout of coughing. Her chest felt as though it were about to explode and her throat burned.

'You were injured?' she asked when the coughing had subsided.

He shrugged. 'Just a small burn.'

Lizzie felt guilty at having been the reason he was in the burning house to start with.

'We should let the doctor know you're awake,' Daniel said. 'And your aunt.'

'Poor Aunt Mathilda, she's lost her home.'

Lizzie fell silent. She wondered for a moment how the fire had started, whether a candle had been left burning or an ember from a fire had floated on to a nearby piece of furniture. Something was nagging her, dancing around the edge of her consciousness.

'When you came and got me was the whole house burning?' Lizzie asked.

Daniel shook his head. 'No, only upstairs, your room, the couple on either side. There was smoke throughout the house, though.'

Lizzie nodded, carefully trying to keep her face composed. She tried to picture her room just before she had closed her eyes and gone to sleep. She quite clearly remembered blowing out the candle by her bed and lying in the darkness. So it couldn't have been her who started the fire.

Still something was nagging at her. Forcing herself to maintain her composure, she thought back to what she had seen when the room was on fire. She'd been panicked, more scared than she had ever been before, but she had noticed something.

Suddenly it came to her; there had been another candle in the room. It had been sitting on the small desk by the window, right next to the curtains. Lizzie knew she hadn't left it burning—in fact, she was sure she hadn't left the candle there at all.

Her thoughts were interrupted by the door opening again and Aunt Mathilda hurrying in, followed reluctantly by Harriet.

'Oh, my dear, we were so worried about you—weren't we, Harriet?'

Harriet nodded vaguely but didn't make any snide comments.

'Were you hurt?' Lizzie asked, quickly running her eyes over both women, looking for injuries.

'Thankfully, no, we got out whilst the fire was still small.' Lizzie saw Aunt Mathilda hesitate before continuing. 'I don't suppose you have any idea how the fire started, my dear?'

Lizzie shook her head. 'I remember blowing out my candle before I went to sleep.'

Aunt Mathilda nodded. 'I just don't understand how it happened.'

'Amelia said she doesn't know anything,' Harriet said in a tetchy voice.

Everyone in the room turned to Harriet in surprise. The young woman had made it no secret that she was not fond of Lizzie and her defence of her now seemed unnatural.

'Well, she did,' Harriet muttered.

'It really doesn't matter,' Aunt Mathilda insisted. 'The main thing is that you escaped largely unharmed.'

'What about your poor house?'

The older woman shrugged, but Lizzie could see the tears in her eyes.

'Please excuse me, I think I'll go and have a lie-down.'

Aunt Mathilda left the room. Harriet stayed where she was for a moment or two, staring at Lizzie, before she followed her mother out. Just as she reached the door Harriet turned back towards Lizzie.

'It looks like once again you came out on top. What a surprise. We've lost our home and the Eastways have lost nothing.'

'How strange,' Daniel murmured.

'She's had a shock. They both have. Losing your home must be awful.'

Lizzie felt the tears well up in her eyes and spill out on to her cheeks. Her hands started to shake and the spasms in her chest returned, making her cough. She knew they had all come close to dying. If Daniel hadn't rushed into the house, there was no doubt she'd be nothing more than a pile of ash.

Daniel was at her side in moments. He took her hand in one of his and stroked her hair with his other. Lizzie closed her eyes and tried to catch her breath.

'Hush,' Daniel said. 'You're safe now.'

Lizzie nodded, but still the tears kept flowing.

With her eyes still closed Lizzie felt rather than saw the moment Daniel moved to sit on the bed beside her. He scooped her into his arms and held her close to his body. Lizzie felt the warmth of his body against her skin and his touch soothed her. After a few seconds her cough subsided and a minute later the tears followed.

They sat in silence, the rise and fall of their chests following the same rhythm, Daniel's breath tickling Lizzie's neck. She felt safe here, ensconced in his arms, protected by his embrace, but even whilst she was enjoying the closeness Lizzie knew it could never last.

Daniel still thought he had rescued Miss Amelia Eastway, most eligible heiress of the season. He might find her plainness and lack of beauty acceptable whilst he thought her rich, but that concession would soon sour once he knew she was almost penniless, a charity case her uncle had taken pity on. She squeezed her eyes tighter shut and wished she could suspend time. She wanted to stay as they were right now, with Daniel's arms wrapped around her and him thinking she was so much more than she really was.

They sat in silence for ten minutes, all the while Lizzie wished again and again that she was her cousin. She wanted Amelia's life so badly, not for her money or her confidence, but she wanted to be the kind of woman Daniel could not ignore. Instead of being plain old Lizzie, eternally condemned to be overlooked by everyone, she wanted to be the woman people sat up and took notice of. Time and again at social occasions Lizzie had stood beside her cousin, watching people's eyes light up as they were introduced to Amelia and then glaze over as they turned to her. Each time that happened the words her uncle had spoken to her as a young girl always flashed back into her mind.

'You're plain, Elizabeth, plain and unappealing. Our best hope for you is for a blind man to happen along in search of a wife.'

She'd been seven at the time. A very gangly and ungainly seven-year-old. Her confidence had never recovered.

It didn't matter that every so often she saw a spark of desire flash in Daniel's eyes. She knew she would always be plain and unappealing. For years she had told herself she didn't care that she wasn't a beauty like Amelia, but that had been before she met Daniel. Now there was someone that she wanted to be desired by she did care. She cared so much it tore her apart.

There was a soft knock on the door and Daniel quickly stood up. Lizzie had to hide a smile. Despite it being his house, they still had to act with propriety.

'Doctor, thank you for returning.'

'How is the patient?' the short bespectacled man asked.

Lizzie managed to croak a short, non-committal sound.

'Hmm, I see the smoke inhalation has caused some damage to your throat,' the doctor said. 'That should recover with rest and fresh air.'

'She's coughing a lot,' Daniel supplied.

The doctor stepped closer to Lizzie, then motioned for Daniel to turn around. Daniel obliged and Lizzie breathed deeply whilst the doctor placed his ear against her back.

'Rattly, as you would expect,' he said without further explanation.

They waited as he checked her pulse, got her to stick out her tongue and inspected the back of her throat.

'No permanent damage,' the doctor declared eventually. 'But I would advise a week or two of good, clean country air.'

Daniel showed the doctor out and returned to her bedside.

'That settles it,' he said.

Lizzie looked at him questioningly.

'You can come and recuperate at my country estate. The fresh air will do you good. Your aunt can come along to chaperon you—'

Lizzie opened her mouth to object. A whole week with Daniel away from the world sounded like bliss, but she knew it would make it all that much harder to give him up.

'No argument, it's the doctor's orders.'

Chapter Fourteen

Daniel was whistling to himself as he drew his horse up outside the inn. He loved it when a plan came together. He was currently riding out to his country estate, which he much preferred to London, and in the carriage that was just rolling to a stop behind him was the woman he was going to marry. A few days in the country and he was convinced Amelia would say yes when he proposed. He'd seen her staring at him with dreamy eyes, even if she did look away rather sharply when he looked in her direction. He knew she desired him, that she replayed each kiss they'd shared over and over in her mind. Now he just had to convince her that he liked her, too.

He wasn't sure when he had warmed quite so much to the idea of having a wife, or more specifically of having Amelia as his wife. True, he still needed her money and he wasn't going to deny that was the reason he was going to propose, but somewhere along the way he had realised that being married to Amelia would have more advantages than just saving his son.

He liked her. He liked her quiet intelligence and how her gentle tone hid a quick wit. And he knew they certainly had chemistry. Their kisses were proof enough and now it took only one look at her and he was simmering with pent-up desire inside. Marrying Amelia would have the distinct advantage that he could take her to bed. And stay there for a week.

Daniel hopped down from his horse and tried to keep his desire in check. He waited for the carriage to come to a complete halt, then opened the door and prepared to assist the women down.

Amelia came shooting from the carriage as if she were being chased by rabid dogs.

'Traitor,' she hissed in his ear.

'Nice to see you, too, my sweet,' he whispered back.

Dutifully Daniel helped down Amelia's aunt and cousin before turning back to escort his future wife inside the inn.

She was already stalking through the door without a backwards glance. Daniel strolled in leisurely after her and found her fuming.

'You left me,' Amelia managed to hiss before the other two women joined him.

The first half of their journey that day, the painfully slow slog through London, Daniel had sat in the carriage with the three women. Aunt Mathilda had snoozed almost from the moment she'd sat down. Amelia, sensible girl that she was, had brought a book, but it had appeared that Harriet wasn't going to give her a single moment to read it. For the awful few hours Daniel had spent in the carriage Amelia's cousin had snipped at and goaded Amelia until the two young women were almost clawing at each other across the carriage. Daniel had decided at their lunch stop that although he very much enjoyed brushing up against Amelia he couldn't spend another minute in the carriage with her odious cousin, so he'd opted to ride for the afternoon. He'd spent a most pleasant couple of hours taking in the countryside and imagining all the things he would do to Amelia once they were married and a couple he was planning on doing before.

'Good evening, my lord,' the landlord of the coaching inn said deferentially. 'We received your message and have our finest three rooms ready for you. Shall I show you the way?'

Daniel strode after the landlord, catching Amelia's arm as he went by and pulling her along beside him. For a moment she resisted, but, sensible girl that she was, she must have realised he had the superior strength and that if she didn't budge he might do something much more embarrassing such as throw her over his shoulder. Daniel glanced sideways at her and let his mind wander through the possibilities of things he could do to Amelia after hefting her over his shoulder.

'Here is the first room, sir,' the landlord said. 'Your room is just across the hall and the room for the two young ladies is the last on the left.'

If looks could kill, Daniel would have been felled twice. Amelia and Harriet shot daggers in his direction. For a moment he thought about putting the two young women in the same room and locking the door. He had no doubt one would be dead by morning, and in his eyes Amelia was the more intelligent of the two, so she'd be sure to survive.

'Good landlord,' Amelia said, sounding like a character from a play, 'I don't suppose you have another room going free tonight?'

The landlord's face fell.

'But, my lord,' he said, turning back to Daniel, 'you only requested three rooms. I'm completely full.'

Daniel gave the poor man a reassuring smile. 'I did only request three rooms. The fault is all mine.' He pulled Amelia close to him, momentarily distracted by the adorable way her brow crinkled when she was frowning. 'You can share with me if you'd rather,' he murmured.

Amelia sent him a withering stare. Aunt Mathilda must have sensed the content of his whisper and stepped forward.

'Harriet, you can share with me,' she announced.

The landlord looked very relieved and slinked away before anyone else could argue, mumbling about dinner being served at seven.

'I shall call for you ladies just before seven,' Daniel said, waiting for Aunt Mathilda and Harriet to turn away before giving Amelia a salacious wink.

She was still pretending to be annoyed with him for his disappearing act in the carriage, but even so she couldn't hide the slight tilt of her lips as she tried to suppress a smile.

Daniel closed the door of his room behind him and flopped down on the bed. He was in a wonderful mood; he loved it when things came together. It would only be a matter of days before he would propose to Amelia and then he would insist on a speedy wedding. With her dowry in his possession he would be able to keep Annabelle at bay a little longer.

The only thing that would make it all better would be to wrest Edward away from Annabelle once and for all. Over the years he had made repeated attempts to convince his ex-lover to give up their son to his care. He had tried appealing to her better nature, explaining Edward would have a good upbringing with him, and then he had resorted to bribing her. Annabelle, however, was an astute woman. She knew she could extract more from Daniel if she kept hold of their son.

So Daniel had sent a man to check on how his boy was doing, to investigate whether she ever treated his son badly, ever raised her hand to him. His agent had reported back that although she seemed a little indifferent to the boy, he was well looked after and the agent had never seen him suffer at her hands.

Daniel had wrestled with his conscience for months. He hadn't been able to decide whether it would be better to take Edward away from his mother, knowing that it would mean revealing the truth to his son about his illegitimacy, or whether to leave him where he was and shield him from the reality of his birth. Neither was an ideal solution and every day Daniel wondered whether he had made the right choice, but when he faltered and thought about claiming Edward as his own he only had to remember Rupert's tortured soul and he sat back and remained in the shadows. It was devastating for a boy to know he was illegitimate. More devastating than it was to be raised by a rather distant mother. He would not put his son through that. So Edward stayed with his mother and Daniel continued to pay and torture himself over his decision.

He shook himself from his reverie and glanced at the clock. It was quarter to seven and he had to prepare himself for an evening of wooing Amelia. He grinned. Just two weeks ago the idea of courting a young heiress had made him shudder and wish for any number of alternative torments, but now he was rather looking forward to stealing a kiss from Amelia and causing her to blush, all the while convincing her they would be the perfect match.

At ten to seven he knocked quietly on Amelia's door. Far from keeping him waiting like most young women would, Amelia eased open the door immediately, looked surreptitiously up and down the corridor, then pulled him inside.

Daniel grinned—she was making the business of seduction so much easier for him. Before she could say a word he looped an arm around her waist and pulled her in for a kiss.

He loved that she couldn't resist him. Despite having pulled him into her room for a reason, and that reason clearly having nothing to do with seduction, Amelia couldn't bring herself to break off the kiss.

'Did you want to say something, my sweet?' Daniel asked, then kissed her again before she could answer him. She was stiff in his arms but kissed him back with grudging vigour. 'Maybe my lady would like to compliment me on my riding skills?' he suggested, then planted his lips firmly on hers before she could get a syllable out. 'Or maybe my goddess would just like to gaze into my eyes for the few minutes before dinner. I'm happy to oblige.'

This time when he kissed her Amelia managed to pull away, spluttering with indignation.

'Now, now, my precious gem, don't go pretending you didn't enjoy my kisses.'

Amelia was nothing if not fair and she inclined her head, knowing she could not deny that she enjoyed every moment their lips were locked together. After a few seconds she raised her chin and looked at him, her eyes blazing.

'You abandoned me, then you planned to torture me by making me spend the night with that snake.'

Daniel gave her his most leery grin. 'I meant it when I said you could spend the night in my room.'

Amelia didn't even bother to acknowledge his remark.

'I can't spend another day cooped up with her. I'll murder her.'

Daniel didn't voice his opinion that the world would be better off if Amelia did murder Harriet. She was her cousin, after all, and despite their differences Amelia might object to Daniel insulting her kin.

'You could always nestle in front of me on my horse,' Daniel suggested.

'Tomorrow I want to ride.'

Daniel saw she was deadly serious and tried to quash the sickness he felt at seeing Amelia mount a horse. The last time he'd seen her ride she'd ended up being thrown and he'd thought he had lost her.

'Amelia,' Daniel said in what he hoped was a conciliatory tone, 'maybe that's not the best idea.'

She stiffened and he reached out and took her hand.

'I've ridden since I was six years old,' she mumbled. 'Just because you saw me the one time I fell off…'

He raised his eyebrows. Amelia was a good horse-woman, but she was also one of the clumsiest people he knew. He didn't believe she'd only ever fallen from a horse once.

'Well, the one time I fell *badly*,' she corrected.

'Maybe I can be convinced,' Daniel said. 'I am a reasonable man after all.'

Amelia's face lit up. 'What would convince you?'

'A kiss.'

He saw her hesitate and for a second he wondered if she would refuse. She was well within her rights to toss him out of her room and scream for her aunt. Of course the sensible girl didn't. She wanted it as much as he did.

Daniel waited for her to come to him. All their previous kisses he had initiated, but this time he wanted to feel her hands on his jaw, see her lips parting as she swayed in closer to him.

Slowly Amelia moved closer so their bodies were pressed together. She raised a hand to his cheek and traced the angle of his jaw, then she looked into his eyes before she closed the gap between them. Her kiss was feathery light and it sent Daniel almost mad with desire. His lips screamed out for more and every nerve ending was on fire. Amelia brushed her lips against his again before pulling away. The minx was teasing him.

'We will be late for dinner.'

Daniel glanced at the clock on the wall and growled something under his breath no well-bred lady should ever hear.

Chapter Fifteen

Lizzie couldn't sleep. There were too many thoughts running through her head. No, that was a lie, there was just one very large and troubling thought: Daniel.

She couldn't get him out of her mind. All through dinner he'd looked at her with smouldering eyes and barely concealed desire. It made Lizzie burn for him and wish for just one moment alone so she could feel his fingers on her skin.

Kissing him again had been a mistake. She'd been truly annoyed with him for leaving her in the carriage with Harriet and had been determined not to succumb to his teasing flirtation. Then he had challenged her to kiss him and she'd not been able to stop herself. It hadn't been about convincing him to let her ride tomorrow, although that was a welcome bonus, it had been about *her* kissing *him*. In all their other kisses she had been a willing participant, but she had never initiated the kiss. She'd wanted that control, so she'd kissed him. Lizzie knew she could have kissed him all night, but she wanted to show him that he wasn't the only one who could be driven mad with desire, and by the looks he had given her throughout dinner she rather thought she had succeeded.

Lizzie turned over in bed and tried to banish Daniel from her mind. She wondered for the thousandth time whether he did actually like her just a little. Not her supposed fortune, but her.

Knowing she was torturing herself for no good reason, Lizzie got out of bed and pulled her thick nightgown around her body. She needed to clear her head and that wouldn't happen tossing and turning in bed all night.

Quietly she slipped through the door and padded down the hallway. The last of the patrons of the inn had gone home well over an hour ago and Lizzie supposed even the landlord was tucked up in bed by now. Reaching the bottom of the stairs, Lizzie made the decision to venture outside. Despite the mild temperature during the day, the night's air had a bite to it and Lizzie found herself shivering for a few moments. Instead of turning round and going back inside she pulled her nightgown closer around her body and walked to the edge of the yard. There were a couple of upturned barrels positioned looking out over the dark countryside, ideally placed for a weary traveller to rest for a few moments. Lizzie sat down and looked up at the stars, trying to put her problems in perspective. She hadn't even stretched her neck out fully before she felt a hand on her shoulder.

An icy spear of fear pierced her heart as she spun round. Daniel was standing behind her, his face shadowed with rage.

Lizzie shot to her feet.

'Are you mad?' Daniel asked in clipped tones, obviously trying hard to keep the full force of his anger in check.

'I…' Lizzie began.

Daniel held up a hand to stop her. 'You must be mad,' he said. 'For I know you are not stupid.'

'Thank you,' Lizzie said quietly, unsure whether it was meant to be a compliment.

'And only a mad or a stupid woman would leave her

room and venture outside a public inn on her own in the middle of the night.'

Lizzie opened her mouth to speak and then abruptly closed it again. He had a point. When she thought about it properly it was rather foolish.

'Do you know what could happen to you?' he asked.

Lizzie sensed he didn't really want her to answer.

'You could be robbed,' Daniel said, holding up a finger for each of his suggestions. 'You could be raped. You could be *murdered*.'

Lizzie tried to look contrite.

'Come inside. Now.'

She didn't argue and allowed him to haul her back inside. Silently they ascended the stairs and Daniel pulled her into her room.

'I can't believe how much danger you put yourself in. It's as though you don't have a single little bit of regard for your own safety.' He was ranting now, albeit quietly.

Lizzie knew she had to stop him. 'I'm sorry,' she said quietly. 'You're right, it was downright stupid.'

That took the wind from his sails.

Daniel ran a hand through his hair and just looked at her. He looked harried and on edge. Lizzie realised he must have been worried for her.

'What were you doing out there?' he asked after a minute.

'I wanted to think. In India I was always outdoors. I can't think being cooped up inside.'

'You need to be careful,' Daniel said, his voice softer now. 'Not everyone is as gentle as you.'

Lizzie nodded and wrapped her arms around herself. Daniel stalked around the room, making the space seem small and crowded by his large presence.

'I shouldn't be here,' Daniel said suddenly, as if only just realising they were in her room together.

Lizzie waited for him to move towards the door, but he didn't even make a pretence at leaving.

'You scared me, Amelia,' he repeated, but more gently this time.

He took a step towards her and grasped her by the top of her arms. Despite the warmth Lizzie shivered.

At that moment she knew something was going to happen between them, something more than the mesmerising kisses they had been sharing already. Daniel's eyes had narrowed ever so slightly as though he had realised what he wanted and was intent on taking it, and Lizzie knew she was powerless to resist his seduction.

'Maybe before I leave I could be granted one kiss, to sustain me during the long walk back to my room.'

Lizzie didn't even have it in her to point out that his room was just across the hall, a mere three feet from door to door.

Before she knew what was happening Daniel had pulled her to the bed and sat down. Lizzie cautiously sat down beside him. She knew she should put a stop to this, she knew she shouldn't let his seduction of her continue. Proper young ladies were not meant to allow gentlemen into their bedchambers, let alone engage in whatever it was that was coming next. She was not going to marry Daniel, he would not have her when he found out who she really was, and that meant any indiscretions could have real consequences for her.

'Daniel,' she whispered, 'we shouldn't.' Not *we can't* or *I don't want to. We shouldn't.* She knew her words were giving him licence to continue.

'Hush, my sweet,' he murmured in her ear, then nibbled on her earlobe.

Lizzie gasped as his tongue traced tiny circles on her

velvety skin and she knew she was lost. She'd let this man do anything to her.

Gently Daniel trailed kisses down her neck to her shoulder, then along her collarbone to the base of her throat. Lizzie felt light-headed with desire. She wanted his lips all over her body, his hands touching her in a place no one ever had before.

Daniel paused for a second, as if deciding whether to go any further, then bent his neck and lowered his lips back to her skin. With nimble fingers he undid the top few buttons of her nightgown and pushed the cotton garment down. Nothing more was exposed than would be in a rather risqué dress, but Lizzie felt naked under his gaze.

'You have beautiful skin,' he murmured.

If he'd told her she was beautiful, Lizzie would have known he was lying, but as she looked down at his lips on the skin of her chest she wondered whether maybe she did have beautiful skin.

Daniel's lips paused in their descent as he stopped to undo a few more buttons of her nightgown. Before he pushed it even lower he stopped and looked into her eyes, giving her the opportunity to tell him to stop. Lizzie bit her lip but said nothing. She wanted this, she wanted him. She wanted to feel his lips on her breasts, his hands to explore where no one else had ever been allowed to go. She knew it was wrong and she knew she should stop him, but she didn't want to. Lizzie had always been a realist. She was aware this was the first and last time a man such as Daniel, a man she actually liked, was going to touch her intimately. If her uncle got his way, it would be the cruel Colonel Rocher who would be allowed to use her body whatever way he saw fit. If she refused to marry the colonel, it was likely she would remain a spinster and never feel the touch of a man again. So whatever her future this was her opportunity, and for once in her life she was going to do what she wanted rather than what was right.

Daniel's eyes lit up as Lizzie gave a shaky nod of her head and he pushed her nightgown fully over her shoulders and down over her breasts. For a second he just looked at her, but before Lizzie could start to feel self-conscious he raised a hand and cupped one breast, and Lizzie lost the power of coherent thought.

Smiling at her moan of pleasure, Daniel started to trace circles around her nipple and Lizzie felt herself arching her back to press her breast into his hand.

'All in good time, my love,' he whispered, then continued his slow journey across her skin.

'More,' Lizzie murmured before she could stop herself, blushing at her forwardness. Daniel just grinned, then obliged.

As he lowered his lips towards her skin Lizzie felt herself holding her breath in anticipation. When his mouth covered her nipple she almost cried out. Gently he began teasing her, nipping and licking and sucking. Somehow Daniel had manoeuvred her back on to the bed and expertly he now straddled her, never moving his mouth more than a couple of inches from her nipple. Lizzie felt her body buck and writhe underneath him. She arched her back and pressed her chest into the air, silently begging for more.

For a second she tensed as Daniel started to slide his hand down her body, but then she was pulled away from every single little concern about what they were doing by his mouth on her other nipple. As he teased her with his mouth his hand found its way under her nightgown and he started to caress the skin on her legs.

Lizzie felt her body tense as his hands drifted closer to her most private place, but gently he coaxed her to relax. She wanted him to touch her and even though she had never experienced anything like this before she had a primal urge that wanted him to enter her and fill her.

The first time he touched her Lizzie's hips bucked. Just a single caress sent waves of sensation all through her body. Smiling possessively, Daniel started to stroke her with slow rhythmic movements of his fingers, then before she knew what was happening he had dipped a finger inside her. Lizzie tensed, the invasion unexpected, but within seconds she felt her instincts take over and her hips start their slow movement up towards him.

Daniel stroked and teased her until Lizzie didn't feel in control of her own body. Her breath was coming in short, sharp gasps and her heart was hammering in her chest. Something was building deep inside her and she knew she needed to release it. Lost in her own little world of pleasure everything else had ceased to exist.

Suddenly the sensation deep inside her burst out and took over her entire body. Lizzie moaned and writhed, clutching at the bedsheets with her hands. She felt as though she was weightless, soaring through the air.

Slowly the pulsations lessened and she felt herself returning to reality. After a minute Daniel rolled off her and scooped her into his arms.

She felt his hardness pressing into the small of her back and a thrill of excitement coursed through her; she had caused that, plain old Lizzie Eastway.

'You are an amazing woman, Amelia,' Daniel said, nuzzling the back of her neck.

Lizzie stiffened but forced herself to relax again. Just tonight she was going to let herself forget who she really was and enjoy the fantasy. She would pretend this was her life.

'Amelia, I've got something to ask you,' Daniel said, the serious tone of his voice making her turn over to look at him. 'Marry me. Be my wife.'

Lizzie felt all the contented glow drain from her body and she crashed back to reality. Slowly, without even realising she was doing it, she started to shake her head in the hope he would take back the words.

He was looking at her in confusion and Lizzie realised she must look a state. All the blood had drained from her face and her mouth hung open in shock. It wasn't that the proposal was unexpected, all the time they had known each other had been leading up to this moment, but Lizzie had foolishly thought she had a bit more time. She couldn't marry him, of course she couldn't, but she didn't want their time together to end.

'Why?' she managed to whisper.

'Why? Because I want to marry you. We'd make a good match and I like you.'

Lizzie felt the tears brimming in her eyes. It wasn't enough. If he'd said he loved her, then maybe they'd have a chance, she would have been able to admit her true identity and maybe, just maybe, he'd still want her.

She shook her head. 'Daniel, I can't, I'm sorry.'

He looked shocked, as if he'd never considered she might turn him down. Lizzie felt miserable. She supposed he thought a plain girl like her would jump at the chance of marrying him. He was right, of course, Lizzie would jump at the chance of marrying him. He was kind and funny and definitely very attractive. A much nicer prospect than Colonel Rocher. The problem was it wasn't she whom he wanted to marry. He had proposed to Amelia— rich, well-connected Amelia.

'You can't?' he asked, picking up on her choice of words.

She shook her head and tried to look away.

'No, Amelia,' he said, turning her back to face him. 'You don't just get to say no with no explanation.'

'I'm sorry, Daniel.'

He looked deep into her eyes for a few seconds, then turned away.

'It wouldn't work. It's not enough.'

'I rushed you. I asked too soon. Forgive me.'

Lizzie nearly broke down and told him the truth, but at the last moment self-preservation stopped her. If she confessed who she really was, or more to the point that she wasn't Amelia Eastway, then she would likely be out on the street with no money and no connections. He wouldn't take her to stay at his estate and the Hunters would have no reason to look out for her, they weren't her relations. Lizzie knew these were all excuses, reasons to put off confessing her deception, but she couldn't help wanting just a little more time as Amelia.

'I'll give you more time,' Daniel said as he stood to leave. 'We'd make a good match, Amelia, you'll see in a few days.'

He left, smiling at her from the doorway. Lizzie blinked back the tears as she smiled back, knowing he would never say the three little words that would mean they could be together; he would never say *I love you* quite simply because he didn't. And without love there was no way he would ever forgive her for her deception.

Chapter Sixteen

Daniel pushed his horse to go faster as the house came into sight. In the pinkish light of dawn it looked beautiful, set atop a small hill with a lake on one side and a small copse of trees on the other. Daniel loved this estate and it saddened him that he had allowed it to become so neglected. It was not derelict by any means, but over the past few years most of his money had been given to Annabelle and the estate had suffered for it. The house, which needed a staff of at least forty, survived with a hard-working and loyal skeleton staff of ten. The grounds were pristine immediately surrounding the house, but neglected as you got further away, testament to how few gardeners and labourers he could afford to employ. Daniel knew one day it was likely he would need to sell off land to keep Annabelle quiet, but he couldn't quite bring himself to abandon his tenants or sell the softly undulating fields he had grown up playing in. One day maybe, but hopefully not yet. Hopefully soon he would also have Amelia's dowry to tide him over.

He desperately wanted to keep the estate intact, to pass on the Burwell legacy as a whole just as his ancestors had. For a few years after Rupert's death, even after both of his parents had passed away, Daniel had avoided the estate, certain that unhappy memories would be dredged up on his return. When he did finally come back to his childhood home he found more happy memories than unhappy. Before Rupert had appeared on the scene Daniel had idolised his father. He was kind and caring and fun to be around. He more than made up for a mother Daniel barely saw, a woman who never once smiled at her husband or child. After Daniel had started at Eton and understood more what was happening with Rupert, he hadn't known how to view his father. On the outside he was the same man, a father who was always waiting to welcome him back from school with open arms, eager to hear about all his achievements and latest schoolmates, but any time Daniel mentioned Rupert he sensed a sadness within his father and now he realised it was regret. After Rupert had killed himself Daniel had partly blamed his parents, wondering how his father could remain so distant. Over time he had understood that his father had only ever been trying to protect everyone whom he loved and in his own way had tried to look after Rupert, too. Daniel could no longer find it in himself to blame his father for being human and making a mistake.

He frowned, coming back to the present. He wasn't sure yet how to secure Amelia as his wife. They had been at his estate for three days and so far he'd seen Amelia for exactly thirty seconds. Once they had arrived, she'd sequestered herself in her room, sending messages at each meal to say she was still recovering from the fire. Daniel could hardly argue with that—the poor girl had almost died—but somehow he didn't believe that was why she was staying in bed. He rather thought it had something more to do with the night they had spent at the inn and his proposal that followed.

Daniel had pretended not to understand her cryptic refusal of his proposition, her saying 'it's not enough'. In reality he knew what she meant. She wanted love, or more specifically she wanted him to love her.

Daniel shook his head in frustration. They liked each other. He made her laugh, he would always be kind to her, he'd allow her to keep whatever interests she had and they certainly were physically compatible. He'd be the model husband, but he could not love her. He'd loved a woman once before and he was still paying for it years on. Amelia might be nothing like Annabelle, but Daniel knew he had no space in his heart for love.

He could have just said it, he supposed, told her that he loved her. She probably would have agreed to his proposal there and then. It felt wrong, though, starting a marriage off with such a deception. Daniel was concealing so much from Amelia already, he didn't want to lie any more than he had to. What was more, Amelia was an astute woman. She'd likely be able to tell if he was lying about something so important.

Daniel knew he could seduce her into marrying him. He had seen how she responded to him, how her resolve faltered as soon as his lips touched hers, but for some reason he didn't want to trick her into intimacy somewhere they would be discovered so the scandal would force her to marry him. He wanted her to want to marry him.

His plan was to court her, make her realise that life with him would be enjoyable, so that when he proposed again she would not hesitate in saying yes. The problem was he had to actually see her to court her and with Amelia shut away in her room that was decidedly difficult.

He was about a mile away from the house when he saw a figure strolling up the hill towards him. He grinned. It was as if his prayers had been answered. Amelia was walking at a leisurely pace, but she did not seem to display any ill effects from the fire. She hadn't caught sight of him yet and by the pursing of her lips Daniel rather thought she might be humming to herself. He grinned—she wouldn't be able to escape him now.

'Good morning,' Daniel called cheerily as Amelia appeared at the top of the hill.

For a second she looked guilty, as if she had been caught out in her deception.

'Feeling better?'

They both knew Amelia had been perfectly well the past few days but had used the ill effects of the fire as an excuse to avoid him.

'Yes, thank you,' Amelia ground out, looking over her shoulder as if wondering whether she could outrun him.

'I'm glad to hear it. I have been bereft without your company, my dear.'

Amelia looked at him through narrowed eyes but remained silent.

'I have been wasting away with boredom.'

'You cannot waste away with... Oh, never mind.'

She turned back towards the house and Daniel nimbly slid from his horse and took her arm in his.

'Shall we go for a walk?' he asked. 'Enjoy the morning air.'

'You have your horse.'

'You'd prefer to ride?' he asked with a gleam in his eye. 'Snuggled up quite scandalously between my thighs?'

Amelia's cheeks reddened, but she held her ground. 'I would prefer to continue my walk alone.'

'That I do not believe.'

'You think your company is so enjoyable?'

'I think *you* enjoy my company much more than you're willing to admit.'

Amelia opened her mouth to protest but then promptly

closed it again. It seemed she couldn't bring herself to lie to him completely.

'How about you grant me ten minutes, and if you're not having fun by then I'll allow you to return to the house on your own?' Daniel offered.

Amelia cocked her head to one side whilst she considered, then nodded gracefully. 'Ten minutes,' she agreed.

'The things we could do in ten minutes,' Daniel mused, leading her gently up the hill and away from the house. 'I don't know where to start.'

'You can't kiss me,' Amelia said suddenly. 'That wasn't part of the deal.'

'We never agreed on that. Indeed, we never stipulated what we could and couldn't do.'

He stopped walking and turned to face Amelia.

'We can do anything at all.'

Amelia swallowed hard as he reached up and brushed a strand of hair from her face.

'Anything in the world.'

For a second they just stood staring into each other's eyes and then their lips were on each other's, frantically searching the other one out. Daniel pulled Amelia into his arms, running his hands down the length of her back and cupping her buttocks.

'The things we could do in ten minutes,' Daniel murmured. Then reluctantly he stepped away, grabbed her by the hand and began to pull her up the hill.

'What about your horse?' Amelia asked, her breathing heavy with exertion.

'He knows how to get home.'

Sure enough his horse had already started trotting back towards the house.

Daniel wanted to stop where they were, sink to the ground with Amelia in his arms and make her his, but he knew that was a bad idea for two reasons. Firstly, he had resolved to show Amelia that they made a good match without seducing her, and secondly, Daniel wanted to stay in control, and he most certainly didn't feel in control when his lips met Amelia's.

So instead of kissing her he pulled her further away from the house and towards the lake. It was romance he needed, something that showed Amelia she was attracted to him emotionally as well as physically. Daniel smiled to himself, the years of seducing less virtuous women were about to pay off; he could use all the lessons he'd learnt wooing merry widows to make it impossible for Amelia to resist him.

'Where are we going?' Amelia said, her breath coming in fast bursts.

'To the lake.' Daniel grinned at her. 'If you grant me longer than ten minutes, I'll let us walk there.'

Amelia looked at him appraisingly, but her pounding heart and screaming muscles must have got the better of her and she nodded.

'Twenty minutes,' she conceded.

'Give me thirty and I promise you won't ever want this morning to end.'

'That's what I'm afraid of,' Amelia murmured under her breath. Daniel knew he wasn't supposed to hear her comment and he pretended that he hadn't, but inside he was celebrating. The way things were going he probably could have her agreeing to marry him in thirty minutes. Not that he was going to push his luck and propose again too soon.

'Isn't it beautiful?' Daniel said as he led her down to the lake. It had trees on its northern shore but otherwise was open to the softly undulating hills.

'It's beautiful,' Amelia agreed.

'And the things you can do in a lake...' Daniel trailed off and wiggled his eyebrows suggestively.

'Such as fishing?' she asked drily.

'It depends what you want to hook on your line. I'm hoping for a little less scaly prey.' It wasn't the finest compliment he'd ever paid a woman, but Amelia didn't seem to take offence. 'Or if fishing isn't your cup of tea we could indulge in a little swimming.'

'Wouldn't it be rather cold?'

'I can think of a few ways to warm you up.' Daniel was thoroughly enjoying himself. It wasn't often women he was pursuing put up even a token resistance.

'I'm not sure Aunt Mathilda would approve,' Amelia said as they reached the water's edge.

'It wasn't her I was planning on taking with me.'

Daniel led Amelia around the perimeter of the lake until they reached a small jetty.

'How about a spot of rowing?' he proposed.

'Is this just a ploy to get me on my own somewhere I can't escape once your thirty minutes are up?' Amelia asked.

'Most certainly,' Daniel said with a grin. 'The question is do you want to escape?'

Amelia didn't answer him but instead gripped his arm and stepped daintily into the small rowing boat. Daniel grabbed the oars and hopped in himself, taking up his position opposite her.

'Now, I know sometimes little mishaps happen when you are around,' Daniel said as he fitted the oars into place and pushed away from the jetty, 'so please refrain from any sudden movements. Even if you're overcome with passion and just *have* to kiss me, please remember we are in a capsizeable boat.'

'Mishaps?' she asked.

'Since I've known you, which isn't all that long, you've

demounted me from my horse, flattened me at the bottom of the stairs and got yourself flung from a horse, not to mention caused me to get my eyebrows singed in that fire.'

Amelia leant in as if trying to get a closer look at his eyebrows.

'My valet was mortified,' Daniel said. 'All that time he spends grooming me to perfection and I go and get my eyebrows burnt rescuing a damsel in distress.'

'They're not singed at all,' Amelia declared as she sat back suddenly, causing the boat to rock from side to side. 'And your housekeeper has told me you don't even have a valet.'

Daniel grinned. 'Caught out again by the tales of disloyal staff. But you can't deny the other things happened.'

Amelia grimaced. 'I have been known to be a little less than graceful from time to time.'

Daniel rested the oars in their holders for a minute and leant across and took her hand. 'I think you move with the grace of a swan, albeit a swan that loses its footing every so often.'

Daniel could see Amelia didn't know what to say to his compliment and it struck him that she wasn't used to people saying nice things about her. He'd seen hints of it before when he'd complimented her; Amelia wasn't used to being told she was beautiful or lovely or graceful. All those compliments that should be showered on young ladies had passed her by. He wondered how that had come to be. She was a pretty young thing, although not what society might think the most attractive, she had an irresistible mouth and an adorable smattering of freckles across her nose. He found it hard to believe he was the only one who had ever seen her charms.

Maybe things were different in India, but that was hard to believe. A young, eligible heiress should be overwhelmed by suitors spouting compliments wherever they lived in the world.

'Amelia, I want to tell you something, but I need you to promise you'll listen to what I have to say.'

She looked as though she was going to protest, to say that of course she always listened, but at the last moment she just nodded.

Daniel leant forward, careful not to rock the small rowing boat, and tilted her chin with his hand so she was looking directly into his eyes.

'I think you're beautiful,' he said sincerely.

Immediately she opened her mouth to protest, but Daniel moved quicker and put a finger against her lips.

'I think you're beautiful,' he repeated. 'I love the shape of your mouth and the tilt of your lips. I love the tiny freckles on your nose. I love how I could get lost in your eyes. And I love how even just the smallest of smiles transforms your face.'

Amelia looked at him with tears glistening in her eyes. Daniel knew no one had ever told her she was beautiful before. He cursed whoever it was in her past that had called her plain or even just neglected to compliment her. A woman needed to feel desirable—every man who had ever succeeded at seducing one knew that—and he'd wager Amelia had never been made to feel desirable before. He just couldn't understand it—did the rest of the world see a different person to him? He almost scoffed now when he thought back to the time he'd convinced himself he would be able to resist Amelia, that physically he wasn't attracted to her. Her appeal had crept up on him and now he found it hard to keep his hands to himself no matter what the situation.

'Do you mean it?' Amelia asked, her voice so quiet it was barely audible.

'I mean it.'

She hesitated as if still trying to find reasons not to believe him. 'I know you are a...man of the world,' she said slowly, 'and such compliments must come easy to you.'

Daniel couldn't help but grin. 'I'm not a monk, Amelia. I've spent my life enjoying the company of lovely women, but it's you I find beautiful.'

She must have seen the truth of it in his eyes for her face lit up with pleasure. Daniel wanted to capture that moment, that look, and keep it for ever.

Chapter Seventeen

Lizzie felt as though she were walking on air. Daniel thought she was beautiful. She'd replayed their conversation over and over again in her mind and she knew he wasn't lying. He'd looked at her with his dazzling blue eyes and he'd made her fall in love with him.

She sighed loudly. Who was she fooling, she'd been falling for him ever since that first kiss. She'd got herself into a right mess. Every day she was falling deeper in love with a man who thought she was somebody else entirely. A man who thought she was beautiful, had told her that he loved her lips and her freckles and her smile, but hadn't actually said he loved her. Which most likely meant that he didn't.

Lizzie was a pragmatist. She knew she'd never been destined for love—in fact, marriage to a decent, kind man had almost been too much to wish for. So Daniel not loving her was not a problem in itself, even if her heart wanted him to utter those three little words. The problem came with her true identity and more specifically her lack of a dowry. Daniel had to be in need of money. Although his estate was beautiful and tended by a small group of loyal staff, there was no hiding the fact that it was in dire need of some money. The furnishings were just a little too worn and the staff overstretched. Daniel needed a wealthy wife and in her he thought he had found one.

He might love her smile and enjoy her company, and maybe even desire her if the episode in the coaching inn was anything to go by, but he was so keen on their marriage because he thought that as well as all those things, she was rich. Which she most decidedly wasn't. Her uncle had never even mentioned a modest dowry, and Lizzie knew that if he did deign to provide something, it would be nothing like Amelia's, nothing like what Daniel was expecting.

So the fact that he thought her beautiful was more a horrible irony than anything else; for years Lizzie had been overlooked, had faded into the background beside her stunning cousin, and now someone had noticed her, had thought she was beautiful, but he needed Amelia's dowry.

'Feeling better?'

Lizzie spun towards Harriet's voice. The young woman was leaning against a pillar in the entrance hall, looking anything but concerned about the state of Lizzie's health.

'Yes, thank you,' Lizzie said, hurrying towards the stairs, hoping she would be able to get to her room before Harriet engaged her in conversation.

'Heard from your cousin recently?'

Lizzie froze, her hand clutching at the banister, her legs suddenly feeling rather weak.

'My cousin?' she asked, trying to keep the tremor from her voice.

'Yes, your cousin, the one who was meant to accompany you here.'

Lizzie allowed herself to breathe again. When Amelia had left her at the docks they had agreed they would pretend Lizzie had been taken ill and was going to recuperate at the house of an old family friend in the country for a while.

'She's recovering slowly,' Lizzie said noncommittally.

'Measles, was it?'

'Mmm-hmm.'

'She'll be excited to hear of her upcoming marriage, I suppose.'

Lizzie just gawked at Harriet. Had she read the letter? But that was impossible. The letter had come straight to her from the housemaid and then it had burnt in the fire.

Something pulled at the edge of Lizzie's memory, some detail that didn't quite add up.

'What do you mean?' she asked.

'Elizabeth's engagement to Colonel Rocher,' Harriet explained calmly.

Lizzie felt the world spinning. Harriet must have read the letter, there was no other way she could know that piece of information.

Suddenly an image flashed into Lizzie's mind—the candle by the window in her room. Surely Harriet hadn't crept in whilst she slept and taken the letter, maybe reading it by the light of the candle? A more horrific thought started to take shape—what if Harriet hadn't put out the candle? Had that been the source of the fire? It would have been a mistake, of course, even Amelia's horrible cousin wouldn't intentionally set fire to Lizzie's room. Even so Lizzie knew she would double-check the lock on her door every night.

Lizzie knew she had two choices: either she could confront Harriet, or she could run away. The old Lizzie would definitely have chosen the latter, she would have scuttled up the stairs and prayed Harriet would leave her alone. Lizzie pushed back her shoulders, lifted her chin and told herself she was a confident and beautiful young woman.

'You read the letter,' she stated.

Harriet's eyes narrowed. 'And what letter would that be?'

'The private letter from my father to me.'

'Something's wrong with you,' Harriet said quietly, moving towards Lizzie with menace in her eyes. 'Something is very wrong and I'm going to find out what.'

'Why do you hate me so much?' Lizzie asked.

Harriet had made her dislike of Lizzie clear from the first day they had met, before they had even got to know each other.

For a moment Lizzie thought Harriet might not reply, but then the young woman's mouth twisted into a sneer.

'What have you got that I don't?' Harriet asked. 'You're not beautiful, you're not funny, you're just rather ordinary, but when you walk into a room you have suitors flocking towards you, just because your father is rich.'

'They're only interested in me because of my dowry, how do you think that makes me feel?'

Harriet snorted. 'You have an earl eager to do anything to make you his wife. Who cares if it's because of your dowry or because you can stand on your head and juggle at the same time. The end result is the same—you become a countess.'

'One day you'll find someone to marry, Harriet,' Lizzie said. 'And you might even love him. Then it won't matter if he's an earl or a duke or a prince.'

'That's easy for you to say, but men will always choose an heiress over someone like me.'

'Is that really why you hate me, Harriet?'

Lizzie watched as Harriet's expression turned into contempt.

'You want to know the real reason?' she spat. 'Why don't you ask your father?'

Lizzie frowned. 'What?'

'The wonderful Colonel Eastway, the clever man who made his fortune in India.'

Lizzie certainly didn't think he was wonderful, but she couldn't tell Harriet that.

'I bet he never spares a thought for all those he stole from.'

'What are you talking about, Harriet?'

Lizzie knew her uncle was ruthless, but she couldn't imagine him a thief.

'We used to be rich, you know,' Harriet said. 'Until your father advised mine on how to invest his money and he lost everything.'

Ah. That would be quite a valid reason for Harriet to dislike her family.

'And then a few years later he makes his fortune in India and doesn't even think about us, about the lives he ruined.'

'I'm sure he never meant to...'

'It doesn't matter what he meant. You're rich and we're poor, all because of the advice of your father. I could have been a great heiress, I could have had hundreds of suitors flocking after me, but instead it's you they're chasing.'

Dramatically Harriet spun around and sailed out of the front door.

Lizzie felt herself slump. Harriet hated her with a vengeance, and she had a feeling she would try to find any way to destroy Lizzie that she could. It wouldn't be long before she found out Lizzie's secret.

Lizzie's hands were trembling and her knees felt weak. All the bravado that had infused her just minutes before had fled and she was left a shuddering wreck.

Slowly she forced herself to climb the stairs and stumble along to her room. Once inside she locked the door, checked it twice, then collapsed on to the bed.

She was worried and not just about her secret becoming public. Of course that was bothering her, she didn't want to be exposed as a liar. Aunt Mathilda had been so kind to her and her whole relationship with Daniel was built on a lie. She didn't want them to find out, but equally she knew they must. When Amelia had begged her to swap identities with her for a couple of weeks Lizzie had been more than reluctant, but her cousin had squeezed her hand and Lizzie was reminded of all the occasions that Amelia had stood up for her when no one else had. So she'd agreed to Amelia's plan, even though it went against her moral compass. At the time she hadn't known the people she would be lying to, hadn't realised that one day she would become fond of them and lying to them would hurt.

More than that, though, was now the worry about her cousin. It had been well over two weeks since Amelia had left Lizzie at the docks, racing off to find the army officer she had formed an attachment to when he was stationed out in India. She'd promised Lizzie she would be back within two weeks and, although Amelia was flighty and was renowned for losing track of time, Lizzie couldn't believe that her cousin would forget to pen a short note to assure Lizzie she was all right.

The problem was Lizzie didn't even know where to start in looking for her. Amelia had been very cagey about the identity of this officer and so Lizzie didn't have a name, let alone an address, for the man.

Her whole life was unravelling before her eyes, the lies catching up with her and her future more uncertain than it ever had been before.

A sharp rap on the door made her jump and Lizzie wondered for an instant whether it was Harriet come back to taunt her some more. Eventually she rose, crossed the room and unlocked the door, opening it a sliver to reveal a footman standing outside.

'A letter, madam,' he said, presenting the letter to her on a tray with a bow.

Lizzie took the letter with trembling hands. Surely this wasn't from Amelia—that would be too much of a coincidence.

The writing was unfamiliar and Lizzie ran her fingers over the thick paper before opening it. Carefully she broke the seal and quickly read. It made her smile.

Dearest Amelia,
I enjoyed our outing this morning and thought it was an unparalleled success. Despite spending over an hour in a small rowing boat neither of us ended up in the water—what more could a man ask for from a rendezvous with a beautiful woman? Well, maybe a man could *ask for more, but it certainly wouldn't be proper.*

Seeing as you denied me your company for so many days I feel another outing is warranted, and soon. Meet me at three today for an afternoon of ex-citement and I guarantee I will be the perfect gentle-man. If you want me to be.
Yours,
Daniel

Lizzie couldn't help but smile. Even when her whole world was falling apart Daniel could make her feel both normal and special at the same time.

Daniel. He would know what to do. Not that she could tell him her whole predicament, not yet at least, but she could ask for his assistance in finding Amelia. Then, when she had summoned up the courage, she would tell him the truth about her identity.

Before she could lose her nerve Lizzie rushed out of her room and down the stairs. It was late morning and she assumed Daniel would be in his study, doing whatever it was one had to do to run a country estate.

She knocked, waited for a response, then pushed the heavy wooden door open and entered the room.

Daniel surveyed her from behind a large mahogany desk.

'Is three o'clock too long to wait, my sweet?' he asked.

'Yes, no.' Lizzie forced herself to take a deep breath and crossed the room towards him. 'I need your help.'

Daniel rose, walked around his desk and guided her into an armchair positioned by the window. Lizzie waited for him to take a seat in the second chair, but instead he stood behind her and started trailing his fingers along her shoulders.

'You seem tense, my dear,' he said and began to gently knead her shoulders with his hands.

Momentarily Lizzie felt her body relax and forgot the reason she had come in.

'Maybe I could help with that tension.'

Daniel dropped his lips to the nape of her neck and started to trail kisses across her skin. Lizzie's eyes fluttered as she tried to resist his touch, but after a few seconds she was melting into his body.

'What was it you wanted to ask me, my dear?' Daniel asked as he took the dainty sleeves of her gown and pushed them down her arms.

Lizzie's mind was trying to function, trying to remember what it was she had come here for, but every time she caught a glimpse of her purpose Daniel distracted her with a kiss.

'Did you want to ask me to kiss you?' he murmured in her ear, nibbling the lobe as she felt the desire mounting deep inside her. 'Or did you want me to touch you?' He dipped a finger inside the bodice of her dress, stroking the skin and distracting Lizzie even more.

'I…' Lizzie tried to focus, to bring their meeting back to her agenda.

'Maybe you wanted to ask me to repeat what we did at the coaching inn.'

Lizzie's eyes snapped open and she managed to push Daniel away.

'I need your help,' she said, trying to pull her dress back into place. 'And I need you to be serious.'

As if sensing her distress, Daniel moved away from her and sat down in the armchair opposite.

'How can I be of assistance?' he asked, all trace of joviality gone in an instant.

'I need to find someone,' Lizzie said slowly. 'Someone I'm worried about, someone I haven't heard from for a while.'

Daniel frowned and motioned for her to go on.

'I can't tell you much more…' Lizzie hesitated. 'But if you could recommend someone who could be trusted, who could make confidential enquiries on my behalf?'

She knew it was asking a lot of him.

'Amelia, are you in trouble?' he asked quietly.

She shook her head. 'But I'm concerned someone I care a great deal for may be.'

She saw his composed expression falter for an instant and realised there was a flicker of jealousy. He hid it well, but Daniel was worried she might have feelings for another man.

'A good friend of mine, she was meant to write to me and I haven't heard anything.'

He seemed to relax instantly. 'Can you tell me anything? This woman's name, why you're concerned?'

Lizzie shook her head. 'One day I promise I'll explain,

but please don't ask me to yet. I can't betray a promise I made.'

Daniel looked at her for about a minute, as if weighing up her words.

'I know a man who will make discreet enquiries for you,' he said. 'But I urge you to trust me, I will help you no matter what the problem.'

Lizzie reached out and took his hand. 'I will tell you soon, I promise, but I need to find my friend first, to make sure she's all right.'

Daniel nodded. 'I will write a letter to this man and ask him to travel down here at his earliest convenience.'

'Thank you,' Lizzie said, feeling a weight lift off her. She stood, feeling a little awkward with her secret sitting between them. 'Do you still want to meet at three?'

Daniel grinned, immediately back to the carefree young-man persona he presented to the world. 'Of course. I'm mad with anticipation already.'

Lizzie moved to the door but stopped with her hand resting on the door handle. As she turned to bid Daniel farewell her eyes fell upon the open desk drawer Daniel had placed something inside when she came in the room. If she wasn't very much mistaken, it was a portrait. Forcing a smile on her face, Lizzie said goodbye and left Daniel's study, wondering whom he kept a picture of hidden in his desk.

Chapter Eighteen

Daniel drummed his fingers absentmindedly on the banister as he waited for Amelia to emerge from her room and join him for their three o'clock outing. Her request earlier had puzzled him. It was certainly strange, wanting to employ a man to find someone but unable to tell him who.

What was puzzling him more was his reaction to her request. Normally this kind of secrecy had him trying to figure out exactly what was going on, but today, after Amelia's request, he had calmly penned a note to a man he knew would handle the business discreetly for her and got on with his accounts. It wasn't that he was not curious—far from it, he wanted to know the details of Amelia's life—but more that he trusted her. And that revelation was baffling all on its own.

Daniel had been trusting once, but Annabelle and her lies and schemes had killed that trust. Now he was lucky if he didn't view even his oldest and most loyal friends with a shred of suspicion. That was why this business of Amelia's, searching for a lost friend but unable to tell him more, should have him prying into every secret she had, but Daniel didn't feel the need. He trusted her. He trusted her to tell him when she was ready and he trusted her to make the right decision.

It was a liberating feeling, trust. He felt like singing from the rooftops, shouting from the windows. Finally he had found someone he trusted. Making her his wife seemed even more vital now. He liked Amelia, he desired Amelia, but most of all he *trusted* Amelia.

Daniel wondered for a moment whether he should just confess his whole sordid past to Amelia. Over the past week the idea of telling her every last detail, from his brother's suicide to Annabelle's seduction to his illegitimate son and the blackmail he was now caught up in, had seemed very appealing. He didn't like keeping something so important from her and on a couple of occasions he had nearly confessed everything, including the reason he had started courting her. It would be liberating to share the burden of his secrets, especially with the woman he was planning on spending the rest of his life with. Then Daniel thought of the way Amelia's face had lit up when they were in the rowing boat and he'd told her she was beautiful. Bit by bit he could see her self-confidence grow. Amelia was blossoming right before his eyes. If he told her the reason he had been so eager to get to know her was because he needed her fortune to pay his old mistress, she would be crushed, all the confidence she had gained would be wiped out in an instant. One day the time would be right to confide in her, but not yet.

'I hope I'm dressed appropriately,' Amelia said as she descended the stairs. 'You could give me some clue as to what you've got planned for this afternoon.'

Daniel grinned, took her hand and placed it in the crook of his arm.

'How would you have dressed if I'd told you we were off to meet the king?' Daniel teased.

'Not in my third-best dress.'

'I think you look lovely in your third-best dress.'

'Where are we going really?' Amelia asked.

'You'll ruin the surprise.'

Amelia looked at him long enough for him to cave. A man couldn't be expected to hold strong under the weight of her deep brown eyes.

'Just a little clue, then. I'm taking you to do something I wager you've never done before.'

Amelia sucked in her bottom lip as she considered the clue. Daniel knew they were in full view of anyone passing through the hallway, but he still wanted to lean forward and coax her lip out from her mouth.

'Whatever you're thinking, remember we're in public,' Amelia hissed.

'What makes you think I'm having inappropriate thoughts?' Daniel asked, moving closer and slipping his arm around her waist.

'Aren't you always?' Amelia mumbled. Then louder, 'You have that look in your eyes again.'

'What look?' Daniel frowned, he was normally so in control of his expressions.

'That look. The one you get when you're thinking of… being intimate. It's as though you want to eat me.'

Daniel almost choked with surprise. Amelia frowned.

'That's more true than you could ever realise…' he paused '…but I promise to remedy that one day soon.'

He bent his head and quickly nibbled her ear, knowing she wouldn't allow him to kiss her for long in public. It was scandalous enough that they were sneaking off for an afternoon alone together, without Amelia's aunt to chaperon them, but Daniel knew none of his staff would say anything and it didn't matter too much as he was planning on marrying Amelia at the earliest opportunity anyway.

He counted. It took five seconds before Amelia had summoned the willpower to push him away.

'Stop it,' she hissed. 'Anyone could see.'

'So your objection is to any possible witnesses, not to what I was doing?'

Amelia mumbled something under her breath.

'If that's the case, I'll find somewhere more private for us, somewhere we won't be disturbed.'

'I thought we were going out.'

Daniel let out a sigh and pulled away. 'As my lady wishes,' he said, then swooped in for a sneaky kiss.

He led Amelia out through the front door and round the side of the house, then they began the twenty-minute walk across the fields to where Daniel had instructed a groom to set up for their afternoon's activities.

As they got further away from the house Daniel felt Amelia's body begin to relax. He wondered what had her so tense. He'd seen the antagonistic glares Harriet sent Amelia's way, but surely a little cousinly dislike wasn't enough to be making Amelia so jumpy. Maybe it was something to do with this missing friend.

'Are we going shooting?' Amelia asked, her eyes lighting up as she saw the target set up ahead of them.

'We are indeed.'

'Oh, I love shooting.'

Daniel turned to her, momentarily speechless. 'You've shot a pistol before.'

'Pistols, shotguns, my cousin and I used to do target practice all the time in India.'

'Who on earth taught you to shoot?'

Amelia gave him an appraising look. 'We lived surrounded by army officers. There were always plenty of volunteers.'

Daniel bet there were lots of eager young officers trying to impress Amelia with their shooting prowess. He suddenly had a foul taste in his mouth at the thought of another man wrapping his hands around Amelia's, of him moving in behind her to help her with positioning. Of the faceless young officer standing that little bit too close and dipping his head to nuzzle Amelia's neck.

'Was there someone in particular?' he asked, hating the strain he heard in his voice.

Amelia laughed. 'My cousin always had officers fighting to be the one to teach her things. Whoever didn't win her favour would have me as the consolation prize.'

Daniel stopped without warning, tugging on Amelia's arm. 'Then they were fools,' he said. 'Stupid, blind fools.'

Amelia opened her mouth to protest. Before she could get a single syllable out Daniel kissed her. It wasn't gentle or particularly elegant, but he needed to make her understand.

'Fools,' he repeated. 'Any man who doesn't see how irresistible you are is a fool.'

Again Amelia started to protest.

Daniel cupped her face gently and made her look into his eyes.

'What did I tell you earlier?'

For a second Amelia looked blank.

'You're beautiful.'

'Compared to my cousin I'm…'

Daniel stroked her cheek. 'I think that's your problem, my sweet, you compare yourself to this cousin of yours far too much.'

He knew by the look in her eyes it was more true than Amelia cared to admit.

'And I promise you I wouldn't look twice at your cousin with you around.'

'You can't promise that,' Amelia said, frowning again. '*You've* never met her. *Everyone* falls in love with her.'

Daniel didn't hear any hint of bitterness in her voice and he realised Amelia must love her cousin very much.

'I wouldn't even notice her. Not with you there.'

He could see Amelia was struggling to believe him. He wanted to give her the confidence she was sorely lacking, he wanted her to see herself as he did.

Daniel pressed a hand into the small of her back and pulled her close into his body.

'Do you feel what you do to me?' he asked, pressing his hips into hers. 'That's all you, not your cousin, not any other woman. You.'

Amelia seemed momentarily stunned, but even as she regained her senses she didn't pull away.

'You drive me crazy,' Daniel said. 'And one day you will be mine. I can't have it any other way. I want you too much to let you go.'

Gently he released her, only keeping hold of her hand.

'So you're going to give me a good bit of competition,' he said, motioning towards the target.

Amelia just stared for a minute, obviously still processing Daniel's words, before rallying.

'I was the best shot this side of Calcutta,' she said with a grin.

'Then how about a wager?' Daniel said.

'What do you propose?'

'If I win you grant me a whole hour, in private, to show you just how desirable you are.'

Amelia swallowed, allowed her tongue to dart out to moisten her lips, then asked, 'And if I win?'

'I grant you an hour, in private, to do whatever you want with me.'

She laughed and the tension that had been sizzling between them was broken.

'Anything I want?' she asked with a mischievous grin.

'Anything.'

'So if I asked you to clean out a pigsty?'

'I'd be honour bound to do it.'

She seemed to contemplate her options for a moment. 'Deal.'

Daniel took Amelia's proffered hand and shook it. Inside he was singing with joy; Amelia had just agreed to a whole hour of blissful seduction. No matter who won Daniel knew how that hour would end.

He wasn't sure whether he was more pleased about the inevitable marriage that would come after such intimacies, or the intimacies themselves. Of course he hadn't lost sight of his ultimate aim, to marry Amelia and secure her dowry, but as each day passed he was growing more enamoured with the idea of actually being married to her. Waking up every day with Amelia in his bed, talking to her over the breakfast table, then taking her back to bed. He'd never imagined he'd actually want to get married, but every moment he spent with Amelia was convincing him that having a wife he desired as much as her could be no bad thing.

In truth Daniel couldn't believe his luck. For years bad things had happened to him or to those around him. First his brother's death, and then Annabelle's seduction and betrayal. And the event that had hurt him the most; the knowledge he had a son whom he would never be a true father to, a boy he would never swing up on his shoulders, never teach to ride, never tuck into bed.

Finally, with Amelia, his luck had changed. This was the woman he was prepared to marry even if she had a face full of warts and poor personal hygiene, if it had meant obtaining her dowry to keep his son safe. Instead he had found a woman he could barely keep his hands off and someone whose company he enjoyed as well.

When he had scooped Amelia up from the burning room Daniel had been scared he might lose her. His heart had pounded like never before and he'd felt sick inside.

Although he'd known Amelia for only a couple of weeks the idea of losing her had made him realise just how much she meant to him.

Amelia picked up a pistol and began to inspect it, feeling its weight in her hands. Expertly she flicked open the barrel and checked bullets before closing it back up.

'Best of six?' she asked.

Daniel ran a finger around his collar and wondered if he was about to be beaten by this surprising woman. Amelia was shy and retiring at first glance. It was only as you got to know her that her hidden depths became apparent.

'Best of six,' he agreed. 'Ladies first.'

Amelia took her time, adjusting her stance first, then lining up the pistol with the centre of the target. After about a minute of fine adjustments she was obviously ready to fire.

Calmly she squeezed the trigger. The bullet hit the target about three inches from the centre. Without moving her feet Amelia made a small correction to the angle of the pistol and fired again. Each successive shot got closer to the centre and the final bullet hit the bullseye just slightly off the very middle.

'Impressive, Miss Eastway,' Daniel said. 'I think I may be surrendering to an hour at your mercy.'

He picked up a pistol, inspected it, took up position and squeezed off his shots.

They both squinted at the target, then stepped towards it. Daniel's shots were all close to the bullseye, with one nearly central.

'I think that's a draw,' Daniel said with a grin.

'What's the tiebreaker?'

'Why have a tiebreaker?' Daniel asked. 'Why don't we have an hour each?'

'An hour each?'

Daniel could see Amelia was trying to say no but couldn't quite bring herself to utter the words. She wanted her hour with him, but she just didn't want to admit it.

'First you will have an hour at my mercy and then we'll swap.'

'Two hours, alone?' Amelia asked, absentmindedly chewing on her bottom lip.

'We did shake on it,' Daniel reminded her.

'We did,' Amelia said.

'Then that's agreed. Tomorrow I will find some way of getting your aunt and cousin out of the house and we shall enjoy two whole uninterrupted hours together.'

He couldn't believe it when Amelia nodded in agreement. He knew she desired him, knew he could make her almost forget her own name with just a single kiss, but he had half expected her to say no, to pull away from him at the last moment and remember all the rules of propriety that would have been drummed into her as she grew up.

By agreeing to these two hours alone she was almost agreeing to the marriage he had proposed before. Daniel knew she couldn't willingly let her virtue be taken and not marry him. It would be madness, especially when he was so keen on the match. He smiled. Tomorrow they would enjoy an afternoon of pleasure and he would gain a fiancée.

Chapter Nineteen

Lizzie knew she was being beyond foolish. She couldn't spend two whole hours alone with Daniel. Whatever was left of her virtue would certainly not remain intact. She knew what a scandal it was just being in the house alone with him, even if they did not see each other, but she couldn't find it in herself to care. She couldn't resist him. Even if she went in with the best of intentions, one of his smouldering looks would have her begging him to make her his.

She would have to tell him the truth. Once he knew who she really was, then it was his decision whether he still wanted her as his wife, but she wouldn't allow him to seduce her and then tell him. Daniel was an honourable man and once he had truly taken her virtue, then he would insist on marriage, even if he didn't want it when he found out her true identity. She would not be the woman who forced him down the aisle.

Lizzie sighed—it had been a nice fantasy. She had been drawn into his world and she had fallen completely and irreversibly in love with Daniel. Lizzie had always assumed she would never fall in love, it seemed like the sort of thing that happened to other people, but here she was completely infatuated with a man who thought she was someone else. What made it worse was that he desired her. Lizzie knew all the compliments he paid her were to advance his cause, but when he looked her in the eye and told her she was beautiful she believed him. Daniel had helped her find her self-confidence.

Glancing at the clock, Lizzie flopped back down on to her bed. Daniel had taken her aside after breakfast and whispered his instructions in her ear. He had arranged for all the ladies to take a trip into Cambridge to do some shopping. At the last minute Lizzie was to cry off sick.

She'd done just as he'd ask, saying her chest was feeling a little sore and that she planned to rest for the afternoon. Harriet had glared at her and Aunt Mathilda had twittered on about it not being right for a young lady to be left alone in a gentleman's house, but Daniel had flashed her his most charming of smiles and made assurances that her niece's reputation would be perfectly safe, so the two women had gone shopping.

Now she just had to wait for Daniel to knock on her door.

Five minutes later she felt she was going mad with nerves. Knowing she couldn't wait much longer, she opened the door and peeked out into the corridor. Lizzie almost shrieked with shock. Standing just outside her door, with his hand raised ready to knock, was Daniel. He held a bunch of flowers in one hand that he must have picked from the garden.

'May I come in?' Daniel asked after a few seconds.

Lizzie's heart was racing, so instead of replying she just nodded. As Daniel entered her bedroom and closed the door behind him the room suddenly felt very small.

'Daniel,' Lizzie said, hearing the tremor in her voice.

'Yes, my sweet.'

'I need to tell you something. Something important.'

Lizzie felt herself backing away as he approached her. She needed to tell him the truth, let him know that she wasn't Miss Amelia Eastway, heiress; she was penniless Elizabeth Eastway.

'I need to tell you something, too,' he purred in her ear.

Lizzie felt her resolve slipping as soon as his lips touched her skin. She wanted this afternoon, wanted to feel his hands all over her body, his lips kissing her. She wanted to know what it felt like to make love to the man she loved. This would be her only opportunity. Once Daniel knew her true identity, he wouldn't be able to marry her; he needed an heiress. A marriage couldn't be built on desire alone and she knew he didn't love her otherwise he would have said so in the coaching inn. So once he knew who she was they would have to go their separate ways, get on with their lives. Lizzie knew she would never love another man; her future was either as the unhappy wife of Colonel Rocher, or as a spinster, maybe an old lady's companion or a governess. This was her one and only opportunity to be intimate with the man she loved.

'I'm not who you think I am,' she said, her conscience overcoming her desire.

'None of us is.'

Before Lizzie could say another word, before she could explain her meaning, Daniel's lips found hers and she was swept away, unable to break off the kiss even if her life depended on it.

Daniel eased her backwards across the room, towards the bed. Lizzie felt his hands on her shoulders, his fingers tracing patterns on her sensitive skin.

He broke the kiss to start to unlace her dress and Lizzie momentarily regained her self-control.

'Daniel, I need to tell you my secret.'

'All in good time. We all have secrets, Amelia, and one

day we'll come clean about everything, but not today. I don't care what your secret is, this afternoon you're mine.'

Momentarily Lizzie wondered what secrets Daniel was keeping from her, but the thought was swept out of her brain when Daniel spun her round and started kissing the nape of her neck.

'You have such a lovely neck,' he murmured. 'So graceful.'

His lips trailed lower, kissing her between her shoulder blades as he pushed the material of her dress down her back. Lizzie felt her dress slip over her breasts and instinctively she raised her hands to cover herself. Daniel reached around and took her hands gently in his, placing them back at her sides.

Lizzie knew she had to stop him now and tell him her true identity or she would be swept up in the moment. She looked at his sparkling eyes full of desire and his lips ready to kiss her, and she swallowed the words she had been about to say. She wanted this afternoon, wanted it more than she had ever wanted anything in her life. She needed Daniel to kiss her, to make love to her. Lizzie knew that once this afternoon was over she would have to tell him her true identity and that would likely mean the end of their wonderful relationship, but she wanted to make love with the man she loved just once in her life, even if he never wanted to see her again afterwards. Her mind made up, Lizzie surrendered to Daniel's deft touch.

Expertly he freed her of her dress and as it pooled around her feet Daniel picked her up and lifted her out of it. Lizzie was still wearing her thin cotton chemise, but she felt naked under his gaze.

Slowly Daniel turned her around so they were facing each other and Lizzie watched as he started to tug at his cravat. Quickly he took off the outer layers of his clothes until he was clad only in his shirt and breeches.

Lizzie hesitantly raised a hand and placed it on his chest, feeling the heat of his body through the thin cotton.

'Why don't you take it off?' Daniel suggested.

With fumbling fingers Lizzie tugged the shirt over his head. Daniel reached out, took her hand and placed it on his chest.

'Feel what you do to me,' he said.

Lizzie could feel his heart pounding under her fingers, but she was distracted by the silky smoothness of his skin overlaid by the hairs that covered his chest. Slowly, as if she were in a trance, Lizzie ran her fingers down on to his abdomen and watched as his muscles tensed and tightened at her touch. She stopped about an inch above his waist-band, not confident enough to do what she really wanted and dip a finger below the band and explore beneath.

'I want to see you,' Daniel murmured. 'I've wanted to see you since you flattened me in the Prestons' garden.'

Lizzie couldn't help but smile. The night she had made her début seemed so long ago now. That was the night she had first been kissed by Daniel, had first fallen under his spell.

With gentle fingers Daniel gripped the hem of her chemise and started to lift it over her body. All her life Lizzie had felt as if she blended into the background. People never noticed her, in particular men never noticed her, especially when Amelia was standing anywhere close by. Lizzie had grown to accept it and the few times she was noticed she had felt self-conscious and uncomfortable. Right now, with Daniel's eyes burning into her skin, she should feel shy, instead she felt beautiful. She wanted Daniel to lift her chemise, to look upon the body she had been unhappy with for so long, for she knew he would see her curves and her beauty where she saw her flaws.

Involuntarily Lizzie shivered as he exposed her body to the air. Although she felt the blood rush to her cheeks as Daniel's eyes raked over her body, she forced her arms to stay at her sides and not cover herself as she instinctively wanted to.

'You're perfect,' Daniel said.

Lizzie knew it wasn't true, but in that moment she felt perfect in his eyes.

He stepped closer to her, narrowing the gap between them so their bodies were almost touching. Gently Daniel raised a hand and ran his fingers from the base of Lizzie's throat, through the dip between her breasts and over her abdomen. He paused just before he reached the soft hair that covered her most private place, then his fingers continued their journey downwards.

Lizzie was overwhelmed with desire. She wanted him to touch her all over, to kiss her lips and bury himself inside her. With fumbling hands she reached for the waistband of his trousers and started to unclasp the fastening. Daniel groaned as she pushed the material down from his hips and he kissed her deeply.

As if it were no effort at all Daniel scooped Lizzie into his arms and carried her to the bed, laying her down gently before kicking off his trousers. Lizzie's eyes widened as she saw him naked for the first time, but before she could say anything Daniel was straddling her and his lips were once again on hers.

'I want you, Amelia,' Daniel whispered in her ear. 'I want you more than I've ever wanted anyone.'

Lizzie couldn't speak, instead she pulled Daniel closer to her, pressing her hands into his back in an attempt to weld their bodies together.

'All in good time, my love,' Daniel said, nibbling on her ear.

Lizzie felt the blood pulsing round her body as Daniel's lips trailed across her skin, kissing and nipping as they went. He captured one of her breasts in his hand and brought his lips to the nipple, grazing it with his teeth and making Lizzie cry out with the jolt of pleasure it sent through her body.

'I want to spend weeks exploring every inch of your skin,' Daniel whispered as he pulled away for just a second. 'I want to know every curve and every perfect imperfection.'

Lizzie knew she couldn't take much more of his teasing. She wanted him, even though she didn't really know what that meant, she wanted him more than life itself.

'I need you,' she said, her voice sounding breathless and foreign to her own ears.

Daniel ignored her pleas and worked his lips across her skin to her other breast, circling the nipple with his tongue before taking it into his mouth.

'I need you,' Lizzie repeated.

This time Daniel took notice of her and raised himself up above her, looking down into her eyes.

'After this there is no going back,' he said.

Lizzie knew he was trying to be chivalrous and she also knew he expected to marry her, so this would be no more than a little indiscretion, but still he was offering her a way out. She knew there was a very good chance he wouldn't want her once he knew her true identity, but she couldn't bring herself to stop him. She wanted this so badly, wanted to make love to the man she loved even if it was just the once. This way she would always have the memory of this afternoon, of their lovemaking, even when she was lonely and far away. When she was once again starved for affection it would keep her going when nothing else could.

'I want this,' Lizzie said.

Daniel smiled at her, kissed her deeply on the lips, then pushed inside her. Lizzie found she was tensing, but slowly Daniel coaxed her to relax. His hands were everywhere, stroking and soothing, until Lizzie knew the full length of him was inside her.

As she got used to the unfamiliar sensation of being so full Lizzie felt a warmth spread deep inside her and her body began to react instinctively. Lizzie started to push her hips up towards Daniel, letting out a small moan as he withdrew nearly all the way and groaning with pleasure as he plunged back inside her. As the blood pounded around her body their pace quickened and Lizzie felt a wonderful pressure building deep inside her.

Daniel thrust in and out of her, his eyes never leaving her face, his body completely in tune with her own. Lizzie started to moan; soft whimpers that she had no control over. Her whole body was tensing as if it were about to uncoil. Lizzie's hands gripped the sheets, her fingers turning white from the pressure, then with a final thrust the release came. It was an explosion deep inside her and it was all Lizzie could do to stop herself from screaming with pleasure.

As Lizzie's body tightened she felt Daniel stiffen inside her and with a groan he collapsed on top of her. They lay panting together, their hearts beating in time, for a few minutes, neither able to utter a single word.

After Daniel had caught his breath he rolled off Lizzie and she felt suddenly bereft, but in moments he was behind her, moulding his body to the contours of hers.

'Have I ever told you you're beautiful?' he whispered in her ear.

Lizzie wriggled in closer to him.

'Beautiful and perfect in every single way.'

She didn't care that all her life she'd been called plain, she didn't care that she was always overlooked when men entered the room. Daniel saw her and Daniel thought she was beautiful.

Chapter Twenty

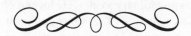

Daniel could lie like this all day. He felt immensely satisfied. He'd wanted Amelia ever since they'd shared that kiss in the Prestons' garden and his desire for her had been building every day since. As he gently kissed her shoulder he smiled. Far from dampening the desire that burned inside him their session of lovemaking had just made him want Amelia even more. Good job she was going to have to agree to be his wife now. He could think of nothing more pleasurable than shutting himself and Amelia in the bedroom for a couple of weeks whilst he fully explored her body and got to know her mind.

Daniel was just letting his eyes droop when there was a sharp rap on the door. Both he and Amelia immediately sat upright in bed, gathering the sheets to cover their naked bodies.

Amelia looked at him with panicked eyes and Daniel leapt out of bed, ready to strongly chastise whoever it was who dared to disturb them. Quickly he pulled on his breeches and flung his shirt over his head, not bothering with the rest of his clothes. With a glance back over his shoulder to check Amelia was completely covered by her sheet, he unlocked the door and opened it a crack.

His butler stood outside. Daniel frowned—there was absolutely no reason for his butler to disturb him in the day anyway, let alone when it was obvious he was breaking every rule of propriety with an innocent young woman.

'I'm sorry, sir,' the butler said, his expression pained. 'You have a visitor.'

Daniel nearly shouted at the man for disturbing him for such a trivial reason, but one look at the man's face told him this was no ordinary visitor. He looked down the corridor and saw a huddle of servants and realised his butler had been nominated to knock on the door and deliver the bad news.

'Who?'

His butler cleared his throat, caught Daniel's eye and whispered, 'A woman and a boy.'

Daniel had to stop himself from staggering backwards. Annabelle was here, in the same house as Amelia. He shot a worried look back over his shoulder at Amelia, who was still huddled in the bed. He wanted to run down the corridor, to snatch his son up into his arms and never let him go again, but he knew Annabelle would never let that happen. As much as he wanted to see his son he needed to get them out of the house, away from Amelia, or all his plans would be ruined.

'Put them in my study,' Daniel said quietly. 'Don't let her talk to anyone.'

His butler immediately hurried off to carry out Daniel's orders and left Daniel alone with Amelia. He shut the door and turned back to the bed.

'What's happening?' Amelia asked, the sheets pulled adorably up to her chin.

'Nothing to worry about,' Daniel said, forcing his voice to sound cheerful. 'Just a bit of urgent business I've got to sort out.'

Amelia looked confused but didn't protest. Quickly Daniel pulled on the rest of his clothes, ran a hand through his tousled hair and pecked Amelia on the cheek. He tried to ignore her mournful expression, not wanting to think what was running through her mind. No doubt she was assuming now he'd taken what he'd wanted he was fleeing and leaving her without her virtue and without a proposition of marriage. Daniel wished he could stay and reassure her, he wanted to gather her in his arms and promise nothing would ever hurt her again, but first he needed to deal with Annabelle.

'I'll be back soon,' he said, dropping another kiss on her forehead. Then he left the room before she could question him about where he was scuttling off to so soon after he'd taken her virginity.

Daniel took a couple of moments to compose himself before he entered his study. Seeing Annabelle always raised his stress levels and he needed to be clear-headed to get her out of the house and as far away from Amelia as quickly as possible.

He opened the door and immediately felt his heart constricting in his chest. Sitting on the floor, playing with a small toy soldier, was his son. Daniel wanted to scoop the boy up in his arms and never let go. He wanted to shower him in kisses and love and get down there on the floor and play soldiers with him until his son fell asleep in his arms.

'My lord,' Annabelle said, dipping into a curtsy and smiling at the look on Daniel's face.

Never before had she brought their son to one of these meetings. She would let Daniel catch glimpses of him at a distance when she wanted to remind him of his obligation to pay her, but she had never brought Edward to see him like this. Daniel took a step towards his son.

'Edward, come to Mother,' Annabelle said, a cruel smile pulling at the edge of her lips.

The little boy obediently picked up his toy soldier and

walked to his mother, smiling shyly at Daniel as he went past. Daniel's heart nearly broke in two. He wanted to be a father to his son, he wanted it more than life itself, but he knew that to protect him Edward could never find out his true identity.

'You're running out of time,' Annabelle said as she motioned for her son to sit down at her feet.

Daniel closed the study door firmly behind him, not taking his eyes off his son for a second.

'I've got what you want,' Daniel said.

Hathaway had loaned him the two hundred pounds before Daniel had left London, the rest he had managed to scrape together.

'I hear you've caught yourself a nice little heiress,' Annabelle said.

Daniel didn't want Annabelle even thinking about Amelia. His ex-lover sullied everything and he knew that no matter what he needed to keep her and Amelia apart.

'Once your circumstances have improved, I'll expect some of that good fortune to come trickling our way.'

Daniel had been afraid she'd increase her demands once he was married. She was a greedy woman who had become used to living in luxury. Daniel knew his son was not badly treated and didn't want for anything, except for perhaps a little more of his mother's attention, but he also knew most of the money he gave Annabelle was not spent on Edward. It went towards her fine dresses, her expensive jewels and her lavish lifestyle.

'There is only a finite amount of money, Annabelle,' Daniel said with a sigh.

'Don't make me do something I'll regret.' She reached down and placed a hand on their son's head.

With the extra attention Edward was distracted from his soldier and looked up at the two adults.

'I'm Edward,' he said to Daniel. 'Who are you?'

'My name's Daniel,' Daniel said, his heart breaking. He hated the thought that his son would never know he was his father, but he knew the shadow of illegitimacy was a worse fate.

'Daniel is one of Mummy's special friends,' Annabelle said.

Edward lost interest then and went back to his soldier. Daniel felt the weight of sadness pressing on his chest, almost crushing him.

'Just give me what you owe now,' Annabelle said, clearly getting bored. 'Then once you come into your fortune we will renegotiate.'

'Don't come to the house again,' Daniel said as he dug out the cash he'd borrowed whilst in London from one of the drawers in his desk.

'Lest your little heiress see us and figure out the real reason you're marrying her?'

Daniel certainly didn't want Amelia ever coming into contact with Annabelle.

'Just send a note and I'll meet you in town.'

Annabelle took the money from his hand, but as Daniel started to pull away she grabbed his wrist, pulling him closer to her.

'We could still be a happy family,' she whispered in his ear.

'I couldn't endure a single hour in your presence, let alone a lifetime,' Daniel hissed back.

Annabelle pulled away, laughing.

'Always so passionate.'

'Just leave,' Daniel instructed, retreating slightly. He watched as Annabelle gathered up their son and for the thousandth time wished the boy was staying with him.

'Remember what you're paying for,' Annabelle said with her hand resting on the door handle.

When Daniel had been young and naïve, and desperately in love with Annabelle, he had told her all about his half-brother. He'd told her of their awkward days at school together when Daniel had not known how to act around Rupert, and he'd told her of their time at university when Daniel tried to reach out to his brother, only to be rejected. He'd also let her see his deepest wounds, the emotional scars left by his brother's suicide and the feelings of guilt he carried around with him every day. Annabelle knew all his secrets and she wasn't afraid to use them to her advantage. She was an intelligent woman and from the very start she had played on Daniel's fears.

Without letting Daniel say goodbye to his son Annabelle opened the door and sailed out of the room, only to stop a few feet into the entrance hall.

'Who are you?' he heard Amelia ask.

The bottom dropped out of Daniel's world.

He considered slamming the door to his study and allowing the two women in his life to fight it out, but Daniel had not allowed himself to shy away from a difficult situation throughout his adult life and he wasn't about to start now.

'She's leaving,' he said bluntly, before Annabelle could even open her mouth to reply.

His ex-lover shot him a glance and then smiled her most dazzling smile. Daniel watched with narrowed eyes as she sashayed through the hall and out the front door. Amelia's eyes were fixed on Annabelle's retreating form as well.

Once the front door had been closed behind Annabelle, Daniel and Amelia stood in silence for over a minute. Daniel could almost see the thoughts as they tumbled through her head. None of them were positive.

'Amelia,' he said, reaching out his hand to her.

She pulled away from him and took a step back.

'You left me in bed alone,' she whispered eventually.

Daniel didn't want to do this out in the hall. He wanted Amelia somewhere private, somewhere he could haul her on to his lap and kiss her until she forgot to be angry. Then he could explain. Looking at her expression, Daniel knew he would get away with nothing short of the whole truth.

'Let me explain,' Daniel said, taking a step back towards his study in the hope she would follow.

'You took my virginity, then you just left me in bed alone.'

Daniel knew that wasn't the whole issue. It had been unacceptable leaving Amelia on her own after they'd made love, but she would have understood if it were a truly urgent matter. Instead she'd emerged to find Daniel had left her to talk to another woman.

'She's your mistress, isn't she?' Amelia asked, her voice unnaturally calm.

Daniel shook his head. He knew things looked bad, but if he could just explain to Amelia, he thought maybe she would understand.

'She's beautiful.'

Daniel couldn't deny Annabelle was stunning. She had the looks so many men desired, the looks he had once found so beguiling. Her hair was a thick shiny mane of dark brown, her eyes were a stunning green and her figure was curvaceous in all the right places. At one time Daniel hadn't been able to resist her, he hadn't been able to say no to any request she made. That was before he'd seen her true nature and now that he knew the evil heart that beat inside her chest she was as attractive to him as an old crone.

'Amelia…' he started but stopped when she held up her hand.

'She's beautiful,' she repeated in a voice that allowed no argument.

Chapter Twenty-One

Lizzie felt the tears welling in her eyes, but she forced them away. She would not cry. She would not let Daniel see her cry. She didn't know what was worse; the fact that she had so naïvely given herself to Daniel when he had another woman waiting downstairs, or that the other woman was so stunningly beautiful Lizzie knew Daniel couldn't be attracted to her when this mysterious goddess was around.

'She was the woman in the park,' Lizzie said suddenly, as the image of Daniel's ashen face popped up in her mind after he had seen the woman and the boy in Hyde Park.

Lizzie understood now why Daniel had looked so alarmed, why he had dragged her out of the park faster than was gentlemanly. This woman was his mistress or his lover and he hadn't wanted them to meet. If they did, Lizzie would never fall for Daniel's sweet talk and assurances that he couldn't resist her, that she was beautiful. Compared to his mistress she was the plainest woman in Britain.

'Stop,' Daniel commanded, finally seeming to pull himself together. 'Whatever thoughts are running through your head, just stop.'

Lizzie couldn't. She pictured them together, laughing at her naïvety, thinking it hilarious that she was falling for Daniel's compliments.

Lizzie didn't resist as Daniel took her hand and pulled her into his study, closing the door firmly behind her.

'She's your mistress, isn't she?' Lizzie asked the question Daniel had ignored earlier.

Daniel raised his hand to cup her cheek, but Lizzie pulled away. She couldn't afford to fall under his spell again. Daniel was a skilled seducer and if she allowed him he'd make her forget what she'd seen and be begging him to kiss her within minutes. She needed a clear head.

'Just tell me the truth.'

Daniel stepped away and she saw his whole body sag. Ever since she had first met him Lizzie had sensed he carried a large burden and maybe now he was about to reveal all to her.

'It's a long story,' Daniel said. 'You'd better sit down.'

For a moment Lizzie thought about refusing, about staying on her feet just out of sheer stubbornness, but she sensed Daniel was telling the truth when he said it was a long story and there was no need for her to be more uncomfortable than she was already.

'First I need to tell you about my brother,' Daniel said, choosing to sit in the armchair opposite hers. He slumped backwards, making no further attempt to touch her.

'I don't see—' Lizzie started to say, but Daniel cut her off.

'I'm not trying to distract you, or to garner any sympathy, but things will be a lot clearer if I tell you about my brother.'

The tone of his voice told Lizzie that he was deadly serious, so instead of protesting she sat back in her chair and tried not to think of the beautiful woman Daniel had left her bed for.

'When I was a boy I thought I was an only child,' Daniel

started slowly. 'I dreamed about having a brother, someone to play with, someone to cause mischief with.'

Lizzie had also been an only child, but from a young age she'd had Amelia and they'd been inseparable. She couldn't imagine growing up without a constant companion.

'One day when I was about eight an old woman came to the house with a boy around my age. My father almost didn't let them in, but the old woman thrust the boy at my father and I can remember him hurrying them into his study.'

Lizzie could almost picture a young version of Daniel watching everything through the banisters, wondering what was going on.

'It turned out my father had sired an illegitimate son. The boy's mother had died during childbirth and his grandmother had raised him.'

'This was Rupert.'

Daniel nodded.

'I found out later that when his grandmother came to the house she knew she was dying. She convinced my father to look after Rupert in her place.'

'You finally had the brother that you wished for.'

Daniel grimaced. 'It wasn't anything like what I'd imagined. My mother refused to have Rupert in the house, so he was sent to live with one of the tenant farmers and his family nearby.'

Lizzie felt sorry for the young boy who had lost his mother and his grandmother and then been rejected by his father, but she knew it was a common enough story. Men the world over fathered illegitimate children they then didn't know what to do with.

'I was forbidden from seeing him,' Daniel said with a sad shake of his head. 'And back then I idolised my father so much I obeyed him and stayed away.'

She knew only too well the sway of a persuasive guardian. Colonel Eastway had had her toeing the line since she'd moved to India.

'We grew up a few miles apart but never laid eyes on each other after that first day.' Daniel sighed. 'So imagine my surprise when Rupert turned up at Eton a few weeks into the first school term.'

Lizzie had known the boys attended school together from Daniel's forced comments whilst they were in the park a couple of weeks previously, but at the time she hadn't realised the significance.

'He was my brother, my own flesh and blood, but I didn't know him.' Daniel shook his head sadly.

Lizzie could imagine only too well what had happened next. Rupert would have been immediately singled out for ridicule and bullying. Not only was he illegitimate, a fact none of the boys would have allowed him to forget, he had so far been raised with the children of a tenant farmer, not nobility. The mannerisms that would have come so easily for the other boys would not have been obvious to him.

Daniel raked a hand through his hair and Lizzie could see how much the memory of those schooldays upset him even now.

'I should have done more, I should have forced the other boys to accept him.'

Although Lizzie was still furious with Daniel for humiliating her with this other woman, she couldn't help but feel sorry for him. He blamed himself for his brother's death, that was clear for anyone to see, and he blamed the young boy that he had once been for not helping his brother even in the early days.

'I just didn't know how to act around him, so at first I avoided him. Then it became the norm. We were brothers, but we hardly even acknowledged each other when we passed one another on the stairs.'

'Children can be cruel,' Lizzie said, remembering the jibes from the other military children she had received out in India. 'But you have to remember you were only a child yourself, you didn't know what would be the outcome.'

Daniel grimaced. 'I wasn't a child when we went to university.'

Lizzie remembered Daniel telling her before that both boys had attended Cambridge, but Rupert had killed himself at the end of the first term.

'For years Rupert had been targeted for being different, for being illegitimate. As I got older I knew what the other boys were doing was wrong, cruel even, and in the last few years at Eton I quietly tried to stop them teasing Rupert.'

Lizzie could see the memories were almost too much for Daniel to bear, but she knew he thought this was related to his mistress and his desertion of Lizzie today, so she let him continue.

'Then we went to Cambridge. I finally felt like an adult and I finally tried to reach out to Rupert.'

'He didn't want to know you?' Lizzie asked.

Daniel shook his head. 'He refused to see me, cut me off whenever I tried to speak to him.'

Lizzie wanted to reach out and comfort the man she loved, but the face of the beautiful woman Daniel had just deserted her for flashed before her eyes and she stayed where she was. She didn't know how the story of his brother's death related to his explanation of his behaviour that afternoon, but she knew it pained him to discuss his brother, so the very fact that he was telling her all the sordid details of his past meant Lizzie owed it to him to listen.

'I tried for the entire term to apologise to Rupert, to tell him I was sorry for not standing up for him before, but he wouldn't even see me.'

Lizzie could see by his earnest expression that Daniel truly had tried to make up for the mistakes he'd made whilst he'd still been a child.

'The bullying he'd experienced whilst he was at Eton only got worse at Cambridge. Rupert was always solitary, but he refused to socialise and this ostracised him even more. He became a sort of recluse, only scurrying out to go to lectures.'

Lizzie could imagine Daniel at university, socialising and drinking with his friends, all the time worrying about his reclusive half-brother, who wanted nothing to do with him.

'At the end of the first term I wanted to try one last time to speak to Rupert, to apologise and try to make amends. It was Christmas and I thought maybe we could share a meal and a drink.'

Lizzie could see by the pain behind Daniel's eyes that they were getting close to the crux of the story.

'I went to his rooms and refused to accept his silence, so I barged in, ready to insist we try to be like true brothers.' Daniel pinched the bridge of his nose and took a deep breath before continuing. 'He was just hanging there, lifeless, staring down at me.'

Lizzie gasped. She had never imagined Daniel had found his brother's body. It was a cruel trick of fate and she knew the image of his brother with a rope around his neck would never leave Daniel.

'I'm so sorry,' she murmured, momentarily forgetting she was livid with him and instead just wanting to comfort this man in pain.

Lizzie slipped off her chair and knelt down in front of

Daniel, who was now staring off into space as if seeing his brother's dead body all over again.

Daniel gripped her hand as if it were his only anchor to this earth and Lizzie allowed him to take comfort in her.

'There's more,' Daniel said after a minute.

She could tell by the haunted expression on his face that the story somehow got even worse.

'Rupert left a note. In it he blamed me entirely for his suicide, said I should have helped him, should have been there for him.'

Lizzie could tell Daniel was trying to hold back the tears. It was disconcerting seeing this man, normally so strong and with a smile never far from his face, reduced to a shadow of his normal self.

'He said if I were a true brother he would still be alive.'

Lizzie wanted to reach up and take Daniel in her arms, to reassure him that it wasn't true, but she knew her words would fall on deaf ears. For years Daniel had been blaming himself for his brother's death, for years he had held himself responsible for his brother's actions. She wasn't going to be able to reverse it with a kiss and a few soft words.

Daniel fell silent, his whole body slumping in the chair as if just telling the tale had exhausted him.

Lizzie sat still for a few minutes, completely conflicted. She loved this man, loved him more than she ever thought was possible. She had given herself to him entirely, only to have him betray her. When she had seen him exiting his study with his mistress her heart had broken in two. Lizzie, who had always guarded her heart knowing no man could truly love her, had let Daniel in and immediately he had betrayed her.

Despite that, and despite Lizzie knowing she would never recover from what Daniel had done to her, she wanted to comfort him. She couldn't stay quiet just because she was angry with him. She needed him to know, no matter what he had done to her, his brother's death was not his fault.

'Daniel, you can't blame yourself,' she said slowly. She could tell the words barely registered in his mind. 'Listen to me,' she said sharply. Daniel looked at her, surprised by the sharp note in her voice. 'Blame the boys who bullied him, blame the schoolmasters who didn't discipline those who persecuted him, blame your father for not including him in the family, blame those who actually made his life hell, but do not blame yourself.'

'I could have made it all better.'

Lizzie shrugged. 'You might have been able to make it a little better, but you wouldn't have been able to change everything.'

'A little better may have been enough to stop him killing himself.'

'When you first went to Eton you were just a boy, just a child. You couldn't be expected to know exactly what to do. And later, when you were older, you tried to make amends.'

'Rupert's still dead.'

Lizzie could see these arguments weren't going to work, so she changed tack slightly.

'That boy who was just here, would it be fair of me to blame him for not stopping his mother coming to see you?'

Daniel looked at her as though she had lost her mind.

'Well, would it?'

'He's three years old.'

'Exactly, only a child. He can't be blamed for failing to stop the destructive actions of another. I certainly don't blame him.'

'I was thirteen.'

'Still a child. A child who was trying to navigate an adult's world.'

Daniel shook his head, not accepting this argument, either. Lizzie raised herself up on her knees so she was looking directly into Daniel's eyes.

'This has been eating away at you for years,' she said. 'And you need to start forgiving yourself or it will destroy you.'

Daniel looked at her bleakly. 'There's more. So much more.'

Chapter Twenty-Two

Daniel could see the hurt and betrayal clearly in Amelia's face even when she was reassuring him that his brother's death wasn't his fault. He needed to make her understand Annabelle was not his mistress, but in doing so he would have to tell her of his much greater secret.

'I continued with my degree at Cambridge,' Daniel said, clutching on to Amelia's hand, worried that any second she would pull away and refuse to hear any more of what he had to say. 'It was as though I were in a trance. I studied, I socialised, but the whole time I felt as though I were living in a nightmare.'

Amelia nodded as if she understood, but Daniel knew that was impossible; he barely remembered what that period had been like himself. Guilt had overshadowed everything he did and he'd been plagued by flashbacks of the moment he'd discovered his brother's body.

'My father died during my last year at university and in a way it was a relief. I didn't have that connection with Rupert any longer. Once I graduated, I threw myself into the business of trying to forget.'

It had been more than a relief when his father had died. When he was a young boy Daniel had idolised his father, but over the years as he had understood what had happened with Rupert, that respect had turned to disdain. His father had refused to take proper responsibility for his actions, allowing his son to live a sort of half-life; he paid for his education but made him live with a tenant farmer family, he never saw Rupert, instead sending his steward to check on his welfare. Since Daniel had become a father himself his opinions had mellowed slightly and he now understood his father had been in an impossible situation. His wife had refused to have his illegitimate son in the house, but he had still wanted to give him a good start in life. Maybe the old man had just been trying to do his best for his entire family and Daniel had seen for himself the regret in his father's eyes whenever he thought about Rupert.

His mother he could never entirely forgive. She had been a distant woman throughout his childhood, almost to the point of being cold. Daniel could never remember her telling him she loved him as he thought mothers were supposed to. He understood how difficult it must have been for her to have the evidence of her husband's infidelity paraded in front of her, but Daniel still couldn't forgive her refusal to even consider allowing Rupert a chance at a normal family life. When Daniel had travelled back home to tell his parents of Rupert's death his father had sobbed—it had been the only time Daniel had ever seen him cry. His mother had sat completely still, no change of expression on her face, no words of remorse. She hadn't even moved to comfort the man she had been married to for more than twenty years.

Daniel returned his mind to the story he was telling Amelia. After he'd graduated he had been wild for a while. He'd neglected his newly inherited estate and all the people who relied on him for their living.

'I spent my days in London, drinking and socialising and enjoying the company of women who promised to make my pain go away.'

He glanced down at Amelia and saw her struggling to keep her composure. Daniel knew he shouldn't talk so candidly of his wild exploits with other women when they had been so intimate only an hour before, but he knew she needed to see the whole picture to understand.

'I was wild and out of control and I didn't care.'

'Something changed you,' Amelia said, understanding. 'Something made you care.'

Daniel could remember the first time he'd set eyes on Annabelle. He'd thought it had been love at first sight as he'd caught her eye across a crowded room.

'I met Annabelle.'

'That was her? The woman who was just here?'

Daniel hated the strained note in Amelia's voice, hated that he had caused her this pain.

'That was Annabelle.'

'You loved her?'

Daniel could see Amelia was close to tears, but he couldn't lie to her now. The only way she might understand why he had kept something so important from her was if she knew the whole sordid story. Even if at first it hurt.

'I fell in love with her. I fell deeply and fast. I thought she was my saviour. I started to care about life again.'

Amelia's hand slipped from his own and in that second Daniel realised she loved him. Amelia loved him. He'd known she cared for him and that she certainly desired him, but until now he hadn't realised that she loved him. Hearing of his infatuation with another woman must be breaking her heart.

'She was the first person I really told the whole story about my brother. The only person other than you.'

Annabelle had seemed like an angel at the time. She'd made him forget his pain, made him focus on something other than his guilt.

'We were of entirely different stations in life, moved in different circles, but I was so deeply under her spell I was convinced I could marry her and everything would work out.'

Amelia slumped backwards a little and Daniel had to stop himself from trying to haul her into his arms. If she resisted him, it would make everything so much worse, so instead he continued with his story.

'I almost proposed to her, I almost made the mistake of asking her to become my wife. That had been her aim all along, of course, to become a countess, to become respectable.'

'She wasn't respectable?' Amelia asked.

Daniel shook his head. 'I was blinded by love at the time, but since I've found out she was quite a notorious courtesan. She'd spent years at the fringes of society waiting for a lovesick idiot to be fooled by her stories and dazzled by her beauty.'

Daniel had just seen a down-on-her-luck, sweet young woman who he had promptly wanted to rescue. She'd told him she loved him, convinced him that despite their differences their love would allow them to be together. Of course, she had never really loved him, Daniel knew that now, she had seen a damaged and vulnerable man and seen an opportunity to become a countess and never have to worry where her next patron was coming from. Annabelle was motivated by money and she had thought that by snaring Daniel she would never have to worry about money again.

'So what happened? Why didn't you propose?'

He grimaced, hating the memory of what had happened. Hating how stupid he'd been.

'I had this grand proposal planned. I was going to take her to the seaside, propose on the beach. I'd even written down what I wanted to say to her, how I'd tell her it didn't matter that she couldn't have children, that she'd always be enough for me.'

'What made you change your mind?'

'It was pure chance really. This man turned up, a real scruffy lowlife. He wouldn't leave Annabelle alone, kept claiming he was her husband. Demanding money to keep quiet.'

It was then everything had started to unwind. Always the consummate actress, Annabelle had shrugged him off and laughed with Daniel about the ravings of a drunken old man, but the doubts had started to creep in. Daniel set his steward to look into the matter and in a few days he had the whole truth.

'Annabelle was a trickster, a con artist. She preyed on lonely men and took whatever she could from them. In me she saw the loneliest and stupidest of the bunch and thought I was her way out.'

Amelia had stopped pulling away from him and sat in stunned silence.

'I was a fool.'

'What did you do?'

'I confronted her. She tried all her usual tricks—seduction, sweet words of eternal love, even hysterics—but for the first time I could see them for what they really were. I could see her for what she really was.'

Daniel shook his head in disgust, still amazed all these years later that he had been taken in by her. If her husband hadn't turned up when he had, Daniel was sure Annabelle would have gone through with the sham wedding. Daniel would have introduced her to the world as his new countess and he would have had a hard time dismissing her from his life after that.

'Love quickly turned to hate as I realised what a fool

she had made of me. I threw her out with just the clothes on her back.'

'There's more, isn't there?' Amelia asked.

Daniel nodded. This was the bit of his past that hurt the most, more than losing his brother, more than his humiliation by the woman he thought he loved.

'I didn't see her for months and slowly I started to get my life back. I have to say one thing for Annabelle, she made me realise what was important. I focused on running my estate, reconnected with loyal old friends.'

He'd also started socialising again, but Amelia didn't need to know that part. She no doubt had heard of his less-than-upstanding reputation, but he didn't need to confirm that he'd started seducing women. Of course, only women who wanted to be seduced. Amelia was the only innocent he'd ever even kissed, but there had been plenty of less virtuous women he'd spent long nights with, always making sure never to get too attached, never to let his heart become involved. Annabelle had broken his trust and broken his heart. He wasn't going to make the same mistake twice.

'Then she contacted me, asked for a meeting. Said it would be to my advantage.'

'Did you go?' Amelia asked, completely engrossed in his story now.

'I went.'

Daniel raked his hand through his hair, remembering every detail of that meeting. The day his life had really changed.

'I told you about my brother so you would understand,' Daniel said.

Amelia looked confused but moved a little closer so she was sitting on the floor right next to his chair again.

'My brother died because he was illegitimate. He was bullied and tormented because of it all his life.'

Amelia's eyes widened with shock as she slowly realised what he was about to tell her.

'Annabelle knew how much Rupert's death had affected me, she knew I was adamant I would not sire an illegitimate child. Before we were intimate for the first time she told me she could never have children.'

Daniel had been a little relieved at the time. Never being able to have children at all seemed better than becoming a father to an illegitimate child. If Annabelle hadn't told him she couldn't have children, he would have made sure they took precautions. As it was he hadn't seen the need.

'I suppose it was all part of her plan, another way to tie me to her.'

Daniel knew now Annabelle had wanted to get pregnant all along. He supposed if her husband hadn't turned up it would have been a reason to hurry along the wedding and secure her future as his wife.

'She fell pregnant?'

'The first I knew about it was when she turned up to our meeting with a baby.'

'Your baby?'

'At first I didn't believe her, but one look at the child and I knew he was mine.'

Amelia was staring off into the distance as if trying to piece together everything he'd told her.

'You had an illegitimate child, your worst nightmare,' she said slowly.

Daniel nodded.

'The boy who was with her.'

'My son, Edward.'

Amelia remained quiet for a few minutes and Daniel sat watching her, allowing her to figure out the chain of events.

'You pay her,' she said finally. 'That's why she was here.'

Daniel could see the frown developing on her face and wondered exactly what she was thinking.

'After everything you've been through,' Amelia said with disbelief, 'you pay her to keep quiet. To shut your own son away, just so society won't think badly of you.'

Amelia shot up from the floor and started backing away from him, as if she couldn't bear to be in his presence.

'You pay her to keep your dirty little secret and to keep your son away.'

Daniel stood and crossed the room in two steps, taking Amelia by the arm so she could not flee any further.

'No,' he said firmly.

'After everything you've been through, after what happened to your brother, still you value the perception of society over the feelings of your son.'

It was the closest to hysterical he had ever seen Amelia. Even when confronted with the sight of Daniel with Annabelle less than an hour after they'd been making love Amelia had remained calmer than she was now.

'You disgust me,' she said, the tears welling in her eyes. 'How could you reject that poor, innocent boy? How could you condemn him to be raised knowing his father is ashamed of him?'

Daniel realised his son's situation must resonate strongly with Amelia. In the short few weeks that he'd known her he'd seen all her insecurities. Someone in her past had made sure she felt inferior, maybe even unwanted. Now she was thinking Daniel had done the same to his own son.

Quickly Daniel released her and crossed to his desk. He opened the top drawer and pulled out a miniature, thrusting it at Amelia. It was of his son as a baby.

'I keep this with me wherever I go,' he said. 'It is the first thing I look at when I wake up and the last thing before I go to sleep. I love my son. I love my son more than life itself.'

'But not enough to claim him.'

Daniel knew he was losing her. Soon Amelia would leave the room in disgust and probably refuse to see him ever again.

'And you were going to make me complicit in this whole sordid mess as well. You were going to use the inheritance to continue to pay Annabelle to hide your son from the world.'

'I don't pay her to hide the truth from the world,' Daniel said slowly, sinking back into his chair.

'Of course you do,' Amelia said.

'I pay her to hide the truth from him.'

Amelia opened her mouth to reply, but as she digested the words she closed it again.

'You pay her to hide the truth from him,' she repeated slowly, as if trying to make sense of his statement.

'At first I tried to get Annabelle to give me custody of Edward, but she refused.'

'As his father you could have just taken him,' Amelia said.

Daniel nodded. 'That is true and often I wish I just had.'

At the time he'd been a mess, not knowing what to do for the best. Annabelle's drunken husband had died earlier in the year, before Edward was born, but Annabelle had told him because she was married when Edward was conceived Daniel would never get his hands on the boy. Technically Edward wasn't even illegitimate, seeing that Annabelle was married, but in the eyes of society, the people who would make the boy's life miserable, he was Daniel's illegitimate son.

'You have to remember Annabelle knew all about my brother. She knew all my deepest fears.'

'She knew you wouldn't want your son growing up to be illegitimate.'

'She said if I took him she'd make sure he knew he was illegitimate, that she would make him notorious.'

'So you had to pay her to keep quiet.'

'Annabelle kept Edward and made it clear that if I ever tried to take him she would ensure he knew he was illegitimate.'

'And she keeps demanding more and more money,' Amelia stated and Daniel could only nod morosely.

Amelia sat down in the chair opposite his again.

'I can't have Edward going through what Rupert went through. I just can't. I send my steward every few months to check Annabelle is treating Edward well and I pay her.'

'Wouldn't you rather Edward lived with you?'

Daniel raked a hand through his hair and sighed. 'Over the years I've struggled so much with what to do for the best. I love my son, but I couldn't be a good father to him.'

When Annabelle had first turned up with their son in her arms Daniel had wanted to reach out and pluck Edward from her, but something had held him back. He'd thought of Rupert's face every time one of the boys at school made a cruel remark, or how the healthy young boy turned into a withdrawn young man. He hadn't been able to protect his brother from the world, what made him think he could do a better job for his son? Annabelle might not love Edward the way he did, but she had never failed in protecting a loved one the way Daniel had, either.

'She doesn't even let you see him, does she?'

Daniel shook his head. His son was growing up without him and there was nothing he could do about it.

Chapter Twenty-Three

Lizzie felt outraged and sick at the same time. She couldn't believe what this woman was putting Daniel through. She had taken his deepest, darkest secret, his guilt about his brother's death, and she was using it against him. It was despicable.

She knew she had to tread carefully. Daniel's emotions had been battered over the past decade and she wasn't going to be able to undo anything with just a few words, but maybe she could plant some seeds of reason that would slowly blossom.

'Annabelle played on your greatest fear,' Lizzie said slowly. 'She's threatening you with making history repeat itself and having your son suffer as your brother did.'

Daniel nodded, as if he agreed with her summation.

Lizzie knew she needed to be close to Daniel to make him listen to what she was saying. Now he had told his story he had withdrawn into himself and she needed to coax him out again.

Slowly she stood and moved over to his chair, perching on the arm and taking one of his hands in her own.

'I know you had an awful experience with your brother. I know he suffered terribly because of his illegitimacy...' Amelia paused and tried to form her thoughts into some semblance of an order '...but it wouldn't have to be the same way with Edward. Even if he knew he was illegitimate, if he was loved it wouldn't matter.'

Daniel looked at her as though she were mad.

'If you loved him and raised him secure in the knowledge that he was loved, no matter the truth of his birth, his illegitimacy probably wouldn't affect him as much as you worry it would.'

For a moment there was a spark of hope in Daniel's eyes and Lizzie wondered whether she had got through to him. Then the bleak look returned and Daniel shook his head and let out a deep sigh.

Lizzie didn't push the matter. It had taken years for the damage to be done—Daniel wasn't going to realise illegitimacy wasn't the worst thing in the world if you were loved straight away—but maybe she had planted the first seeds of change in his mind.

'I'm sorry I jumped to conclusions about Annabelle,' she said softly.

Daniel smiled grimly. 'What were you supposed to think? I left you minutes after taking your virtue to see another woman.'

'I understand why now.'

'I wanted to get rid of her before you had a chance to run into her.'

Lizzie gently stroked the palm of his hand with her thumb.

'You didn't want me finding out why you needed that dowry so badly.'

Lizzie knew she had to tell him the truth about her identity now. Annabelle's presence might have forced Daniel to tell her his secrets, but he could have fobbed her off with half the truth. Instead he'd trusted her with the full tale, with every one of his secrets. It wouldn't be fair on him to keep hers any longer.

Lizzie knew once she told Daniel she wasn't Amelia Eastway it was likely their relationship would be over. Daniel was a good man, a principled man, and now he had taken her virginity he would probably still insist on marrying her, but it wouldn't be a marriage of love. He'd never said he loved her and once he realised the depth of her deception she would be lucky if he could bear to be in the same room as her. She also knew she couldn't be responsible for Daniel being unable to pay Annabelle. If she left, Daniel would be free to find another heiress and the secret of his son's birth would remain safe.

'You're a good woman,' Daniel said, looking up into her eyes. 'Not many would stick around after they heard what I was mixed up in.'

'I've got a secret of my own,' Lizzie said quietly. She was unable to look Daniel in the eye, knowing as soon as she said it the affection she saw there would vanish.

He smiled at her gently. 'Nothing could be as bad as what I've just told you.'

Lizzie knew it was much, much worse.

She sat silently for a few moments, trying to figure out the best way to tell Daniel she wasn't who he thought she was. Just as she opened her mouth to speak there was a knock on the door.

'Interrupted again,' Daniel said, squeezing her hand. 'I'll get rid of them and then I'm all yours.'

He rose from the chair and crossed the room, opening the door to his study just a crack as if he were the gatekeeper to the world.

Lizzie was struggling to find the right words to tell Daniel her true identity.

Daniel, I lied to you.

Daniel, I'm not who you think I am.

Daniel, I'm impersonating my cousin.

Daniel, I'm a penniless orphan.

She needed to phrase it right so he listened to her whole story. Lizzie couldn't bear the thought of having to run after him, trying to explain her deception.

Daniel quietly closed the door and turned back to face her.

'Your revelation may have to wait a few minutes,' Daniel said, the concern showing clearly on his face.

'What's happened?' Lizzie didn't want any more delays, she wanted to finally tell Daniel who she really was.

'There's a policeman here to see you.'

'To see me?' Lizzie could hear the panic in her own voice.

A hundred different scenarios ran through her mind as she began to panic. It had to be about Amelia. She hadn't heard from her cousin in weeks. Something awful must have happened.

'He's been shown into the Green Room. I'll accompany you. There's nothing to worry about, Amelia, I won't let anything happen to you.'

Lizzie felt his strong hand wrap around hers and for a moment she felt safe and secure. She knew whatever news the policeman brought she would be able to cope with Daniel at her side, but if it was about Amelia her secret would be told for her.

Gently Daniel pulled her to her feet and led her to the door. Just before he opened it and ushered her out into the hall he placed a soft kiss on her lips and looked deeply into her eyes.

'I'll be there the whole time,' he reassured her.

As they entered the Green Room a man in his late forties stood to greet them.

'Henry Golding, Bow Street Runner.'

'I am Burwell. This is Miss Eastway.'

They all sat awkwardly and waited for Mr Golding to explain his presence.

'I'm very sorry to have to disturb you in the country, my lord, but there has been a very serious allegation made against Miss Eastway and we are duty bound to investigate.'

Daniel nodded and glanced at Lizzie. She wondered what the allegation could be.

'I understand you were both present at the unfortunate fire at Mrs Hunter's house in London last week.'

'Miss Eastway was almost killed in that fire,' Daniel said. He edged towards her protectively and Lizzie wondered what this could all be about.

'Quite. Unfortunately there has been an allegation that Miss Eastway started the fire deliberately.'

Lizzie's mouth dropped open with surprise and she saw Daniel's defences rise. He was going to fight this battle for her. It felt wonderful to be protected, to have someone in the world who would stand up for her no matter what. Lizzie knew once Daniel found out her true identity he wouldn't feel the same way, so she allowed herself this one final act from him.

'Impossible,' he said with authority.

Lizzie knew those born into nobility often were self-assured and confident. Daniel had certainly never lacked conviction or assertiveness, but Lizzie had never seen him in full lordly glory until now. His bearing was regal, his expression told of a man you wouldn't want to argue with and the tone of his voice suggested whoever he was conversing with was wrong and he was right.

'You are entitled to your opinion,' Mr Golding said.

'Do not be a fool,' Daniel said quietly.

This time Mr Golding raised an eyebrow but did not back down.

'Miss Eastway is an intelligent young woman. Tell me why she would start a fire in her own bedchamber and almost perish in the flames if it was deliberate?'

Mr Golding had no answer.

'I was the one to pluck Miss Eastway from the jaws of death and I can assure you there was no way she started the fire.'

'Maybe if Miss Eastway would be so kind as to tell me what she remembers.'

The request was put to Daniel and he almost looked as though he was going to refuse.

'Of course,' Lizzie interjected. 'It would be no trouble.'

Mr Golding sat back and turned to face Lizzie for the first time. She felt the full intensity of his stare and for the first time she began to worry. Mr Golding did not seem like the sort of man to back down from anything, even when faced with an angry earl.

'I had been reading a letter one of the maids had brought up to me before bed.'

'So you had a candle lit?'

'As would everyone in the house at that time of night,' Lizzie gently chastised him. 'It was dark and getting ready for bed without the light of a candle would have been next to impossible.'

Mr Golding nodded and Lizzie felt Daniel shift closer to her protectively.

'I remember blowing out my candle before going to sleep. The next thing I remember is waking up feeling so hot I thought I would melt. I tried to make for the door, but the smoke was so thick I tripped on something and went sprawling on the ground.'

Lizzie had spent the past week trying not to remember the fire. If Daniel hadn't been passing the house, or if he'd even been just a minute later, she would have died.

'That's where I found Miss Eastway,' Daniel said.

Mr Golding nodded. 'There's nothing else of significance you remember?'

The image of the extra candle sitting on the table by the window flashed into Lizzie's mind. She had her suspicions that Harriet had actually sneaked into her room to read the letter. And if she had, had she left a candle burning by the window and the extremely flammable curtains?

Lizzie shook her head. Mentioning the extra candle and her suspicions about Harriet wouldn't help. She didn't know anything for sure and, as much as Harriet disliked Lizzie, Lizzie was sure she would never have set her own house on fire on purpose. Whatever had happened it must have been a terrible accident and nothing more.

'Thank you, Miss Eastway, for clarifying events for me.'

'Tell us about the accusation,' Daniel growled, making Mr Golding edge back in his chair.

'An anonymous letter was received a few days ago detailing the events of the fire. Someone was able to pinpoint exactly where the fire started and stated they saw Miss Eastway deliberately put a candle to the curtains.'

'Any idea who sent the letter?' Daniel asked. 'I'd be looking at them as a suspect if I were you.'

Lizzie was wondering the same thing herself. Someone wanted her to take the blame for Aunt Mathilda's house burning down.

'We don't have any leads on that front.'

Lizzie smiled, trying to distract the men from this train of thought. The only person who would have sent that letter was Harriet and, however misguided Amelia's cousin was, Lizzie didn't want to get her into trouble. She would have a word with Harriet in private and no one else would ever have to know.

'Apart from this anonymous letter, do you have any proof?' Daniel asked.

Mr Golding shifted in his seat.

'We are gathering fresh evidence all the time.'

'But no proof—in fact, nothing to go on except the word of someone who will not identify themselves.'

'A crime has been committed,' Mr Golding said self-righteously. 'And I will make sure whoever is responsible will be suitably punished.'

Mr Golding stood, bowed to Lizzie, inclined his head towards Daniel, then quickly left the room, no doubt to be shown out by Daniel's butler.

'How very strange,' Daniel said, looping his arm around Lizzie's waist and pulling her closer to him now they were alone.

Lizzie nodded absentmindedly. The day had been a very strange one all round. First she had lost her virginity to the man she loved, then found out he had an illegitimate son, and now she had been accused of arson. There was only one more thing to do today and that was tell Daniel the truth. No doubt that would be the most damaging revelation of the afternoon.

Chapter Twenty-Four

Daniel reached out and touched Amelia's forehead in the spot just between her eyes. That little furrow was back between Amelia's brows, the one she got when she was worrying about something. Daniel felt he could devote his life to making that furrow stay away.

'Daniel, I need to talk to you,' Amelia said.

'I know, you want to tell me your secret.'

He was a little curious about what had her so worried. Daniel knew it wouldn't be anything major. Amelia was a sweet, innocent young thing. She was probably worried because she had let some young soldier kiss her back in India. As the thought came into his head Daniel realised he didn't like the idea of Amelia kissing anyone else. He wanted to be the only one to taste her lips, to make her shiver with anticipation as he drew his mouth across her skin.

'Please, Amelia, I want to listen. Just give me ten minutes, then I'm all yours.'

She looked as though she were going to protest, but even though it was obvious she really wanted to get whatever it was off her chest she couldn't deny him ten minutes.

'It's a beautiful day outside,' Daniel said. 'And I think we could both do with some fresh air. Meet me in the rose garden in ten minutes.'

Without giving her a chance to protest Daniel kissed

her quickly on the cheek, rose and walked out of the room. He had a lot to prepare in ten minutes.

Daniel had thought his world was about to implode when Amelia had stood not a few yards from Annabelle. The look in her eyes had been pure devastation. He knew now Amelia loved him, it was obvious in her every look, her every touch, and for her to come across the woman she supposed to be his mistress was devastating. If Daniel had been in her place, he probably would have cursed and shouted and refused to listen to any explanation, but Amelia had kept a lid on her pain and had heard him out.

Even though everything had pointed to Daniel being the worst possible scoundrel, Amelia had believed in him enough to listen to his explanation.

When he'd told her about his brother she had shared his pain, then when he had explained about Annabelle and Edward she had surprised him yet again. Far from trying to distance herself from his messy private life she had sympathised with him and felt angry with Annabelle on his behalf.

Daniel couldn't believe she was still in his life, she hadn't made her excuses and abandoned him as he'd been certain any woman would when they found out about his son. She knew what he wanted her dowry for and she hadn't once voiced an objection.

He knew he had to get her to agree to marry him. Amelia Eastway was one of a kind and he'd be the biggest fool in the world if he let her slip through his fingers. Now they had made love Daniel was pretty sure she wouldn't refuse him again. There was no real reason to. She loved him and she desired him. Now she even knew his deepest, darkest secret and hadn't gone running for the hills. There was no reason they shouldn't be together.

'William,' Daniel said, once he had sought out one of

the footmen, 'I need you to bring a bottle of champagne out to the rose garden in half an hour's time.'

That should give him plenty of time to persuade Amelia to marry him. After she'd got whatever it was that was worrying her so much off her chest, of course.

With his first task accomplished Daniel dashed upstairs and started rummaging around in his room. He was searching for a token to give to Amelia to seal their engagement. He would take her to get a ring made just for her in the next couple of weeks for the wedding, but he wanted something special to give to her now and he had just the thing in mind.

With five minutes to spare Daniel rushed back downstairs and out into the garden. Thankful there was no sign of Amelia yet, he busied himself picking the most beautiful blooms, checking over his shoulder that the gardener wasn't looking and feeling like a naughty schoolboy for picking roses in his own garden.

When Amelia emerged from the house and walked towards the rose garden Daniel could see the tension on her face and for the first time wondered whether this secret of hers might actually be something serious. He suddenly had a vision of her secretly marrying another man and he felt a sickness start to build in the pit of his stomach.

'Daniel,' Amelia said as he rose to meet her.

Her face was white and drawn and her eyes looked hollow and haunted.

'Before you speak I want to tell you something,' Daniel said.

'Please…' Amelia's voice was quiet and pleading '…no more delays. I need to tell you the truth about who I am before I lose my nerve.'

Daniel nodded. He didn't want her to speak, he didn't want to know her secret, not if it was something that would keep them apart. As he sat next to her on the stone bench, his thighs pushing against hers, he just wanted to envelop Amelia in his arms and never let her go.

'I love you,' Daniel blurted out.

He hadn't meant to say it, he hadn't even realised he was thinking it, but as soon as the words were out of his mouth Daniel realised he meant them. He loved her. He actually loved her. He didn't know when it had happened, or how, but he did know it was the truth.

'You love me?' Amelia asked, clearly thinking she had misheard.

'I love you.' Daniel cupped her face and looked into her eyes. 'I love you, I love you, I love you.'

Now he'd said it once he couldn't seem to stop.

'I love your kind heart and I love your forgiving nature. I love your beautiful face and I love each and every one of your freckles. I love the way your body fits perfectly with mine and I love how you respond to my kisses. I love each and every little bit of you.'

Daniel was grinning now. He never thought he would fall in love again. After Annabelle's betrayal he had sealed his heart off, keeping everyone at a distance and only allowing himself the shallowest of feelings for anyone. In just a few short weeks Amelia had broken through all of his defences and she'd mended the heart he'd thought was broken for ever.

'I love you, too,' Amelia said, tears forming in her eyes.

'I'm sorry,' he said. 'I'm sorry I interrupted you. I just had to let you know. You go ahead. I won't say another word until you've told me whatever it is you want me to know.'

Daniel sat and watched as Amelia prepared herself to reveal whatever it was that was worrying her so much. He clasped her hand in his, smiling encouragement, all the time replaying Amelia's voice as she said *I love you, too.*

'Daniel, I'm not who you think I am,' she said, repeating what she'd started to tell him before they'd got caught up in their moment of passion.

She took a deep breath and continued. 'I'm not Amelia—'

She was cut off by a loud shout and both she and Daniel jumped up with surprise.

'Impostor, liar, she-devil.'

Daniel pulled her towards him protectively whilst he assessed the threat.

Amelia's cousin Harriet came dashing from the house and out into the garden. She was still screaming insults with a satisfied look on her face as she reached Daniel and Amelia.

'What the hell is going on?' Daniel asked.

'She is not who she says she is. She's an impostor.'

Daniel looked at Amelia and saw her shrinking before her cousin's words.

'I was trying to tell you,' Amelia whispered.

'Pah! Unlikely,' Harriet said, jabbing a finger none too gently into Amelia's chest. 'Con artists never confess unless they're caught.'

'I was trying to tell you.' This time Amelia looked directly at Daniel with desperation in her eyes.

He almost ordered Harriet back to the house but quickly decided against it. He needed to know what was going on, no more delays, no more interruptions.

'She is not Amelia Eastway,' Harriet said triumphantly. 'We ran into a soldier who had served under Colonel Eastway whilst we were in Cambridge.'

Daniel was listening to Harriet, but he couldn't take his eyes off Amelia. She seemed to shrink before him, folding into herself as if she were seeking a way to disappear.

'This officer remembers Amelia Eastway well. Apparently she is the belle of all the balls, the most beautiful woman he's ever laid eyes on.'

Daniel frowned, wondering what Harriet was getting at.

'Amelia Eastway, the real Amelia Eastway, is a petite blonde with blue eyes,' Harriet finished triumphantly.

Daniel shook his head. It wasn't possible, none of this made sense. If it weren't for the devastated look on Amelia's face, he would have dismissed Harriet's claims and concluded the officer had been mistaken.

'Amelia?'

She shook her head, the tears flowing freely down her cheeks now.

'My name isn't Amelia. It's Lizzie...well, Elizabeth.'

Daniel felt his world rock and he stumbled slightly. The woman standing in front of him wasn't Amelia Eastway. She was a liar, an impostor. The woman he thought he loved didn't even really exist.

'I'm sorry,' she said quietly.

Daniel tried to look at her, but he couldn't bear it. She still had the same face, the same expressions. She looked like the woman he loved, but in reality he didn't know her at all.

'Please let me explain,' she said so quietly he barely heard her.

'More lies?' Harriet asked nastily.

'No.' Lizzie's voice was firm. 'The truth. The whole truth.'

Daniel sank down on to the bench. He'd trusted her. He'd loved her. What a fool he was. For years he had protected himself against this sort of deception and when he finally dropped his guard he had been taken in by a liar again.

'Who are you?' he asked.

'My name is Elizabeth Eastway. I'm Amelia's cousin.'

'Amelia's poor cousin,' Harriet added. 'Not a penny to her name.'

Daniel watched as Lizzie grimaced, but didn't offer any words of comfort. He just wanted the whole story now, to try to understand why she had deceived him.

'I was sent to accompany my cousin Amelia whilst she made her début into society and searched for a suitable husband,' Lizzie said, her eyes pleading with him to understand.

Daniel couldn't give her any reassurance. He felt numb, betrayed, and he wondered if she was now even telling them the truth.

'Amelia had been secretly in correspondence with a young officer who had served out in India a few years ago. She wanted to go visit him. She said they were in love.'

Harriet snorted and Daniel wondered how she could get so much enjoyment out of this.

'Go away, you stupid girl!' Daniel snapped. Harriet looked outraged but turned on her heel and stalked back to the house, a smug expression on her face. 'Continue.' Daniel nodded to Lizzie.

'She begged me to take her place, to pretend to be her, for a few days, a fortnight at most. She said she'd be back before I made my début and no one apart from Aunt Mathilda would ever know.'

Daniel wondered how Lizzie had been persuaded by her cousin to do such a thing.

'I didn't want to do it, but Amelia is very…persuasive. She begged me and I couldn't say no.'

He wondered if the two women had giggled about the deception that had ended up breaking his heart.

'Then Aunt Mathilda insisted I make my début earlier than we'd assumed and I was presented to society as

Amelia. I didn't know what to do and I just kept hoping to hear from my cousin, but there was no word.'

Daniel saw the panic etched on her face even now and he realised this was the 'friend' she'd wanted his assistance in finding.

Lizzie turned to him and took a step forward, but she must have seen something on his face that made her pause, because she didn't come any closer.

'I never set out to deceive you. I just didn't know how to stop the lies once they had started.'

Daniel looked into her eyes but couldn't find any words to say. She wasn't his Amelia.

'Harriet is right,' Lizzie said with a sob. 'I don't have a rich father or a significant dowry. Marrying me won't solve your problems.'

Up to that point Daniel hadn't thought about the dowry, he'd been so focused on the fact that Lizzie had lied about who she was he hadn't even realised that she did not have the dowry he'd started courting her for in the first place.

'Was any of it true?' he asked, his voice gruff and catching in his throat.

Lizzie sank to her knees in front of Daniel and took his hand in hers. He tried to pull away, but she held on firmly, gripping him as if he were her only link to the real world.

'I may not be Amelia, but everything else we shared was real. I love you.'

Daniel looked down into her deep brown eyes and felt himself softening, weakening. It would be so easy for him to forgive her, to take her in his arms and pretend none of this mattered, but he knew deep down that he couldn't do it. It wasn't about the dowry, it was the lies. He'd been hurt once by a woman's lies. He wouldn't let himself be hurt again.

'It wasn't real,' Daniel said. 'None of it was real.'

Lizzie recoiled as if she had been slapped, letting his hand slip through her fingers. As her hand fell away Daniel had a moment of panic; he was losing her. He loved her and he was losing her. Then he hardened his heart. He didn't love her, he loved his Amelia, a woman who didn't exist.

'Hate me,' Lizzie whispered. 'Despise me, refuse to ever see me again, but don't tell me none of it was real.'

Daniel thought of all the moments they had shared, the moments that had made him fall in love with her. The kiss in the Prestons' garden, their outings to the park, the night in the coaching inn, their rendezvous around his estate, and earlier that morning the moment she had given herself to him completely.

He wanted to believe it was all real, not engineered by a woman who was trying to entrap him, but he had experienced first-hand what happened when he trusted a woman. He couldn't make the same mistake again.

'Pack your bags. You're leaving first thing in the morning.'

He couldn't bear to look her in the eye as he delivered the words.

Chapter Twenty-Five

Lizzie sat morosely on the side of her bed. The tears had stopped falling sometime in the middle of the night and she now just felt empty and hollow. She hadn't slept at all. Every time she closed her eyes she just saw the look of betrayal on Daniel's face.

She understood why he wanted her gone, but that didn't make the pain any better. Over the past few days as she had been wondering how best to tell Daniel the truth about her identity she had imagined his reaction hundreds of times. Lizzie had known he would be hurt and betrayed, but nothing had prepared her for the look of utter disgust on his face. He had hardly been able to look at her and when he did Lizzie had felt as though she'd been slapped. The familiar gazes of longing and desire of the man she loved had been replaced by the cold stare of someone she didn't know.

Lizzie choked back a sob. He'd told her he loved her, just before Harriet had turned up and blurted out Lizzie's secret, Daniel had looked into her eyes and told her he loved her. Just a few minutes later it was clear that short-lived love had turned to hate.

Lizzie stood and checked over her meagre belongings. Most of what she had brought to London or purchased whilst living with Aunt Mathilda had been destroyed in the fire. She had one small case of items hastily bought or

borrowed, nothing of hers before she had started impersonating Amelia, nothing to make her feel like plain old
Lizzie Eastway again.

There was a sharp rap on the door and Lizzie crossed
to it quickly, knowing it would be one of the servants, but
holding out a flicker of hope that it might be Daniel, willing to give her another chance.

She opened the door. It was William, one of the footmen. Lizzie gave him a small, sad smile as he looked at
her awkwardly.

'Time to go, miss,' William said, picking up her light
case and carrying it out of the room for her. They descended the stairs in silence and Lizzie was mortified to
see Aunt Mathilda and Harriet at the bottom.

'I'm sorry for lying to you,' Lizzie said, stopping in
front of Amelia's aunt.

The older woman smiled at her and gently patted her
on the arm. 'My brother-in-law was always writing to say
what a handful Amelia was, wilful and persuasive. I've no
doubt who made you go along with this,' she said kindly.

Lizzie burst into tears at Aunt Mathilda's understanding and felt all the despair and sadness come bubbling to
the surface again as the older woman took Lizzie in her
arms. She didn't release her for a few minutes, holding
Lizzie as the tears ran down her face and her chest heaved.

When Lizzie had finally composed herself she stepped
back and eyed up Harriet. They certainly weren't going
to have a tearful hug.

'I always knew there was something wrong about you,'
Harriet said smugly. 'Well, you've got what you deserve
now.' Harriet looked her up and down with disdain. 'Look
at you, you're plain and boring and have nothing that I
don't have. Yet you very nearly married an earl.'

Lizzie looked at Harriet sadly. She was spiteful and jealous, but Lizzie couldn't bring herself to hate the young girl.

'Sometimes people can see past the plain and boring and find something that no one else can see,' Lizzie said, thinking of when Daniel had told her he loved her. 'You'll find the person who sees his perfect woman when he looks at you one day, Harriet.'

'Look how well it's turned out for you,' Harriet sneered.

Lizzie turned away. She was never going to make Harriet like her and right now she didn't have the energy or motivation to even try.

'Miss Eastway,' Daniel barked as he emerged from his study.

Lizzie covered her mouth in shock as she turned to face him. Far from being his normal, well-presented self, Daniel looked as though he had spent the night in the gutter. His eyes were bloodshot, his skin pale and his hair sticking up in all directions. Lizzie wanted to run to him, to take him in her arms and make everything right, but she knew she was no longer in the position to comfort him.

'Let's go.'

Lizzie turned and smiled a final farewell to Aunt Mathilda, then docilely followed Daniel out to the waiting carriage.

Daniel stood aside as a groom helped her up into the carriage, as if he couldn't bear to touch her, but then to her surprise he jumped in himself and sat opposite. He must have seen the question in her expression.

'I'm taking you to London,' he said.

Lizzie had expected him to send her alone. He'd made it painfully obvious that he didn't want to spend any more time than was necessary in her company.

'Thank you,' she said quietly.

Daniel looked as though he might soften for a second,

but before Lizzie could say anything else he'd banged on the roof and the carriage lurched into motion.

They sat in a horrible, uncomfortable silence. Lizzie looked down at her hands, her feet, out the window, at the roof, anywhere but at Daniel. She couldn't bear to see the pain on his face, pain she had caused.

Lizzie had known her deception would hurt Daniel, she'd known it ever since he'd began pursuing her, but she had never realised quite how much it would shatter his world until his revelation about Annabelle. He'd been hurt badly before, so much so he had never really trusted another person. That was why he had a reputation as a rake, never bedding the same woman for more than a few weeks. He didn't want anyone to get close in case he got hurt again.

At first Lizzie knew she was nothing more to him than a means to keep his son's illegitimacy a secret and protect the young boy, but as time had passed she liked to think his affection had grown. She knew for sure that he had desired her from the very start, from that magical night in the Prestons' garden, which seemed so long ago now. When he had come to her in the night at the coaching inn he'd done it with seduction in mind, but when they had finally made love Lizzie knew it was because of deeper feelings for her.

She'd never expected love from him, especially after his revelations about Annabelle and her schemes, but yesterday, just before Harriet had come screeching into the garden, he had declared his love.

Lizzie took the memory of him uttering those words and wrapped herself in it. For a few moments at least someone had loved her. Despite what Daniel said about not really knowing her, Lizzie had been herself the entire time.

If Daniel loved anyone it was Lizzie, not Amelia. He just knew her by the wrong name.

She was certain those few minutes would for ever stick in her mind. Daniel had declared his love for her, something she had been craving for so long, and then her world had shattered with the revelation of her lie.

Lizzie had known Daniel would be hurt and upset, that he would be angry at her for lying to him for so long, but she hadn't been prepared for the force of his emotions. Now he could barely bring himself to look at her. It was as though her very presence brought him pain.

For a moment she wondered whether he had never really loved her at all, whether it had all been part of the plan to get her to marry him and get his hands on her dowry to protect his son. She could tell his thoughts were never far away from the boy and how to protect him from the world. She let out a small sigh, not noticing when Daniel's eyes flicked to her face and quickly looked away again. Lizzie had to give him more credit than that. He would not lie to her about love. Although losing her dowry would be a big blow, Daniel was more hurt about her betrayal of his trust.

She glanced at him across the carriage. It would be so easy to reach out and take his hand in her own, to beg him to forgive her, but Lizzie knew she didn't deserve forgiveness. She had let him believe she was Amelia, even when he had revealed his darkest secrets to her. Although she had tried to tell him a few times she had always allowed the interruptions that postponed her revelation.

Sitting up straighter, Lizzie decided she couldn't keep quiet. There was something she needed to say to Daniel. She might not deserve his forgiveness, she might not deserve to ever see him again, but she would never be able to look herself in the eye if she didn't try to make him understand one thing.

'Daniel,' she said softly.

Immediately his eyes snapped to her face. For a long moment they both sat there, looking at each other and wondering if there was any way back from this mess.

'I want to say something and I need you to listen,' Lizzie said.

He looked as though he were about to protest already, so Lizzie quickly continued.

'It's not about me, or our relationship. I know I have irrevocably damaged your trust in me and that we don't have a future.'

She wondered if the pain she saw in Daniel's face was reflected in her own. She certainly felt as though her heart was being ripped out.

'I need to say something about Annabelle. About Edward.'

For a moment she wondered if he would snap at her, whether he would tell her Edward was no longer any of her business, but after a long thirty seconds he inclined his head as if he were willing to at least listen.

'Love can conquer anything,' Lizzie said quietly. 'You may think the worst thing in the world for Edward would be living with the knowledge of his illegitimacy, but trust me, a child would rather be illegitimate and loved than legitimate and unloved.'

Lizzie thought back to all the moments in her childhood where she'd wished she had a parent to love her. The moments when Amelia ran to her father and he'd looked down at her, proud and caring, and Lizzie had stood back, trying to hold in the tears. Even the little moments, when she had finally mastered a piano piece, or when she fell and scraped her knee, Lizzie knew every part of her life would have been better with someone to love her.

'When I was a child my parents died. I went to live with

my uncle. No one loved me. No one cared if I succeeded or failed. I would have much preferred to be illegitimate but had a parent's love.'

'Being illegitimate killed my brother,' Daniel said stubbornly.

Lizzie shook her head. 'Being alone killed your brother. Your father didn't welcome him, accept him into the heart of the family. Your brother had no one to love him.'

They fell silent. Lizzie knew Daniel wanted his son so badly it was tearing him apart. She could see by the pain in his eyes every time Edward's name was mentioned that he couldn't stand missing out on his son's life.

'Love can conquer anything,' Lizzie repeated.

Chapter Twenty-Six

They had spent most of the journey in silence. Daniel hated to see Lizzie so withdrawn and fragile, but he couldn't bring himself to do anything about it. Every time he thought about reaching out to her his brain screamed that she'd lied to him and there was nothing stopping her from lying again.

After their talk about Edward some of Lizzie's words kept circling round in his head. *Love can conquer anything.* He wondered if it were true. For the first time in years, for the first time since Annabelle had started to blackmail him, Daniel felt a surge of hope. Maybe Lizzie was right, maybe Daniel could still be part of his son's life.

He thought back to Rupert's suffering and he realised that on that front at least Lizzie's words were true. Rupert hadn't had anyone to love him. He'd been bullied about his illegitimacy, but if their father had accepted him and showered him in love, the bullies' words would probably have just slid right off Rupert rather than taking hold and festering.

One thing he could give his son was love. He loved that little boy so much and he barely even knew him. The thought of being the one to raise him, the one to kiss him goodnight and tuck him safely into bed, was almost intoxicating. He wondered whether he could have all that and still protect Edward.

He wanted to ask Lizzie to talk more about it, to explain how love conquered anything. He wanted to listen as she convinced him he could claim his son and not ruin the young boy's life. Daniel glanced across the carriage to where Lizzie sat, staring morosely at her hands.

Before he could find the words the carriage lurched to a stop. Daniel peered out of the window into the dusk. It had been a long afternoon of travelling. He had wanted to get as far as possible on their journey back to London and to avoid the coaching inn they had stayed at only a few nights previously at all costs. He didn't need the memories of his time there with Lizzie, things were painful enough without reliving that night together.

Daniel opened the door and hopped down from the carriage, stretching his leg and back muscles, which were stiff from the long day spent cooped up in the carriage. Once he had regained his normal range of movement, he turned round and automatically held out his hand to assist Lizzie from the carriage. As their hands met Daniel felt a jolt coursing through his body. Even though he despised how she had deceived him his body still responded to her. He craved the touch of her skin against his, the taste of her lips on his own. He wanted her even now, even when he knew they had no future together.

Once on the ground, Lizzie quickly pulled her hand away as if aware of the tension between them the contact had caused.

Daniel turned and walked into the inn, not waiting to see if Lizzie followed him.

'Two rooms, please, for myself and my sister,' he said as the landlord appeared.

Daniel knew travelling alone with Lizzie was scandalous enough. The pretence that she was his sister would at least shield her from a little of the gossip generated in these places.

'Two rooms? Ah.'

Daniel's heart sank. There wasn't another inn for miles and he didn't think the horses would make it that far without rest.

'We have one very nice room, perhaps you and your sister would not mind sharing,' the landlord said.

'We need two rooms.'

'I'm very sorry, sir, but we're completely full. It's uncommonly busy.'

Daniel took a deep breath and reminded himself that it wasn't the innkeeper's fault that there was only one room. A few days ago he would have relished the prospect of spending a whole night with Lizzie so close. Now he couldn't think of anything more tortuous.

'We'll take the room,' he said. 'And dinner.'

'Of course, sir.' The landlord looked very relieved Daniel wasn't going to make more of a fuss. 'I can serve you dinner in the private dining room in half an hour.'

The landlord led them up to the room, showed them in and then quickly retreated before Daniel could change his mind about sharing with Lizzie.

'I can sleep elsewhere,' Lizzie said, her voice barely more than a whisper.

Daniel turned to look at her. 'And where exactly do you propose to sleep?'

'In the carriage?' Lizzie suggested. 'Or maybe the barn.'

Daniel shook his head. 'I may not be pursuing you as my wife any longer, but I refuse to let you put yourself at risk whilst in my company. We will both sleep here tonight.' As he said it Daniel eyed up the small bed and had to suppress a groan. 'I'll sleep in the chair.' The very upright, uncomfortable-looking chair.

Lizzie opened her mouth to protest again, but Daniel silenced her with a look. He might be furious with her, but he wasn't about to let a lady sleep in a chair whilst he was in a bed.

Daniel flopped down into the hard chair and tried to make himself comfortable. He grimaced; it was going to be a very long, sleepless night.

Lizzie walked over to the window and looked out, allowing Daniel to study her back. He had so much he wanted to ask her, so many questions whirling round his head, but he couldn't bring himself to utter a single query. He knew if he started asking her to explain he would be on the slippery slope to forgiveness, leaving himself open to being hurt again.

'Shall we go down for dinner?' Lizzie asked after twenty long, silent minutes.

Daniel roused himself, levering his body from the hard chair and following Lizzie out of the room.

They sat in silence whilst they waited for dinner. Daniel could see Lizzie darting glances in his direction every few seconds as if she wanted to ask him something but didn't know how.

'What is it, Miss Eastway?' Daniel asked eventually after their mutton had been set down in front of them.

Lizzie pushed her food around her plate and tried a mouthful. She grimaced but chewed and swallowed before answering him.

'What happens when we get to London?' she asked eventually.

Daniel tasted some of the dinner himself. It was grim—

the mutton overcooked, the vegetables soggy and the potatoes hard.

'I will deliver you to some of your relatives.'

Lizzie nodded as if this were a sensible plan, although by the way she pursed her lips Daniel could see she thought there might be a flaw in his idea.

'Which relatives will you deliver me to?' Lizzie asked.

Daniel shrugged. 'Whomever you'd like to go and stay with.'

He was getting distracted by her lips. They kept pursing and relaxing, and once he even thought he saw the flicker of her tongue darting out.

'Maybe if you would be so kind as to take me to a reputable guest house,' Lizzie suggested.

Daniel looked at her properly for the first time since they'd sat down for dinner and realised there was real fear in her eyes.

'What's wrong with your relatives?' he asked sharply.

'I don't have any. Amelia and my uncle are my only living relatives.'

Daniel cursed under his breath. He might want to try to distance himself from Lizzie so he could start thinking clearly again, but he couldn't abandon her in the middle of London all on her own.

'You didn't think to mention this earlier?' he asked.

'You didn't want to share your plans with me.'

He knew she was right and this was one thing he couldn't blame her for, but Daniel felt annoyed all the same. He'd envisioned dropping her off with some elderly aunt, then going and reassessing his life. The truth was he couldn't think with Lizzie near him. He hated that she'd lied to him, hated that he had allowed himself to be deceived again, but he couldn't bring himself to hate her. He wanted to, but the feelings just weren't there. In fact, he still felt rather protective towards her and there was something deeper, something he didn't care to examine yet.

When he had found out that Annabelle had lied to him all those years ago, Daniel had immediately realised everything they had shared was part of that lie, but somehow with Lizzie things felt different. He was beginning to wonder whether she did care for him, love him even, and her deception had just got out of hand.

Looking across the table at her, Daniel wanted to forgive her, he wanted to sweep her into his arms and tell her everything would work out, but he knew he couldn't let his heart rule his head. He needed distance, some time to assess the situation, some time away from Lizzie.

'I do not want to be a burden on you any longer,' Lizzie said quietly. 'If you would be so kind as to recommend suitable accommodation, you will never see me again.' There was a choke in her voice as she spoke and Daniel knew she was hurting, too.

'We will figure it out tomorrow,' he said wearily, running a hand through his hair.

Lizzie nodded and went back to pushing her food around her plate, every so often taking a mouthful and grimacing at the taste.

They finished dinner in silence and returned to the room. Daniel eyed up the chair he was going to be spending a very uncomfortable night in and decided he needed some air.

'I'm going for a walk,' he said. 'I'll be back in half an hour. I suggest you are in your nightclothes and in bed by then.'

The last thing he needed was to be in the room whilst Lizzie undressed. Hearing the rustles and imagining what she was taking off would weaken his resolve and he couldn't be sure he wouldn't sweep her on to the bed and ravish her, despite not knowing how he felt about her any longer.

He slipped out of the room and out of the inn, determined to clear his head before returning to where Lizzie, the woman he'd thought he loved, was sleeping.

Chapter Twenty-Seven

There was no way Lizzie was going to sleep. Her body might be exhausted, but her mind was whirring with activity. She knew she should be making plans for the future, deciding what it was she wanted to do with her life, but Daniel, and the life she could have had with him, kept returning to her thoughts.

She turned over in bed and buried her face in the pillow, letting out a muffled scream. She wished she didn't feel so alone. If only Amelia was here, her one confidante. Lizzie knew Amelia would tell her to fight for Daniel, to make him realise what he was throwing away, but Lizzie wasn't her cousin. No matter what she had been pretending in the past few weeks Lizzie wasn't brave or outgoing or flirtatious.

As she saw it she had two options and neither of them involved the man she loved. Either she could consign herself to a life of misery and return to India to become Colonel Rocher's badly treated wife, or she could strike out on her own. The second option was riskier, but Lizzie knew that after experiencing freedom and love these past few weeks she couldn't willingly give herself up to a man who wouldn't love her and would probably beat her. Before she came to England she would have married Colonel Rocher without argument, but over the past couple of weeks she had found a confidence and self-respect she had never realised was buried deep inside her.

Lizzie heard the door open quietly as Daniel slipped into the room. She kept her eyes closed and her breathing steady. For a moment she wondered if he would come to her, slip into the bed beside her and tell her everything would be all right. She wanted his forgiveness so badly, but she knew it couldn't ever happen. Other men might forgive her deception, but Daniel had been hurt in the worst possible way before, and now she knew he could never forgive her.

Lizzie also knew that if he forgave her, if he agreed they could have a life together, then he would be giving up what he viewed as his son's protection, all for her. That sort of responsibility was too much and she wouldn't be able to bear it if little Edward got hurt because of her.

She listened as he kicked off his boots and sank into the chair. Daniel shifted position every few seconds and Lizzie knew he must be uncomfortable. Another thing for her to feel bad about.

'We can share the bed,' Lizzie said quietly. 'I promise I won't even touch you.'

Daniel grunted and Lizzie wondered if he expected her to seduce him in the middle of the night. As if she would know how.

'I'm fine,' he said. 'Go to sleep.'

Lizzie lay staring up at the ceiling for a few minutes, listening to him shift his body trying to get comfortable.

'Please. The bed is big enough for two. There's no point in depriving yourself of sleep on top of everything else.'

Silence. Five seconds passed, then ten. Lizzie could tell he was weighing the options up in his head. He could spend the night in the chair and start the morning sleep-deprived and aching, or he could share the bed with the woman who had lied about who she was.

Eventually he stood and walked over to the bed.

'I'll sleep on top of the covers,' he said.

Lizzie waited for Daniel to lie down, but he seemed to hesitate.

'I promise I won't touch you,' she repeated sadly.

'It's not you I'm worried about.'

Slowly he got on to the bed, careful not to touch her at all. Although there was a thick blanket and a couple of sheets separating them, Lizzie could still feel the heat of his body radiating through the layers. She thought back to the last time they had shared a bed together, when she had given herself completely to the man she loved. He'd caressed every inch of her body then, now he was taking pains not to touch her at all.

Tears welled in her eyes and silently Lizzie let them fall down her cheeks and into the pillow. She didn't know how she had messed everything up so much, but she would not take Daniel down with her. She loved him, even though he was rejecting her, and the best thing for him would be to be free of her. Tomorrow she would disappear out of his life and allow him to forget her. He would be free to find another woman, a real heiress, to marry and secure his son's future with.

'Tell me,' Daniel said hoarsely, 'was any of it real?'

Yesterday, when Lizzie had told him of her true identity and the web of lies she had spun to protect her cousin, he had immediately assumed she was a trickster, a seducer, a woman like Annabelle, out to take him for all he had. Lizzie had tried to make him see it was only her identity she had lied about, not her feelings for him, but she knew Daniel hadn't been able to separate the truth from the deception.

Lizzie turned over in the bed to face Daniel in the dark.

She couldn't see his face, or his expression, but she knew every feature as well as if it had been etched on her brain. Slowly she reached out a hand and touched his cheek.

'I loved you from the moment we met in the Prestons' garden,' Lizzie said. 'I've never met anyone like you. I've never met anyone who has noticed me.'

She held her breath, knowing this was a pivotal moment. Daniel was angry at her, he felt betrayed, but he was still here beside her. He could have sent her back to London with a maid as a chaperon. In fact, it would have been less scandalous to do so. Instead here he was, lying in bed beside her.

Lizzie felt her jaw clenching with tension and her free hand balling into a fist. This was the moment, their one chance at happiness. If Daniel could bring himself to forgive her, or even just begin to understand that she had never meant to hurt him, they might have a future. She hardly dared to hope. She loved Daniel and over the past couple of weeks she had come to realise that she deserved love. Daniel had made her realise that. He'd pulled her from the shadows and made her appreciate herself, even made her feel beautiful.

'I love you,' she repeated.

The silence stretched out before her and slowly Lizzie let her hand drop from Daniel's cheek. She'd laid herself bare, told him that she loved him, and he'd responded with silence.

She didn't blame him, she'd broken his trust, but that didn't make his rejection hurt any less.

Lizzie bit her lip to stop herself from sobbing and turned back over in bed so she was facing the wall. She heard every breath Daniel took and part of her was still hoping he would reach out and pull her body towards her, wrap her in his arms and tell her everything would work out.

They lay side by side without touching for what seemed like hours. Every muscle in Lizzie's body was tense and she knew if Daniel just touched her with a single finger she would fall happily into his arms.

He didn't touch her. The minutes ticked by and slowly his breathing steadied and deepened. Lizzie didn't sleep at all. Her mind was active, planning for the days ahead, and her heart was mourning the loss of the man she loved.

Lizzie had lain there through the darkest part of the night and waited until the grey light of dawn started to filter in through the thin curtains. As the first birds began to chirp she carefully got out of bed and pulled on her dress.

She couldn't be there when Daniel woke up. Another day of him being barely able to look at her would destroy what was left of her heart. She had to get away, allow both of them to make a fresh start.

Quickly Lizzie collected all of her meagre belongings into her small bag. She hesitated by the door and looked back at Daniel. He was sleeping peacefully, all the worry from the past few days wiped from his face. Lizzie couldn't help herself, silently she crossed back over to the bed and kissed him softly on the lips. He didn't stir, but as Lizzie pulled away he smiled in his sleep.

Before she could talk herself out of her decision, Lizzie turned away and left the room. Once outside she rested her forehead against the wall and made herself breathe. She was making the right choice, this way both she and Daniel got a fresh start. If she stayed and allowed him to take her to London, the whole situation would get more and more complicated. Now she had accepted they could not be together Lizzie had to move on. It might be heart-breaking, but it was possible.

Once she had calmed her nerves and silenced the voices

of doubt in her head, Lizzie descended the stairs and went into the bar. The landlord was already up, cleaning the mess left by his patrons the night before. He nodded a greeting to Lizzie but didn't say anything as she exited the inn.

The night before, just after dinner, Lizzie had discreetly asked the landlord when the first stagecoach to London passed by. If it was on time, it should stop outside in a few minutes' time.

Lizzie waited by the side of the road, every so often glancing up at the window of the room she had shared so briefly with Daniel.

Chapter Twenty-Eight

Daniel stirred and stretched as the light filtering through the thin curtains reached his eyes. He felt warm and contented and as if he could stay in bed all day. He was still half-asleep and instinctively reached out across the bed. He could smell Lizzie and for one moment he forgot everything that had gone before and just wanted her in his arms.

The other side of the bed was cold. With a groan Daniel forced open his eyes and surveyed the room, expecting to see Lizzie sitting in the hard chair trying to ignore the half-clothed man in her bed. The chair was empty and Daniel sat up quickly with a curse. The events of the past few days came rushing back, culminating in Lizzie's declaration of love the night before. The declaration he had said nothing in reply to.

Daniel jumped out of bed, stumbling slightly as his muscles raced to keep up with his brain. Quickly he surveyed the room—all of Lizzie's belongings had gone. She hadn't had much with her, but the small bag with her change of clothes and few personal items wasn't anywhere to be seen.

Within two minutes Daniel had thrown on the rest of his clothes, ran a hand through his hair and pulled on his boots. He certainly didn't look as presentable as an earl should, but he wouldn't offend anyone out here in the country.

'Have you seen the woman I was with?' Daniel asked as he strode into the bar.

The landlord had just finished tidying up from the night before and was sitting at one of the small tables eating a meal of bread and cheese.

'Left early this morning,' the landlord said, getting to his feet as Daniel entered the room.

'She left?' He couldn't quite believe what he was hearing. He'd expected her to be holed up in one of the private rooms, trying to stay as far away from him as possible.

'Asked about the first stagecoach to pass and went outside to meet it.'

Daniel shook his head in disbelief. She couldn't be gone, she just couldn't. There were so many things he wanted to say to her, so many things not yet resolved.

He hurried outside and looked around the deserted yard. There wasn't even a stable boy in sight. Daniel ran out to the road, wondering if he would find her sitting on a rock, waiting for him to come and rescue her, but she wasn't there.

Daniel felt a pressure begin to build around his heart. He couldn't have lost her, not yet. He might not know what his feelings for her were any more, but he did know he didn't want her leaving his life quite so abruptly.

Making his way back to the inn, Daniel didn't go back inside immediately, instead heading towards the stables. A young lad was just opening the door, rubbing his bleary eyes, as Daniel arrived.

'Saddle one of my horses,' Daniel said. 'Have it ready to go in five minutes.'

He cursed at not having any of his fast horses with him. The beasts used to pull the carriage they had travelled in yesterday were good strong animals, but they weren't particularly fast. He needed to catch the stagecoach before it reached London, otherwise he knew Lizzie would disappear for ever in the vast city.

Whilst the stable boy went about getting one of the horses saddled and ready to go Daniel returned to the inn, collected his belongings and paid the landlord, asking him to keep the rest of his horses and the carriage safe until his return. Hopefully with Lizzie in tow.

It was less than fifteen minutes later that Daniel was on the road, pushing his horse hard through the flat countryside. He rode like a man possessed, all the time trying not to analyse why he was quite so upset.

Daniel knew this was all his fault. He had set out to take Lizzie to London to get some space away from her. He found it difficult to think straight when she was around. He didn't know whether he could trust her, didn't know whether her small lie had just got out of control, or whether there was a deeper deception going on.

When he'd found out she was lying to him about her identity his mind had instantly darted back to when he had discovered Annabelle's deception. The irrational part of him had screamed that he'd been conned again, allowed another woman to fool him and trick him into giving her his heart. Daniel had immediately tried to protect himself in the only way he knew how; he'd closed himself off.

Last night when Lizzie had said she loved him his resolve had cracked a little. Maybe Lizzie wasn't like Annabelle, maybe she was just a good woman caught up in a lie that had got out of hand. He'd looked into her eyes and seen sincerity and hope and he'd wanted to trust her, but some little part of him had held back.

Now he was in turmoil. He knew he still loved her, but he wasn't sure that he could forgive her. After everything he had been through in the past, honesty was important to him, maybe too important for him and Lizzie to have a future.

Daniel just didn't know. He needed time to sort through his feelings and work out whether Lizzie was right, whether love could conquer anything. He needed time, but he also needed Lizzie waiting for him at the end, which if he didn't catch the stagecoach soon would never happen.

He tried not to think of how he would feel if he never saw her again, but as he forced his mind on to other areas he began to imagine Lizzie alone in the world, vulnerable and at the mercy of strangers. Daniel needed to find her. Whether he could forgive her or not, he would never be able to forgive himself if something bad happened to her.

He rode hard for three hours without a break. He could tell the horse was tiring and that soon he would have to stop for water. Just as Daniel was about to despair that he had lost Lizzie for ever he saw a cloud of dust up ahead.

Quickly he spurred his horse on for one last gallop and within five minutes had caught up with the stagecoach.

Daniel approached carefully, knowing the last thing he needed was to be mistaken for a highwayman and shot by an overeager driver.

'Good morning,' Daniel said as he drew up alongside the horses and the driver.

'Morning,' the driver greeted him gruffly.

'I'm so sorry to bother you, but I'm looking for my runaway sister. I think she might be on board.'

The driver looked Daniel over carefully. Daniel cursed his rumpled clothes and wild hair, knowing he probably looked more like a highwayman than a gentleman.

'Sorry, sir, can't stop the coach in the middle of nowhere. More than my job's worth.'

Daniel knew it was no use arguing. The man had his

instructions and wasn't likely to disobey them if there was even the smallest possibility Daniel was there to rob his passengers.

'Where's your next stop?' Daniel asked.

'Coaching inn about an hour away.'

Daniel glanced down at his flagging horse and wondered if the beast could make it another hour. Now they were going at a slower speed it had recovered, but Daniel knew another hour would probably be pushing it.

'I've got a purse full of money that's all yours if you stop.'

Daniel reached into a pocket and withdrew the purse, jangling it temptingly.

The driver looked conflicted. Daniel knew there would be more money in the purse than the driver made in a year, but equally he wouldn't want to be blamed for a robbery if this was all a hoax.

In the end the greed won out and the driver pulled sharply on the reins bringing the horses to a walk and then finally to a stop. Daniel tossed him the purse and quickly dismounted, crossing to the coach in two long strides and flinging open the door.

'Lizzie?' It was gloomy inside but Daniel could see immediately Lizzie wasn't in there.

'Did you pick a young woman up at the Bull Inn?' Daniel asked, turning back to the driver.

'No, sir.'

Daniel cursed as he slammed the door shut. He'd lost her. If she wasn't on this stagecoach, he had no idea where she was. Maybe she was on an earlier stagecoach, maybe a passing carriage had picked her up, or maybe she had decided to walk into the village back near the Bull Inn. Whatever the explanation, Daniel knew he wouldn't ever pick up Lizzie's trail in time now.

He watched as the stagecoach pulled away and felt the despair mounting inside him. Lizzie was lost to him and before he could figure out exactly how he felt about her.

Daniel snorted. That was a lie. He knew exactly how he felt about her: he loved her. What he didn't know was whether he could bring himself to trust her enough to spend his life with her.

Turning back the way he'd come, Daniel let his horse walk at its own pace. There had been an inn just a few miles away and he should be able to get a fresh horse there. Then he would return to his estate and begin the search for Lizzie whilst he tried to work out whether he had a future with the woman he loved.

Chapter Twenty-Nine

It had been nearly two weeks since Lizzie had last set eyes on Daniel, two weeks of misery and fear and hunger. She'd had only a little money when they'd left Cambridgeshire and Lizzie knew it wouldn't last her very long. After a ticket on the stagecoach, a bite to eat and nearly two weeks' accommodation in a rat-infested dive the money was almost gone.

Lizzie had wept that first night. She'd wept for the life she had lost and she'd wept for the hellhole she now found herself in, but, ever practical, Lizzie had allowed herself only one night of self-indulgence.

Standing at the mouth of the alley, Lizzie glanced around her. She'd never imagined she would have to frequent such a neighbourhood, but the past few weeks had taught her she could survive anything. With a deep breath Lizzie walked into the darkness and knocked on a door halfway down the alley.

After a minute the door opened and a small man peered up at her from the gloom within.

'I was told you might be able to help me,' Lizzie said, trying to keep the tremor from her voice.

'What have you got?'

Lizzie ran her fingers over the bracelet on her wrist. It was delicate, a thin gold chain, simple but elegant.

'How much for this?' she asked, unclasping the bracelet and holding it out to the small man.

She tried to ignore the feeling of betrayal. This was all she had of her mother, the only thing she had to remind her of the woman she could barely remember. Lizzie knew her mother would understand, that she would want Lizzie to put her survival over her sentimentality, but it didn't make parting with the last link to her parents any easier.

'I'll give you ten shillings for it.'

Lizzie bit her lip. She knew it was worth more, but equally she didn't know where else she would go to sell it. Cautiously she nodded her head.

She waited whilst the man counted out her money and handed it over, then gave him the bracelet, telling herself it would be worth it.

Lizzie exited quickly before she could change her mind, squinting as she emerged out into the light from the gloomy interior.

With her ten shillings hidden away from any pickpockets Lizzie made her way through the streets of London towards the office she had been visiting every day for the past week. Today she would find a position, hopefully as a governess, but she would even take something as a housekeeper. Lizzie knew ten shillings wouldn't last her very long and, without knowing where Amelia was, she had no friends or contacts in England whatsoever. Well, except for Daniel, and there was no way she could contact him—she'd promised herself a clean break, and even just seeing him once would make her resolve shatter.

'Miss Eastway,' the woman in the ladies' employment agency said with a sigh as Lizzie pushed open the door.

'Good morning, Miss Farnham,' Lizzie greeted the bespectacled woman, ignoring the sigh. 'I've come to see whether you have any new vacancies today.'

Miss Farnham looked down at the sheets of paper on her desk and Lizzie felt a surge of hope. She just needed one chance, one person to employ her, and she would be safe. Lizzie didn't even want to think what might happen if she didn't find a job before her money ran out completely.

'Do you have your letters of reference yet?' Miss Farnham asked.

Lizzie took a deep breath and considered her reply. The only big lie she had told in her lifetime was pretending to be Amelia and look where that had got her: standing in a shabby office in the middle of a strange city with no money, no prospects and a broken heart.

She had two options: she could tell the truth and most likely face starvation and spending nights on the street, or she could tell her second big lie of her lifetime.

'They came in this morning,' Lizzie said, hoping the guilt she felt didn't show on her face.

Lizzie dug out the two letters and handed them over, hoping Miss Farnham wouldn't look too closely.

The older woman unfolded the first letter and began reading. She nodded in approval and repeated the process with the second.

Of course the letters were forgeries. Lizzie had sat up for hours the night before, trying to think what to say in her references. She'd been complimentary, but not too gushing, stating that she was a good, hard worker who kept to herself.

'This should make things easier,' Miss Farnham said and smiled for the first time since Lizzie had walked into her office a few days ago.

'Are there any positions available?' Lizzie repeated the question she had asked every day.

Miss Farnham cleared her throat and started searching

through the papers in front of her. Lizzie found herself holding her breath.

'There is one thing, the notice came in yesterday afternoon.'

Lizzie waited whilst the older woman found the job she was talking about.

'The only problem is it's a long way away.'

Lizzie would travel as far as she needed as long as it meant there was a job at the end of the journey.

'The position is as governess to two young girls down in Devon.'

Devon. Just about as far from Cambridgeshire as you could get.

'They're looking for someone to start as soon as possible.'

Perfect, Lizzie thought. Even if Devon seemed worlds away.

'The only problem is you will of course have to pay your fare to get down there. The mistress of the house has very kindly said she will reimburse whomever we send once they have taken up the position, but you will have to shoulder the cost up front.'

Lizzie thought of the ten shillings she had hidden in her purse. Surely the fare to Devon wouldn't be more than that.

'It might be a little less costly to find a ship,' Miss Farnham said kindly. 'That way you don't have to pay for your board as well.'

After the passage from India Lizzie had hoped not to have to go on another sea voyage for a long time, but she supposed a journey along the south coast of England would be better than the long voyage halfway around the world.

'I'll book myself a passage immediately,' Lizzie said.

'Good. Take your letters of recommendation and report to this address.' Miss Farnham wrote out an address in Devon and handed it over to Lizzie. 'Good luck, Miss Eastway.'

Lizzie left the small office with a smile on her face. She might never see the man she loved again, but at least she had a job. For the first time in her life she was in charge, she was the one making the decisions. Ever since she could remember Lizzie had obeyed her uncle's every instruction, but not this time. She would not return to India to a life of misery as Colonel Rocher's wife. Maybe a few months ago she would have surrendered to her uncle's wishes, but not now. The past month with Daniel had taught her a lot, but the main thing was self-respect. For the first time in her life Lizzie felt as though she mattered and her opinions mattered, too. She deserved to be happy as much as anyone else and if no one else would fight for her happiness, then she would.

As she walked briskly towards the docks Lizzie couldn't help thinking about Daniel. She wondered what he was doing and whether he missed her. Every time she pictured his smiling face Lizzie felt the pain of leaving him all over again, but she knew it had been the right decision. If she'd stayed, he would have tried to protect her out of a misguided sense of chivalry and Lizzie would have fallen in love with him more and more every day. She doubted Daniel would ever be able to forgive her properly, not after he had been so betrayed by Annabelle, and if she stayed in his life he might come to resent her. Lizzie didn't want him resenting her. She had her memories and she had her new-found self-respect. That would have to be enough.

Lizzie entered the docks and pulled the shawl she had draped across her shoulders tight across her chest. It was the middle of the day and the docks were swarming with people, but she still felt a little nervous coming into such a man's world unchaperoned.

She made her way to the cramped little office of the shipping company that had transported her and Amelia from India to England over a month before. She didn't know the first thing about arranging a passage to Devon, but this seemed a good place to start.

'Good morning,' she said as she entered the office.

A harried-looking clerk glanced up at her with surprise before holding a finger up and returning his attention to the papers in front of him. After a minute he finished what he was doing and looked up again.

'Are you lost?'

Lizzie shook her head, feeling completely out of her depth.

'I need to book a passage to Devon,' she said, trying to smile, but feeling too nervous to manage much more than a grimace.

'We don't sail to Devon. We have routes to France, Spain, India. Nothing to Devon.'

Lizzie sensed the clerk was about to return his attention to the papers in front of him so spoke quickly.

'I've never booked a passage on a ship before,' she said, giving the clerk her sweetest smile. 'I don't suppose you could recommend a reputable company who do sail to Devon?'

The clerk sighed but grabbed a piece of paper and hurriedly wrote something down.

'Salters and Son. Their office is about five hundred feet to your left. They won't scam you and there will likely be other passengers on board.'

'Thank you,' Lizzie said gratefully, taking the slip of paper in one hand. The clerk had already bent his head and returned to his work.

Lizzie walked further down the docks until she saw the

battered sign of Salters and Son above a small office almost identical to the one she had just been in.

'Good morning,' a clerk greeted her as she pushed through the door.

'I'd like to book a passage on a ship to Devon,' Lizzie said.

'Our next ship sails tomorrow.'

Before she could talk herself out of the idea Lizzie handed over her money and booked herself a small cabin.

Tomorrow. It was so soon. Whilst in London, although alone, Lizzie knew there were people nearby whom she at least recognised. Acquaintances who would come to her aid if she were in real peril. Once she set sail for Devon, she would be truly alone. Daniel would be almost a whole country away and there would be no chance of ever seeing him across a room or catching a glimpse of him in a crowd. Lizzie told herself this was what she needed, a completely fresh start, but as she walked out of the shipping office she couldn't help but feel as though she was making a mistake.

Chapter Thirty

Daniel bent down and placed a kiss on top of Edward's head, unable to stop himself from grinning as he did so.

'Daddy, what's a monkey?'

They were sitting in Daniel's study on a rainy afternoon looking at books together. Edward, being just three years old, liked the big old illustrated encyclopaedias with pictures of creatures and sights from around the world.

'A monkey is an animal that lives in the jungle,' Daniel explained slowly. Over the past week he had got used to adapting his language for the young boy, although he was careful not to talk down to him. Even at the tender age of three Edward got offended if Daniel oversimplified things.

'Monkeys swing through the trees and they make this noise.'

Daniel did his best impression of a monkey. Edward was immediately on his feet jumping around after his father, imitating him.

They collapsed breathless after a minute and Daniel enjoyed the feeling of holding his son in his arms.

Once he'd lost Lizzie's trail, Daniel had been frantic. He knew he had to find her, he wouldn't be able to forgive himself if something bad happened to her, and in his mind there was no doubt that it would; she was a pretty young woman without any money.

Luckily the man he had summoned to help Lizzie search for her cousin had been waiting for him when he returned to his estate. Immediately he had instructed the agent to begin searching for Lizzie, and not to stop until he found her. Daniel only hoped he wouldn't be too late.

What he was going to say to her once they were reunited was another matter entirely.

Whatever he decided, he certainly needed to thank her. For days after she had disappeared from the coaching inn Daniel had not been able to stop replaying her words in his head. *Love can conquer anything.*

He'd remembered their conversations about Edward and how she had been convinced a father's love was more important than thinking oneself of legitimate birth. Hour after hour Daniel had tried to figure out if she was right, then eventually he had acted.

Daniel had summoned a lawyer, taken the lawyer to Annabelle, and half an hour later had returned home with his son. The law was made by men and it favoured men, but in this instance Daniel didn't care about the inequality or unfairness of it. Edward was now in his custody, and there was nothing Annabelle could do about it. In the end Daniel had asked his lawyer to draw up a contract that gave Annabelle a small yearly sum of money if she did not try to publicise the scandal. He had also granted her the right to visit their son, as long as the visit was prearranged, and suggested he help her find lodgings in the local area so she could still be part of Edward's life.

'Daddy, can I have a dog?' Edward asked, his nose buried back in the illustrated encyclopaedia.

Daniel glanced at the entry his son was looking at and smiled. On the page was a picture of an Old English sheepdog, complete with shaggy coat and lolling tongue. The dog would outsize his son at least threefold, but Daniel had a sneaking suspicion this was part of the appeal.

'We'll see. Let's get you settled in here first of all and then we can think about a dog.'

A dog wasn't a bad idea, Daniel thought. It would be a companion to keep his son company as he settled into his new home, someone to explore with and get him over the transition period. Edward had not had too much trouble since he had left his mother, but sometimes at bedtime Daniel saw a scared little boy tucked up in bed and he wanted to do anything to help Edward feel completely at home and relaxed.

'I was bitten by a dog,' Edward said as he traced the picture of the sheepdog in the book. 'But I still want one.'

Daniel ruffled his son's hair affectionately and wondered how to go about buying an Old English sheepdog puppy. A friend for Edward to grow up with.

'Did it hurt when the dog bit you?' Daniel asked.

Edward looked up at him with wide eyes and nodded.

'You're a brave boy.' Daniel bent down and placed another kiss on his son's head.

'Mama wanted to have it killed,' Edward said, pulling a face. 'But I cried until she said no.'

'You forgave it,' Daniel said, 'even though it hurt you.'

Edward looked at Daniel with his lips pursed and a question in his eyes.

'What does that mean?'

'To forgive someone?'

Edward nodded, looking up at Daniel as if his father had the answers to all the questions in the world. Daniel felt a rush of love for his son and had to take a deep breath before replying; this was the first of many lessons he was going to be able to teach his son.

'To forgive someone is when you show you don't feel

angry or upset after someone has hurt you or done something wrong.'

Edward smiled up at his father.

'So I forgave the dog for biting me?'

'Exactly.'

'And you forgave Mama for keeping you away from
me?'

Daniel knew he had to be the bigger man here. His son
didn't need to feel anger towards either of his parents.

'That wasn't her fault. It wasn't anyone's fault, so there
is nothing to forgive.'

Daniel watched as Edward went back to looking at the
illustration of the dog. He knew he could never forgive
Annabelle for keeping him and Edward apart for all these
years, even if he told his son there was no one to blame,
and he was having a hard time forgiving himself for thinking the scandal of illegitimacy would be worse for Edward
than having a real father. He had Lizzie to thank for making him realise it.

Lizzie, kind and caring Lizzie. The woman who had
got caught up in her own lie and hadn't been able to find a
way out. Perhaps all this time he had been too harsh on her.
He had made mistakes. In fact, his entire way of thinking
the past three years was mistaken, but his little boy, who
was only three years old, had forgiven him and allowed
them to move on. Maybe he could do the same with Lizzie.

As soon as the notion came to him Daniel knew it was
the right thing to do. He loved Lizzie, and it wasn't a love
based on lust as it had been with Annabelle. Certainly he
desired Lizzie, but his feelings ran much deeper than that.
He craved her company, wanted to share every exciting
event and every mundane moment with her. He missed her
low-pitched laugh and her quiet appreciation of the world.

Daniel couldn't help but smile. He loved her, he loved

Lizzie Eastway, and it didn't matter that she didn't have the name he'd first known her by. If it meant spending his life with her, Daniel would be content to call her by a different name each week, as long as her surname was Blackburn for eternity.

He needed to find her and tell her how he felt. He'd been a fool pushing her away and there was a very real possibility he'd lost her for good. Daniel was afraid she might have boarded the first ship for India, intent on fleeing the country after he had rejected her. If she was halfway across the world by now, he knew the chances of getting her back were slim, but he also knew he wouldn't be able to rest until she was back in his arms.

Daniel knew he shouldn't have pushed her away, especially when they had lain side by side together in the coaching inn and Lizzie had told him that she loved him. She'd bared her soul and reached out to him and he had rejected her. Daniel would certainly not blame her if she had fled the country after that incident. He would make it up to her, he would spend a lifetime declaring his love for her, as long as he could get her back in his arms where she belonged.

Daniel was also acutely aware that she had forgiven him for his deception. She had listened to his story about Annabelle and his son, and she had sympathised with him. There had been no anger and no blame. Lizzie had forgiven him immediately, but when she had needed him to understand why she had lied he'd pushed her away.

'You look sad, Daddy,' Edward said as he glanced up from the book.

Daniel wondered how much to tell his son and knew he should be honest with the boy. Even at just three years old Edward was a perceptive boy.

'I'm thinking about a friend of mine who I should have forgiven a while ago.'

'Why does that make you sad?'

'I don't know where she is to tell her I forgive her and I'm sorry for not telling her sooner.'

'Then she can forgive you, too.'

Daniel hoped so. He didn't know what he would do if Lizzie had sailed back to India, but he knew he'd be completely devastated if she was still in the country and rejected him once he found her.

'I hope she can forgive me,' Daniel said quietly.

Edward lost interest in the conversation and started flicking the pages of the book through his fingers, giggling as he got faster and faster.

Daniel hoped Frampton, the agent he had sent to search for Lizzie, returned with some news soon. He couldn't bear not knowing what had happened to her. He didn't know if she had any money or any contacts or if she was sleeping rough on the streets. The idea of her spending her nights alone in London sent shivers of fear to his heart.

He was also worrying about Golding, the Bow Street Runner who had visited his estate a few weeks before to question Lizzie about the fire. The man had been back, demanding to see Lizzie, even storming in when Daniel had told him she was no longer there. Mr Golding had informed him that he had a warrant for her arrest and wanted to question her further. Daniel just hoped he found Lizzie before Mr Golding did. The accusations against her were ludicrous, but the thought of Lizzie even just having to defend herself in front of a magistrate made him feel sick.

As Daniel watched Edward flicking the pages of his book there was a knock on the door. Quietly his butler entered and looked at Daniel meaningfully.

'Mr Frampton is here to see you, my lord.'

Daniel felt his heart start to pound in his chest. He hoped Frampton had found Lizzie, but just a small part of him worried that the agent would come bearing bad news.

'Show him in.'

Daniel rose from the floor and sat behind his desk, hauling Edward up on to his lap and handing him a small wooden toy soldier to keep him occupied whilst Daniel spoke to the agent.

Frampton entered and Daniel motioned for the tall man to take a seat opposite him.

'Tell me,' he said, his voice hoarse with trepidation.

'I've found her,' Frampton said.

Daniel felt every muscle in his body relax a fraction as the relief washed over him.

'I rode all afternoon to tell you, otherwise it might be too late. Miss Eastway is due to sail for Devon tomorrow morning. She's taking up a position as a governess.'

'Tomorrow morning?' Daniel repeated. It wasn't long enough. He might be able to reach London if he rode all evening and into the night, but he only had to have a small mishap and Lizzie would have already sailed.

Daniel gritted his teeth. It didn't matter. He would follow her all the way to Devon if that was what it took. He wasn't going to lose the woman he loved.

'Westwood,' he called loudly.

The elderly butler stuck his head round the door a few seconds later.

'Tell the grooms to ready a horse. I need to ride to London immediately.'

As usual Westwood didn't blink as he issued the strange order, but just shuffled out of the room to do as Daniel bid.

'I'll write down the ship and location of the dock Miss Eastway is sailing from,' Frampton said, and Daniel handed him a pen and paper so he could do so.

Quickly Daniel pocketed the slip of paper and handed over Frampton's fee, waiting until the agent had left the room before turning to his son.

'I need to go to London to sort things out with that friend I was telling you about,' Daniel said to his son.

'Can I come?'

Daniel shook his head. 'I'll take you to London soon, but I need to ride very, very fast so I can speak to this friend before she sails away to the other end of the country. You'll be safe here with Nanny Jones.'

He wondered if his son would protest, but Edward thought about Daniel's words for a moment, then shrugged and went back to playing with the toy soldier.

Fifteen minutes later Daniel was ready to go. He gave Edward one last kiss and hug before handing him over to his nanny, then he mounted his horse and galloped down the long sweeping drive. He had to get to Lizzie before she left for Devon, he had to tell her he loved her. He couldn't bear to be without her any longer.

Chapter Thirty-One

Lizzie stood on the deck of the ship and looked out over London. Although she had spent only a short couple of weeks in the city she felt sad to be leaving. This was where she had met Daniel and this was where many of her memories of their time together were based. In Devon she would have no reminders of the walks they took together in the park, or the balls they danced at or the afternoon rides on horseback. There would be nothing to remind her of Daniel except her own bruised heart.

She knew she should be focusing on her new life and grateful that she had found a position as governess. Certainly this life would be better than the alternative: a loveless marriage to a man at least two times her age who was rumoured to beat his wives. At least this way she would be free to make her own decisions.

Despite all this Lizzie couldn't help thinking of Daniel and the life they could have had together. She would have been happy spending her days by his side and her nights in his bed. If only she had never lied to him, or at least confessed the truth much earlier, then she would be in his arms instead of about to sail down to Devon to start a whole new life.

'We're just loading the last of the cargo,' the captain of the ship said as he came to join Lizzie at the rail. 'And then we'll be off.'

Lizzie nodded and smiled absently at the captain, too caught up in her own thoughts to make small talk. She knew she was watching for Daniel, that some romantic part of her was hoping that he would gallop up on his horse and sweep her into his arms. He'd declare that he forgave her and realised that he couldn't live without her.

The horizon remained empty.

Lizzie sighed and turned away from the rail, leaning back against the wood and angling her face up into the sun. It was a warm day, nowhere near as warm as it used to be in India, but she could at least enjoy the feel of the sun on her face. Life was about small pleasures now.

'Running away, Miss Eastway?'

Lizzie jumped with fright, her eyes snapping open at the sound of the man's voice. Mr Golding, the Bow Street Runner who had questioned her about the fire at Aunt Mathilda's house, was standing in front of her.

'No,' she said, clutching her hands together to stop them from shaking. 'I have a job as a governess waiting for me down in Devon.'

'And is this as Miss Elizabeth Eastway or Miss Amelia Eastway?'

Ah. So he'd found out about her lie concerning her identity.

'Elizabeth,' she said quietly.

'I'm afraid that will have to wait. I am arresting you for starting the fire on May the twenty-third at Mrs Hunter's London home. I will take you to prison to await further questioning by the magistrate.'

Lizzie felt her knees go weak and she clutched at the rail behind her to steady herself.

'I didn't do anything,' she said, beseeching the man to believe her.

'Funny, most criminals say the same thing.'

'I didn't do anything.'

'You can tell the magistrate your side of the story, but for now you're coming with me.'

He grabbed her none too gently by the upper arm and guided her across the deck and down the gangplank. The captain of the ship watched as she went, but did not intervene.

As her feet touched solid ground Lizzie wondered if she should try to escape. She was all alone, a woman who had no friends to vouch for her, someone who had lied about who she was. Why would the magistrate believe what she had to say?

'Don't even think about trying to escape,' Mr Golding said, hauling her up into a waiting carriage. 'I will shackle you if you give me any trouble.'

Lizzie sank back into the seat of the carriage and tried not to cry. For the past week she had thought her life couldn't get any worse; she'd destroyed her relationship with the man she loved and had been living in a rat-infested boarding house with barely any money for food. Now she wished she could go back, wished she was anywhere but here.

They sat in silence throughout the journey through the city. Lizzie occasionally glanced out the window, wondering whether this was the last time she would see the sights of London, whether she would be waking up tomorrow in a fetid cell.

After well over an hour of travelling the coach drew to a halt and Mr Golding got out. He motioned for Lizzie to follow him, and as soon as her feet touched the ground she was flanked by two other men who grasped her firmly by the upper arms.

Instinctively Lizzie started to struggle. She had nowhere

to run and no one to seek help from, but her survival instincts told her she should try to escape nonetheless.

'No point trying to get away, miss,' Mr Golding said sternly. 'Not a single soul has escaped from custody in the twenty years I've been working for the magistrate.'

Lizzie forced her body to obey and allowed the two guards to guide her towards the imposing building in front of her.

'This is a prison,' Lizzie said, her words coming out in a panicky voice.

'That's right.'

'But I haven't done anything wrong.'

'That's your opinion, miss.'

'You haven't got any proof, any evidence. You can't just throw me in prison.'

'You'll be kept in our custody until you are taken in front of the magistrate to face trial, as is usual in a case like this…' Mr Golding paused as if wondering whether to say anything more. 'And we do have evidence, Miss Eastway, plenty of it. We don't just go around arresting people on a whim.'

Lizzie shuddered as she was led through the imposing archway. A small man dressed in tatty clothes and with almost entirely black teeth unlocked the gate as they passed through, then closed it behind them with a loud clang.

'Elizabeth Eastway,' Mr Golding said. 'Awaiting trial under Magistrate Kirby.'

'Welcome to Trinity Prison,' the man with the awful teeth said with a horrible grin. 'I can take her from here.'

As much as Lizzie hated Mr Golding right now she dreaded more being left to the mercy of this scruffy prison guard. Mr Golding just nodded, turned and walked away, waiting at the gate for it to be reopened and then disappearing out of sight.

Lizzie felt a wave of panic wash over her. She was all alone in prison with no one to help her.

'Follow me, miss,' the guard said. 'Smith's my name, and I'll make sure you're well looked after.'

Lizzie had no choice but to follow Smith through another set of gates and into the prison proper.

'I'm guessing you've never been in prison before,' Smith said cheerily. 'Don't fret, miss, I'll steer you right.'

They walked down a dingy corridor lined with damp bricks, passed through another gate and then reached the cells. Lizzie could smell them before she could see them: a foul mixture of human excrement, unwashed bodies and despair.

'We've got half our cells for people awaiting trial with the magistrate,' Smith said. 'The other half are long-stayers.'

They walked past door after door of thick wood, all with a grille at eye level for the guards to see in. Lizzie didn't dare look into any of the cells, she was frightened enough. If she peered inside, she might lose control completely.

'This is you, miss, got the cell to yourself at the moment.'

Smith led her into a small, dark room. There was no window, no natural light at all, just the dim illumination from the candles that lined the passageway outside.

'Right, let's get down to business,' Smith said. 'We provide water, food you have to pay for. Have you got any money on you?'

Lizzie had just the few small coins she had received in change from when she had booked her passage on the ship. She handed them over.

'Good, I'll make a note of how much you've got, subtract the cost of your meals. By the looks of it you'll have enough to pay for three days' worth of food.'

Lizzie swallowed. She didn't know how long she was

likely to be held before trial, but three days' worth of food didn't sound like very much.

'If I were you, I'd use some of the money to send a message to a friend, tell them you're here and ask them to top up your account.'

Lizzie didn't know who she could ask. The only people she knew were Aunt Mathilda, whose house she was accused of burning down, and Daniel. Daniel had made it very clear what he thought of her the last time they'd been together, but deep down she knew he wouldn't hesitate to help her when she was in need. She would just have to swallow her pride and ask him for help.

'Could I write a note?' Lizzie asked.

'I'll bring you a pen and paper later—it'll come out of your account, of course.'

Lizzie nodded. The rate things were going, she wouldn't even get a meal tonight.

'Don't worry, miss. Magistrate Kirby doesn't keep prisoners hanging around. You'll get to stand trial within the week.'

A whole week in this place. Lizzie didn't know if she could bear it. As Smith left, locking the thick wooden door behind him, Lizzie sank to the floor in despair. If she was found guilty, she would be spending a lot more than a week in prison. She wasn't sure what the penalty for arson was, but she was sure it would be severe, most punishments set by law were.

Lizzie rested her forehead on her knees and started to cry. She didn't know how any of this had happened—surely Mr Golding couldn't have any real evidence that she started the fire, quite simply because she didn't. Lizzie had known Harriet hated her, even after she had found out Lizzie wasn't Amelia, the real target of her hatred, but surely she wouldn't allow her lie to go this far?

With the tears running down her cheeks Lizzie allowed herself to sob loudly. In the past few weeks she had lost the man she loved and she had lost her freedom. She dreaded to think what she might lose next.

Chapter Thirty-Two

Daniel wove his horse through the crowds, all the time conscious that if he didn't make it to the ship before it set sail Lizzie would be out of his reach for even longer. He pushed onwards, passing ship after ship moored at the dock, hardly taking in the frenzied activity as the crews loaded and unloaded whole hulls of cargo.

He pulled his horse up in front of the *Lady of the Sea* and quickly dismounted, flipping a coin to a passing young lad to hold the reins for him until he returned. Quickly he hurried up the gangplank and grabbed the first man he saw.

'You've got a passenger, a lady, where is she?'

The man looked surprised and shook his head. 'Best you speak to the captain.'

He pointed the captain out and Daniel strode over to him.

'I'm looking for a passenger of yours, a Miss Eastway,' Daniel said, wasting no time.

The captain looked him up and down, taking in his finely tailored, but currently dishevelled, clothes.

'Who are you?'

'The Earl of Burwell.'

The captain stood a little straighter and swallowed nervously.

'Miss Eastway was due to be sailing with us,' he said in a tone that made Daniel immediately worried. 'She even boarded the ship about an hour ago. Unfortunately a man came looking for her, had a warrant for her arrest.'

Daniel closed his eyes. He'd known they hadn't seen the last of Mr Golding.

'Where did he take her?'

The captain shrugged apologetically. 'I didn't ask.'

Daniel thought for a minute, trying to work out what patch of London Mr Golding must cover and therefore which magistrate he needed to find.

'Thank you,' he said as he dashed from the ship, grabbed his horse and retraced his route along the dock.

Three hours later Daniel was in the foulest mood he had ever experienced. He'd finally found Magistrate Kirby, and the pompous fat man had refused to listen to reason. Daniel had suggested Lizzie be released to his custody until the trial. The magistrate had refused. Daniel had suggested the magistrate drop the case and get on with dealing with real criminals. The magistrate had refused. Daniel had suggested the magistrate should be stripped of his position and thrown into prison himself for letting such a ridiculous case come to court. The magistrate had thrown him out.

Now Daniel was standing in the prison courtyard talking to a much more reasonable man, a guard called Smith. At least he knew how to accept a bribe.

'She's settling in fine, my lord,' Smith said. 'Although she doesn't have much money for food or the like.'

Daniel brought out a few more silver coins and flipped them to Smith.

'See she gets everything she needs.'

'Do you want to see her?'

Daniel nodded. As much as he hated the idea of seeing Lizzie in this awful place, he knew her reality of being locked up here was so much worse. He wanted to comfort her, hold her in his arms and tell her everything was all right.

'Follow me.'

Daniel followed the guard through a few sturdy gates, down a dank corridor and past at least twenty identical cells before they stopped in front of a locked door.

'I can give you ten minutes, no more,' Smith said.

Daniel didn't argue. As much as he wanted to stay and comfort Lizzie, he really needed to be out in the world, finding out exactly what 'evidence' Golding thought he had and how he could quash it in court.

Smith opened the door and Daniel stepped into the cell. It was so dark inside at first he thought it was empty, but then he saw the figure curled up in the corner and he realised it was Lizzie.

Two eyes looked at him warily.

'Daniel?' Lizzie's voice quavered as if she couldn't quite believe it was him.

Daniel stepped towards her, but before he could reach her Lizzie was on her feet and throwing herself into his arms.

'It's all right, you're safe,' Daniel murmured into her hair as she clung to him and sobbed.

'I didn't know if you would come,' Lizzie managed to gasp in between the tears.

'Of course I would.'

'But it's only been an hour since I sent the letter.'

Daniel frowned. 'What letter?'

'The letter telling you I was in here.'

'I never got your letter. I came looking for you. The captain of the *Lady of the Sea* told me you'd been arrested.'

He could see the spark of hope flare in her eyes, but then she looked at him warily. The last time they had been together he'd rejected her. He could tell a small part of Lizzie dared to hope his presence here meant everything was forgiven, that he had realised he couldn't live without her, but she wasn't about to risk her heart again so readily. This time Daniel would have to speak first.

'I rode all night,' he said.

Daniel knew he was dishevelled, his hair and his clothes were a mess and he had thick stubble covering his chin.

'I've been searching for you ever since that night in the coaching inn,' Daniel said.

Lizzie pulled back and looked up at him. Although the more pressing problem was Lizzie's incarceration, Daniel had to make her see that he loved her. Now it mattered more than ever. He wanted her to know that he would fight for her freedom, that he loved her more than life itself.

'I had to get away,' Lizzie said. 'After...' She swallowed and changed tack. 'I needed to get away.'

'I was a fool, a complete and utter fool.' Daniel took another step towards her and captured her hand in his own. 'I should have told you I loved you then. I should have shouted it from the rooftops and sung it in the streets.'

Daniel hated that he had to do this with Lizzie locked in prison, but he felt as though he had waited long enough to tell her he loved her. He didn't want her going a single moment longer thinking he was angry with her, or that he didn't want to spend his life with her.

'I was angry and I felt betrayed. I was too caught up in the past to see you never meant to hurt me. To see that you weren't like Annabelle.'

Lizzie's eyes flared with hope and Daniel wanted to gather her in his arms and kiss her until the end of time, but he knew their time together was limited, so instead he pressed on.

'I know you never meant to hurt me, that the lie just

spun out of control, but at the time I couldn't get past the fact that you'd lied to me just as Annabelle had, to see that it was nothing alike. Yours was a simple mistake that got out of hand. It was never malicious.'

'It was never malicious,' Lizzie repeated.

'I'm sorry I didn't see all this sooner,' Daniel said, stepping closer and putting an arm around her waist. 'I was blind and stupid and I should never have let you go.'

If he hadn't let her go, she probably wouldn't be locked up now. He would have been able to protect her from Golding. If she was safely tucked away at his estate, the odious man would never have got to her. Daniel knew he would carry that guilt for the rest of his life, but right now he had to focus on securing Lizzie's freedom.

'I'm sorry I lied to you,' Lizzie said, allowing Daniel to pull her in closer so their bodies were almost touching.

'I understand now. You did it because someone you loved asked you to.'

'I thought it would be a harmless little deception, that I would be back to being plain old Lizzie Eastway before I met anyone.'

'Not old and certainly not plain,' Daniel said, making Lizzie smile despite their surroundings.

'Then when I did meet you I kept putting off telling you who I really was. I tried a few times, but my heart wasn't in it, I was too afraid of losing you.'

Daniel grimaced. 'You thought I only wanted you for your dowry.'

Lizzie nodded. 'Well, Amelia's dowry. Mine is non-existent.'

'I have to admit that was the reason I started to pursue you, but it wasn't long before I realised the woman I planned to marry for financial reasons was the woman who drove me half-mad with desire.'

'Only half-mad?'

Daniel grinned. 'We can work on that as soon as I get you home.'

Lizzie's face fell as she remembered where they were and why she was locked away.

'I'm scared, Daniel.'

'Of course you are.' He placed two fingers under her chin and tilted her head backwards so she was looking up into his eyes. 'Lizzie, I promise you that I'm going to get you out of here. I won't rest until you're back home with me.'

For a moment she just looked at him, then she nodded. Daniel felt the weight of the responsibility as she placed her trust in him.

'I wish I was home with you now,' Lizzie said and Daniel saw the tears starting to fall down her cheeks again.

'I wish that, too.'

He held her in silence for a minute or two, wrapping his arms around her and pressing her close to his body. He wished he could swap places with her, go through this ordeal for her, but he knew he couldn't. The best he could do was quash whatever evidence Golding thought he had against Lizzie.

Suddenly Lizzie pulled away.

'Daniel,' she said seriously, 'you do realise if we are together you won't have the money to pay Annabelle.'

Daniel felt his heart constrict as he realised how much she loved him. Even now, when her future was uncertain at best, she was still thinking of him and his son.

'I got some good advice on that front,' he said, pulling her close again .

'What happened?'

'A very wise woman told me love could conquer anything and it got me thinking. I summoned a lawyer and paid a visit to the mother of my son, and she soon came round to my way of thinking.'

Even in the darkness Daniel could see Lizzie's eyes flare with hope.

'Edward is now living with me and he knows I am his father.'

Lizzie sprang forward and started smothering Daniel's face with kisses. He loved how selfless she was. Even whilst her life was so grim she was pleased he had worked things out with his son.

'And Annabelle?' she asked after a few minutes.

'It was all very civil with the lawyer present. Of course, as Edward's father I have more parental rights anyway, but the lawyer drew up a contract, which means Annabelle no longer has any hold over me.' Daniel shrugged and broke into a smile. 'I told her she could visit Edward sometimes and I'm going to help her find lodgings nearby. I think it's important that Edward still sees her from time to time.'

'Is Edward coping without his mother?' Lizzie asked.

'He's blossoming. It'll take time, of course, but we've got years to show him we love him.'

'You mean…'

Slowly he looked into her eyes and brought her hand to his lips, placing a kiss on her knuckles. This wasn't how he ever imagined himself proposing, but he wanted Lizzie to realise he was there for her. He wanted her to know he would fight until the bitter end for her freedom, all because he loved her.

'Lizzie, will you make me a very happy man and be my wife?'

'Are you sure, even after all of this?'

'I'm sure.'

He kissed her, gently and reverently, trying to make her see that none of this mattered. He didn't care that she'd lied to him about who she was and he didn't care that she was accused of arson, all he cared about was securing her freedom and spending the rest of his life showing her how much he loved her.

'You still haven't answered me,' he said.

'Yes.'

Daniel allowed himself a moment of pure happiness, then he hardened his resolve as he focused on the task ahead of him.

'One minute.' Smith's voice came through the door.

'Be strong, Lizzie,' Daniel said, grasping her hand tightly. 'I'll get you out of here, I promise.'

'It's Harriet,' Lizzie said. 'I'm sure she's the one who accused me. She hates my uncle for losing all of her family's money. This is her revenge.'

Daniel nodded, knowing he would find Harriet and drag her to court if that was what it took.

'Before you know it we'll be back home and I'll never let you from my sight again.

The heavy door swung open and Daniel pulled Lizzie towards him for one last kiss. As he walked out the door he saw her sink to the floor and he seriously contemplated sweeping back into the cell, gathering her in his arms and fighting his way out, but he knew that wasn't the way to help her. He needed to prove the accusations were false and he couldn't do that if he was locked up, too.

Chapter Thirty-Three

Lizzie tried to stand up straight and hold her head high, but it was difficult when you were dressed in clothes covered in grime and hadn't had a wash for days. The jeering crowds didn't help much, either.

As Mr Golding led her into the courtroom Lizzie desperately looked around for Daniel. She knew he would have been working tirelessly to try to secure her freedom, but part of her was panicking he might not have had enough time. Rather than the week Smith had predicted, Lizzie had been held in the prison for only two days before being summoned to court.

Mr Golding pushed her to a bench at the front of the court, where she sat, her shackled hands resting in her lap, beside the other people standing trial.

Every few minutes she looked around the room, hoping for a glimpse of the man she loved. Part of her still couldn't believe they were actually engaged and once or twice she had wondered if Daniel visiting her in her cell had been a dream, but then she had remembered how he'd held her and how he'd kissed her and she knew he'd been there.

The room fell quiet as the magistrate entered and Lizzie swallowed nervously. He was an imposing man with a shock of grey hair and a huge double chin that wobbled every time he moved. He looked down at the people sitting on the bench in shackles with disdain and Lizzie knew immediately he was likely to be a harsh judge.

Forty minutes later and Lizzie was physically trembling. Three of her fellow shackled prisoners had been led away, all openly sobbing. Two were going to be transported for stealing, one had received a harsh prison sentence for pickpocketing and all this had been decided on within forty minutes.

Before her incarceration Lizzie hadn't thought much about the law and the punishments meted out to the accused. In India every now and then she had witnessed a scaffold being erected, but her uncle had always ushered them off in the other direction, eager to shield his precious Amelia from anything unsavoury.

Now she wished she knew if these sham trials were the norm. The accused were barely allowed a defence. The evidence would be set out before the magistrate, the magistrate would ask if anyone had anything to say to defend the criminal and so far no one had spoken up, then he would proclaim their guilt and sentence them harshly.

'Elizabeth Eastway,' the magistrate called.

Lizzie felt her knees wobble as she was hauled to her feet.

'You are accused of arson. Burning down one Mrs Hunter's house. The penalty if you should be found guilty is death.'

Lizzie felt her head start to spin. Surely this wasn't real. She felt as though she should wake up from a nightmare any moment.

'Mr Golding, please present your evidence.'

Mr Golding stepped forward, handing a piece of paper to the magistrate. The magistrate dipped his head and read slowly.

'I have here a signed statement from one Miss Harriet Hunter swearing that she saw you light the fire that destroyed her mother's house.'

Lizzie shook her head. She'd known Harriet didn't like her, but she never thought she would go to these lengths to hurt her.

Mr Golding handed the magistrate another piece of paper.

'I have another signed statement from a housemaid, Rosie Thomas, stating that she saw you with a candle the night in question.'

Hardly a crime, to be carrying a candle on a dark night, but Lizzie knew it just helped the magistrate seal her fate.

'Does anyone have anything to say to defend Miss Eastway?' the magistrate asked.

Silence. Lizzie looked around frantically. If Daniel didn't speak up now, she was going to die. She scanned the faces in the crowd, desperately pleading with someone to say something, to defend her.

Nothing. Just silence. The magistrate looked down at her severely.

'I'm innocent,' Lizzie said, finding her voice. 'All you have is the word of a spiteful young girl against mine. If you convict me on the lies of one person, you are making a mockery of the justice system.'

The magistrate rose to his feet, his face turning an unhealthy purple colour with rage.

'You may not speak,' he bellowed.

'And why not?' Lizzie asked, trying to keep the tremor from her voice. 'You are about to sentence me for a crime I did not commit. Why may I not defend myself?'

The magistrate spluttered. He was clearly not used to having educated people in his court and certainly not accustomed to being spoken back to.

'I will hold you in contempt of court,' he shouted.

'And what will you do?' Lizzie asked. 'Hang me twice?'

The silence that followed stretched out for what seemed like eternity and was only broken when the doors to the courtroom burst open.

'What now?' the magistrate yelled, turning to face the newcomers.

Daniel strode down the steps, dragging a crying Harriet behind him.

'Get out of my court,' the magistrate ordered.

'I am the Earl of Burwell and if any of you lay a hand upon me I will see to it you are never employed again,' Daniel said as a couple of guards moved towards him.

'I don't care who you are. Here I am in charge.'

Daniel turned to the magistrate with an icy stare and Lizzie felt her heart pound in her chest. He had come back for her. He was here to rescue her, remove her from this awful nightmare and make sure nothing like this ever happened again. She felt all the courage she had summoned to speak up for herself blossom under his gaze and she knew they would be leaving the courtroom together.

'Your case rests on the testimony of Harriet Hunter,' Daniel said, not wasting any time. 'Well, here she is, all ready to tell you she lied.'

None too gently he shoved Harriet forward towards the magistrate.

'This is not how things are done,' the magistrate bellowed. 'Get out of my court.'

'Are you saying you will not listen to evidence that proves this woman's innocence?' Daniel asked calmly. 'That sounds pretty illegal to me. I was sure your remit was to weigh the evidence from *both* sides.'

The magistrate said nothing, so Daniel stepped forward and prodded Harriet.

'Tell the court your name.'

'Harriet Hunter,' Harriet said miserably.

Lizzie wondered what Daniel had threatened Harriet with to get her here.

'And tell the court about your awful lie.'

Harriet looked up at the magistrate and glanced sideways at Lizzie, then she crumbled.

'I'm sorry,' she said. 'I lied. Lizzie didn't start the fire. It was an accident, a terrible accident.'

The magistrate stared for a second, then, finding a new target for his anger, rose to his full height.

'You mean to tell me you lied in a sworn statement?'

Harriet nodded morosely, refusing to meet anyone's eye.

'You have committed an awful—'

'Oh, do shut up.' Daniel cut the magistrate off. 'Now let me tell you what is going to happen.'

Lizzie watched as the man she loved went about securing her freedom. Since her parents had died she had never really had anyone fight for her, but now she had Daniel. She knew he would do anything to keep her safe and that knowledge made her feel like a queen.

'You are going to release my fiancée, the future Countess of Burwell, immediately, and you are going to apologise for treating her quite so abominably. Then I am going to leave with Miss Eastway and Miss Hunter and I will spend the next few days considering who to tell about your dubious views on the law. If I were you, I wouldn't expect to be a magistrate for much longer.'

The magistrate sank back down in his chair, the fight leaving him, and motioned for one of the guards to unlock Lizzie's shackles. As soon as she was free she ran to Daniel and threw herself into his arms.

'Let's get out of here before he regains his composure,' Daniel whispered.

Lizzie felt him slip an arm around her waist protectively and hustle her outside and up into a waiting carriage. He directed Harriet to another carriage before climbing up and sitting beside Lizzie.

Lizzie felt her body go weak and she collapsed into Daniel.

'You're safe now,' he whispered as he gathered her into his arms and pulled her on to his lap. 'I'm never going to let you go again.'

'I thought you weren't going to make it,' Lizzie said as she gripped Daniel's hand.

Daniel grimaced. 'I thought I would have more time, but Kirby seemed in a hurry to sentence you.'

'How did you persuade Harriet to come?'

'I didn't. I just told her mother what she had done. After that Harriet didn't have a choice. Mrs Hunter does care for you rather a lot, you know.'

Lizzie nodded. Aunt Mathilda was a kind woman who had forgiven Lizzie's lies immediately. Of course she wouldn't let Harriet's malice send her to the gallows.

'I care for you rather a lot, too.'

Lizzie smiled as Daniel bent down and covered her lips with his own. He kissed her deeply, as if trying to tell her he would never let her go again.

'In fact, I love you.'

Lizzie felt all the worry and upset from the past few days wash away with his words. He loved her. The man she loved, loved her back.

'I love you, too.'

'Now let's get you home.'

Epilogue

Lizzie placed her hands over her eyes and started counting slowly. Behind her she heard scuffling and laughing as Daniel and Edward dashed out of the room.

'Six, seven, eight...'

Lizzie couldn't believe how lucky she was. Just a few months ago she had been plain Lizzie Eastway, a young woman with no self-confidence and no hopes of love. Now she was Lizzie Blackburn, Countess of Burwell, a wife, a lover and, tentatively, a mother to Edward, too.

'Twenty, twenty-one, twenty-two...'

In all the long years she had lived under her uncle's roof Lizzie had never even dared to dream her life might turn out like this. She was happy. Her days were filled with love and laughter and fun, and her nights were filled with passion.

'Thirty-five, thirty-six, thirty-seven...'

Lizzie's heart still pounded in her chest when she caught Daniel looking at her with his dazzling blue eyes and desire written all over his face. She loved it when he stole a kiss from her when they were out and about, loved the fact that he still couldn't keep his hands off her.

'Fifty, fifty-one, fifty-two...'

Her time spent in prison now seemed like a bad dream. All the awful memories had been replaced by moments of love and laughter with her new little family. Of course, there had been gossip. Daniel was the only earl with a wife who had nearly been sent to the gallows, but as with everything the gossip settled down with time.

'Fifty-nine, sixty, sixty-one…'

They'd been lucky with the wedding, too. Daniel had used his connections and Lizzie had found herself walking down the aisle in a private ceremony just two weeks after Daniel had proposed. Her only regret was her cousin Amelia hadn't been there for the wedding. The agent Daniel had tasked with finding her hadn't managed to track her down in time, but this afternoon Amelia was coming to visit. In her last letter she had hinted that she had some news of her own, but wouldn't tell Lizzie what it was. Knowing Amelia, Lizzie guessed that she'd probably impulsively joined the circus or become an opera singer. Nevertheless, Lizzie couldn't wait to see her cousin and find out where she'd been all this time.

'Sixty-five, sixty-six, sixty-seven…'

Lizzie sometimes thought of the life she could have had if Daniel hadn't come after her. She would be a governess in Devon, not much more than a servant, with no one to hold her close at night, no one to wake her with a morning kiss. Or the life she could be living as Colonel Rocher's wife, bruised and battered, her spirit beaten out of her. Or, even worse, she could be awaiting execution for a crime she hadn't committed. All her life Lizzie had assumed she would never experience true love and here she was, more infatuated with her husband every single day.

'Seventy-nine, eighty, eighty-one…'

Of course, there had also been a bit of a scandal when Lizzie's true identity had been revealed and the *ton* had realised she was not the heiress she had presented herself to be. In truth, Daniel had shielded her from the worst of the gossip, both about her time in prison and her lies about her identity, and Lizzie hadn't really cared anyway. She was married to the man she loved and a positive side to the whole situation was that the gossips were talking about her and Daniel rather than little Edward. Her notoriety was protecting him from being the centre of attention.

'Eighty-five, eighty-six, eighty-seven…'

Lizzie stroked her stomach through her dress and wondered if she would be allowed just one more miracle. Daniel was a wonderful father to Edward and she knew he wanted more children, and with the amount of time they spent in the bedroom Lizzie knew if she were lucky it would happen soon. She wanted to give Daniel another child, a little brother or sister for Edward, and although it was far too early to tell, Lizzie had a good feeling about this month. Her monthly courses were just a few days late, but maybe, just maybe, this was the start of a whole new adventure with her little family.

'Ninety-eight, ninety-nine, one hundred. Ready or not, here I come.'

Lizzie spun around and walked out of the room. With Edward being just three years old he wasn't all that good at hide-and-seek, but on rainy mornings like this one he could play for hours, hiding in rather obvious places and squealing with delight as either Daniel or Lizzie found him.

Lizzie walked slowly through the hallway, looking for telltale feet sticking out from under pieces of furniture or a small giggle as Edward couldn't contain his excitement. She made her way into the dining room and stopped just through the doorway.

'I wonder if anyone is hiding in here?' she mused loudly.

She started circling the table, moving round to where a pair of legs were sticking out at the other end.

Carefully she bent down and grabbed both legs by the ankle.

'Oof,' Daniel said. 'You found me. You're far too good at this game.'

He half slid out, flipped over so he was lying on his back, then instead of standing up he looped an arm around Lizzie's waist and pulled her down on top of him.

'We're meant to be searching for our son,' Lizzie said as he kissed the tip of her nose.

'Stop wriggling, woman.' Daniel held her more firmly against him and after a few seconds Lizzie stopped trying to get up.

'He'll enjoy the suspense and thinking he's really foxed you this time.'

Lizzie glanced over her shoulder. Anyone could walk in the room and find them on the floor, half underneath the table and giggling like naughty children.

Daniel waited until she turned her head back towards him, then kissed her quickly on the lips. Lizzie felt her body melting into Daniel's and all her token resistance faded away as he ran his hands firmly down the length of her back and cupped her bottom before giving it a squeeze.

'Maybe we'll have time to disappear to the bedroom before your cousin arrives once Edward gets tired of hide-and-seek,' Daniel whispered, his breath tickling Lizzie's ear.

Lizzie couldn't help but smile. 'You think Edward is ever going to get bored of that game?'

Before Daniel could protest Lizzie pushed herself upwards and stood, looking down at her husband.

'Help an old man off the ground.'

'You shouldn't hide in places you can't get out of,' Lizzie said with a grin, repeating Daniel's words to Edward from an hour previously when the boy had found himself stuck in the fireplace.

Daniel heaved himself off the floor with an exaggerated groan, then darted forward and swept Lizzie up into his arms with ease. Lizzie liked the feel of Daniel holding her, knowing that she was completely safe and loved.

'Right, we've got a scallywag to find,' Daniel announced, walking out of the dining room still carrying Lizzie.

'Put me down,' Lizzie said with a laugh, knowing Daniel would do nothing of the sort.

'No. Now, where can that son of ours be?'

'I think he's in the library,' Lizzie said loudly.

They heard a giggle coming from Daniel's study. Quietly Daniel crept inside, still carrying Lizzie in his arms. Without making a sound he set Lizzie down on the carpet and together they approached the small pair of legs sticking out from under Daniel's desk.

Lizzie felt overcome with love for her perfect little family. She loved her husband and she loved Edward, the boy she was beginning to think of as her son.

'Got you,' Daniel said as he grabbed his son's legs.

Edward giggled and wriggled out from under the desk. Immediately he threw himself into Daniel's arms and Lizzie felt her heart swell. In the past few weeks she had watched as Edward started to trust his father more and more. Soon it would be as if they'd never spent the first few years of his life apart.

'Again, again,' Edward shouted as he dashed off out of the room.

Daniel turned to Lizzie and caught her hand before she could leave the room to hide.

'I love that little boy,' he said quietly, 'and I love you.'

* * * * *

HEIRESS ON
THE RUN

For Nic, for all those marathon
make-believe sessions.

One day I'll forgive you for Jasmine's head.

And for Luke and Jack, you make all my
dreams come true.

Chapter One

Amelia ran through the trees, ignoring the branches that whipped at her face and the brambles that caught at her skirts. She was exhausted, her lungs felt as though they were on fire and the muscles in her legs protested with every stride, but still she kept running. Risking a glance over her shoulder, Amelia stumbled, her ankle twisting dangerously to one side, but she caught herself and managed to stay on her feet.

A loud clap of thunder sounded overhead and seconds later the sky lit up with a fork of brilliant white lightning. Amelia felt exposed in the bright light, despite the camouflage of the trees, and was glad when the world returned to darkness again. Now the rain started in earnest, big droplets of water that pounded against Amelia's skin and soaked her within minutes. Her dress hung heavily against her, rubbing like sandpaper with every movement, and for once she wished she was wearing something more practical, less pretty, something that might keep her a little warm in this awful climate.

Pausing for a moment to catch her breath, Amelia listened carefully. She'd been walking over these God-forsaken Downs for the past two days, unsure where to go, where would be safe and offer her sanctuary. It had been bad enough when it was just cold and windy, but now, with the storm raging overhead, Amelia wondered whether she might die out here on these hills.

At least the village was far behind her now, the village that she had hoped might give her shelter for the cold night. That had been a bad idea. The first person that had caught a glimpse of her bloodstained dress and windswept hair had backed away, calling for her to keep her distance, and alerting the entire population to her arrival. She'd fled quickly, sparing a glance for the warm glow coming from the roadside inn, and continued her dash over the sodden hills.

Amelia was convinced the villagers would have sent people to follow her. Her face was probably on posters by now, her crime known far beyond the seaside resort of Brighton where it had been committed. She let out a small sob, wondering where everything had gone so wrong, and allowed herself a moment of self-pity. This was not how her life was supposed to be. Four days ago she'd had everything to look forward to: a new life in England, a reunion with the man she loved and a Season in London, whirling through ballrooms and sparkling in pretty new dresses. She had imagined being complimented and courted, not condemned and chased.

Straightening up, Amelia noticed a low wall on her left and a little further on a set of wrought-iron gates, easy to miss as they were so overgrown with curls of ivy and creepers. It only took her a second to decide what to do. Her feet were hurting, her entire body shivering and she hadn't slept for two days. The gates looked as though they belonged to an abandoned estate. If she was lucky there might be a barn or outbuilding still standing, somewhere to provide her shelter from the elements and to rest.

Cautiously she pushed open the gates and slipped through. As Amelia walked up the driveway a sense of unease began to uncurl inside her. The place had a ghostly feel to it and, if she wasn't so desperate to stop for the night, she might have turned back to look for alternative shelter.

The house was magnificent, in a dark and Gothic sort of way. Gargoyles loomed from precipices and the windows all tapered to elegant arched points. Statues and carvings decorated the spaces around the windows and doors, and towards the back of the house Amelia could see two imposing towers climbing up into the sky.

The estate was abandoned, Amelia could see that straight away. The house had an empty, disused feel about it even from this distance and the east side was blackened by fire damage. She wondered how long ago it had been abandoned and whether there might still be a soft bed to rest on inside.

Cautiously Amelia approached the front door and pushed it open, surprised to find it swung inwards without a creak or protest, revealing an empty hallway.

'Hello?' she called out before stepping over the threshold. 'Is anyone here?'

She waited for a second and then, hearing only the howling of the wind outside, she chided herself for the unease that prevented her from pushing the door closed behind her.

After another minute of silence she shut the door and stepped further into the hall. She had to wait for a moment until her vision had adjusted to the darkness before she could see anything properly. Summoning her courage, she walked down the hall, selected a door and pushed it open.

Amelia could see the room beyond must have once been a drawing room, or maybe a sitting room. A com-

fortable-looking armchair tempted her to take a step inside and once she was in the room she could make out the
other contents. Most of the furniture had been covered
over with white sheets, designed to keep the thick dust at
bay, and on the floor was a heavy, luxurious rug covering the floorboards.

Her eyes skimmed over the details of the room and
came to rest on the large fireplace set into one of the walls.
A spark of hope flared inside her as she saw the basket of
wood sitting beside it and visions of a roaring fire, warming her frozen limbs and drying her sopping toes, sprang
into her mind. She almost cried with relief when she saw
the tinderbox sitting on top of the mantelpiece. Finally her
luck was beginning to change.

The practicalities of starting a fire were much more difficult than Amelia had first envisioned. She'd seen fires
laid before—even in India they had needed fires in the
kitchen and sometimes in monsoon season a fire would
be lit to help dry out the clothes—but she'd never actually
taken much notice of what the servants were doing. Hesitantly she piled some wood in the grate, ensuring there
were some small pieces at the top, and then she set to work
on the tinder box.

Fifteen minutes later and she was just about ready to
throw the infuriating little box across the room. Her fingers
were aching from trying to strike up a spark into the tinder
and she had begun to shiver almost uncontrollably, which
didn't help with the delicate manoeuvres needed. With a
growl of frustration she struck the steel against the flint
one last time and almost cried with relief as a few sparks
flew out and ignited the tinder. Carefully she fanned the
flames, blowing softly, then touched the sulphur match
to ignite it, before lighting the taper. With delicate move-

ments Amelia knelt down in front of the fireplace and set about coaxing the wood to begin burning, feeling an unparalleled sense of satisfaction as slowly the wood began to blacken and the flames danced brightly in the grate.

Amelia almost flopped to the floor in exhaustion. The last few days had taken their toll on her not only physically but emotionally, and all she wanted to do was curl up and sleep, but she knew she would be at risk of a fever if she didn't get herself out of her wet clothes. With tired fingers she fumbled at the fastenings of her dress, wriggling and stretching to undo the buttons at the back. Finally she felt the heavy material drop to the floor and she was left standing in her long chemise and petticoat, with her mud-covered stockings on her legs.

She let out a gasp of horror as she looked down. The blood that had stained her dress had soaked all the way through to her undergarments and there were hideous pink patches covering her chemise and petticoats. Amelia felt momentarily sick and had to reach out to the mantelpiece to steady herself. For a few seconds she was back in Captain McNair's study, brandishing the letter opener that had slipped so easily into his soft flesh. Amelia heard a sob escape her lips at the thought of what she'd done, at the image of his bright red blood seeping through his shirt and the knowledge that she had committed the ultimate sin. For two days she had been running, desperate to get away from that cursed room, and she hadn't stopped long enough to allow herself to think. Until now. Here, with the heat of the fire finally warming her skin, Amelia knew her life would never be the same again.

Edward woke with a start. He had always been a light sleeper and any noise, even an animal call from half a mile away, was enough to rouse him from his dreams. For a moment he lay still, not moving a single muscle, but it only took a few seconds for him to be sure: there was someone in the house. He could hear them moving around downstairs, soft footsteps and the swish of material. Within seconds he was on his feet and felt a low growl issuing from his throat at the thought of an interloper in his domain. The cool night air hit his body, making him shiver, and a surge of irritation welled up inside him.

Swiftly he strode across the room, threw on a dressing gown and grabbed the poker from the fireplace in the place of a more conventional weapon. Despite his years of living alone Edward was confident of his ability to defeat any intruder even if they were armed. He wasn't a violent person and much preferred his books and his sketches, but at just over six foot tall he had a commanding presence.

Edward moved quietly, hoping to surprise the intruder before they had a chance to find a weapon of their own, making his way down the main staircase and pausing outside the sitting room.

The sight that met his eyes as he pushed open the door was not what he expected at all. Standing in front of the fire was a young woman in the process of undressing. Edward swallowed. She had already shed her dress and petticoat and was now clad in just her chemise and stockings. Both items of clothing were soaked with rainwater and the chemise clung to her body in a scandalous fashion, revealing much more than it was designed to.

As he watched her chemise slipped from one shoulder, revealing the creamy white skin beneath. The young woman then bent down and started to unroll her stockings, sighing with pleasure as she peeled the wet material from her legs.

Edward knew he had already been watching for far too long to be considered a gentleman, but later he would tell himself it was the shock of finding a half-naked woman in his sitting room. Long-forgotten emotions were beginning to stir in his body and as he watched the mystery woman arch her back and let her head drop backwards Edward felt a surge of desire. He wanted to scoop her into his arms, peel the remainder of her wet clothes from her body and lay her down in front of the fire.

Immediately Edward felt guilty for the thoughts. He loved his wife, missed her every day, but it was a long time since he'd had any human contact.

Just as he made to clear his throat he paused and frowned. He hadn't taken much notice of the state of the woman's clothes before, more surprised at her degree of undress than what she was actually wearing, but he now noticed the pink stains on her chemise and on the discarded dress that was draped over a chair. If he wasn't very much mistaken she was covered in blood and it didn't look as though it was her own.

Edward cleared his throat. The young woman turned round, her eyes widened and she screamed. It was an ear-piercing sound that bore right through Edward's skull and irritated him immensely.

'Will you be *quiet*?' he bellowed.

Immediately the young woman clamped her lips together. She started to back away from him, fear etched on her face, and Edward sighed. He wished he was back upstairs in bed instead of dealing with this melodrama.

He wanted to order this young woman out of his house, push her and her problems out of the door and forget she had ever been there.

'What are you doing here?' he asked, grimacing as the words came out more as a growl than a question.

'Please don't hurt me,' she stuttered.

'I'm not going to hurt you,' he said, in the friendliest

voice he could muster. He tried to smile, but the baring of his teeth just seemed to make her cower away more and whimper with terror.

Abruptly he pressed his lips together and took a couple of short steps across the room. He needed this young woman to be conscious and coherent if he was to have any chance of getting his solitude back as soon as possible. As he approached she backed away and Edward saw her sway slightly on her feet. For a terrible moment he thought she might faint, leaving him to deal with an even bigger problem, but at the last moment she seemed to rally.

'What are you doing here?' Edward repeated, more softly this time. He tried to remember how he'd interacted with people in the days when he'd run a successful and thriving estate and slowly opened his hands, palms outwards to show he wasn't a threat, and made eye contact with the shivering young woman.

As he looked into her eyes he saw her relax just a little and Edward felt a spark of curiosity about the woman standing in front of him. Now he was closer he could see what a state she was in—not only was her chemise covered in blood, but her entire body was caked in mud and grime. Her legs had a myriad of scratches and bruises on them and he had to wonder what trouble she was running from.

'I needed a place to rest for the night, somewhere to shelter from the storm,' she said quietly.

Instinctively Edward knew there was so much more to it than that. A well-bred young lady did not wander the hills of Sussex all by herself covered in blood and soaked to the bone. He opened his mouth to press her further and then thought better of it. Whatever drama this young woman was mixed up in, whatever it was she was running from, he didn't want to know. He wanted his house back to himself and he wanted her gone.

'I thought the house was empty,' she continued after a few seconds. As she spoke her teeth chattered together and gave her voice a juddering quality.

'It just looks empty,' he said a little gruffly. 'You should go home.'

Quickly her frightened eyes darted to meet his and he saw a flash of desperation in them.

'I can't go home.'

'Then a friend, a family member. There will be someone to take you in.'

His heart sank as she shook her head. Part of him was whispering she wasn't his problem, to usher her out into the night and forget she'd ever even been here.

'You could stay at the inn in the village.'

The look of panic that crossed her face momentarily piqued his interest, but he refused to be drawn in and quickly moved on.

'No,' she said firmly.

'What's your name?' he asked.

'Amelia.'

'Well, Amelia, you can't stay here.' He tried to say the words softly, but they came out as a harsh bark, almost an order. He watched as she recoiled from him as though she'd been slapped and felt a flash of guilt at the despair that permeated every inch of her body.

Silence followed as Edward waited for her response. As the seconds ticked by he could see her entire body shaking. The blood had drained from her face and suddenly Edward realised her eyes had become unfocused. If he wasn't much mistaken his intruder was close to collapsing.

With quick, purposeful strides Edward crossed the space between them, took hold of Amelia's shoulders and lowered her into a chair. He told himself he didn't want to have to deal with a head injury on top of everything

else, but Edward knew his humanity was buried somewhere inside him and chose moments like this to rear up
and make him act like a decent person. As he touched the
bare skin of her arms he was surprised at just how cold
they were. He was no medical man, but Edward could see
if Amelia didn't get warm and dry soon she would be in
real danger of catching a chill, or worse. He remembered
the time he and his late wife had got caught out in a storm
on the edge of the estate—by the time they reached the
house both were drenched to the bone, but whereas Edward had shaken the cold off Jane had been lain up with
a fever for a week.

'You can't stay here,' Edward repeated quietly, almost
to himself. In reality he knew if he sent Amelia back out
into the storm in this state then she probably would die.

With a growl of frustration Edward hurled a cushion
from the sofa towards the fire. It smacked into the mantelpiece with a loud thud before falling to the floor. He didn't
want to be put in this position, held hostage by his own
conscience. He wanted to return to bed in a house only he
inhabited and not feel guilty about it.

Amelia looked at him with her large, dark eyes and
Edward knew there was nothing else to be done.

'One night,' he said eventually. 'You can stay for one
night. But you leave first thing in the morning.'

The relief on Amelia's face should have pleased him,
years ago it would have. Edward could remember being
the type of person that cared about others, that would go
out of his way to help someone in distress, but that part of
him seemed to have withered and died along with so many
other characteristics. Once he had been kind and caring,
but now all he could think about was how he didn't want
this young woman in his house.

'What's your name?' Amelia asked, her voice not much more than a hoarse whisper.

'Edward. Sir Edward Gray.'

'Thank you, Edward.'

Next to him Amelia shuddered violently and Edward made a conscious effort to shift his full attention to her, pushing his own concerns to the back of his mind. A warm bed and a good night's sleep would be all Amelia needed to recover. If he sacrificed a little of his treasured privacy now he could send her on her way tomorrow with a clear conscience.

'We need to get you warm.'

Amelia looked at the paltry fire struggling to burn in the grate and shuffled a little nearer.

'Properly warm,' Edward said with meaning.

He hesitated for a few seconds. The last woman he'd touched was his wife, and she'd been dead for three long years. He couldn't even remember the last time he'd shaken someone's hand or laid a hand on someone's shoulder.

Quickly, before he could overthink things any further, he stood and carefully scooped Amelia into his arms. She let out a murmur of protest, but her heart wasn't in it. Already Edward could see the cold was affecting her brain, slowing her thought processes and making her sluggish.

He carried her through the house, up the stairs and into the West Wing where he kept his rooms. After the fire three years ago Edward had closed up most of the house, choosing to live his half-existence in the comfortable rooms of the West Wing rather than venture into the grander family rooms. The West Wing was warm and cosy, he'd had a fire burning in his bedroom grate earlier that evening and the embers would still be glowing.

'I feel so cold,' Amelia whispered, her body shuddering in his arms.

'You'll warm up in no time,' Edward said and for the first time in years he felt a sense of purpose. He would not let this young woman die. Even though he didn't know her or what she'd done he would offer her a warm bed and a safe place to rest.

Edward kicked open the door to his bedroom and set Amelia down in his armchair, pulling the heavy seat closer to the fire. He wondered if he had done enough now. With a glance at the door he weighed up his options: he could either leave Amelia here to fend for herself and retreat to the safety of the rest of the deserted house, or he could ensure she would not die from the cold in what remained of the night.

Now she was up here in his bedroom Edward had to suppress the trepidation that was creeping through his entire body. He had shut himself away from the world to avoid exactly these sort of interactions. After the fire he hadn't wanted anyone to venture into the house, into the space he had shared with his family. This was their private domain and he had tried to keep the memories alive by not allowing anyone else in.

Tonight, with Amelia shivering in the armchair his late wife used to sit in, Edward felt as though he'd already somehow desecrated those memories.

'You need to get out of those wet clothes,' Edward barked, knowing he was taking his displeasure out on Amelia, but unable to temper his tone. As he spoke they both glanced down to the almost-transparent chemise and Amelia shifted in embarrassment.

'I'll give you a nightshirt to wear. It'll be far too big, but at least it will be warm and dry.'

Edward crossed to his chest of drawers and selected a nightshirt, shaking out the creases as he returned to Amelia's side. Living alone, with no servants to surprise, Edward normally slept naked, but he had a nightshirt from the days the house had been bustling and full of life.

In the chair Amelia hadn't moved and Edward had to pause before he could see the gentle rise and fall of her chest.

'Will you be able to undress yourself?' Edward asked.

The image of him having to peel the wet chemise from her body, lifting it inch by inch to reveal the silky skin underneath, had imprinted itself in Edward's brain. He swallowed, closed his eyes, and rallied. He had been without a woman's touch for a long time, but that was no excuse for the entirely inappropriate thought.

He didn't wait for her reply, instead throwing the nightshirt down on the empty armchair by the fire and striding out of the room.

Once outside Edward rested his forehead against the cool stone wall and tried to quash the contempt he was feeling towards himself. For three years he had consoled himself by promising to always remain true to his late wife, and the first time he was tested, the first time a pretty young woman stepped into his world, he allowed his imagination to run wild.

He waited a few minutes, then knocked on the door. When he didn't get a reply he hesitated before opening the door and stepping back into the room.

Amelia had managed to finish undressing herself and don the nightshirt Edward had found for her. The blood-stained chemise was hanging over a chair. Now it wasn't plastered to her body Edward could see just how much blood there was.

'What happened?' he asked sharply, pointing at the bloodstains.

Amelia turned and looked at him with vacant eyes and just shook her head.

Part of Edward wanted to drop the topic. What did it matter to him how she had got to be covered in blood and running through a storm? She'd be gone tomorrow, out of his life never to return.

'Tell me or you can leave,' Edward said firmly.

The frightened eyes that looked back at him were almost enough to make him regret the threat.

'I was attacked,' Amelia said.

'You're hurt?'

She shook her head. 'I fought back.'

For now that would have to be sufficient. Edward knew enough about human nature to be sure Amelia wasn't a threat. He didn't want to be drawn in to whatever trouble she was in, so he let the matter drop.

'Get to bed,' he said. 'I'll see you in the morning.'

He turned and began to walk towards the door, pausing only when he realised Amelia had not even made an attempt to move.

'You'll be warmer in bed,' he said more softly.

She nodded her head, a minuscule movement which seemed all she was able to do. Edward waited for a few more seconds, just to see if she would move, before realising she was just too exhausted to take the few steps to the bed. Cursing under his breath, Edward strode back to her side and without asking permission he swept her up in his arms, carried her over to the bed and deposited her underneath the covers. The encounter must have only lasted ten seconds and throughout Edward gritted his teeth and concentrated on not becoming aware of the contours of Amelia's body in his arms.

Efficiently he pulled the sheet and blanket up to Amelia's chin, stood back and nodded in satisfaction. For a man who had barely spoken to anyone for three years he was rather pleased with his hospitality.

Amelia's teeth began chattering and he could see her body spasming under the covers. Gently he leant over and touched her cheek. Her skin was still icy cold and had that worrying clammy feel to it. Edward hesitated. He wanted to leave, to retreat to another part of the house and sit out the night, waiting for the moment he could send Amelia on her way. He glanced down at Amelia again. Her lips had an unhealthy blue tinge and there were deep black rings surrounding her eyes.

Edward didn't want Amelia here in his bed or in his house, but now she was he wasn't going to let her die. He couldn't have another death on his conscience. He knew the best way to warm a freezing body, but it felt wrong. Amelia let out a pained moan, her whole body convulsing, and Edward heard her begin to sob.

'You're going to be all right,' he said as he slipped into the bed behind Amelia and looped his arm around her.

Through the covers he felt her stiffen as he made contact with her body. He wondered if she would throw him out, demand he leave her alone despite her desperate need for warmth. After a few seconds of indecision Edward felt her relax a little and bury her body closer to his, luxuriating in his warmth.

It was an unfamiliar sensation, having a young woman's body pressed up against his own, and Edward found he kept having to remind himself exactly why he was doing this. He would take no enjoyment out of this situation, but despite his determination he found himself gripping Amelia just a little tighter. For years he had denied himself any human contact. Only now he was lying with a strange woman curled up against him in bed did he realise quite how much he'd missed another's touch.

Chapter Two

Amelia awoke slowly, revelling in the warmth of her bed and the comforting presence beside her. For just a few moments she was back in India, lying beside her cousin Lizzie, and her life was easy and pampered. Her eyes fluttered open and as she stared at the unfamiliar ceiling the events of the past few days came crashing back.

Warily Amelia turned her head and almost jumped from the bed with shock. Lying beside her, an arm flung casually across her waist, was the man who had rescued her from the cold, wet night and given her shelter. Forcing herself to remain calm, Amelia tried to piece together what had happened the previous night. She remembered seeking refuge from the storm and nearly dying from fright when Edward had surprised her as she'd undressed in front of the fire. After that her recollection of events was patchy at best. She had a vague feeling he had carried her through the house, but she couldn't remember how she had got out of the rest of her wet clothes or just what had happened to mean they ended up sharing the same bed.

Risking another glance at the man beside her, Amelia studied his face. He looked youthful and innocent whilst he slept, the frown she remembered from the previous night smoothed over as he relaxed in his sleep. He had a shock of dark hair, too long to be fashionable, and strong, manly features. Edward was the complete opposite of McNair, who was lithe and slender and beautiful.

Choking back a sob, Amelia remembered the events of three days ago and had to close her eyes as a wave of nausea overcame her. She'd killed someone. Never again would she wake up and not be a murderer. She might be a fugitive, running from the law, but McNair, beautiful, vibrant McNair, was dead and it was all her fault. Amelia could feel her hands shaking as she remembered McNair's gasp of surprise as the letter opener slid into his flesh and how after that one movement she had frozen, unable to let go, unable to pull away.

Beside her Edward stirred and Amelia rallied, pulling the bedcovers up to her chin.

It wasn't my fault. She repeated it to herself, forcing the disturbing images and memories from her mind.

She watched as the man beside her slowly emerged from his sleep. Amelia had never woken to a man in her bed before and it was fascinating to see how he stretched and wriggled before finally opening his eyes.

Edward's body froze and his eyes shot wide open the moment he saw her.

'Good,' he said gruffly. 'You're still alive.'

Amelia bristled. She wasn't sure what the etiquette was in this situation, but she rather thought he should greet her with something more poetic, more reassuring.

Without any further communication Edward swung his legs out of the bed and stood, gathering the dressing gown he'd slept in around himself. Amelia caught a glimpse of muscular legs and strong forearms before he was halfway across the room.

'What happened last night?'

Edward turned to face her.

'I remember you finding me in the drawing room, but not much else.'

He shrugged. 'You were cold. I put you to bed.'

A man of few words it would seem.

'And how did you end up in bed with me?' Amelia asked frostily. Two could play at that game.

Edward had the decency to colour a little, but otherwise he seemed unperturbed.

'You were shivering despite the fire and the blankets. I didn't want you to die so I added my body heat.'

He made it sound so detached, so clinical. Without another word he crossed to the door and opened it.

'Thank you,' Amelia said softly.

Edward turned around, gave a short nod, then left. Amelia stared open mouthed after him. Despite all her flirtations she was an innocent, but even so she knew a man of good breeding did not just run out on a woman he'd spent the night in the same bed with. She felt the irritation at being so easily dismissed build inside her and it was a welcome distraction from the guilt and despair she'd subjected herself to over the last few days.

With a huff she got out of bed, gathering the loose material of the nightshirt around her body and letting her bare feet sink into the plush woven rug. Slowly she started to explore the room, running her fingers over the well-made if slight tatty furniture and examining the paintings on the wall. As she came to the large desk set at one end of the room she paused, her eyes settling on the numerous pieces of paper scattered across it. Eyes stared up at her from beautifully rendered sketches, drawing after drawing depicting people as they really were, not the stylised creations you often saw in professional portraits.

'I've brought you some clothes,' Edward's voice came

from near the door. For a tall, powerful man he moved surprisingly quietly.

Amelia jumped back guiltily. She hadn't done anything wrong, the sketches had been lying on the desk, not locked away in a drawer, but still she sensed she'd trespassed on something very private and personal.

'Thank you,' she said, crossing the room and taking the clothes from Edward's arms.

'I will be downstairs in the kitchen. Once you're dressed join me. It's at the back of the house.'

'I'm sorry...' Amelia started to say, but Edward had already gone, closing the door behind him with a resounding thud.

Laying the clothes out on the bed Amelia was surprised to find the styles modern and the garments in good condition. She wondered why this strange, solitary man had women's clothes stored in the house. She couldn't picture him with a mistress squirrelled away somewhere—maybe a wife, someone mousy and quiet, but evidently not around any more.

Everything was too big on Amelia's petite form, but the clothes were clean and dry, and vitally not covered in blood. She badly wanted a bath, a long soak in a deep tub to clean all the grime from her body and soothe her aching muscles, but she sensed she was as likely to get that as the possibility of a man walking on the moon. So instead she scrutinised herself in the small mirror hung on one wall and tidied herself up the best she could.

Grimacing as she noticed the slight swelling to one side of her face, Amelia touched her cheek gently. She could still feel McNair's fist crunching against her delicate bones and quickly she squeezed her eyes shut to stop the memory of what happened next flashing before her eyes.

With great effort Amelia opened her eyes and tried out

a breezy smile. She needed Edward to let her stay here in this strange, half-derelict house, at least for a few days. McNair's death would have been discovered by now and someone would be hot on her trail. Even though Amelia knew she had committed an awful crime, she didn't want to hang for it. She felt remorse and regret, but truly it *had* been in self-defence. Nevertheless she had fled the scene and, as a young woman with no husband and her father many thousands of miles away in India, Amelia wasn't so naive to think she would get off lightly. No, the best course of action would be to hide away somewhere until her trail had gone cold and then find a way to fund her passage back to India. Her father would be irate, but he loved her and would make sure she was safe.

No one would think to look for her here in this house inhabited only by a reclusive bachelor. She just had to persuade Edward to let her stay for a few days, maybe a week. She wished she had something to offer, some practical skill that would make her indispensable, but her upbringing had consisted of painting watercolours, playing the piano and dreaming of a more exciting life.

Straightening her back, Amelia raised her chin and took a deep breath. She was Amelia Eastway. She'd never struggled to get men to do her bidding. Although she rather suspected she had never come across a man quite like Edward before.

Edward clattered around in the kitchen, his mood blackening with every second he couldn't find the bread Mrs Henshaw had left him the day before. For three years he had lived undisturbed in his private refuge. Only Mrs Henshaw, his old housekeeper who had retired to a cottage in the village, came to visit him nowadays, bringing fresh food every few days and keeping the house from falling into complete disrepair.

Now his refuge had been invaded by an impish and vivacious young woman who had already started going through his private possessions. Granted the sketches had just been left lying on his desk, but when he'd first got into bed the night before he hadn't expected to start the morning with a stranger in his bedroom.

He needed her gone, Edward decided as he located the loaf of bread and cut two thick slices. His reaction to her was uncomfortable and he knew it was more than a desire for a return of his privacy that drove that reaction. This morning as he'd woken to a warm, soft body in his bed he'd felt a primal stirring deep inside him. It was absurd and now Edward was even more determined to hasten Amelia's departure from his house.

'Do you live completely on your own?' Amelia asked as she swept into the room. For such a petite little thing she had a way of commanding your attention. A breezy smile was affixed to her lips and Edward wondered again what pain she was trying to hide.

'Completely. My old housekeeper visits twice a week to deliver some food and other essentials.'

'You don't go down to the village?'

Edward shook his head, trying to ignore her incredulous expression. He had ventured out in the painful months after the fire, but the looks filled with pity and the expressions of concern had soon put a stop to his trips to the village.

'I have everything I need here,' he said brusquely, trying to discourage her from asking any more questions.

Amelia wrinkled her nose and looked around.

'Don't you get lonely?' she asked. 'Or bored?'

'No. Not everyone likes chattering away incessantly.'

Amelia looked at him as if she expected him to elaborate further.

He had his sketches and his books, he still kept an eye on the running of the estate, although he had a reliable steward who did most of the work for him. As for loneliness, it was a welcome penance for the guilt he felt for surviving the fire.

'Maybe you would like a little company?' Amelia asked, with a quick glance at his expression.

Edward's first instinct was to march Amelia straight out the front door that instant, but then he paused. She'd survived the night and was back on her feet, there was nothing to hinder her departure today so he could afford to be a little more courteous.

'I can be very good company,' Amelia said.

She might think herself a woman of the world, this little minx, but he could tell straight away that she was innocent in many of her ways.

'Company?' he asked, raising an eyebrow.

Immediately he saw the colour start to rise in her cheeks and her bottom lip drop slightly.

'Not like...that is to say...'

'I know we shared a bed last night, but I am not that sort of gentleman,' Edward said.

'I wasn't suggesting...'

'I'm teasing you,' he said, knowing his serious expression didn't quite tally with his words. Maybe he should stick to his more sombre demeanour.

'Oh. Of course.'

Amelia drummed her fingers on the table as she struggled to regain her composure and Edward took the opportunity to study her properly. She was pretty, there was no denying it. Petite and slender with large brown eyes and soft blonde hair. The sort of young woman who would cause a stir when making her debut in society. His keen artist's eye also caught details others might not notice: the nervous energy that stopped her from standing still for more than two seconds, the little pucker in the skin between her eyebrows that appeared when she was thinking and the way she sucked her bottom lip into her mouth as she decided what to say next.

She was nervous, Edward realised, more nervous than the circumstances should warrant. True, she was in a strange house with a reclusive man, but she'd survived the night unmolested—most young women would solely be concerned with how to leave with their reputations intact. Edward didn't think it was her reputation she was worried about, there was something much bigger going on in Amelia's life.

He thought back to the blood-covered clothes and the panicked state she had been in when he'd first found her almost collapsed in his sitting room. Last night she'd said she had been attacked and had fought back, but Edward sensed there was more to the story than that. For a few seconds he deliberated, wondering if he should delve deeper, find out exactly what sort of trouble Amelia was in, but he knew that would just prolong the time until he could usher her out of his life so he kept his mouth shut.

'Maybe I could stay for a few days?' Amelia suggested, looking up at him hopefully.

For all her beauty and feminine wiles, Edward could read her easily. She might think she was an enigmatic young siren, but every emotion was written across her face just as soon as she experienced it.

'No.'

'No?'

'No,' Edward repeated. It would be a bad idea. A terrible idea.

'You can't just say no. Why not?'

He guessed she was an only child. There was a sense of entitlement about her that suggested she had been spoiled most of her life.

'I can. It's my house.' Edward grimaced and then relented. He was not a child and he would give her a proper answer. 'I live alone. I like living alone, and in a few hours I will go back to living alone.'

Her face fell and he tried to soften the blow.

'Besides, your reputation would be in tatters if you stayed here with me unchaperoned.'

'What reputation?' Amelia murmured under her breath. 'I don't care,' she said louder. 'I could tidy the place up a bit,' Amelia suggested.

'Do you have much experience at domestic chores?'

Amelia bit her bottom lip again. Edward felt the pulse of his blood around his body as his eyes flickered to her lips. 'No,' he said much more brusquely than he had intended, 'I didn't think you did.'

'I could cook you a decent meal at least.'

Edward looked down to the two roughly cut chunks of bread and sighed.

'I'm sorry, Amelia, but the answer is still no. After breakfast I will take you down to the village and you can catch the stagecoach to London.'

'I don't have any money.'

'I'll pay.'

'What if I don't want to go to London?'

'Then you can get off at one of the stops beforehand.'

She fell silent, but Edward could see the cogs turning inside her head as she tried to think of another excuse not to leave. He wondered why she wanted to stay so badly and what it was she had been running from the night before. Just as he opened his mouth to ask, he once again caught himself and silently shook his head. It wasn't his place to get involved. Later, when Amelia was safely on the stagecoach to London, he could brood over his life-style decisions, but the fact was right now he didn't want to delve deeper into Amelia's problems and if that made him unsociable that was fine by him.

Chapter Three

Amelia fidgeted as Edward placed a thick coat over her shoulders. She didn't want to leave. Somehow this strange half-derelict house felt safe, and once she was out in the real world again she knew it was only a matter of time before the consequences of her deeds caught up with her.

'Maybe I could stay for lunch?' Amelia suggested.

'I don't have any food in the house.'

The man was infuriating. Every suggestion she came up with he shot down with that calm tone of voice and unshakeable demeanour.

'I think I left something upstairs.' Amelia was beginning to panic now. The outside world was looming closer and she didn't know if she could cope with another indeterminate period on the run.

'You didn't bring anything with you.'

Amelia scrabbled for something, anything she might have left behind, just to buy herself a few more minutes. She needed to think of a reason to stay, something that would convince Edward it would be in everyone's best interests.

'Please,' she said quietly, 'I can't go out there.'

This quiet plea made Edward pause and for a moment Amelia thought he might relent.

'Why not?' he asked.

Amelia swallowed and bit her lip. She couldn't exactly tell him the truth. Admitting she was a murderer would only speed her departure from the house, not prolong her stay.

With wide eyes Amelia felt the desperation and despair all come crashing together and knew she had everything to lose. If Edward insisted she leave, she had no doubt whoever it was that was chasing her would catch up with her within a day or two. She couldn't sustain her progress any longer, she was exhausted and her feet covered in blisters. Here she had a chance at avoiding the hangman's noose and she realised she would do anything for it.

Straightening her back and lifting her chin, Amelia looked Edward directly in the eye and smiled shyly at him.

'If I stay we could get to know one another better,' she said, trailing a finger up his arm.

Edward stood completely still, his eyes following the progress of her finger. The heat began to rise in Amelia's cheeks, but she knew she had to give this her best shot. Humiliation and ruin was nothing compared to being found guilty of murder.

'I promise I'm very good company.' She didn't even really know what that meant, but she'd overheard some of the less virtuous women use the phrase at a regimental party a few years ago.

Edward took her hand, removed it from his arm and let go, allowing it to drop back to her side. His face was stony and devoid of expression and his movements almost stiff. Amelia felt the flood of shame wash over her. In a way it would have been better if he'd laughed, at least then she would have known he wasn't disgusted by her proposition.

'It must get lonely, living here all by yourself,' Amelia said, giving it one last try. She was desperate and she knew she sounded desperate, but she didn't care. Self-preservation was at the top of her list of priorities, she would have time for embarrassment and regret when she was safe.

'Come on, otherwise we will miss the stagecoach.' Edward said, ignoring her last few comments. He didn't sound angry or disgusted, just tired and worn down, and for a moment Amelia wondered why he was so keen to get rid of her.

Amelia dawdled a little longer, wasting as much time as possible fiddling with the laces on the boots he'd found her and adjusting the bodice of her dress.

Eventually Edward sighed, gripped her arm and led her firmly out of the front door.

It was a cool day, clear and crisp after the storm of the night before. Amelia huddled into the cloak draped around her shoulders and reluctantly allowed Edward to lead her down the sweeping driveway.

'I could tidy up your garden,' Amelia said without much hope as they passed another overgrown flowerbed.

'I like it this way.'

'No, you don't.' No one could. The garden had potential, great potential, and Amelia could see a few years ago it would have looked much different. Someone had lovingly planned and planted, landscaped and tended, but it had fallen into ruin along with the rest of the house.

Edward shrugged again, that infuriating movement he seemed to favour when she challenged him about anything, and continued his steady pace down the driveway. Amelia glanced back at the house and found her heart sinking. Every step they took resulted in her being further away from the place that she'd hoped would be her sanctuary for a few days. She felt like turning and running back inside, slamming the door and locking it shut.

'The village is only twenty minutes away,' Edward

said as they reached the wrought-iron gates Amelia had squeezed through the night before. 'If you don't walk at the pace of a lethargic snail,' he added under his breath as she lagged behind, dragging her feet.

She watched as he tore some of the overgrown vegetation from the bars of the gates, frowning thoughtfully as he did so. Amelia wondered if he saw the house and gardens as she did, with all the cracks and faults, or if when he looked around he saw the place as it used to be.

As Edward pushed open the gates Amelia felt an icy stab of panic jolt through her body. Inside the estate grounds she felt peculiarly safe and now she was being asked to step over the threshold. Out here, in the wider world, who knew what awaited her.

As if sensing her reticence to step through the gates, Edward paused for a moment and looked at her with his searching brown eyes.

'The road is clear,' he said, 'So unless there's any further reasons you can't possibly leave shall we be on our way?'

For a second she almost blurted it all out. It would be a relief to share what had happened with someone, to tell the whole sordid tale. She wondered how Edward would react, if he would respond kindly and calmly, or push her away. Maybe he would let her stay, take pity on her and agree to shelter her from the world. Or maybe he would turn her over to whoever was hunting her down.

Unconsciously she raised a hand to her throat, rubbing the skin of her neck at the thought of a noose tightening around her throat.

'Nothing,' she replied eventually. She would be safer if no one else knew what she had done.

'The coach runs to London in one direction and

Brighton the other,' Edward said, disturbing Amelia from her thoughts.

She nodded absentmindedly.

'Would you prefer to go to Brighton or London?'

Dear Lord, not Brighton, Amelia thought.

'London. Definitely London.'

'Do you have any family there?'

Amelia shook her head. It was a lie, but a necessary one. It wasn't as though she could turn up on her aunt's doorstep, it would be the first place a magistrate would look for her.

'How about friends?'

Again Amelia shook her head.

'Where are your family?'

She sensed Edward was starting to feel a modicum of responsibility for her. He might not want to let her stay in his strange house, but he wanted to make sure she was safe all the same.

'India.'

'Ah. I see.' He paused for a few seconds. 'Surely you didn't come over here on your own?'

Amelia stopped walking and waited for Edward to turn.

'I'm out of your house and soon I'll be out of your life,' she said coolly. 'After today you will never have to think of me again. I have no friends or family in this country, but as you have made clear, that is not your concern.'

She saw the flicker of hurt in Edward's eyes and for a moment she felt remorse. Her cousin Lizzie always said she had a sharp tongue and Amelia knew she often spoke before she'd had chance to think through what impact her words might have. Edward was kind, for all his brusque manner, and he had taken her in for the night when others might have thrown her out. It wasn't his fault she was in such a mess, but she was just wishing for a reprieve, a few days to decide what to do with her life, and Edward couldn't give that to her.

'Come on,' he said stiffly and began walking again.

Amelia watched his back for a few seconds before hurrying to catch up. He was a tall man, with broad shoulders, a strong man. He emanated power and Amelia found herself wishing to be enveloped in his arms, pressed up against his chest and kept safe.

Trying to suppress the thought as she drew level with him, Amelia risked a sidelong glance. In his own way he was handsome, she supposed, although not in the same way McNair had been handsome. Edward had strong features and kind eyes, but he had a slightly wild look about him with his tousled hair and creased shirts. McNair had always been beautifully presented, but thinking back there was a coldness about him, a calculating, detached look on his perfectly symmetrical face.

After ten minutes they reached the outskirts of the village, with a few simple cottages appearing on either side of the lane. Amelia felt herself instinctively hunch her shoulders, trying to appear less conspicuous. Although there wasn't anyone around at the moment, she felt nervous and frightened all at the same time.

The small cottages gave way to bigger dwellings once they reached the village proper and as they turned on to the high street Amelia froze. People were milling about, women walking arm in arm and talking, men going about their business with purpose. Beside her Amelia felt Edward go still at the same moment she did and she wondered fleetingly how long it had been since he'd visited the village.

All thoughts about Edward's lifestyle were swept away as he took her arm and guided her down the high street.

People were looking at them strangely, a couple of women actually pointed and stared, and Amelia knew it would only be a matter of seconds until some officer of the law clamped his hand on her shoulder and hauled her off to face the consequences of her crime.

As they reached the clock tower that stood proudly in the middle of the village square Amelia caught a glimpse of a smartly dressed man coming out of a small shop. He looked out of place in this small village, his clothes were too well tailored, his hair too well groomed. It was obvious from a single glance he was an outsider.

With a pounding heart Amelia grasped Edward's arm and pulled him behind the clock tower, squeezing her eyes shut as she did so, wishing she could just will the well-groomed man away.

'Amelia?' Edward asked, his voice a mixture of concern and irritation. He probably thought she was just trying to waste more time.

'Shh,' she hissed.

'What's wrong?'

'Everyone's looking at us.'

Edward chuckled, the first real laugh Amelia had heard him utter.

'Do you think it might be because you're acting so strangely?'

Amelia opened her eyes and looked up into Edward's face, frowning.

'They're looking at me,' she insisted.

He shook his head, a self-deprecating little smile playing on his lips.

'I think they're probably looking at me. I am rather notorious. The recluse of Beechwood Manor.'

Amelia paused and glanced out from behind the clock tower. No one was coming for her—in fact, everyone had just returned their attention to whatever it was they'd been doing. Maybe Edward was right, maybe it was him they had all been staring at.

'What are you afraid of, Amelia?' Edward asked.

He reached out and touched her gently on the arm and Amelia found herself looking up into his concerned face. Edward had been generous to her, she couldn't deny it. He'd allowed her to stay and ensured she was warm and dry for the night, but until now she hadn't really caught more than the occasional glimpse of his kind side. His outward demeanour had always been stern and distant, but right now there was warmth in his eyes, genuine concern and compassion. She sensed this was the man he really was, his true nature, and the gruffness was a wall he erected to keep everyone at bay.

For a moment the rest of the world disappeared, the noise of the villagers going about their daily lives faded into the background and it was just the two of them, hidden in their own little world behind the clock tower. Amelia wondered what it would be like to raise herself up on her toes and kiss Edward, to allow him to fold her in his strong arms and protect her from the world. She felt her body sway slightly, her lips part with anticipation, but just as she began to lean in McNair's face flashed before her eyes.

The last time she'd kissed a man it had ended in tragedy. She wouldn't allow it to happen again. She couldn't be trusted, her instincts had been proven to be wrong before and just the fact that she felt attracted to Edward should be enough to tell her to stay well away.

Edward saw the moment Amelia's eyes glazed over and her lips parted. He had been without female company for a long time, but in his youth he'd experienced enough to know when a woman wanted to kiss him. She'd even began to lean in, swaying towards him, but then something had happened. Amelia had stiffened, a look of horror had passed over her face and now she'd backed away to a more respectable distance.

He found himself a little disappointed. He shouldn't want to kiss this enigmatic little minx, but the idea of tasting her lips, just once, was rather enticing. Before he could stop the thought it had taken hold and all the guilt and feelings of betrayal it conjured up were right there with it. Quickly he balled both his hands into fists, digging his nails into his palms to try to distract himself. He knew his wife was dead and gone, nothing would ever bring her back, but he owed it to her to honour her memory.

'Shall we find the stagecoach?' Amelia said formally once she'd recovered some of her composure.

Edward stepped out from behind the clock tower and waited for Amelia to follow. Before she ventured out into the open square, she checked each direction, her head swivelling this way and that like a skittish horse.

'There's no one poised and waiting to attack you,' Edward said impatiently as she eventually stepped out into the square.

She gave him a withering look, still checking each direction every few seconds. He wondered what she was afraid of. There was an air of innocence about Amelia, the demeanour of someone who hadn't experienced much of the world on their own, so he couldn't imagine she'd got mixed up in anything too heinous, although maybe the bloodstains on her clothes were evidence against that opinion.

Edward gently took her hand and placed it in the crook of his arm and guided her further along the high street to the point where the stagecoach stopped to pick up passengers. Now they were nearing the point of farewell Edward felt a great weight being lifted from his shoulders. He had found it difficult sharing his home even just for one short night and was quite looking forward to getting back to the peace and quiet of an empty house. For a second he felt a pang of sadness. Once, long ago, he had enjoyed noise and company and laughter. With a sideways glance at Amelia he rallied. Now was not the time to waver in his resolution to put this troubled young woman on a stagecoach and wave her on her way.

If Jane were here, standing beside him and giving advice in that calm and sensible way of hers, she'd tell him to start living, to stop stagnating. She'd probably convince him to take pity on Amelia, shelter her from whatever trouble she was running from and learn once again to tolerate the company of others. Edward knew one day he would have to pick up the reins of his life again, to do more than spend his time sketching and reading, but with living came memories and he wasn't sure he was ready to confront those yet.

'You're looking rather serious,' Amelia said as they slowed to a stop at the side of the road.

'Do you need any money?' Edward asked, knowing he was avoiding Amelia's comment.

She bit her bottom lip and fidgeted a little. It was the curse of the human race not to be able to ask for monetary help when they needed it.

'Maybe just a little something to help you on your way,' he said, placing a hand into his coat pocket.

One second he was standing at the side of the road, reaching for his coin purse, the next he was lying in some rather prickly bushes with Amelia on top of him.

'What...?' he began, but Amelia pressed a finger against his lips.

He tried to speak again, but was silenced by the look

of pure terror in Amelia's eyes. For almost a minute they lay there, Amelia frozen by fear and he trapped under her body. They were half-hidden from the road, but if anyone walked passed they would have a lot of explaining to do.

When another minute had passed without Amelia explaining or letting him up Edward began to feel the damp from the ground soaking into his trousers.

'Will you tell me what's going on, woman?' he asked, quietly but firmly.

Amelia's eyes widened with shock and fear and immediately Edward regretted his tone of voice.

'Come, let's stand up,' he said more softly.

Amelia allowed him to help her to her feet, although he noticed she did not step back out on to the road, and her restraining hand on his arm stopped him from doing so too. For an instant Edward missed the warmth of her body as it had been pressed against his, but soon the feeling was replaced by irritation. The woman was crazy. First darting behind the clock tower and now wrestling him to the ground whilst they waited for the stagecoach.

'Is he still there?' Amelia hissed.

'Who?'

She didn't answer so Edward stepped forward and looked up and down the lane. It was completely empty. Maybe there was something not quite right in Amelia's head. She seemed normal, if not conventional, most of the time, but then she went and did things like this. Then he remembered the blood-soaked clothes and the state Amelia had been in the night before and softened slightly. Something bad had occurred in Amelia's life recently. That must be what was driving this fear.

'There's no one there.' Edward wondered if this was another of Amelia's time-wasting ploys, but the terror in her eyes convinced him otherwise.

Warily Amelia edged forward, peering out from the bushes until she was satisfied they were alone.

'I think you should tell me what's going on,' Edward said, in a voice that brooked no argument.

Amelia shook her head, tears forming in her eyes and spilling out to roll down her cheeks. Edward almost reached out to brush them away, but he stopped himself. It was an intimate gesture, too intimate. He couldn't believe he'd even contemplated it.

'Who did you think you saw?'

Again Amelia shook her head, still glancing furtively up and down the road.

Edward ran his hands through his hair and studied the young woman who stood before him. She was petrified, that much was clear. He didn't know if her demons were real or imaginary, but he did have experience with living with events he'd rather forget.

His brain screamed to let her go, to get back to his reclusive existence, but his heart recognised another wounded soul. He wanted to leave, to walk off down the road without as much as a backwards glance, but something was holding him back. Edward even tried placing one foot in front of another, but his body just wouldn't obey his commands. Something sparked inside him, something that he thought was long dead and buried. He wasn't sure if it was compassion or pity, but he realised he didn't have it in him to abandon Amelia here in such a state of dread. For years he might have suppressed his humanity through lack of interaction, but he'd been brought up to be kind and chivalrous and there were a few strands of those characteristics that refused to leave him despite years of disuse.

'Amelia, look at me.' He grasped her by the arms and turned her to face him. She looked distractedly around her. 'I will make you a bargain,' he said.

This caught her attention.

'You tell me exactly what is going on, what trouble you're in, and I promise to help you as much as I can.'

She shook her head, 'I can't.'

'Then you're on your own.'

Edward had only taken two steps before he felt her clutching at his sleeve.

'Please don't leave me here.'

It would be so easy to give in to her beseeching eyes, but Edward knew he had to stand strong.

'Then tell me what has you so scared.'

'I've done something terrible,' Amelia said quietly.

He looked at her youthful, innocent face, and wondered what it was she could have done that was making her quite so worried.

'What?'

He watched as her whole body began to tremble. With difficulty she rallied, squeezing her eyes tight for a few seconds before looking up at him with an expression full of pain and regret.

'I've killed a man.'

Chapter Four

Amelia sank back into the comfortable, worn armchair and closed her eyes for a few seconds. She felt exhausted, even though it wasn't yet midday. For the duration of the trip out to the village she had been petrified, in a state of high alert, seeing danger where there was none and ready to flee at the slightest provocation.

When she'd leaped into the bushes at the side of the road, taking Edward with her, she really had thought someone was looking for her. A tall, serious man with an official-looking uniform had started walking down the lane towards them and Amelia had been convinced this man had tracked her across the South Downs and was here to take her away to face justice. When she'd pointed him out to Edward on their return dash through the village he'd actually laughed before telling her he was the local postman.

After her confession Edward had gone quiet, studied her for some time, then started to lead her back through the village.

'We'll talk back at the house,' he'd said and hardly uttered a word after that.

Amelia wondered if she should be scared. He might be summoning the local magistrate right now, eager to hand over the murderer sitting in his cosy armchair and be done with the drama she had brought into his life. Although she hardly knew the man, Amelia couldn't find it in herself to be overly worried. He seemed fair and honourable, and she thought he would at least give her the chance to explain the circumstances before deciding what to do with her.

'Whisky,' Edward said as he entered the room, 'and biscuits, it's been quite a morning.'

Amelia watched as he poured out two glasses of whisky and handed her one. Cautiously she sniffed the rich, caramel-coloured liquid before taking a gulp.

'Careful,' he cautioned.

She felt the wonderful burn in her throat followed by a warm sensation in her stomach and felt herself relax a little.

'Not the first time you've had whisky?'

She shook her head. 'Back home in India the soldiers were always happy to share.'

'So you actually did grow up in India?'

'I've lived there my whole life. Until I disembarked the ship a week ago I'd never been to England before.'

'I think you should start at the beginning,' Edward said quietly. 'Tell me everything and then we will decide what is to be done.'

Amelia felt herself complying with his order and bristled. She didn't like being told what to do and especially not by a man who she barely knew, but there was something authoritative about his tone, something that promised to sort things out, that made her relax back into the chair and do as he suggested.

She wasn't quite sure where the beginning was. In all honesty she probably would have to start far back in her childhood to make complete sense, but she felt Edward might lose patience if she began recalling the details of her mother's death and the emptiness that followed. He wasn't a man to hide his irritation.

'Two years ago I met a man out in India. My father is a retired colonel and he still has much to do with the army and the officers stationed in India. He hosted a ball and it was there I met Captain McNair.'

Amelia didn't confess how she'd been swept off her feet immediately by his easygoing manner and charming façade. She had been bored, tired of the same routine day in and day out, and she'd been ripe for a seduction.

'We met in secret, in the months following the ball, and after a few meetings McNair professed his love for me.'

'Why the secrecy?' Edward asked, getting to the point in that calm, shrewd, way of his.

Amelia felt her cheeks start to colour with the shame of her naivety. At the time she'd believed McNair's wishy-washy excuses to keep their relationship a secret; his desire to gain a promotion before approaching her father, not wanting to conduct their courtship under his commanding officer's watchful eye. Amelia had believed him because she'd wanted to believe him. At first she'd even kept the relationship secret from her cousin Lizzie, her closest confidant.

'I was young and naive and I thought he wanted to marry me,' Amelia said simply.

He had *wanted* to marry her, of course—most men in India did when they discovered she was the wealthiest heiress in the subcontinent.

'We courted in secret for almost eight months, snatching precious moments whenever we could, and then suddenly he disappeared. I waited for him, searched for him and eventually found out he had been sent back to England. I even wrote to his commanding officer for information, but his reply was a curt note telling me to forget about Captain McNair.'

Amelia glanced at Edward sitting across from her. It felt strange to be admitting all this to a virtual stranger, especially when she hadn't even told her nearest and dearest the truth.

'Can I surmise you didn't take the commanding officer's advice?'

Amelia shook her head. 'I couldn't forget about him. I thought we were meant to be together.'

It was galling, really, when she thought of how much time and energy she had wasted trying to track McNair down.

'My behaviour became a little…erratic, and after some time my father decided to send me to England to stay with my aunt and have a London Season.'

And find a respectable husband. The words had never been explicitly said by her father, but he'd made it quite clear he wanted her happy and settled, and that he expected a good match from her. Edward leaned back in his chair and watched her intently as she told her story. There was something searching and assessing in his gaze, and she had the impression he was committing her to memory, maybe for one of his sketches he seemed so fond of.

'When I got to England I persuaded my cousin Lizzie to assume my identity for a few weeks whilst I slipped away. I'd found McNair's address and was determined for us to be reunited.'

Amelia didn't recount the dizzy anticipation she'd felt on her journey to Brighton. Her thoughts had been full of breathless reunions, impassioned kisses and romantic vows never to be apart. The reality had been so much different.

'When I got to his address McNair was more than a little shocked to see me, but he recovered quickly.'

She closed her eyes as she remembered the honeyed words he'd used to placate her after his first expression had not been of complete pleasure. He'd led her into his rooms, entwining his fingers with hers and had whispered all manner of scandalous endearments in her ear. Amelia had fallen for him all over again, her infatuation deepening every minute she was in his company.

Amelia glanced at Edward, unsure how much to say. He seemed to pick up on her hesitation and wordlessly stood, crossed the short distance between them and re-filled her glass with whisky. Amelia took a fortifying sip as she remembered McNair's kiss, the way his lips had trailed over her skin, the light dance of his fingertips over her back and the warmth of his body pressed close to hers.

She would have given herself to him, completely and utterly. It was only pure luck that she had not fallen into bed with the man she'd thought she loved.

'We were disturbed and McNair left the room for some moments. Whilst he was gone I wandered around, looking at this and that. Then I saw the will on his desk.'

She'd stared at it for a whole minute, uncomprehending. Reading the letters, but their meaning not fully sinking in.

'It was his wife's will. It transpires that she had become unwell just over a year ago, coinciding with McNair's return to England. She had passed away at the end of last month.'

'You didn't know he was married?'

Amelia shook her head. She'd stared at the piece of paper detailing McNair's wife's bequests to certain charitable organisations and she'd felt as though her heart was actually ripping in two. Years of flirtation and infatuation had immediately soured and as McNair had walked back into the room she'd finally seen him for what he was: a trickster, an adulterer. She'd hated him in an instant, but more than that, she had felt all of her self-confidence and trust in her own judgement destroyed in one fell swoop. She'd allowed herself to be taken in by this villain and that hurt almost as much as the scoundrel's betrayal.

'I confronted him when he returned and at first he tried to deny it. I became a little hysterical and suddenly he turned nasty.'

He'd shown his true colours then. Gone was the man who had whispered his desire to spend eternity in her arms and the real McNair replaced him. This McNair snapped and snarled like a wounded animal and let her know it was just her father's substantial fortune he was interested in.

'He admitted his plan had been to seduce me, entice me to run away with him, then extort money from my father for my safe and scandal-free return.'

It had been the ultimate humiliation. Just one more man who wanted her for her money.

'What a bastard,' Edward said, not apologising for his language. Amelia felt her spirits buoy a little as she continued. It was the most animated she'd seen him.

'I threatened to expose him as a scoundrel and a liar, empty words, but I think he had a new scheme afoot, some new girl he was trying to con, for he became enraged.'

Amelia raised a hand to her cheek where McNair had left his mark.

'He hit you?'

She nodded. 'He punched me, right on the cheek. He was livid, like a wild beast.'

It was no excuse, not for what she'd done, but Amelia truly had been afraid for her life.

'There was a fancy letter opener on his desk and I grabbed it, thinking to brandish it and warn him away, but he just laughed at my efforts and came at me again.'

She closed her eyes as she relived the moment the blade

had sunk into McNair's flesh, the soft resistance, the warm trickle of blood that had flowed over her hand, McNair's surprised exhalation before he collapsed on to the ground.

'I stabbed him,' she said so quietly she wasn't sure Edward would hear her words.

She couldn't open her eyes, couldn't bear to see what another person thought of her taking a man's life and all because of a seduction gone wrong.

'I stabbed him and I killed him.'

Some men would come and take her hand, try to comfort her despite there being nothing that could change the fact she was a killer. Some men would chastise and condemn her, even restrain her until they could summon a magistrate. Edward did neither. He sat in the chair across from her in silence, giving her time to collect herself, to steady her nerves and to continue.

'I fled, I ran as far as I could as fast as I could, then when I couldn't run any more I kept walking.'

'And that's how you came to be here, on the night of the storm.'

Amelia looked up at him, trying to read his expression, to garner exactly what he thought of her.

'How long was this letter opener?' he asked, taking her by surprise.

She measured out a few inches with her fingers, trying to recall the look of the blade before it had been covered in blood.

'And where did you stab him?'

'What does it matter?' she asked, feeling sick.

'The blade was small. Unless you hit a vital organ I think it unlikely you killed the man.'

She shook her head. She'd killed him. No one could bleed that much and not be dead.

'He collapsed to the floor...there was blood every-where.'

'Did you check to see if he was breathing? If he had a pulse?'

She hadn't. In fact, she hadn't been able to look at his body at all once the blood had started seeping from the wound around her fingers.

'There was too much blood,' she repeated.

Edward fell silent, seeming to realise if he pushed her much further Amelia wouldn't be able to keep her tenuous grip on her composure.

'What do you want to happen now, Amelia?' Edward asked.

'I don't want to hang.'

A smile tugged at the corner of his lips. Amelia watched as Edward fought it and returned his expression to the more familiar frown.

'An admirable ambition. I don't think any judge would hang you.'

Amelia wasn't sure. And even if she wasn't sentenced to death, a long spell in one of the country's notorious prisons was just about as bad as the noose.

'It was self-defence. You're a young woman of a good family and by all accounts McNair seems to be a known scoundrel.'

It sounded as though Edward was justifying handing her over to the magistrate to face the penalty for what she'd done.

'It's up to you, of course, but if you run then you will spend your entire life looking over your shoulder, wondering whether this crime will catch up with you.'

Amelia hadn't thought of that. She'd been so preoccupied with the here and now, avoiding being apprehended for murder and getting as far away from the scene as possible, she hadn't thought what her life would be like with this always hanging over her. She would always be a murderer. Even if she returned to India, to her father's protection, she would never be able to undo what she had done.

'I want to go home,' Amelia said in a small voice.

She wanted her father, with his gruff voice and stiff embraces. She wanted the rolling hills of Bombay with the humid heat and monsoon rains.

'To India?'

She nodded. He looked thoughtful.

'You can stay a couple of days,' he said eventually. 'I will summon my steward and instruct him to make discreet enquiries, see what the state of affairs is with this McNair. We will make a further decision when we have all the facts.'

She didn't know how he could reduce her momentous revelation to such a cool, calculating plan, but as his words sunk in Amelia felt a surge of hope blossom inside her. He was going to help her and, more importantly, he was going to let her stay.

With a yelp of relief Amelia sprang from her chair and launched herself across the room at Edward. He was stiff under her embrace and momentarily Amelia remembered how his body had moulded to hers the night before as she lay in bed shivering from the cold. He was capable of warmth and closeness, but he wasn't comfortable with it.

'There are conditions,' Edward said quickly. 'I don't like to be disturbed. We shall take dinner together and nothing more. The rest of the time you may do as you please, but you will not venture into the East Wing. Is that clear?'

Amelia nodded, willing to agree to anything if it meant she could stay. For a while at least she was safe. She would remain hidden in this strange, half-empty house until they could be sure exactly what the situation was with McNair's death. It was a reprieve, the sanctuary she had hoped for during her mad dash over the Downs. Of course it wouldn't bring McNair back to life, wouldn't change the fact that she was a murderer, but for now she would have to be content with safety over absolution for her crime.

Amelia pulled away, pausing as she got to arm's length. Something made her stop, to hesitate. Her eyes met Edward's and for a second there was a spark, a flare, between them. Amelia felt skin begin to tingle and her blood rushing around her body. She was aware of every tiny movement, every breath, every muscle. There was something captivating about this gruff, generous man, something not obvious at first glance, but hidden beneath his cool exterior.

Then Edward shifted and the moment was lost. Amelia stood, turning away to cover her confusion. She wasn't sure what had just passed between them, but she did know she had no right to experience whatever it was. Taking a deep breath, she forced a smile to her lips before turning back to face Edward.

Chapter Five

A s Edward's pencil danced over the paper he felt all the tension and worry from the last couple of days flow from his shoulders. Drawing preserved his sanity, it was a hobby that had become much more. In the last few years he had lost himself in his sketches, picking up his pencils whenever his grief or solitude threatened to overwhelm him. Sometimes he drew from memory, a person from his childhood or scene from the village. Often he would sketch faces, allowing his pencils to flow over the familiar lines of the faces of the people he had lost over the years.

Today he was sitting by the window, drawing the view he could see. He'd needed this time alone, some space to regroup and sort through the events of the last couple of days. So he had retreated to his rooms soon after Amelia had finished telling him her story.

It was strange having another person in the house. Ever since he had dismissed the servants a few weeks after the fire he had lived alone. Edward knew he'd turned the house into a sort of mausoleum, a place of memorial for all that had he had lost. Maybe it wasn't the healthiest way of dealing with his grief, but he'd never felt he deserved anything more than the loneliness he had imposed on himself.

Now, with Amelia's presence, he felt uncomfortable and guilty. It should be Jane here with him, not some pretty young woman.

He didn't believe for a second Amelia had actually killed this Captain of hers. A petite little thing like her wouldn't be able to best a seasoned soldier with just a letter opener. Far more likely the scoundrel was still alive and hell-bent on vengeance. That was the real reason he'd allowed her to stay, to ensure she was kept hidden from McNair and whatever plans he had for the woman who'd injured him. Part of him had wanted to hold back and send her on her way, but he knew his conscience couldn't bear the burden of another death.

So he had promised to look into Amelia's claims and before he had retired to his rooms he'd walked to the edge of the estate and found a willing boy to deliver a message to his steward for a couple of shiny coins. Hopefully the man would visit later and they could get the business sorted as soon as possible.

Then life can return to normal. Edward grimaced. As if anything in his life could be termed normal.

Mulling his future over in his mind, Edward glanced out the window again, his hand with the pencil in falling to his lap as he saw Amelia pacing about the garden. As he watched he saw her heft a spade from the ground and start to dig.

For years the lawn had been overgrown, but covered in lush, green grass. Now it was beginning to be peppered with several muddy holes of varying depths all scattered about in front of the flower bed. It looked a complete mess.

It wasn't the mess, however, that made Edward spring up from his chair, it was the realisation of exactly where she was digging. Now there was only a thorny tangle of overgrown bushes and Edward couldn't remember the last time he'd seen a flower, but he knew for certain the area she was attacking had once been the rose garden. The rose garden Jane had once loved so much. With a growl of displeasure Edward stood, pushing his sketches to one side, and quickly made his way downstairs. Out in the garden the full extent of the damage became apparent.

'What are you doing?' he asked, not bothering to hide his exasperation.

'Digging,' came Amelia's cheery reply.

She carried on plunging the spade into the ground, a look of steely determination on her face.

'Why are you digging?'

'To rescue the roses.'

She didn't look up at him as she spoke, too intent on her task.

'Stop,' he said, adding a quiet 'please' as an afterthought.

'Won't be long now.'

She carried on wielding the spade.

'Stop now.'

The hole in front of them got a little larger and Edward's shoes were sprinkled with mud.

'Stop,' he bellowed.

Amelia halted, the spade frozen in mid-air, and looked at him with puzzlement.

'What's wrong?' she asked.

'What's wrong? What's wrong?' Edward tried to keep his temper in check, but as he looked around at the devastation in front of him he lost the battle. 'You've destroyed my garden.'

Amelia took a step back, but Edward couldn't regret the volume of his outburst. She had desecrated the rose garden, the patch of ground he and Jane had spent hours planting and tending together.

'It was a mess to begin with.'

Edward felt guilty. He knew he had neglected a lot in the past three years, allowing the house and gardens to fall into disrepair. He regretted allowing the garden he and Jane had planted so lovingly become this overgrown mess of tangled brambles, but that did not give Amelia the right to swoop in and attack it with a spade.

'If I had wanted it any different, I would have done it myself.'

'Like the rest of the house?' Amelia challenged him.

He could see she regretted her comment as soon as she'd said it, even going so far as clamping her hands over her mouth as if trying to pull the words back in.

'Do not touch anything else,' Edward said, his voice low and dangerous. 'Now leave.'

She hesitated for just a second and then dropped the spade and hurried back to the house.

'I'm sorry,' Edward whispered, closing his eyes. 'I'm sorry for letting things get like this.'

He knew the house and gardens were in a terrible state. No one could live there and be unaware of the dust and the weeds and the crumbling stone, but over time he had become used to it. Each time he'd noticed another cobweb or another fault he'd closed his eyes to it and tried to forget. He knew this was partly due to his need to punish himself. The problems arose when he realised he'd let the things Jane had loved fall into disrepair. He should have been a better custodian.

Carefully he began replacing the clumps of earth Amelia had dug up, patting the turf on top and trying to return the grass to how it had looked before. Once he had finished he sat back and regarded the overgrown rose bushes thoughtfully. After a few minutes he got up, walked to one of the outbuildings and began his search for the gardening equipment.

* * *

Half an hour later his fingers were scratched and bleeding, but the tangle of rose bushes had been trimmed back to a more respectable size. Each individual plant was distinguishable from its neighbour now, and although there were no buds on the bushes it looked more like the garden it had once been.

As he sat back on his knees he sensed Amelia's presence behind him.

'They must look beautiful when the flowers are in bloom,' she said quietly.

They had been beautiful. The whole garden had been beautiful. He and Jane had often taken evening strolls through the grounds in the summer months, stopping to admire the roses or sniff the fragrant flowers.

He turned to face her, trying to work out what to say. Amelia was already walking back towards the house, her head held high, but the slight hunching of her shoulders belying the burden she was carrying.

Amelia didn't want to return inside just yet. She had been shocked by Edward's reaction to her trying to do a spot of gardening and was still smarting from his harsh words. She couldn't quite understand why he had reacted in such a fashion; it was only a rose garden. Part of her had wanted to be helpful, to repay Edward's kindness with an act to show she was grateful for him letting her stay. Her other motivation for wanting to attack the flowerbeds was much more selfish.

Amelia couldn't bear to be idle, not at the moment. Every second she wasn't occupied with some task or other her mind wandered back to the encounter with McNair in his study. Over and over she would relive the moment he had lunged at her and she'd plunged the letter opener into his abdomen. It made her feel sick and light headed, but no amount of willpower could stop her from dwelling on her crime.

Only when she was occupied, preferably doing something physically demanding, did her mind take a break from brooding over the events of earlier in the week. So she'd decided to attack the flowerbeds, thinking Edward would be pleased to see some part of the estate tidy and thriving.

Amelia kicked at a pebble on the path, taking her frustration out on the small stone. She wanted to be angry with Edward for speaking to her in such a tone, but part of her wondered what had fuelled the outburst. There was something deeper going on at Beechwood Manor, something she didn't quite understand yet. Edward was a damaged soul—no one shut themselves away from the world like he did without a good reason. She rather suspected he had lost someone close to him and that loss had prevented him from moving on with his life.

Ever since she had first arrived Amelia had felt the grief and heartache emanating from Edward, but she had felt something else as well. There was a power there, a sense of authority that made Amelia wish he would just fold her in his arms and keep her safe from the world.

Pausing, Amelia flopped down on a bench and closed her eyes. Here she went again, jumping to conclusions about people before she really knew them. With McNair she had been taken in by his good looks and easy charm. She'd fallen for him within ten minutes of meeting him and declared her undying love less than a week later. Her judgement when it came to men couldn't be trusted. She didn't know Edward, not really, and she wouldn't allow herself to ever fall victim to a man ever again. From now on she wouldn't pin her hopes on anyone but herself.

'Good afternoon, miss.'

A voice startled Amelia from her reverie. She sprang to her feet, ready to flee if the need arose, and was confronted by a stout, portly man in his sixties. Slowly Amelia relaxed. If he did pose a threat she rather thought she would outpace him with nothing more than a brisk walk.

Forcing her racing pulse to slow, Amelia smiled warily at the newcomer.

'Tobias Guthry at your service, miss, and what a pleasure it is to meet you.'

Amelia took his proffered hand, allowing his podgy fingers to enclose hers briefly.

'I am Sir Edward's steward, been summoned by the master himself. Sorry if I startled you at all.'

Mr Guthry was looking increasingly anxious and Amelia decided he was most likely harmless.

'You must forgive me, Mr Guthry, I was miles away and I wasn't expecting anyone.'

'You gave me quite a surprise yourself, miss. In the past three years I've been working for the master I've not seen a single other person about the grounds.'

'Yes, I understand Sir Edward is a very private person,' Amelia said, wondering if this amiable little man might be willing to tell her any more about her host.

'Oh, very private, miss, the most private a man could be.'

'Tell me, has he always been this way?'

Mr Guthry gave her a sidelong look and his already pink complexion turned beetroot.

'I wouldn't like to speculate, miss, I've only known him since after the…er…the incident.'

He glanced at the fire-damaged portion of the building as he spoke.

So the fire had been the turning point in Edward's life.

She wondered if he'd been injured in it, or whether he'd lost someone he loved as she had first suspected. A slither of guilt slid into Amelia's consciousness. After all he was doing for her she ought to know more about him and the reasons behind his peculiar choice of lifestyle. The worst thing was he'd probably dropped hints, even alluded to whatever terrible event had affected him so badly, but she had been too caught up in her own world to notice.

'Do you come to see Sir Edward often?' Amelia asked, changing tack.

'Only every couple of months.'

She was surprised at this. Edward seemed the sort of man who liked to be in charge of things, completely in control. True, to manage an estate such as this, which must encompass land outside the boundaries of Beechwood Manor with tenants and farmers and livestock, you would have to not live in such reclusive circumstances, but all the same she couldn't picture him giving up complete control.

'Sir Edward must trust you very much, Mr Guthry.'

The portly man visibly swelled with pride at Amelia's words.

'Come inside and please make yourself comfortable, I will let Sir Edward know you are here.'

Amelia ushered him into the sitting room she'd entered the night before. It was the only room in the main part of the house vaguely suitable for guests. At least the chairs were no longer covered in dust sheets, but still there was rather a ghostly feel to the room.

She left Mr Guthry wiggling his ample backside into one of the armchairs and set off in search of Edward.

Cautiously she knocked on the door to his set of rooms in the West Wing, and when there was no answer after a few seconds she took a few steps inside. Edward's sketches were scattered across the desk, with an open pad of paper resting on the windowsill, but there was no sign of Edward. Amelia knew he wasn't outside or in the main portion of the house, which only left the fire-damaged East Wing.

Quickly Amelia padded along the landing, feeling like a rebellious child for even thinking about venturing into the East Wing. His warning never to enter that part of the house was ringing in her ears, but she couldn't exactly leave Mr Guthry waiting indefinitely.

At the end of the landing another long corridor swept off at an angle to the main house, identical upstairs and down. Amelia paused before stepping over the threshold, a shiver travelling down her spine and making her glance back over her shoulder to check she was alone.

She took a step and then another. Already the fire damage was evident: blackened walls, the faint smell of smoke, damaged paintings hanging over the peeling wallpaper.

'I told you not to enter the East Wing.' Edward's voice made Amelia jump with fright.

He emerged from the shadows like a phantom, taking Amelia firmly by the arm and guiding her quickly back to the main section of the house.

'You are never to enter the East Wing.'

Amelia was about to protest, about to question why, but she saw the haunted look in Edward's eyes and decided for once to keep her mouth securely shut. She waited for him to reprimand her further but he just continued to lead her away from the fire damaged corridor.

'There's a Mr Guthry waiting to see you,' she said, once her heart had stopped pounding and she'd caught her breath.

The normality of her response, or the familiarity of Mr Guthry's name, seemed to pull Edward back from whatever precipice he was teetering over. Slowly he regained

his focus and Amelia was relieved to see the haunted look
fade from his eyes.

'Good,' he grunted as they descended the main staircase, 'He can find the proof all this murder business is
nonsense and then you can be on your way.'

Normally Amelia would have bristled at his tone and
his dismissive attitude towards her plight, but even she
could recognise a man who had just confronted some past
demon and deserved a little forgiveness for his sharp manner, so instead of making a withering retort she led Edward calmly to Mr Guthry, all the time wondering what it
was in the East Wing that Edward didn't want her to see.

With Edward and Mr Guthry ensconced in the sitting
room Amelia wandered the house for a few minutes before finding herself back in the homely West Wing. Safe
in the knowledge that Edward would be busy for at least
the next half an hour Amelia ventured into his bedroom,
the room they had both shared the night before, and made
her way to the desk. Trying her hardest not to pry any
further through his personal documents, she sat and rum-
maged through the drawers until she found a blank sheet
of paper and a pen.

Amelia was not a keen writer of letters. Sitting and con-
structing beautifully worded, descriptive prose was not
in her character, she much preferred to be outside doing
something. Nevertheless today she would grit her teeth
and get on with her task.

Dearest Lizzie,
How long it seems since I left you in London and how
much has happened during that time. I hope you are
faring better than I, and that my aunt has not discov-
ered our deception and is treating you well.

Amelia paused, sucking on the end of the pen as she wondered how best to word the description of what had happened over the past few weeks. She did not want to trouble her cousin more than was necessary, but Lizzie was currently masquerading as Amelia Eastway and, if Edward was right and there was a chance McNair had survived, her cousin could become a target.

A hundred times I have wished for you to be by my side these past few days. I have been sorely in need of your calm words and sensible cautions. As you had suspected, McNair was not the man I had hoped and ever since I tracked him down in Brighton a series of unspeakable events have occurred.

I cannot go into detail on paper, but I hope we will be reunited soon and I will tell you everything then.

The most important thing, dearest Lizzie, is for you to be vigilant. I fear I am being hunted, most likely by a magistrate or one of his officers, but also possibly by McNair. As you are currently going by the name Amelia Eastway I urge you to be careful. I could never forgive myself if something happened to you because of my foolishness.

I will write again soon, hopefully with a solution to this predicament rather than all these concerns, but until then know that I am safe. A gentleman has given me shelter in his old dilapidated house for a few days until things have settled down. I feel peculiarly safe here.

All my love,
Amelia

Chapter Six

Edward wanted some privacy, but with Amelia hovering outside the door he knew he wasn't going to get much time to himself.

'Come in, Amelia,' he bellowed after she'd strolled past the open door for the twelfth time.

'Am I disturbing you?' she asked innocently.

'Yes.'

'Oh.' She looked taken aback. 'I can leave.'

She turned back towards the door and Edward sighed, knowing she would just pace up and down until he agreed to listen to whatever it was she had to say.

'Stay,' he said more softly.

Hesitantly Amelia perched on the edge of one of the sofas, sitting primly as no doubt her governess taught her all society ladies sat.

Edward waited, knowing she would come out and tell him what she wanted eventually.

'How did it go with Mr Guthry?' she asked.

Under her poised veneer Edward could detect a hint of nervousness. She nibbled on her lower lip in that distracted manner of hers and one of her legs was fidgeting up and down under her skirts.

'He's a very sensible man, Amelia, you have nothing to worry about.'

She nodded. 'But he could be linked back to you and then the magistrate would know exactly where to find me.'

'Mr Guthry will be discreet in his enquiries.'

Again Amelia nodded, but Edward could tell she wasn't convinced. He wanted to reach out and place a hand on her knee to stop the constant jittering, but instead leaned back in his chair.

'Someone might wonder why he is asking questions.'

'We need to know what the situation is,' Edward said a tad impatiently.

Amelia fell silent and Edward wondered if it would be unforgivably rude to usher her out so he could get the privacy he was so in need of. His head was in a spin, memories of the night of the fire sparring with regrets of letting the estate fall into such disrepair.

'It's getting late,' Amelia said after a few minutes, 'I was just wondering where I would sleep tonight.'

The memory of her soft body pressed up against his sprang uninvited to Edward's mind. He felt the hot flash of desire, a primal urge encouraging him to sweep Amelia up and hold her close to him again. It lasted only a moment, but it was enough to trigger a cascade of guilt and self-loathing.

'Of course, there are plenty of bedrooms. You may take your pick.' He paused, but chivalry made him continue, 'Unless of course you would prefer my bedroom and I will find another.'

'No, I'm sure I will find a suitable room.'

He expected her to stand and go off in search of a room to call her own for the next few days, but she remained perched on the edge of the sofa.

'Was there something else?' he asked.

Most people would understand the comment to mean he wanted to be left in peace, but Amelia cocked her head and smiled.

'Come and help me choose a room,' she said.

Edward looked down at the papers scattered across his desk and wondered how offended she would be if he just said no.

'Ten minutes,' Amelia pressed. 'And then you can go back to ignoring me for the rest of the day.'

Years ago Edward had known how to play the generous host. He had entertained and amused his guests and ensured they were never left feeling uncomfortable in his home. He supposed that was why he felt a little uneasy at leaving Amelia to amuse herself whilst he continued with his life as if nothing had changed, but it wasn't as though she were an invited guest.

'You can spare me ten minutes,' Amelia said. 'Just grit your teeth and show me the bedrooms.'

Edward felt the beginnings of a smile start to form on his lips and quickly suppressed it. In a world where people tiptoed around others it was refreshing to have someone speak quite so bluntly.

He stood, stretched, and then offered her his arm, feeling the unfamiliar wave of contentment as she slipped her delicate fingers into the crook of his elbow. He'd forgotten what it felt like to have a woman's hand rest trustingly on his forearm.

'The house has sixteen bedrooms,' Edward said, 'but four are in the East Wing. There's two in the West Wing, one of which is mine, and ten in the main part of the house.'

As they walked up the stairs he tried to remember the last time any of the rooms were occupied. There had been a garden party a couple of months before the fire, family and friends had gathered to celebrate some occasion or other and as they'd stayed long into the balmy evening his wife had offered most of their guests a room for the night. Edward doubted anyone had set foot in many of the bedrooms since then. He certainly hadn't.

Amelia poked her head into each of the bedrooms Edward indicated, glancing around for a few moments before returning to him in the corridor. In one room she hesitated for a little longer and Edward found himself stepping in after her.

He had to reach out and hold on to the door frame for support as he crossed the threshold.

'Edward?' Amelia's voice seemed to come from a long way away even though she was standing right in front of him.

As if in a trance he moved further into the room, trailing his fingers across the faded wallpaper and feeling his feet sink into the plush carpet. He hadn't stepped into this room since the fire, hadn't been able to face the memories of the chamber he'd shared with his wife for their four years of marriage. Unlike many couples they hadn't kept separate rooms, preferring instead to come together at the end of the day, and this had been their meeting place. A place where they had shared their hopes and fears and their love for each other.

With a heavy heart Edward sat down on the bed, placing a hand on the embroidered covers and remembering the last night they had spent together.

'Please, leave me,' Edward said, his voice coming out as a hoarse croak.

Instead of following his orders, Amelia sat down beside him, her petite form perched on the edge of the mattress. Gently she took his hand and without a word folded it in her own.

His memories were private and still raw, his grief was

overwhelming at times, and he knew that over the past three years he had coped by hiding from the pain rather than confronting it.

They sat side by side, hand in hand for a good long time and slowly Edward felt the grief begin to subside and the pull of reality build. Standing, he began to look around the room, allowing different objects and pictures to spark fond memories and even pausing before the small portrait of his late wife he used to keep on his bedside table. Gently he ran his fingers over her face, tracing the lines that had once been so familiar.

'I would rather you didn't choose this room to make your own,' he said.

'Of course.'

With one final glance behind him Edward led Amelia from the bedroom, closing the door firmly after her.

'We could—' Amelia began to say, but Edward cut her off with a shake of his head.

He didn't want to talk, didn't want to share his memories.

'Let's find you a bedroom,' Edward said resolutely.

He led Amelia through the house to the West Wing. His current bedroom and sitting room were in this part of the house and he had a feeling Amelia subconsciously wanted the security of being close to him at night. Although maybe not as close as they had been the previous night.

'This room is quite small,' he said, opening the door to the only other bedroom in the West Wing.

It was small but beautiful. Two large windows let in bright streams of sunlight and a four-poster bed dominated the room. Dainty furniture was squeezed into the rest of the space and the whole room had a definite feminine feel to it.

'I love it,' Amelia declared, walking over to the bed and

perching on the edge. Carefully she inspected the bedcovers and when all was to her satisfaction she smiled with pleasure. 'It's just perfect.'

And only a door away from his room. Probably too close for comfort, but at least there were two heavy wooden door separating them.

With the sunlight reflecting off the golden highlights in her hair and the smile lighting up her face Amelia looked like some goddess from mythology.

'I will leave you to get settled in,' he said. 'I have a few things I need to do.'

Quickly Edward left and made his way into his own rooms. There was a sense of urgency building inside him, the need to capture something special, almost magical. For years his sketching had been about losing himself in something that occupied his mind and allowed him to escape from his memories, or a way to relieve stress and tension, but before that, long ago, he'd drawn because he'd *had* to draw. Something or someone had inspired him and he couldn't help but put pencil to paper.

Just now, looking at Amelia, for the first time in years he had that feeling again. It was a primal need, something Edward had to satisfy, and as he picked up his pencils and a fresh sheet of paper he allowed himself to enjoy the warm buzz that was building inside him.

Chapter Seven

Amelia wandered downstairs, feeling a little lost. She was pleased that she had a room of her own now and a very comfortable room at that, despite a small part of her craving the warmth and protection she'd felt the previous night in Edward's arms. As a well brought-up young lady Amelia knew her even just being in this house alone with Edward would destroy her reputation and, if anyone ever found out they'd actually shared a bed, there would be moral outrage. Even so, Amelia had felt particularly safe with Edward's strong arms wrapped around her and it wasn't as though anything inappropriate *had* happened.

With a sigh Amelia admitted to herself her reputation would already be in tatters because of her crime. She would never be able to go out in society again, never take tea with respectable ladies, never whirl around ballrooms or flirt with eligible bachelors. Her life as it had been before was over. The best she could hope for was to escape back to India where no doubt she would have to live a life of quiet repentance. It was against her character and against her spirit, but Amelia had to acknowledge if it kept her from doing something awful again maybe it would be worth it.

Even now as Amelia wandered through the house her

mind kept returning to Edward. Strong, safe Edward. A man she had known for only a day and already she found herself trusting him as though he were her guardian angel. She was too quick to trust, she too easily judged a man honourable based on very little information. Edward had a powerful physical presence and when she caught him in a moment when the frown dropped from his face he was a very attractive man, but that shouldn't be enough to make her trust him. Amelia knew her attraction to McNair had been primarily due to his good looks and easy charm— surely she should have learnt from that experience.

As she reached the hallway Amelia froze. Someone was pushing the door open and with Edward retired to his rooms it couldn't be anyone good.

'Golly gosh, what a fright you gave me,' a plump woman in her late fifties said as she bustled through the door.

Amelia felt herself relaxing a little. The older woman looked no more of a threat than a fluffy pussycat.

'Not in all my years have I ever felt my heart beat so fast.'

'I'm sorry for startling you,' Amelia said, recovering enough herself to move forward and greet the woman properly.

'No harm done, my little ducky, I'll live to see another day. I'm Mrs Henshaw, but why don't you just call me Goody? Everyone else does, except the master, of course, but rules are different for some folk.'

Goody bustled through the hallway, took Amelia by the arm and began to lead her through the house. Already the half-derelict mansion felt more alive, even warmer somehow, with the older woman's presence.

'Now you must tell me who you are and what on earth you are doing here.'

Amelia thought about lying, she knew she shouldn't let

another person in on her secret, but Goody's kindly face made her want to spill every secret she had.

'I'm Amelia,' she said as she was directed to sit on one of the wooden stools in the kitchen. Next to her Goody began unpacking a small sack, placing a loaf of bread and various other foodstuffs on the table. 'I'm in a bit of trouble and Edward, Sir Edward, is letting me stay for a few days.'

That made Goody stop what she was doing and stare at Amelia for a few seconds.

'Well, I never,' Goody said eventually. 'I never thought the day would come.'

Tears began to fill the older woman's eyes and immediately Amelia wondered just what was going on.

'What day? What do you mean?'

Goody shook her head and patted Amelia kindly on the hand.

'I'm just glad to see the master being roused by something. By someone. Now why don't I fetch us some biscuits and make a nice cup of tea and you can tell me all about yourself.'

Goody busied herself lighting the stove and boiling the kettle and after a few minutes she set a steaming cup of tea in front of Amelia, accompanied by a large plate of biscuits.

'I baked them fresh this morning.'

'Goody, have you known Sir Edward for long?' Amelia asked as she took a bite of one of the buttery biscuits.

'Oh, Lordy, yes. I can remember when he was no more than a lad, must have been about seven or eight. That was when I joined the family.'

Amelia knew she shouldn't pry, but Edward intrigued her and with his often monosyllabic conversation she wouldn't get much information from him.

'You worked for his parents?'

'Indeed I did, worked for the late Sir Edward and Lady Gray for twelve years. And then when they passed away I carried on as housekeeper for young Master Edward.'

'Edward must have been young when his parents passed away.'

Goody nodded sadly, the tears springing to her eyes again. Amelia wondered what this family had done to earn such love and loyalty from a former servant.

'He was only twenty when his father died, still at university studying, of course. And then poor Lady Gray died not two months later. It was all very sudden, a great loss.'

So at one point in his life Edward had been out enjoying the world, studying and gaining an education. Something had changed him, pushed him into this reclusive state. She assumed it was the fire that had ravaged the East Wing, but it was interesting to hear how he had been when he was a younger man.

'That's when Edward inherited the house and the estate?'

Goody beamed proudly as if she had brought Edward up herself. 'He was such a good master and landlord, despite his young age. All of his tenants agreed he was just and fair, and you can't ask for more than that, ducky.'

Amelia reached out and took another biscuit from the plate, crumbling it before popping a small piece into her mouth.

'Was it the fire? Was that what changed everything?' Amelia had never been good at being subtle in her approach and she decided now just to come out and ask the question she wanted to know the answer to.

'Mrs Henshaw, I didn't realise you had arrived.' Edward's deep voice made Amelia jump guiltily up from her seat. 'I see you have met my guest.'

Amelia swallowed nervously and wondered how long he had been standing there.

'What a lovely young lady she is, sir.' Goody paused, and then pressed on. 'I don't wish to speak out of turn, master, but have you spared a thought for her reputation? A young lady staying with just a man for company…I wouldn't want there to be gossip.'

Edward waved a dismissive hand, but smiled indulgently at his old housekeeper.

'Always looking out for me, Mrs Henshaw. I don't deserve you. However, I think it would be fair to say Amelia has bigger problems to worry about than her reputation.'

Amelia marvelled at the change the older woman brought about in Sir Edward. There was a fondness there, an easy companionship that came of knowing someone for a very long time. Amelia wondered if it was the first time she'd seen Edward smile properly and glanced at the old housekeeper again. She must be a special woman to have this effect on her guarded host.

'Ah, that's easy for you to say, sir, but a young woman always has to think about her reputation. Miss Amelia is young and no doubt one day she will want to marry. A woman can find even a small stain on her reputation a significant impediment.'

Edward looked at Amelia and raised an eyebrow.

'I honestly don't mind,' Amelia said, 'It is very kind of Sir Edward to let me stay here. He shouldn't have to disrupt his life in any other way.'

'I could come to stay for a little while, sir,' Goody pushed on. 'No one could say anything improper was going on with me in the house. And it would give me a chance to tidy up a little at the same time.'

Amelia saw the determined glint in the older woman's eyes and wondered if she was just the excuse Mrs Henshaw had been looking for to ensure her old master was properly looked after.

'I wouldn't like to inconvenience you,' Edward said.

'Nonsense. I'll pack my bags this evening and return tomorrow.'

Edward gave a curt nod and then turned his attention back to Amelia.

'Would you grant me a moment of your time, Amelia?'

It was an order rather than a request and immediately Amelia felt her heart begin to pound in her chest. Slipping from her perch on the kitchen stool, she followed Edward from the room and into the sitting room she'd first met him in the night before.

'Is there something you want to ask me, Amelia?' Edward asked, turning to face her.

He was standing close to her, so close it emphasised their difference in stature and build. Amelia felt small compared to Edward, but despite his powerful build and obvious physical advantages over her she didn't feel threatened at all. There was an underlying gentleness about Edward, obvious even through his gruff exterior. However angry he might become, however much she might irk him, Amelia knew he would never raise a hand to her.

She shook her head.

'Are you sure? I would rather you ask anything of me directly than gossip with anyone else.'

Amelia felt the heat begin to rise in her cheeks as the shame and embarrassment washed over her. She was selfish and sometimes she didn't think how her actions affected other people. Amelia knew her flaws well, but it didn't seem to stop her from acting or speaking before she had considered the impact on other people.

'I was wondering why you keep yourself shut up here, away from the world,' Amelia said eventually.

Edward turned away from her and stared out the window for a long couple of minutes. Amelia was convinced he wasn't going to answer her, but finally he exhaled and cleared his throat.

'Sometimes something happens in life that even the strongest person finds it difficult to deal with,' he said slowly, 'My solution was to shut myself off from the world, to deal with my pain in my own time without anyone making it worse by inadvertently reminding me of things I didn't want to remember.'

Amelia wanted to push him, wanted to ask him just what pain he was recovering from, but something made her hold back. Edward would tell her when he was ready, pressing him now would only make him close up completely. This was the most frank conversation they had shared since her arrival.

'Has it worked?' Amelia asked instead.

Edward turned back to face her, a small smile tugging at his lips.

'Do you know, I've no idea? Who is to say what I would be feeling if I'd done things differently?'

Amelia felt an urge to reach out and take his hand, to reassure him everything would get better, but she knew she was not in a position to give that reassurance. He seemed lost and empty, as if he had strayed from his path in life and was now struggling to find his way back. Amelia wanted to help. Despite her preoccupation with her own problems, she wanted to guide him to a place where he could be happy.

Quietly she snorted. All her life she had been pampered and protected. Everyone had done her bidding and she could count on one hand the times she had not got her own way How could she, a now disgraced socialite, hope to comfort a man who had obviously suffered greatly?

Edward leaned back from his desk and admired the drawing in front of him. Whatever disruption Amelia might have brought into his life he could not deny she was doing wonders for his creativity. The sketch sitting on his desk was one of the best pieces he had ever done. It was a portrait of Amelia and he had managed to capture some of her essence, some of her vitality on the page. In the drawing she was captured in motion and he'd even managed to reproduce the little frown that furrowed her brow when things weren't quite going her way.

Carefully he set the drawing down, reluctantly acknowledging he could do no more by candlelight and the finer details would have to wait until morning.

He was tired now, but he doubted he would sleep. So much had changed in the course of a couple of days, his entire life had been turned upside down. From tomorrow he would have two people living in his house alongside him, but despite his grumblings Edward had welcomed Mrs Henshaw's suggestion she come to stay. Amelia would have someone else to talk to and he would be doing his bit to protect her reputation. Although he would have to get used to the idea of even more social interaction.

Edward sighed. He knew his manners sometimes left something to be desired. He could be abrupt and blunt and believed in using the fewest words possible to get his point across. More than once he had seen the shock in Amelia's eyes as he didn't soften his words for her ears. He supposed if she would be staying for a few days he would get used to socialising again, maybe even used to considering someone else's needs.

Slipping into bed, Edward allowed himself to consider

the future for the first time in three years. Ever since the fire he had lived day by day, focusing on surviving rather than enjoying his life. Looking back, he could see it had been necessary for him, the best way for him to grieve and process all of the emotions that had threatened to suffocate him in the months after his bereavement, but today Amelia had made him question how he coped with things and what came next.

Edward sat, moulded his pillow into a more comfortable shape and then laid down again. Maybe his coping strategies weren't the healthiest or the most robust, but they had kept him from falling into the deepest pit of despair over the past few years. For now that would have to be enough.

Edward awoke with a start. There was a scream, followed closely by another one. Quickly he jumped out of bed, his reflexes sharp despite years of living on his own. He'd reached the door before he realised he was naked and, cursing for the delay it caused him, he quickly pulled on his dressing gown.

Amelia's room was next to his, the only other bedroom in this part of the house. His heart was pounding as he threw open her door, wondering what he was going to find. Thoughts of an intruder attacking Amelia crowded his mind and as he dashed into the room he was ready to fight whoever was there.

The room was empty apart from Amelia's small form under the bedcovers. She was still lying down, curled up like a small child in bed, screaming in her sleep.

For a moment Edward didn't know what to do, but then his instincts took over and he was by her side immediately.

Gently he scooped Amelia into his arms and held her firmly, but not tightly. He murmured soothing sounds and stroked her hair, all the time making sure she could feel the strength and safety of his body.

As soon as he'd gathered her to him the screams had stopped to be replaced by sobs that racked her whole body. Edward held Amelia whilst she whimpered and nuzzled into him, wondering what memory or event had caused such terror.

'I'm sorry,' Amelia whispered after a few minutes. She'd woken up at some point during the ordeal, but Edward just continued to soothe her.

'Hush,' he said gently. 'Nothing to be sorry about.'

It felt oddly right to be sitting with Amelia in his arms in the middle of the night. Edward felt useful again, as if he had made a difference to someone's life, and that feeling was beyond compare.

'Do you want to tell me about it?' he asked.

For a long time Amelia just sat with her head resting against his chest, but Edward didn't push the matter. He knew all about nightmares, all about the very real terror they could inspire in you. For well over a year after the fire he had woken up certain his bedsheets were burning. He would hear screams in his sleep and be convinced the fire was raging all over again. Dreams and nightmares were not something to be easily dismissed, they could have a big impact on your mental state and ability to cope with events.

'I can hear your heart beat,' Amelia said, tilting her head slightly to look up at him.

Edward held her a little tighter and wondered whether he would have coped better with his bereavement if he'd had someone to hold him and help him through.

As Amelia stared up into his eyes Edward had the urge to bend down and kiss her. It wasn't lust, just an urge to touch his lips to hers, to connect with her.

'It was McNair,' Amelia said eventually.

'You dreamed about him?'

Hesitantly she nodded.

'It felt so real, as if I were back there in the room with him.'

Edward was well acquainted with the pounding heart and sweaty palms that accompanied these sorts of dreams, the features that made you question what was real and what was imagined.

'It's over now,' he said soothingly.

'Every time I close my eyes I can see my hand holding the letter opener.' Amelia gave a little sob. 'And I can see the blood oozing out of his body.'

As she nuzzled in closer to him Edward felt his body begin to respond. Trying to distract himself, he ran a hand up and down her back, but found the warmth of her body having the opposite effect.

'It's normal to have nightmares and flashbacks after such a traumatic event,' Edward said, trying to keep his voice neutral. 'It will get better with time.'

Amelia looked up at him with such trust and hope in her eyes that Edward felt the weight of responsibility he had for her.

'You promise?'

'I promise.'

She didn't push him as to how he knew, didn't ask for his personal experience even though Edward suspected she knew more about his circumstances than he'd told her.

Sighing, Amelia rested her head back on his chest and Edward found himself dropping a quick kiss on her tousled hair. It was intimate and immediately he regretted it, but Amelia didn't seem to notice.

As she relaxed into him, her body growing heavy as she slipped back into sleep, Edward continued to hold her.

She wouldn't sleep unless she felt safe and after the terror of her nightmares she needed to rest.

After a few minutes of Amelia's steady breathing Edward closed his eyes. He knew he would not sleep, but he tried to force himself to relax. His mind was a hive of activity, thoughts and doubts and self-recriminations.

Amelia shifted in his arms, making a little mewl of contentment as she slept. It felt good to be the one who had made such a difference to her, the one that could make her feel safe. He knew he had become a little self-absorbed during his years of solitude—with only his grief for company it was difficult not to. As much as he grumbled about having Amelia invade his privacy he wondered whether maybe it was a good thing to challenge himself, just for a couple of days.

With these thoughts circling his head Edward settled himself back against the headboard, trying to ignore the warm glow he felt inside from holding Amelia in his arms.

Chapter Eight

Amelia brushed the dust from her hands and stood back to admire her handiwork. Slowly she looked around the room and frowned. Things weren't going quite how she'd envisioned them.

That morning she'd woken once again in Edward's arms. Memories of her nightmares the night before had flooded back and she'd felt a supreme sense of gratitude towards Edward for comforting her. When she was a child Amelia had experienced night terrors, awful dreams about the monsters coming to hurt her and her family, and every night her cousin Lizzie had climbed into bed with her and held her until Amelia had banished the bad dreams. The night before had been the worst nightmare she'd ever had, so vivid and detailed it had been as though she were back in McNair's lodgings, plunging the small blade into his flesh once again.

At the memory Amelia shook herself. Edward had gathered her up and held her close and soon the nightmare had been weakened to a faint echo. She felt inexplicably safe with him and when he'd released her from his grip that morning she'd heard herself suppressing a murmur of protest.

As Edward had slipped away and Amelia had woken fully she had felt a crashing sense of unease. She had wanted Edward to remain holding her all morning, wrapping her in his arms and never letting go. Her body had stirred as he'd moved against her and Amelia felt that familiar heat rising all the way up from her toes.

The last time she'd reacted like that was when she'd fallen for McNair.

Not wanting to examine her feelings too deeply, Amelia had thrown herself into a flurry of physical tasks. Today she was tackling the sitting room. If she was going to stay with Edward whilst Mr Guthry made enquiries about McNair and the authorities then she had decided she would help brighten the place up a little. After the initial disaster in the rose beds yesterday Amelia was not going to be deterred. She had seen Edward's wistful look as he took in the dust and grime as they'd searched through the bedrooms the day before. He might not know he wanted the house to be spruced up, but Amelia was sure deep down it was the truth.

Not having any budget to work with, or any means of obtaining new furnishings, Amelia had decided to first strip back the room to the bare essentials and then forage around the house for items to brighten the place up and replace what she had removed. In her mind she had pictured a wondrous transformation. The reality was a little disappointing.

Grimacing, Amelia wiped her dusty hand on her dress and swept her hair from her face. She knew she must look a state, but that was one advantage of living such a life of solitude, she did not have to care too much about her appearance. Apart from for Edward, of course.

There it was again, that rebellious thought about her host. There were many emotions when Amelia thought

of Edward, gratitude and relief being in the top five, but
there was something else, something deeper, too. Considering she had only met the man a few days ago, she felt a
connection with him, despite the myriad of obvious differences between them. When she caught him looking at
her a warmth swept through her body and he made her
feel safe and secure even in these most difficult times.
Then there were her reactions to him holding her close,
the subtle quickening of her pulse, the warming of her
skin. She knew he had only held her to comfort her from
her dreams, but it had been so lovely to feel another person's arms wrapped round her, especially as that person
was Edward. It was almost devastating to think none of
these feelings could be trusted.

'Dear Lord, what on earth has happened here?' Goody
gasped as she bustled into the room.

Amelia looked around sheepishly.

'I wanted to brighten the place up a little, to do something for Edward, Sir Edward.'

Goody patted her kindly on the hand whilst still looking around in horror.

'Well, I'm sure he will see you have the best of intentions, my dear. That's what counts.'

'I want him to know I really appreciate him taking
me in.'

'You should just tell him, ducky. And never forget he is
getting something out of this arrangement, too.'

Amelia looked at her, puzzled. As far as she could tell
Edward was taking all the risk sheltering her for no real
benefit. It wasn't as though she had any money to pay him
for her lodgings, or any contacts in this country to see him
justly rewarded for his kindness.

'He gets your company,' Goody said. 'Something he
sorely needed,' she added half under her breath.

Amelia had to smile. Although Goody was very polite to Edward and acted in many ways the good family servant, she did have quite strong opinions about her former master with regard to his well-being.

'Why don't we get these dust sheets cleared out of here and you can help me give the room a good airing?' Goody suggested. 'After that we can worry about putting things back together.'

Amelia relished the physical work of folding the dust sheets into neat squares which they stacked in one corner and then cleaning and polishing the furniture that had dulled with disuse. As they worked Goody chatted away, talking about life in the village and giving Amelia the gossip on the locals. It made Amelia feel normal for a while and part of her craved this sort of life. A life where she belonged somewhere, where people knew her. In India she had felt at home for many years, she had a loving if distant father and her cousin Lizzie was her closest friend and confidant in the world. True, she missed her mother who had died when Amelia had been just seven, but she hadn't been unhappy, not until McNair had come along and seduced her with his honeyed words. Then she couldn't wait to get away, to chase after the man she'd thought she'd been in love with. The rolling green hills and dusty tracks that surrounded her home had lost their charm and Amelia had lost interest in the people who surrounded her. Now, looking back, she could see how self-absorbed she'd been. No wonder her father had despaired and sent her to England for a Season in London.

As she worked she wondered what she wanted from her future. The things that had once seemed so important to her, excitement and adventure, now felt soured and naive. If she could have anything it would be to turn back time, to have never met McNair, never fallen under his spell and never followed him back to England. She would give anything not to have his death on her conscience. No matter what Edward said, she still believed she must surely have killed him.

'I think that's enough for today,' Goody said when they had wiped down all the surfaces and rid the room of dust. 'Tomorrow we can work on the carpet and curtains. I've got dinner to prepare now and you look as though you could do with a bath.'

At the suggestion Amelia almost squealed with delight. A bath would be glorious. She had managed to scrub most of the grime from her body with cold water, but it had not been a pleasant or relaxing experience. Now she was covered in dust and certainly not looking or feeling her best.

'Would it be possible?'

Goody laughed at her hopeful expression and took her by the arm.

'It won't be the most glamorous bath ever, but it's possible.'

Edward regarded the house with a critical eye. When he had woken this morning, stiff from holding Amelia in a sitting position all night, he'd felt the need to clear the cobwebs from his head. Donning his heavy boots and a coat to barricade him from the cold, he'd set out to take a walk about the estate. It had been an eye-opening experience.

Although he had left the house in the past three years he had never really done so with an appraising eye. Today he'd forced himself to look at the overgrown garden, the tumbledown portions of the house and the neglected estate, despite the feelings of regret they inspired inside him. Edward knew he'd let things go, stopped caring about what had once been so important to him. For a long while he hadn't seen the point of worrying about the state of his birthright, his estate, as he had lost his family, the people he had worked so hard to give a good lifestyle. His family would no longer grow up in Beechwood Manor and to Edward that had been a good enough reason to let it fall into disrepair.

Sighing, he acknowledged all the work that needed to be done to get the estate back to its former glory. It seemed almost insurmountable and, if he had been faced with such a challenge even a couple of weeks ago, then he would have retreated back to his rooms and tried to forget about it. But he wondered whether he needed a project to focus on, something that he could be proud of. For too long he had allowed himself to languish and now he could see just how his estate had suffered.

Knowing he didn't need to make a final decision on what to start with straight away, Edward re-entered the house. Maybe it was enough that he was acknowledging the disrepair and the damage, one day he would decide what he needed to do. The idea of employing a gardener or an architect to fix the structural damage filled him with dread, but part of him wondered if he needed to take the first step to restoring the house he had once been so happy in.

Hearing a soft, sweet melody coming from the direction of the kitchen, Edward stopped where he was and listened for just a second. In all the years Mrs Henshaw had been his housekeeper he had never heard her sing. The dulcet tones must be coming from Amelia.

Suddenly he wanted to talk to her, share some of his plans for the estate. He hesitated, nearly heading for the solitude of his rooms anyway, but decisively he changed direction and made his way towards the kitchen. There was no harm in talking to her about the house and gardens.

Maybe Mrs Henshaw would have a plate of warm, buttery biscuits he always remembered so fondly from his youth.

As he pushed open the door to the kitchen the humidity hit him and made him pause. It was a warm, damp heat, not usual for this part of the house. Inside there was a big screen pulled across one half of the kitchen and the sound of soft splashing and Amelia singing coming from behind it.

Edward swallowed, looking around for Mrs Henshaw. She was nowhere to be seen.

The scene was so domestic, so routine, but Edward felt his senses heighten and his blood begin to rush around his body. It was natural for Amelia to be taking a bath. In fact, if he was any kind of host he would have provided her with the means to bathe earlier after her dash over the stormy Sussex Downs. What was not natural was his presence in this room with her. He should leave, slip out before Amelia or Mrs Henshaw found him here.

With once last glance at the screen Edward left the room, stopping to rest his forehead on the cool plaster of the wall outside. He could still hear Amelia's singing, the sweet soft tones drifting from the kitchen and trying to entice him back in like a siren's call.

Part of him wanted to deny the physical reaction he was experiencing at this very moment, but it was not the first time he had responded in this way to Amelia. That very first time he'd laid eyes on her as her wet dress slipped from her shoulders he'd felt the same. And again each time he'd held her body close to him at night. This was not a one-off.

The cool wall against his forehead was helping to disperse the vivid images racing through his imagination and the pictures of Amelia drizzling water over her naked body in the bath started to fade. Edward stood up straighter, turned and almost collided with Mrs Henshaw.

'Are you well, Sir Edward?' the kindly older woman asked with real concern in her voice.

Edward managed an unconvincing nod.

'You look like you've seen a ghost.'

Not seen, Edward thought, just aware of. Everything he did, every decision he made, his late wife's presence was there with him. He had loved Jane and he had lost her, and now he was defiling her memory by feeling desire for a woman he barely knew.

'What have you got there?' Edward asked, trying to distract himself.

'Three dresses for Amelia. I took the liberty of purchasing them from the dressmaker's in the village. They'll be far too big, of course, but I can adjust them.' She paused for a second. 'Amelia doesn't want to be walking around in Jane's clothes.'

Edward nodded. He supposed he should have thought of it himself.

'They're a present from you,' Mrs Henshaw said with a smile, patting him on the arm in a motherly fashion.

'How generous of me.'

'I'll be serving dinner in the dining room at eight,' Mrs Henshaw said, opening the door to the kitchen. Edward managed to restrain himself from peering over her shoulder, balling his hand into a fist and digging his nails into his palm.

'The dining room?'

'Second door on the left in the main hallway.'

He remembered where it was, he'd eaten in there enough throughout his life.

'It's shut up.'

'Not any more. I cleaned it earlier today. You can't expect Miss Amelia to take all her meals down here in the kitchen with me.'

Edward thought Mrs Henshaw would likely be better company than him.

'Anyway, it'll do you good to dress for dinner. How long has it been since you put on your full dress suit?'

Years. In fact, it had probably been eaten by moths many moons ago.

'It will be too much trouble for you to make dinner and serve it, after you seem to have spent the day cleaning as well,' Edward said.

'Don't worry, Sir Edward, I'm hardy,' Mrs Henshaw said cheerfully. 'Although I wouldn't say no to an extra pair of hands to help around the place. Maybe a maid or an odd-jobs boy, just someone to do the fetching and carrying my old arms are too tired for.'

There was a mischievous glint in his old housekeeper's eyes and Edward began to wonder how long she had been planning her assault on his life. Mrs Henshaw had been with his family for more years than he could remember. She cared about him, that he knew, and throughout the years of his seclusion she had insisted in keeping the house ticking over even if he hadn't kept on any other staff.

'You wouldn't want to see me suffer in my old age, would you, sir?'

Was it his imagination or had she become more stooped in the last thirty seconds? He watched as she grimaced and steadied her back with one hand.

'You are hardly old, Mrs Henshaw, I have a feeling you will outlive us all.'

This made the older woman smile.

'But about that maid?'

Edward had a soft spot for Mrs Henshaw and her overt

meddling didn't annoy him as it would if it came from anyone else.

'Fine. One maid. But she'd better keep out of my way and not touch my sketches. And make it clear it is only a short-term post, just whilst Amelia remains here.'

Mrs Henshaw immediately straightened and almost skipped with glee into the kitchen. As much as he'd never admit it, it felt warming to have someone worrying about his well-being.

Chapter Nine

Edward struggled with the fabric of his neckcloth and growled softly. He couldn't remember getting dressed for dinner to be such a complicated and arduous task, but he supposed in the days they'd hosted house parties and had friends over he'd had a valet to ensure he was properly presented.

With a grimace he glanced in the small mirror on his wall, pushing his hair back from his forehead as it flopped into his eyes. He was far from the debonair figure he was sure was popular in today's society, but he had to admit he did look smart even if his waistcoat was a little crumpled and his neckcloth not completely straight.

As he walked from his room towards the main part of the house he felt a moment of nerves and had to chastise himself softly. This was purely a dinner with the young woman he was assisting in her plight, nothing more. There was no need to worry his polite conversation might be too rusty or his manners too abrupt. Amelia was not some woman he was trying to impress. If he said or did the wrong thing it would not matter.

All thoughts of his lack of social graces fled his mind as he reached the bottom of the stairs and turned to find

Amelia beginning to descend behind him. She was dressed in a gown of deep red and, although it was once again too big for her petite frame, tonight someone had expertly pinned it to pull tight against her curves and sit well on her body. Her skin was pink and fresh and her hair still a little damp, with a few stray curls bobbing as she walked.

Amelia's eyes met his and immediately she smiled, an unfettered, instinctive smile of warmth and pleasure. Edward felt something snap inside him and found himself smiling back.

'Thank you for inviting me to dine with you,' Amelia said.

He hadn't, but of course he didn't say anything. Mrs Henshaw would be mortified if he ruined her cunning plan at the first hurdle.

'Thank you for the dresses. Mrs Henshaw has just pinned this one to fit for now, but she said she would adjust them for me,' she said, pulling at the material of the dress. She was obviously a little uncomfortable wearing a garment that didn't quite fit, but Edward thought she looked exquisite all the same.

'You look fine,' he said.

'Oh, good.'

He cursed himself for his lack of ability to compliment her, but Amelia recovered quickly.

'Mrs Henshaw filled me a bath this afternoon,' she said, placing her hand into the crook of Edward's elbow, 'It felt divine to finally wash all the mud and grime off properly.'

Edward grunted, trying not to blurt out that he'd walked in on her having the bath and nearly been ungentlemanly enough to venture round the screen.

'And whilst I was in the kitchen I took a peek at what Mrs Henshaw was cooking up for dinner. It looked incredible and smelled absolutely delicious.'

'Good. I'm hungry.'

Amelia fell silent and Edward wondered if he'd always been so clumsy in making polite conversation. He didn't think he'd struggled at university and of course with Jane things had been different. He'd known her since they were both young children, barely any effort had been needed.

Silently Edward escorted Amelia to her seat and pulled the chair out for her, ensuring she was comfortable before he sat down himself. Reaching across the table, he poured out two glasses of red wine, pushing Amelia's towards her before taking a large gulp.

'I saw you outside today,' Amelia said as she toyed with the stem of her wine glass. She was always moving, always fidgeting, and sometimes Edward just wanted to reach out and place his hand over hers to show her how to keep still.

Edward nodded.

'What were you doing?'

'Just looking. At the house.' And thinking. All the plans he'd once had for the estate, all the work he'd undertaken to improve the house and gardens.

'Did you like what you saw?'

He looked at Amelia sharply, wondering if she was trying to provoke him. She was a little minx sometimes and he wouldn't be surprised if she was goading him into blurting something out just to get him to talk to her. He hadn't exactly been stellar company so far.

'Your home in India—have you always lived there?' Edward asked.

Amelia frowned as she tried to follow his trail of thought. 'Yes, my father built it before I was born.'

'Then you will understand how one's memories can be tied to a building, a place. A lifetime of good times and bad times, all contained within one house.'

'Is it the good times or the bad times you think of when you look at Beechwood Manor?'

'Both.' Edward paused and considered his answer further. 'I suppose all the good memories are tainted with the bad, though.'

Amelia reached across the table and took Edward's hand, her soft, warm skin connecting with the sensitive pads of his fingertips.

Guiltily they sprung apart as Mrs Henshaw entered the room with two steaming bowls of soup, setting them down in front of Edward and Amelia before bustling back out. Edward waited for Amelia to start, but although she picked up her spoon she did not dip it into her bowl.

'What happened here, Edward?' she asked.

He could have pretended to misunderstand her question, or just refused to answer, but Amelia was not the sort of person to let something go.

'There was a fire.' *A terrible fire.*

'In the East Wing?' she prompted.

'Yes.' He nodded curtly, to try and signal that the conversation was over.

'You were here when it happened?'

Edward gripped the edge of the table, the memories of the heat and the flames taking over his mind.

'You lost someone, didn't you?' Amelia asked gently.

Edward stared down into his bowl of soup before closing his eyes. Then abruptly he stood and strode from the room.

Amelia finished her dinner alone, shrugging as Mrs Henshaw brought the main course and enquired where Edward had gone. She'd upset him and that hurt her. She hadn't meant to be so insensitive, but she knew herself how cathartic it was to talk about these things. Edward bottled everything up, if he would just rant and rave about what had gone wrong in his life, let it all out, then maybe he might be able to start healing.

After dinner she roamed around the house, too restless to go to bed and too preoccupied to settle to any particular task. Once or twice she picked up a book, but put it down again almost immediately. Still there was no sign of Edward. With resolute steps she turned her attention to the West Wing. If he wouldn't come to her she would go to him. It wasn't as though she was going to sleep until she had seen he was at least partially recovered.

She knocked on his door, softly at first and then a little louder. When there was no reply she gently pushed it open. His bedroom and the small sitting room off it were empty. It didn't look as though Edward had returned since dinner. Amelia hesitated, knowing she should not trespass in his private rooms, but the temptation of the desk, and the piles of papers on top of it, was too much.

Carefully she leafed through Edward's sketches, feeling the warmth spread through her body as she realised all of the recent ones were of her. He had sketched her digging in the garden, strolling through the rosebushes and even just lounging on one of the chairs in the sitting room. His drawings were good, even Amelia's amateur eye could see that, and he had caught something deeper than just her physical likeness on the paper.

As she reached the bottom of the pile she placed the drawings back on the desk and made her way out of the room. If Edward wasn't in the main part of the house or the West Wing then he must be in the East Wing. Despite him warning her to stay out of the fire-damaged Wing, Amelia barely hesitated before stepping into the corridor.

The light of her candle flickered and cast long shadows in the darkness of the East Wing and Amelia found herself creeping silently down the long corridor. There were doors off to either side, bedrooms most likely, but something drew Amelia further down the corridor to where the fire damage was at its worst.

Here an entire portion of the house had been ravaged by the fire, the walls still blackened with soot and even the faint aroma of smoke remained. As the floorboards creaked underneath her feet Amelia had visions of plummeting through the damaged floor to the hard flagstones of the ground below.

Amelia paused beside an open door, every fibre in her body telling her this was where she would find answers and maybe Edward, too.

As she stepped inside the room it took her a moment to work out exactly what it had been before the fire, and then as her eyes rested on a half-burned rocking horse she heard herself gasp softly.

It was a nursery. A beautiful, fire-ravaged nursery. Amelia bit her lip as suddenly she understood the depth of Edward's pain and suffering. No one should have to lose a child, not like this.

Her eyes began to adjust to the gloom and she could make out other features, familiar shapes morphed and warped by the fire. There was a small bed, the remains of a rocking chair and a pile of what Amelia could only assume had once been toys. A sooty teddy bear sat on the bedsheets as if sadly waiting for an owner who would never return.

Amelia spun around as a noise from by the window startled her. Edward's silhouette was outlined against the glass, his shoulders hunched as if he was physically trying to block out the pain. She hesitated, wondering if he would explode in anger at her for venturing into the forbidden East Wing, for trespassing on his grief and memories, but when he remained silent Amelia crossed the room and wrapped her arms around him.

'What was his name?' she asked quietly.

'Thomas.'

She felt him drop his head and rest his chin on top of her hair, allowing her to hold him tight. Amelia couldn't even begin to imagine his suffering and knew whatever she said would never be enough. No wonder he had locked himself away.

'Come,' Edward said after a few minutes, leading her out of the room and back to the main part of the house. He held her hand, his large fist enveloping her small one, but the pressure of his fingers were light on hers.

'You don't need to tell me anything,' she said as they reached the West Wing and their bedrooms. Edward hesitated a moment, and then pulled her gently into his rooms.

'Sit,' he instructed, motioning to the armchair by the fire she had sat on a few nights previously.

Amelia obeyed. She knew it was entirely inappropriate to be in Edward's bedroom, especially at this time of night, but in truth they had overstepped the line between appropriate and scandalous days ago. This little indiscretion was just another in a long list.

Edward pulled his desk chair over beside her and sat looking at the embers glowing in the grate for a few minutes.

'I shouldn't have pried,' Amelia said eventually. She wanted to know what had happened, wanted to know every detail of how Edward had lost everything dear to him so she could better understand him, but not if retelling it was going to cause him pain.

'Thomas would be six now,' Edward said softly.

'Thomas was your son?'

He nodded and Amelia saw the flash of pride and love cross his face.

'He was the sweetest little boy, mischievous and playful, but ever so loving.'

Amelia remembered the drawings of the young boy she'd seen on her first morning at Beechwood Manor.

'I was so happy. We were so happy. Our lives were complete, we had each other and we had Thomas, I never wanted anything more than that.'

And it had all been ripped away from him. Amelia felt a wistful longing. She doubted she would ever feel love and satisfaction like that, not now her life would be spent always in the shadow of her crime. One day she might marry, but it would be to a second-rate suitor, someone who had flaws of his own so would overlook her past.

'The fire...' Edward trailed off, running a hand over his brow.

Amelia slipped from her chair and knelt on the floor in front of him, her hand resting gently on his arm. She wanted him to know he didn't need to tell her anything, but she sensed now they were here, now Amelia had seen the scorched nursery, he wanted to share his pain with someone.

'Thomas had been ill. We were taking it in turns to sleep in his nursery at night whilst he recovered.'

Of course Edward would be a wonderful and caring parent. Amelia thought back to all the ways he had looked after her during their short acquaintance. He was a kind and giving person underneath the sometimes gruff demeanour.

'It was your wife's turn?' Amelia prompted.

He nodded. 'I still remember kissing them both goodnight. I never thought...'

Amelia couldn't even begin to imagine what it would

feel like to wake up every day knowing those you loved were no longer in the world. No wonder Edward had shut himself away for these three years.

'No one could tell how the fire started, but it was in the nursery. By the time the alarm was raised a good portion of the East Wing was on fire.'

She could see the panic in his eyes as he relived the memory in his mind.

'I went in through the flames and they were just lying there on the bed, side by side.'

Amelia could imagine him charging to the rescue, battling the fire and the smoke to save the people he loved the most.

'I carried them out, but it was too late. The doctor said the smoke killed them while they slept, that they wouldn't have suffered...'

Edward fell silent, his head dipped and his eyes closed. Amelia wished she could reach up and smooth the pain away, but she knew nothing she said or did would make much of a difference. Every day Edward would have to mourn his wife and his son and every day the pain would rip him apart.

Suddenly Amelia felt helpless. She wanted to do something, say something. When she had confessed her crime to Edward he had listened carefully and then made a sensible and reassuring plan. He was the reason she wasn't mentally falling apart, or worse, festering, rotting in a cell somewhere. Now he needed her, he'd trusted her with this emotional wound and she didn't know what to say to him.

'A day lasts until it's chased away but love lasts until the grave,' she said eventually. Edward opened his eyes and looked down at her. 'It's an old Indian proverb, my nanny used to say when I was a child. It means no matter what you never stop loving those close to you until the day you die.' Amelia felt the colour rising to her cheeks and wondered if she had spoken out of turn.

'A day lasts until it's chased away but love lasts until the grave,' Edward repeated, nodding slowly. 'Very apt.'

'Do you have any other family, anyone to help you mourn?' Amelia asked softly.

Edward shook his head, 'I pushed everyone away. I couldn't bear the looks of pity in their eyes.'

They fell silent, both lost in their own thoughts. Amelia wondered whether anyone could ever recover from a loss like this. Edward was a good man, a kind man, and if anyone deserved a second chance at life it was he. He'd taken her in and protected her when she was a complete stranger. She just wished there was something she could do to help him, but part of her wondered if he would ever be able to enjoy himself without feeling guilty because his wife and son weren't there beside him.

'I can see why you shut yourself away,' Amelia said eventually.

'I doubt it was the right thing to do.'

'Maybe at the time it was the only way for you to cope.'

Edward seemed to think about this for a while. 'It just seemed impossible to carry on life as normal when I'd lost...' He trailed off and Amelia squeezed his arm.

Amelia couldn't tell how long they sat like that, with her curled by Edward's feet, her head resting on the arm of the chair, but eventually she must have nodded off for the next thing she remembered was Edward's arms lifting her up gently and carrying her to her own bed. She was still half-asleep as he lay her down carefully on top of the sheets, paused and then kissed her softly on the cheek. As the door closed behind him Amelia lifted her fingers to where he had kissed her. Her skin was tingling and she had the urge to preserve the moment, but slowly her body relaxed and she slipped into a dreamless sleep.

Chapter Ten

Edward prowled through the house, a frown on his face. He'd agreed to one maid, one harmless young woman to help dust and tidy around the place. He should have known things would spiral from there. In the past week Mrs Henshaw had taken full advantage of her return to the house and now the place was practically crawling with people.

He sighed. He wasn't angry with Mrs Henshaw, he couldn't be when he knew she had his best interests at heart, but he just wanted a little privacy.

'Good morning, sir.' A maid curtsied as he walked past.

Edward grunted and then regretted his surliness. 'Good morning, Betty.'

All in all there were now five members of staff at Beechwood Manor, including Mrs Henshaw. Two maids, one upstairs and one in the kitchen, a footman and a gardener. Edward had argued against the need for each one, but as the house began to regain some of its old sparkle and lustre he had to admit they were doing a good job. Mrs Henshaw always had run a tight household.

As Edward stepped outside he saw Smith, the gardener, hurrying towards him.

'Good morning, sir. Might I just have a quick word?' Smith said, pulling his flat cap from his head as he spoke.

'What can I do for you, Smith?'

'It's a delicate matter, my lord…don't want to offend.'

'Go ahead,' Edward prompted, with a sinking feeling in his stomach. He knew what this was going to be about and there wasn't an easy solution.

'Well, I don't wish to cause offence, but it's the young lady, sir, your guest.'

They had agreed to keep Amelia's identity a secret from the staff for now, after taking Mrs Henshaw into their confidences. Amelia had been introduced to the staff as a friend and guest, staying with him for a few weeks to take in the country air.

'I keep finding her digging up my flowerbeds, sir.'

Edward had noticed. Each afternoon Amelia would return to the house covered in mud, looking rather dirty and dishevelled. He often sat by the window in his bedroom, just watching her as she worked. There was something so energetic about Amelia, so alive. Often he would draw her whilst he observed, but sometimes he just found himself watching. Sometimes an hour would pass without him quite knowing how.

'I wouldn't mind at all, sir. Soil always needs a good turning over and who am I to say what a guest of the master can do? But…' The gardener trailed off, his cheeks flushing.

'But she's disturbing the plants?'

'Exactly, sir.' Mr Smith sounded relieved.

Edward looked around the garden with a critical eye. He couldn't deny Mr Smith had worked miracles in a matter of days. The middle-aged man had only been in Edward's employ for less than a week and already the garden was transformed. Overgrown bushes had been trimmed, weeds pulled and he had just made a start on planting a few new flowers.

'Miss Amelia likes to keep busy,' Edward said. 'I wonder whether there might be an area of the garden where you would be happy for her attention to be directed. Somewhere she can focus on without getting in your way.'

The gardener's face broke into a wide grin, 'What an excellent idea, sir. I knew you'd have the solution.' He slowly perused the garden, his lips moving as if weighing up where would be best to redirect Amelia's efforts. 'How about near the old gazebo, sir? There's a patch of flowerbeds there where she could dig as much as she wanted.'

'Wonderful. I'll let Miss Amelia know when I next see her.'

Just as the gardener turned away Edward saw a flurry of colour heading towards him and found for the first time in a long time he didn't have the urge to avoid any further human interaction. Amelia was a frenzy of pent-up energy, always on the move, always eager to do something to occupy herself. He knew much of it came from her feelings of guilt over what had happened in Brighton. She still thought she had killed a man and Edward could see that was eating away at her. By exhausting herself during the day she didn't leave much time to dwell on her feelings and was so tired by the time she got to bed she managed to sleep at least a little.

On four separate occasions this week Edward had needed to go into her room at night and soothe her screams and tears. She seemed to be reliving the events leading up to her crime and each night it was distressing her even more. Sometimes she would wake up as he held her, but most nights she just burrowed into his chest and calmed as he wrapped his arms tightly around her.

Edward hoped Mr Guthry returned soon with good

news concerning the young Captain Amelia thought she had killed. If she could hear the scoundrel was still alive, still going about his daily life, then no doubt her guilt would ease.

'Edward,' Amelia said, coming to a stop a few feet away. 'I've got something to show you.'

She grasped his hand and began pulling him back towards the house.

'What is it?'

'A surprise. Now come on.'

Edward began to grumble something, but Amelia flashed him a withering look and he promptly fell quiet.

'Close your eyes,' Amelia instructed.

'Why?'

'Stop being so difficult and close your eyes.'

He didn't doubt Amelia had ever had a problem with getting her own way. She had a confidence in her voice that suggested she hadn't often been challenged.

Edward heard a door open and Amelia's hands on his back guiding him into a room.

'Open your eyes.'

Edward obeyed. They were in the sitting room, the one he had first found Amelia in, stripping off her sodden clothes. In front of him Amelia was smiling proudly and looking around, waiting for his reaction.

Edward felt his body freeze and time slow down. An uncontrollable urge to storm out almost overtook him, but he struggled and managed to remain still.

'You don't like it?' Amelia asked, her face dropping.

'You did this?'

She nodded, biting her lower lip.

'You changed the furniture and the curtains and even the damn rugs.'

Again Amelia nodded.

'What made you think you had the right to do that?'

A small part of him knew he was being churlish and unnecessarily harsh. True, she hadn't asked his permission to renovate the sitting room, but she didn't know what it meant to him.

'You didn't even stop and think, did you? You didn't even consider this room might be preserved in a certain way for a reason.'

'I...' Amelia tried to speak, but Edward held up his hand, silencing her.

'You're so self-centred, so absorbed in your own little world. You didn't even consider asking me if it would be a problem.'

'I can put it back,' Amelia stuttered.

Some part of her anguish must have penetrated through the red haze of Edward's anger because he felt himself deflating, the anger subsiding as if he had been popped with a pin.

'No,' he said, running a hand through his hair. 'Leave it. It doesn't matter.'

Edward knew many women would flee the room in tears after an incident such as this. He wouldn't have blamed her for doing so, he was acting so brutishly, but Amelia stood her ground. Slowly he saw some of her normal confidence return. Her shoulders squared, her chin raised up a notch and she looked as though she were about to do battle. Edward didn't know if he could bear having Amelia berate him for his behaviour, not now. He was just about to apologise and leave quickly when she lunged forward and grabbed his hand. Too late. He was trapped.

Amelia knew sometimes she was not the most aware of or sensitive to other people's feelings. She supposed it came from being a spoiled only child, always the one to get her way. She'd never really had to consider anyone else before, but right now she was having a moment of clarity.

'Come and sit with me, Edward,' she said softly.

She knew the look in his eye—he was weighing up whether he could get away with fleeing the room, locking himself away in his sanctuary and avoiding the confrontation that was to come. It wasn't a healthy way to deal with things and Amelia was determined to get to the bottom of Edward's outburst one way or another.

'I apologise,' Edward said.

Not good enough. She wanted to know more, only then could she actually make a difference to his life the same way he was to hers.

'Yes, yes,' Amelia said, pulling Edward towards the sofa, 'apology accepted. We all get a little ratty sometimes.'

'I need to go.'

'No. You need to stay and talk to me.'

At the suggestion a look of panic crossed Edward's face.

'I really don't think that's necessary.'

'You've just snapped at me for rearranging a few pieces of furniture,' Amelia reprimanded. 'I think it is necessary.'

'I said I was sorry.'

'It's your wife, isn't it?' Amelia plunged in with the question that had been on the tip of her tongue for the last few minutes.

Edward recoiled a little, but wouldn't meet her eye.

'Did she decorate this room?'

For a while Edward just sat silently, looking around at the changes Amelia had made. Slowly he nodded.

'And then I came along and charged in without even thinking.'

'It doesn't matter.'

'It does to you. And that means it matters to me.'

Amelia wanted to reach out and embrace him, to fold

him in her arms and show him he wasn't alone. The memories of his family and his solitary existence in this ghost of a house for the past few years would be enough to drive anyone a little mad. She had to remember she'd exploded into his life, changed so much in a short space of time. He had been remarkably patient with her; Amelia knew she was difficult to live with sometimes, but Edward had barely complained.

'Tell me about her.'

For a moment Amelia wondered if he would refuse. She knew she was pushing him, forcing him to face up to some of the grief he had been hoarding inside for years, but Amelia couldn't help it. Edward needed something to change in his life or he would spend his days in a never-ending cycle of guilt and regret. Maybe, just maybe, she could help him start living in the present. It was no less than what he'd done for her.

'She was kind,' Edward said eventually. 'Probably the kindest person I've ever met.'

'How did you meet?'

Edward smiled softly as if remembering. 'We were just children. Jane's family moved into the area and soon after our parents introduced us.' He shrugged. 'There was always the plan we would marry when we were an appropriate age.'

Amelia resisted the temptation to screw her face up in response. Her father had threatened her with an arranged marriage on a couple of occasions when she had particularly vexed him, but she'd known he would never go through with it. To her not having at least some say in who she spent the rest of her life with was the worst possible scenario. Although she had to concede her judgement when it came to matters of the heart was maybe not as reliable as she had once thought. McNair's face flashed before her eyes and for a moment Amelia felt the light-headed panicky sensation she always did when she thought of him. Focusing on Edward, she tried to push the building anxiety away.

'So that's what you did?' Amelia asked.

'When I came back from university we married as had always been planned.'

It wasn't the most romantic of stories, but Amelia could sense there was more to come.

'When did you fall in love?'

Edward looked at her strangely, then gave a low chuckle. 'You know, no one has ever asked me that before.' He paused as if thinking. 'We weren't in love when we married. I liked Jane, was very fond of her, but then I didn't love her. I suppose it crept up on me slowly. I just remember when Thomas was born looking down at him in my arms and realising how much I loved the woman who shared him with me.'

Amelia felt the tears spring to her eyes. She wasn't normally emotional. Sometimes her cousin Lizzie even said she was the least sentimental person in India, but she knew she could never hope for a love like Edward's.

'You must have been very happy.'

'We were. I spent my days running the estate. Jane looked after Thomas and in the afternoons we would all come together.'

It sounded like the perfect little family. No wonder losing his wife and son had hit Edward so hard. It wasn't as though he were an absentee husband or father, living it up in the city whilst his family festered on the country estate. They had been a proper family.

Edward closed his eyes as if remembering the good times and Amelia wondered if she had pushed him too far.

'I'm sorry for rearranging the room without asking you first,' she said softly.

Edward opened his eyes and looked at her for a long minute before nodding as if accepting her apology.

There was a rawness about his expression, something pained and resigned at the same time, and Amelia just wanted to smooth away the pain. Slowly she reached up and placed a hand on his cheek, running her fingers over the light stubble that was already growing after his morning shave. Their eyes met and for a long while they just sat, their bodies close together, Amelia's hand on his face.

Amelia knew she should get up and walk away. Nothing good could come out of gazing into Edward's eyes and wishing for something that he could never give her. He was a good man, probably the kindest man she had ever met. Part of her knew that she was still rebounding from her experience with McNair, looking for someone who was the polar opposite of that brutal, lying scoundrel, but deep down Amelia could acknowledge that wasn't all that was going on here. Edward had rescued her, swept her away from danger and cocooned her in the safety of his protection. There was something rather intoxicating about that.

Against her better judgement Amelia felt her body sway forward. Her eyes were still locked on his and she thought she saw a mutual spark of desire and affection burning there. Maybe he wouldn't reject her.

For a moment she thought there was a softness to Edward's face and then his expression hardened into something more akin to disgust. He pushed himself back, away from her, and shot to his feet.

'Edward?' she said, hating the pleading tone in her voice.

'Good day Amelia,' he said stiffly, all the intimacy and closeness of just a few minutes ago gone from his voice.

As she watched him give a curt bow and leave the room she felt embarrassment and anger and shame. Her anger wasn't directed towards Edward, he'd never given her a reason to think he wanted anything more than to do his civic duty and give her a safe place to stay. No, she was furious with herself.

Chapter Eleven

As she tossed and turned in bed Amelia realised she was full of regrets. Regret that she had ever trusted or cared for McNair, regret that she had so foolhardily followed his trail to Brighton, regret that she had confronted him over his lies and, of course, the climax of those events: picking up that letter opener to defend herself with.

However, her biggest regret of all didn't centre around McNair, or the myriad of mistakes she'd made with him, it was about the events of yesterday morning with Edward.

She'd finally felt as though she were getting through to him; he'd opened up a little about his wife, showing her snippets of the life he had once lived. Slowly and surely Amelia had thought he was softening towards her. She'd learnt to ignore his gruff moments and his requests to be left alone and had thought she detected a blossoming of affection.

Well, that would be all gone now. Amelia closed her eyes and once again saw the look of disgust on his face as she'd swayed towards him. Yet again she had thrown herself at a man she barely knew and hadn't considered the consequences.

She felt disappointed in herself. Ever since the moment

in McNair's study she had vowed to be more careful and considered. She couldn't take back how she had acted with McNair, but she could learn from it. For a long time she had allowed her attraction to the Captain to cloud her judgement, refusing to see him for what he really was. It was only when she was presented with indisputable proof McNair was a scoundrel that she had believed it.

Amelia sighed, not that she thought Edward was a scoundrel, far from it. His behaviour over the past week had been beyond reproach. He'd allowed her, a complete stranger, to stay in his house at her moment of need and had acted like a gentleman, albeit an aloof one, for the entire time.

With a dramatic groan Amelia sat up and threw off the sheets. She'd never been very good at lying and mulling over her problems. She was an impulsive person, someone more likely to cause a scene than to quietly think through a solution, but tonight something was holding her back.

It was Edward, Amelia realised, kind, gruff Edward. The man of few words who had opened up to her about his wife and son. She didn't want to hurt him, didn't want to add to his already substantial pain. He had suffered the ultimate loss, the loss of a beloved wife and child. It didn't matter it had been three years, Amelia rather suspected it could be thirty years and the pain would still be acute. She felt the blood rush to her cheeks as she relived the moment of embarrassment she'd felt before Edward had left the sitting room yesterday morning. How could she even begin to think she would be good enough to occupy a place in his heart alongside his treasured late wife and son?

She was a murderess, a wanted woman. He was the type of man to mourn his family for three years and to take in a desperate stranger; a good man, a kind man. In reality there was no comparison between them and Amelia found a bubble of hysterical laughter fighting to escape as she realised how ridiculous it had been to think Edward would ever want her.

The funny thing was Amelia had found herself imagining all kinds of domestic situations, situations she had no right to want. It had surprised her as she had never really thought about settling down. With McNair she had been dazzled by the promise of adventure and glamour, but yesterday morning as she'd sat in the sitting room with Edward she'd found herself wondering what a life of quiet domesticity would be if Edward was by her side.

Amelia snorted. That was something she certainly had no right dreaming about. Her circumstances meant she had no right to even fantasise about a life like that—besides, Edward would never love her. He'd not once given her any indication that he might be interested in her romantically, but still Amelia had found herself wishing for something that could never be.

He still loved his wife and probably thought one love in a lifetime was more than many people got to experience, he wouldn't be looking for a second. And if he was it certainly wouldn't be with a foolish murderess as his mate.

Amelia pulled a shawl around her shoulders and paced gloomily to the window and then back to the bed. She felt the tears begin to prick at her eyes and knew she would struggle to face Edward again. He was a gentleman and wouldn't bring up the moment they had shared in the sitting room, but it would always be hanging quietly there between them.

Maybe she should just leave. It would pre-empt any awkwardness and she would no longer be a burden to the man who has treated her so well. The idea of fending for herself again in a strange country made her stomach flip over with nerves and for a moment she almost threw herself back under the bedsheets. She knew Edward would struggle to look at her in the same way again, he'd probably wonder when she would next throw herself at him. His love for his late wife was all-encompassing, but even so Amelia knew he would never blame her, he was too good, too self-condemning. Edward would probably find a way to punish himself for her moment of weakness.

Amelia wandered back over to the window and leant on the sill, looking out at the garden she had tried to desecrate, and suddenly she realised what she must do. For once in her life she had to put someone else first.

Edward would not ever want her, he wasn't gaining anything from this arrangement. Amelia might want to stay, to hide in the sanctuary of Beechwood Manor and enjoy Edward's company, but for once she would not put herself first. It would be a hard step to take, but after all he had done for her Edward deserved it. Besides, she knew if she stayed her feeling for Edward might develop into something more and Amelia didn't know if she could bear to experience any more heartache. Finding out what sort of man McNair really was had almost broken her. Her heart wasn't strong enough to be rejected again.

Her decision made, Amelia gathered up her paltry belongings and swept out of the room before she could change her mind.

'You're up early, ducky, are the bad dreams troubling you again?' Goody bustled along the hallway as Amelia crept downstairs.

'I thought I'd get some air,' Amelia said, the words catching in her throat.

'At this time in the morning? You'll catch a deadly chill. Come and sit in the kitchen and I'll make you a nice warm glass of milk.'

'No,' Amelia said, more forcefully than she meant to. 'I really need to go outside.'

Goody looked at her appraisingly and then led her firmly towards the kitchen.

'There isn't a problem in the world that can't be sorted by a bellyful of warm milk and a seat by a newly lit fire.'

Amelia allowed herself to be led into the kitchen, all the time wondering if she should just break away and run. If Goody said one more kind thing to her, she might just break down and cry and then her resolve would waver.

'You sit there, ducky, and I'll be right back.'

Amelia watched as Goody bustled around the kitchen and before long a cup of warm milk and a plate of biscuits had been set down in front of her. Not knowing when her next meal might be, Amelia tucked in.

'You're thinking of leaving,' Goody said as she pulled out a stool and sat down opposite Amelia.

Amelia froze, mid-bite of a biscuit. The woman was a mind-reader.

'I...'

'Don't worry, my dear, it's not my place to talk you out of going.'

Amelia found herself a little disappointed. Maybe she did want someone to talk her out of fleeing the only place she had felt safe in the last few weeks.

'Now, I don't know what's happened to prompt this change and I'm sure you've already thought through all the consequences, but I couldn't have you leaving on an empty stomach.'

Amelia looked down into the frothy cup of milk and wondered if she had considered all the consequences. She had still killed a man, there would still be people out there looking for her, that hadn't changed just because she had foolishly developed feelings for Edward that could never be reciprocated.

'*Have* you thought through all the consequences?' Goody prompted softly.

'All my life I've put myself first,' Amelia said softly. 'Do you know I begged my cousin to swap identities with me so I could chase after Captain McNair? I didn't even consider the difficulties she would face, the lies she would have to tell, all for me.'

'She agreed?' Goody asked.

Amelia smiled. 'Lizzie is the kindest, most generous person I know. She'd do anything for me.' She paused, feeling a lump building in her throat. She wished Lizzie was here now, her cousin would know what to do, what to say, how to make everything right again. 'I guess I want to be more like her.'

'We are who we are,' Goody said quietly. 'It's no use wishing to change.'

'But I can be kinder, more thoughtful. I can put others' needs before my own.'

Goody looked at her thoughtfully. 'You're worried about the master.'

Amelia couldn't meet the older woman's eye. Goody had known Edward when his wife was alive, she'd run his household when it had been inhabited by a happy, living family. She wouldn't approve of Amelia pining after Edward, of her sullying the memory of his marriage.

'I don't know what has passed between you and it's not my place to know, but I do want to say this: Master Edward has been barely surviving these past three years. He has shut himself away from the world, retreated into his rooms and refused to move on. Now I understand grief, truly I do, but what he was doing was not healthy.' Goody leaned forward and took Amelia's hand. 'It has been good for him to have someone else to think about, to worry about. It's reminded him what it is to be human, to be alive. You've done more for him in a week than anyone has been able to do in three years.'

'But I haven't *done* anything.'

'Maybe nothing out of the ordinary. But you've showed him how to care again, how to break free from the constant cycle of grief and guilt and think of something else for a while. Don't underestimate the value of that. So whatever it is you think you've done wrong, just remember the good you've achieved by being in his life.'

Goody gave her one last pat on the hand, then got up and bustled out of the room, leaving Amelia to her thoughts. She wanted to believe Goody's words, wanted to think maybe she could make a difference to Edward's life. Even if she could bring him just a moment of happiness that would be worth a lot of sacrifice, but then she thought of the look on his face as she'd swayed towards him and she knew she couldn't stay. Far from easing his grief she had only made it more acute, reminded him how much he missed his family. She couldn't have his pain on her conscience along with everything else.

Nevertheless deep down she wanted to stay—in fact, she couldn't think of anywhere she would rather be. Even the rolling hills of Bombay didn't hold the same appeal as staying here with Edward where she felt safe.

Amelia almost surrendered to her desires, but something held her back. She thought of Lizzie, her kind and selfless cousin, and wondered what she would do. Lizzie always put others first, considered their needs long before her own. And if Amelia was honest with herself she knew Lizzie would leave. She would unobtrusively walk away and let Edward carry on with his new lease of life unhindered by her own emotional baggage.

Slipping out of the kitchen, Amelia felt the tears start to run down her face. Although she'd only been here just over a week it felt like home and she would be sad to leave Beechwood Manor and the people in it. Before she could change her mind Amelia pushed open the heavy wooden door and left the house, wondering what the next stage of her life would hold.

Chapter Twelve

Edward prowled round the house like a wounded bear, growling at any staff that crossed his path. He had barely slept and now something didn't feel right. The house felt empty, deserted, despite there being the maids and other servants present that Mrs Henshaw had hired. He had spent the time since he'd woken up alternating between wanting to seek Amelia out and wanting to avoid her at all costs.

He didn't blame her for the moment they shared the morning before. He had told her things he'd never told anyone else and a closeness, an intimacy, had followed. That in itself wasn't a problem, it was his reaction to her that had caused him to toss and turn all night.

Edward pictured her eyes fluttering closed, the delicate eyelashes resting on her cheeks, and her swaying towards him. His body reacted instantly to the memory, a coil tightening inside him and a surge of desire flowing all the way to his very core.

This was what disgusted him. He was still mourning the deaths of his wife and son. They would never laugh or cry or shout with joy again and here he was sullying their memory with fantasy about the first pretty young woman who came along. Every day since the fire Edward had wished it had been him who had been taken and not them. He knew his retreat from the world had partially been from grief, but also stemmed from a need to punish himself. Then Amelia had crashed into his life and everything had changed. Yesterday wasn't the first time he'd felt the hot burn of desire for his houseguest and he didn't know how to cope with it.

Most of him wanted to retreat further, to punish himself for the betrayal of his wife and son's memories, but a small rebellious part kept asking what he was so disgusted with himself about. Jane wouldn't want him to live like this, she'd much rather he enjoyed the company of others, but that didn't mean he had permission to lust after Amelia.

'Good morning, sir,' Mrs Henshaw said as she bustled out of the kitchen.

'Good morning.'

'Would it be too bold to venture that you're looking for Miss Amelia, sir?'

Edward tried not to let the surprise show on his face as his housekeeper asked the question.

'Has she said something?' he asked abruptly.

'Nothing at all, sir, and it's not my place to pry.'

Edward saw the knowing glint in Mrs Henshaw's eyes and wondered if there were any goings on in his household she wasn't aware of.

'It's just Miss Amelia left early this morning. I thought you might like to know.'

Edward froze, every muscle in his body seizing up at once.

'She left?'

'Yes, sir. At about half past seven. She wasn't to be swayed from her decision to leave.'

Edward let out a growl of frustration. He'd driven her away.

'Maybe it's for the best,' Edward said quietly. He

couldn't quite bring himself to believe his own words, though. Amelia was out there on her own, scared and vulnerable, at the mercy of strangers. All because of him. He'd seen the expression in her eyes as he'd backed away from her, the hurt and confusion. He should have uttered a few words of comfort.

'Maybe it is, sir. As long as that scoundrel doesn't find her, of course. Or the law doesn't catch up with her. Or she doesn't starve or freeze to death.'

Edward was too caught up in his own thoughts to reply immediately. McNair, the villainous cad who had seduced Amelia, struck her and provoked her into self-defence, was most likely somewhere out there. Either that or someone would be looking for Amelia for his murder. Whichever scenario was true, things were grim for Amelia and he'd just pushed her away from the one place she'd felt safe.

'Of course you could go and get her back,' Mrs Henshaw said nonchalantly. 'The first coach doesn't leave until noon and, unless she plans on walking to London, I doubt she's got further than the village.'

Part of Edward wondered if it would be easier just to let her go. Then he wouldn't have to deal with the maelstrom of feelings building inside him. If Amelia was out of his life he could go back to just feeling guilty about the fire and his lack of ability to protect those he cared most about. Edward snorted. He knew this was no way to live, but the guilt had been part of his life for so long he didn't know how to live without it.

He loved his late wife, he missed her every day, but now he had agreed to help Amelia he felt a modicum of responsibility for her. If she was put in danger because of him, he wouldn't be able to forgive himself.

'I'll just check she's not wanting for anything,' Edward

said, half to himself, as he pulled on his overcoat and strode towards the door.

'I'll make lunch for two, then, shall I?' he heard Mrs Henshaw shout cheerily after him before the heavy wooden door closed behind him.

As he hurried through the estate towards the village Edward felt a knot of tension building in his stomach. He was worried about her safety, but that wasn't all that was troubling him. After all, how much trouble could one young woman get into in a couple of hours? No, he realised he was also worrying that she might refuse to return to Beechwood Manor with him.

He didn't want to admit it but he had got used to having Amelia around the house. Where a week ago he was irritated by her soft voice humming as he tried to focus on his accounts or her incessant chatter over dinner, now he quite looked forward to meeting her in the hallway or watching her as she strolled through the gardens.

Within fifteen minutes he was on the outskirts of the village and he slowed his pace a little so as not to attract any undue attention. Already he knew the whole village was gossiping about how he'd finally been seen out and about and how he'd opened the house up once again, employing staff and allowing the gardens to be tended. He didn't need any additional gossip about him dashing through the narrow streets like a madman.

Keeping vigilant for anyone who looked out of place, Edward made his way to the village square, wondering if Amelia would be waiting for the coach or if she had resumed her journey across the Downs by foot. A momentary wave of panic engulfed him as he pictured her caught in another storm, drenched to the bone and shivering in a ditch somewhere, and he decided not to examine the depth of his concern in too much detail.

As he caught sight of the clock tower Edward saw a familiar flash of light blue fabric rounding a corner at the end of the street. Amelia came into view and Edward found himself suffused with relief. He'd found her. She wasn't injured in a ditch or halfway to London or in the hands of the evil scoundrel who had seduced her. Within a few minutes they would be on their way back home and he could ensure she was safe once again.

Just as he was about to raise his hand to catch her attention a man in a bright blue jacket and crisp white shirt caught his eye. The man was young, handsome and very well presented. As he walked through the village Edward could see some of the young women surreptitiously following his movements and glancing in his direction.

Suddenly Edward knew this man was McNair. He knew it as surely as if they'd been introduced. There was an arrogant air about him, an irritating swagger, and Edward could see innocent young women would be taken in by his easy charm and good looks. Simmering underneath all of that was a restrained anger and a sense of purpose and Edward knew this was a man he had to protect Amelia from at all costs.

With a spurt of speed Edward strode past the man he thought to be McNair and hurried towards Amelia. She was unaware of either man approaching yet, distracted by something in a shop window, and Edward just hoped he could get to her before she spotted the man she thought she'd murdered. Knowing Amelia, she would make a scene.

He reached her just as she turned away from the shop window, threw an arm around her waist and barrelled her into a small alleyway.

'Edward,' Amelia exclaimed, with a loud exhalation, her body shaking with the shock of being manhandled and taken by surprise.

His body had pressed up against hers in an entirely inappropriate way and for a few seconds Edward lost the ability to speak. She was soft and warm and every curve of her body seemed to fit his perfectly. Rousing himself, he pulled away a little, but only as far as to maintain an appropriate distance between their bodies whilst still being able to talk quietly to her.

'He's here,' he said quietly, hearing the strain in his own voice.

Amelia understood immediately and the colour drained from her face.

'He can't be. He's dead. I killed him.' There was a slight note of hysteria in her voice and Edward saw her begin to panic. 'You must be mistaken, you don't know what he looks like.'

'Amelia, he's here. I need you to keep calm.'

She writhed, pressing herself away from the wall and against him, seemingly unaware of the contact between their bodies. Edward forced himself to focus, waiting until she collapsed back against the bricks, her body going limp. Edward knew he had a limited amount of time before she either dashed out into the street or made such a fuss other people would come to investigate.

'Amelia, you need to take a look and tell me if it's him or not,' Edward said. 'But you need to do it carefully.'

'He's dead.'

'Well, let's reassess that after you've looked at this man.'

'He's dead.'

Edward leaned forward and gently cupped her chin with his hand, his large fingers feeling oversized and clumsy against her delicate features. He waited until her eyes met his and until the panic had subsided.

'Whoever this man is, I won't let him hurt you. I just need you to have a look.'

He watched as she regained control of herself, noting her squared shoulder, straightened back and raised chin. She was ready.

'When I last saw him he was heading towards the clock tower on this side of the street,' Edward said.

Amelia edged towards the end of the alleyway and cautiously peered out. She looked left and right, her entire body tense as if ready to flee at the slightest hint of danger. Slowly Edward could see her relax as she studied the people in the village square and along the shopfronts without seeing anyone she recognised. Then she stiffened. Edward heard a sharp intake of breath and quickly pulled her back towards him. She allowed him to scoop her in to his chest and as he held her body against his Edward could feel her shuddering.

'He was dead,' she whispered.

Although Amelia was in shock now, Edward knew seeing McNair would be a good thing in the long run. Here was the proof she needed to know she hadn't killed a man. For days Edward had watched her as she suffered, not knowing how to ease the guilt and regret she was living with. Now, although they had to worry about McNair seeking revenge, Amelia would at least be able to move on with her life.

And move on from you, a rebellious little voice said inside Edward's head. He squashed it down, but the seed had been planted. She could move on from Beechwood Manor now. He would get what he'd wished for on numerous occasions in the past week: his house back to himself and a life of solitude again.

'What do we do?' Amelia asked, turning her beseeching blue eyes up towards him.

'Let's get you home,' Edward said, taking charge of the situation. 'He hasn't seen you and no one knows you're here. There should be no reason for him to tarry in the village for more than a day. We'll keep you hidden until he's passed through.'

He could see his words were having a soothing effect on Amelia and was relieved when she nodded in agreement.

'Come with me.' Edward took her hand and led her further down the alleyway between the shops and round the corner at the back. They had to scramble over some old crates, but after a few minutes they were out of the village and on the path back to Beechwood Manor.

'Why is he here?' Amelia asked as they walked. Every few seconds she would turn and glance over her shoulder as if checking if they were being followed.

Edward shrugged. 'It's the logical place to start looking for you, a village on the route to London. You'd have to pass through if you took the stagecoach. He's probably trying to trace your movements.'

Amelia fell silent. As she moved closer in towards Edward, taking his arm as she stepped across a puddle, Edward felt inordinately pleased at the implied trust in her gesture. She wanted him close, she wanted him to be the one to protect her. He'd forgotten quite how intoxicating being needed could feel.

Chapter Thirteen

Amelia was a mess. She'd been a bundle of nerves for
the last few days and it didn't seem to be getting any better. She knew she should be pleased—after seeing McNair
in the village it was quite clear she hadn't killed the man,
but that fact did leave him alive and most likely looking
for revenge.

'Amelia,' Edward called as she roamed through the
house aimlessly. 'Come here. I have a surprise for you.'

Relieved she wouldn't have to be alone with her
thoughts any longer Amelia hurried to the hallway where
Edward was waiting for her.

He grabbed her hand, obviously excited by whatever it
was he wanted to show her, and pulled her outside. Amelia was aware of the tingle in her fingers as his skin met
hers and wondered if any woman would be strong enough
not to fall for him in these circumstances. He was her
knight, her hero, and it was so typically unfair that she
could never have him.

'Where are we going, Edward?' Amelia laughed as he
pulled her along. She hadn't seen him this excited before,
there was something boyish and carefree about his demeanour. It suited him.

'You'll see.'

They dodged the gardener, who stared after them with a raise of his eyebrows and a knowing expression, and continued on to the outbuildings.

'Here we are,' Edward said, as he pushed open the door to one of the huge barns.

'A barn?' Amelia asked. 'This is my surprise.'

Ever since Edward had tracked her to the village and escorted her back to the house Amelia had sensed a change in him. It wasn't huge or obvious, but she noticed he was allowing himself to smile a little more, to spend a few more minutes conversing with her rather than hurrying off to his private rooms. It was as though he'd realised he was allowed to enjoy her company, that the threat of her leaving had been enough to prompt him to appreciate how human contact could enhance his life.

'It's what's inside the barn.' He pulled her inside and whilst her eyes adjusted to the darkness Amelia let her imagination run wild, hoping Edward might take advantage of the low light and kiss her just as she wanted him to. Of course it didn't happen, Edward clearly didn't see her as a romantic prospect, but since he'd brought her back from the village there was a greater sense of companionship, maybe even friendship between them.

In the gloom she heard a rustling noise and then a louder tapping, as if a hoof was hitting the floor.

Edward pulled her forward again and directed her to a stall. Amelia peered in and let out a squeal of delight. Inside was a beautiful light bay horse with a glossy coat and silky black mane.

More stomping and a quiet whinny was enough to tear Amelia away from the first stall and to look into the second. Inside was a massive black stallion, standing proud and tall and just a little bit haughty. All in all the perfect horse for Edward.

'You bought two horses.' Amelia turned to Edward with a smile. He glanced guiltily at the stall on the end.

'Well…' Edward said with a sheepish smile. 'I actually bought three.'

Amelia was over there immediately and couldn't help but smile. Inside the third stall was a heavily pregnant mare, barely able to stand but munching away happily on some fresh hay.

'Who buys a pregnant horse?' Amelia asked with a laugh.

'I didn't want to separate them,' Edward said a little uncomfortably.

Amelia glanced back in at the black stallion and realised the depth of love the man standing before her was capable of. He'd even bought a pregnant mare just so his new stallion wouldn't be separated from the foal. Edward might appear stern and sombre, but over the past week Amelia had caught glimpses of the man underneath, the man who sheltered damsels in distress, inspired loyalty in his servants and bought a pregnant mare for sentimental reasons.

'And they threw her in for free with the other two.'

Amelia knew Edward would have bought her even if she had been at a premium.

'Afternoon, sir,' a young man said as he pushed open the door to the stable.

'Amelia, this is Tom, our new groom. Tom, this is Miss Amelia.'

He doffed his cap and gave a little bow, before going straight in to see the pregnant mare.

'Would you like to take the horses out, sir?' he called from the stall, all the while petting and soothing the heavy horse.

Edward looked at Amelia with a raised eyebrow and allowed himself a low chuckle at her enthusiastic response.

'I think the lady would.'

Amelia watched as the groom fitted the saddle on to the bay mare and Edward did the same with the stallion. He talked softly to the huge horse throughout, running his large hands over its back and calming the great beast. Amelia took one last look at the heavily pregnant mare still lying in her stall and sent a quick prayer that the foal would be delivered safely, then she helped to lead the two horses out into the yard.

Edward handed the reins of the stallion over to the groom and came up behind her.

'Can you ride?' he asked.

Amelia loved riding. There was an unrivalled freedom on horseback. In India she would often saddle up her horse, persuade someone to join her and roam the countryside for hours at a time.

'I can ride,' Amelia said. 'The real question is can you keep up?'

As Edward helped her mount her horse Amelia felt some of the tension from the day slipping from her shoulders. Soon it would just be her and Edward and the open countryside. She wouldn't have to worry about McNair or the future or even her burgeoning feelings for Edward.

'Let's ride,' Edward said as he swung himself up on to his horse.

Amelia soon found her confidence in the saddle, despite not being correctly attired for riding and it being her first ride out for a few months. They rode in silence for a while, both enjoying the crisp, fresh country air and the sun on their faces.

'We'll stick to the estate,' Edward informed her, 'so

there's no need to worry about bumping into anyone we don't wish to.'

'Thank you,' Amelia said quietly.

For now she just wanted to ride. She wanted to forget the feeling of dread that had planted itself deep inside her when she'd caught sight of McNair, she wanted to forget the sadness that had led to her leaving Beechwood Manor, sadness that she could never mean as much to Edward as his late wife. No, later she could dwell on all of that, but for now she was going to enjoy the fresh air and freedom being on horseback allowed.

Edward was a surprisingly good host, pointing out all the features of the estate, grimacing as he saw how some parts were overgrown or walls had fallen into disrepair, but generally cheerful. Amelia knew he was doing this all for her, trying to instil some normality into her life after the supremely stressful episode a few days ago. He didn't bring up their encounter in the village whilst they rode, or the reason why she had left, but instead stuck to more mundane subjects.

'This wall marks the edge of the estate,' Edward explained as they reached the top of a small hill. 'Those cottages over there are tenant cottages and the farm you can see in the distance belongs to the estate, too.'

Amelia noticed the long silence that followed as Edward surveyed his domain. She wondered if this was the first time he'd been out this far since the fire and whether he regretted his decision to ride up here.

'I haven't been to see my tenants for three years,' he said after a few minutes.

'I'm sure they understand.'

'Mr Guthry ensures the cottages are well looked after and collects the rent, but I always imagined myself a hands-on landlord.'

'You've had a lot to deal with.'

Edward fell silent and then turned his horse away so he was facing back towards his estate and the house. From up here there was a good view of the rolling countryside and Beechwood Manor in the middle. Amelia grimaced as she, too, turned around and saw they were looking at the East Wing of the house.

'I need to get that repaired,' Edward said quietly. 'One day.'

Amelia leaned over and placed a hand on his arm. Edward stiffened for a second, but did not shake her off.

'Why did you leave?' Edward asked eventually.

Amelia had known this question would come and Edward deserved an answer, but she wasn't sure if she could tell him the truth.

'I didn't think you'd want me around,' she said.

'I don't want you to ever put yourself at risk like that again.'

Amelia sensed he wanted to say more, but something was holding him back. She willed him to open up, to tell her he felt *something* for her, but he remained quiet. Allowing herself a moment of sadness, Amelia knew it was too much to expect. She should be content that Edward had realised he was allowed to enjoy her company, that they could live side by side in easy companionship—anything else was just pure fantasy on her part.

'What do we do about McNair?' Amelia asked.

'Nothing. At least nothing for now. No one knows you're here, apart from Mrs Henshaw and she's the most loyal person I know.'

'One of the servants might talk.'

Edward shook his head. 'They don't know who you are and they would have no cause to talk to McNair anyway.'

'I thought I'd killed him.'

Edward must have heard the tremor in her voice because immediately he dismounted, took her horse's reins in his hand and lifted her out of the saddle. His strong hands encircled her waist and once again Amelia felt safe and secure.

'You didn't kill him,' Edward said softly. 'And even if you had it was self-defence. He struck you, he hurt you. A man like that doesn't deserve your pity or your regrets.'

Once again Amelia could picture the letter opener slipping into McNair's flesh, the warm trickle of blood over her hand.

'Stop it,' Edward said sharply. 'Whatever you're thinking, stop it.'

'Why is he here? Why is he looking for me?'

'I don't know the man, but I've encountered enough of his type in my life. To him a physical wound won't be anywhere near as bad as a wound to his pride. You got the better of him and I'm sure he wants revenge for that.'

Amelia felt herself shiver. The murderous look that had flashed in McNair's eyes just before he'd struck her was enough to scare someone much braver than her.

'But he won't get anywhere near you. I promise I will not let him hurt you.'

As Amelia gazed up into Edward's eyes she believed him and some of the fear and the worry began to ebb away.

'But—' Amelia began, but Edward cut her off, tilting her chin up with a gentle finger so she had to meet his eye again.

'I promise I will protect you.'

Amelia had been about to ask when she had to leave Beechwood Manor, but all thoughts were dashed from her head as Edward's fingers touched the skin of her chin. For a moment she thought he might kiss her and her entire body willed him to dip his head and claim her as his, but it was not to be so.

Slowly Edward stepped away and Amelia fought to hide her disappointment. It was for the best. At least that was what she had to keep telling herself. Not that she truly believed that in her heart. If Edward leaned forward and kissed her she would be smiling for the rest of her days. Amelia knew she had doubted her burgeoning feelings for Edward these past couple of weeks, telling herself that her judgement couldn't be trusted, that she'd fallen for a scoundrel before, but ever since Edward had promised not to let McNair hurt her Amelia had known the truth. He was a good man, a man no one would ever regret loving, if he loved you back, of course.

As Edward helped her back into the saddle he smiled up at her softly and a little sadly and Amelia wondered if he were thinking about his wife and son. Maybe wishing it was them he was out riding with instead of her.

'I was thinking about your cousin,' Edward said as they began the ride home.

Amelia frowned, wondering why on earth he would be thinking about Lizzie.

'You said you had swapped identities to allow you to travel to Brighton.'

'Yes, I hadn't seen my aunt since I was very young so Lizzie was going to pretend to be me until I returned to London.'

'Would you like me to ask Mr Guthry to send someone to check on her well-being? I doubt McNair would harm her, but if he pays someone else to look into the matter for him they might fall for your ruse and think your cousin is you.'

Suddenly all the blood drained from Amelia's face and

she felt a little light headed. Had she underestimated the danger Lizzie was in? She loved her cousin more than anyone in the entire world and she wanted to protect her from this mess above anything else. The letter she had penned a week ago would hopefully be well on its way to Lizzie by now, but maybe that wasn't enough.

'I'll write again when we get back to the house. Perhaps Mr Guthry could pass on my letter so I know Lizzie receives it.'

'I received a note from Mr Guthry yesterday. He is still following McNair's trail, but promises to come and update us in the next couple of days. We shall ask him to organise someone to check on Lizzie's safety then,' Edward said decisively.

Amelia felt the tears welling in her eyes and tried to suppress them. Edward was thoughtful and considerate, he was even thinking of the safety of a woman he'd never met, and from what she had heard about his late wife she had been the same. Amelia would never be able to live up to her character, it was ridiculous to even dream she might.

As soon as they returned to Beechwood Manor, Amelia excused herself, went to her room and hurriedly began writing to Lizzie, hoping that nothing befell her cousin before the warning reached her.

Dearest Lizzie,
I do not know if you received my last letter, but I am in a perilous position and am worried for your safety, too. Captain McNair turned out to be exactly the scoundrel you suspected and as always I wish I had listened to you at the time. Then this entire mess could have been avoided.

Lizzie, I did something terrible, something I cannot bear to write down, and now McNair is out for revenge. I worry for you, for your safety as you pretend to be me. Please be careful.

Do not expend too much energy worrying for me. For now, at least, I am safe and cared for. When I was fleeing from Brighton I stumbled upon an old house inhabited by a gentleman. Edward has sheltered me and cared for me over the past two weeks and I could not ask for a better host.

Oh, he grumbles and sometimes is a little crabby. In fact he reminds me of that bear we saw once in the marketplace in Aska. Of course he's completely harmless...in fact, underneath it all he's one of the kindest people I've ever met.

Not that I mind his bearish demeanour. He's been beset by tragedy. Three years ago he lost his wife and young son in a fire. Until I came into his life I think he'd barely spoken to another person for years. It's terrible how such a kind and generous person can be struck by such sad circumstances.

Oh, Lizzie, I wish you were here with me. I need your sensible counsel, your words of wisdom. I think I might be falling for Edward.

I know, I know... I hardly know the man. But if you only could see him, Lizzie, and understand what he's done for me already I truly think this time you would approve.

Of course none of that matters. Edward still mourns his wife and his son. His late wife sounds so lovely, so kind. I know I could never live up to her. And Edward does not deserve second-best. I am aware of all of this, but still my heart sings every time I see him.

What should I do?
Please keep yourself safe and I hope we will be reunited soon.
All my love,
Amelia

Chapter Fourteen

Three days later Mr Guthry made an appearance. Edward had been sitting at his old desk in the study, a room he hadn't entered for at least two years. The furniture was recently polished and the room aired, but there was still a slight musty, disused feel about it.

He had spread out a number of documents pertaining to the estate and was going over his accounts for the past twelve months. Although he had kept abreast of what was happening to his birthright, Edward knew he had been a neglectful owner these past few years. It was the small things, like the Richardsons, who were one of his tenant-farmer families. They'd had to source someone to repair their roof when it had collapsed the previous year. In the past Edward would have never let one of his properties fall into such a state that a roof might even threaten to fall in. Someone could have been hurt.

A tap at the door made him look up from his papers.

'Mr Guthry here to see you, sir,' one of the new maids said with a deferential curtsy.

'Show him in. And have you seen Miss Amelia?'

'I think she's out with the horses, sir.'

He hadn't been sure of himself when he'd bought the

horses, it had been an impulsive action, one that he hadn't quite thought through. After chasing Amelia into the village of Denton he had allowed himself to acknowledge he actually enjoyed her company. When he had noticed the advertisement for the sale of the horses from a neighbouring estate he had felt an urge to do something to take her mind off McNair and what the rogue wanted with her. It had worked. Amelia had fallen in love with the three beasts and spent a lot of time out there rubbing them down or riding.

Mr Guthry entered and shook Edward's hand, his face grim.

'Miss Amelia should hear what I have to say,' he said with a grimace as Edward indicated the man should sit.

Edward thought about screening the information his steward was bringing first, but decided it was Amelia's future at stake, so instead strode outside to find her.

She was hurrying back towards the house from the stables, her hair windswept and her cheeks rosy from the fresh air. She looked happy, the fear that had been stalking her for the past few days was finally lifting, and Edward was loathe to shatter that happiness.

'Mr Guthry's here,' Edward said as they met.

Immediately the worry was back. He could see it in the small frown lines between her eyebrows and the way she sucked in her lower lip.

'What did he say?'

'He hasn't told me anything yet. I thought we should hear whatever he has to say together.'

Edward wondered if he'd made the right decision. When Jane was alive he had always dealt with any unsavoury business without involving her. He'd protected her from the worst in the world, but Amelia was stronger than Jane had been. She'd been through so much in the last few weeks and was still fighting. It only seemed right to let her hear what Guthry had to say first hand. It was her life after all.

Mr Guthry was waiting for them and looked anxious to begin.

'Well, firstly, McNair is alive. I thought you'd like to know straight off. But I have some worrying news, miss… worrying news indeed. I don't wish to alarm you, but I need to warn you. I'd never forgive myself if something happened and I hadn't warned you.'

'Start at the beginning, Mr Guthry,' Edward said soothingly. He glanced at Amelia and saw she had initially blanched at Guthry's warning, but had managed to regain her composure.

'Well, I travelled to Brighton to track down this fellow of yours, Captain McNair. It wasn't all that difficult to find where he resided, but the man himself was long gone.'

Edward supposed McNair had set off after Amelia soon after he had recovered from the wound she had inflicted upon him.

'I started to ask around, try to build up a picture of the man, and I can tell you it wasn't good.' Guthry shook his head vehemently and clasped his hands together.

'He's in debt with everyone, a gambler and a drinker, and no one would come out and say it, but I gathered he's seduced one or two women he shouldn't have.' Guthry's ears turned pink as he glanced at Amelia. 'Begging your pardon, miss, but that's what I was told.'

Amelia gestured for him to continue, her face impassive and only her stiff posture betraying the tension she must be feeling.

'It took me a while to pick up his trail, but after a few days I caught up with him in the village of Southease. He was asking everyone if they had seen a young woman fitting your description.'

Edward knew the village well. It was only a few miles away and he supposed McNair must have followed Amelia's trail from there to here.

'I bought some of the locals drinks to find out what he'd been asking them and it turns out McNair was rather vocal when under the influence of a few too many cups of ale. He said he was tracking his wife, who had attacked him and then fled, and that when he caught up with her then her life wouldn't be worth living.' Guthry flicked an apologetic glance in Amelia's direction. 'I'm sorry, miss, I wish I had better news.'

Amelia shook her head. 'You've been very diligent, Mr Guthry. Thank you for everything you have done.'

'There's one more thing, miss. One of the locals told him they'd seen a young woman covered in blood about a week previously. Pointed him in this direction.'

Which explained why McNair had been in the village a few days ago.

'I've spent the last few days travelling backwards and forward between the local villages, trying to pick up his trail again, but he's disappeared.'

'Thank you, Mr Guthry, you've been very thorough,' Edward said.

'My pleasure, Sir Edward. I only wish I had better news.'

'I have another request, Mr Guthry, if you don't mind.'

The portly man nodded, his face serious and his demeanour showing he was ready to do whatever was asked of him.

'Miss Amelia's cousin is currently residing in London. I won't go into details, but she has assumed Miss Amelia's identity for a few weeks. We are concerned that there is a small chance she may be in danger from McNair due to her relationship with Miss Amelia.'

'I'll travel to London straight away,' Mr Guthry said.

'It would be enough to send a trusted associate,' Edward said. 'We may well need you here in the next couple of weeks.'

'I have a young assistant who is much faster on a horse and would be honoured to assist us in this matter,' Mr Guthry said, 'I will ensure he sets out as soon as I return.'

'Thank you,' Amelia said, taking Mr Guthry's hand and squeezing it warmly. 'Here are the details he will need to find Lizzie and this is a letter outlining the circumstances for her.' She handed over the envelope and the name and address of her aunt in London.

Edward showed Mr Guthry out, asking his steward to return in a day or two to discuss estate business, but for now he knew he needed to check Amelia was not too shaken by Guthry's account.

Amelia was slumped in one of the comfortable armchairs he had moved himself from his rooms in the West Wing to his newly re-opened study.

'Amelia…' he began, not sure where to start.

'I'm a terrible person,' she wailed, taking Edward by surprise. He had expected fear, uncertainty, maybe even gratitude for the confirmation she wasn't a murderess, but not this.

'You're not a terrible person.'

She levelled him with a black look and Edward had to contain a sigh. He had thought Amelia's dramatic outbursts were a thing of the past. He glanced a little wistfully at the pile of simple, undramatic papers on his desk before turning his attention back to Amelia.

'I am a terrible person. I wished him dead,' she whispered this last part. 'I wished that I had killed him. Even when I saw him with my own eyes I wished McNair dead.'

Edward collapsed in the armchair opposite her and regarded the woman in front of him for a minute. His instinct was to flee, to leave her to work through this dilemma on her own, but something kept him in the chair. He knew all about guilt, about punishing oneself for things that were not your fault. He knew how it could eat away at a person, strip them of hope of happiness and make them question their reasons for living.

'The man tricked you, stole away your innocence, struck you and threatened your life. Show me a hundred people McNair has injured like you and I'll show you a hundred people who wished him dead.'

'But for weeks I've hated myself for killing him…' Amelia paused and then corrected herself. 'Well, thinking that I'd killed him.'

'And if you didn't show remorse for your actions I would be much more concerned I was sheltering a monster,' Edward said, trying to inject some joviality into the room.

'Do you think I'm a monster?' Amelia asked quietly, her face pale and her lips trembling.

Edward silently cursed his choice of words and resisted the temptation to lever himself out of his chair and take her hand. Amelia was the sort of woman who stirred a man's protective side, but it wasn't his place to comfort her. He had promised to shelter her, to provide her somewhere safe to stay whilst she worked out what to do, and he would even go so far as to protect her from the cad that had seduced and betrayed her, but he could not allow himself to go any further than that. If he took her hand, well, Edward didn't want to think of how his body might react and that would lead to the now familiar feelings of grief and self-reproach. So instead he remained where he was, but spoke softly and kindly.

'You're not a monster, Amelia. You're a wonderful, fun, kind person who was treated very badly by that scoundrel.

It is human nature to want him punished, just as it is human nature to regret actions taken on the spur of the moment.'

'I'm scared, Edward. What does he want from me?'

Edward was all too aware of what McNair wanted from Amelia. In all likelihood he wanted to hurt her as she had hurt him, wound her pride just as his had been wounded.

'It doesn't matter what he wants, he's not going to find you.'

Amelia bit her lip and nodded unconvincingly.

'He's not going to find you, Amelia. You have to believe that.'

'But he was right here, in the village.'

'That was three days ago. If he'd picked up your trail, if he knew you were here with me, then he would have made his move by now.'

She looked as though she were digesting that piece of information, weighing it up and looking for flaws.

'He's not going to give up.'

Edward had to agree with her there. He didn't know the man, but he'd come across plenty like him in his time. McNair wouldn't rest until Amelia had paid for her attack on him.

'It doesn't matter. He has no idea where you are and by now he would have moved on, somewhere further away.'

'I'll always have to be looking over my shoulder.'

Edward grimaced. She was right, her life would be spent waiting for McNair to catch up with her.

'I don't know what to do, Edward.'

'Stay here with me, at least for a while longer,' he said with authority. 'Write to your father, explain exactly what has happened and ask for his assistance.'

As soon as the words were out of his mouth Edward found himself gawping. He had never meant to ask her to stay a while longer.

'Run back to India?'

Something inside him wanted to withdraw the invitation for her to stay with him whilst she awaited her father's reply, it had been issued spontaneously without him fully thinking through the consequences, but he kept quiet. Amelia was alone and in danger, he couldn't be the man to turn her out into the world. And after all it was only a few weeks, maybe a couple of months, and then Beechwood Manor would become his private sanctuary again.

She looked down at him with those piercing blue eyes, an uncharacteristic uncertainty behind them.

'I can stay here, with you, until my father sends for me?'

'I suppose I have the space for you,' Edward said.

Amelia launched herself out of the chair and into his arms. After his initial shock Edward found himself instinctively embracing her, pulling her closer. She was warm and soft and inviting and as Edward held her in his arms he felt his heart begin to hammer faster in his chest.

'Thank you, thank you, thank you,' Amelia said, pulling away a little.

Their eyes met and Edward felt a spark fly between them, but then Amelia looked away, stiffening slightly. She stood, gave a hurried little curtsy, something she'd never done before in his presence, and fled the room.

Chapter Fifteen

Amelia read through the letter to her father one last time, grimaced and then signed her name. She was glad she wouldn't be there to see his reaction first hand. No doubt he would curse and shout when he read she wasn't in London finding herself a well-to-do husband.

Dearest Papa,
I hope you are keeping well. I miss you and find myself wishing I could be back in the hills of Bombay, awaiting the first of the monsoon rains with you. Do you remember when Mama was still alive and we would sit on the veranda watching the first heavy drops hit the dusty ground? I can still smell that earthy scent Mama used to love so much as if it were yesterday.

Papa, I'm so ashamed to have to write this, but I need your help. I'm in trouble and, although I know you will be angry and disappointed, you are the only person I can turn to. On arriving in London I did a silly thing: I asked Lizzie to assume my identity for a few days whilst I travelled on to Brighton alone.

I don't know if you remember Captain McNair

from the regiment in Bombay, but I am ashamed to admit I was a little infatuated with him. I thought ours would be a wonderful reunion after the time we spent together last year, but I judged him wrongly.

After travelling down to Brighton to find Captain McNair I discovered he had been married all the time I had known him in India. He was planning on seducing me, convincing me to run away with him and then extorting money from you for my scandal-free return. Only the intervention of his commanding officer saved me from my fate and McNair was sent home to his ailing wife.

When I found this out on arriving in Brighton I threatened to expose him as a scoundrel and things got a little heated. I did something awful, Papa. I stabbed him with a letter opener.

Now I do not know what to do. I am currently staying with a gentleman by the name of Sir Edward Gray. He is sheltering me from McNair, who I think will be seeking revenge. I regret my actions every minute of every day, but I am scared of what McNair will do to me.

Papa, I know I have been foolish and I know I have been selfish, but I truly need your help.

I was hoping you might be able to find a way to organise a passage back to India. If I could come home to you, I promise to try and be a more docile and obedient daughter.

Please help me, Papa.
I love you and miss you.
Amelia

Folding the letter, Amelia then slipped it into an envelope and wrote the address on the front before making her way to the kitchens to find how Goody was getting on with the favour she'd asked of her.

Amelia hovered around the kitchen whilst Goody bustled backwards and forward, chatting away at the same time. It was relaxing being in here with Goody. The woman was content to carry out a conversation with just the minimum of prompting, allowing Amelia's mind to wander but without her being able to focus too long on one thing.

'We've got jams, fresh bread, a fruit cake and some pickles. I think the tenants will be delighted with the hampers.'

Amelia peered inside, wondering if it was a good idea to spend the entire day out and about with Edward. She wanted to do something to say thank you, to show she appreciated him letting her stay whilst she awaited a reply from her father, but maybe an activity that threw them together all day was not the best idea. She hated to admit that she yearned for him, when he wasn't close by she missed him physically.

She wanted him to look at her the way he looked when he spoke of his late wife and son, that adoration, that eternal love, but it was clear that would never happen. Over the past week Edward had opened up a little, shown her more of his real self, and Amelia had just found herself wanting him even more, but today she would suppress all those feelings and focus on being a good guest and friend.

Once Goody indicated everything was ready Amelia gathered up the baskets and thanked the older woman for all her hard work. Whatever she felt for Edward she still wanted to say thank you to him for letting her stay. She'd seen the regret and wistfulness in his face a few days previously when he'd talked of how he had neglected his tenants and this was an area where Amelia could excel.

She loved entertaining and meeting new people. She

was naturally confident and outgoing, whereas Edward was more reserved. He might struggle to approach the tenants he'd neglected for so long on his own, but he would feel increasingly guilty the longer he left it. Amelia thought she could help smooth the way and take some of the awkwardness out of the situation.

'Knock-knock,' Mr Guthry said as he peered round the kitchen door and smiled sheepishly as he caught sight of the two women.

'Mr Guthry, what a pleasant surprise. I had no idea we were expecting you today.' Although Amelia greeted him warmly she felt a ball of dread settle in her stomach.

'I just popped by to discuss a few pieces of business with Sir Edward,' Mr Guthry said. 'He was eager to go through some new acquisitions.' He caught Amelia's worried expression and hastened to reassure her, 'I have no more news on that front, Miss Amelia, but you try not to fret. Sir Edward will look after you.'

'He will indeed.'

Goody patted Amelia on the arm and Amelia rallied. They were right, she couldn't go thinking the worst every time there was a visitor to the house.

'And my young associate is heading to London as we speak, ready to seek your cousin out and warn her of the potential danger she could be in.'

'Thank you, Mr Guthry.'

'My pleasure, Miss Amelia, I am truly delighted to be of service.'

'Would you like a drink, Mr Guthry?' Goody asked.

'Oh, that would be very kind, Mrs Henshaw, if it isn't too much trouble.' He paused and then pressed on. 'And maybe one of those delicious biscuits, if there are any left from the other day.'

'I'll see what I can do, Mr Guthry.'

Amelia watched as Goody fussed around the older man, pulling him out a stool and pouring him a cup of tea. Once a plate of biscuits was set on the table Goody took a seat opposite the land agent.

'I do declare these are the finest biscuits I've ever tasted,' Mr Guthry said as he devoured a buttery shortbread. 'And as you can probably tell I've tasted a fair few in my time.'

He patted his ample midsection and eyed up the plate.

'Go ahead and take another, Mr Guthry,' Goody said warmly. 'There's nothing wrong with a man with a healthy appetite.'

'I do believe you have a magical touch when it comes to baking, Mrs Henshaw. The fruitcake you sent me home with the other day was just divine. I have to confess I've polished it off already.'

Goody's cheeks shone at the compliment and Amelia wondered how many times Mr Guthry had come to visit the widowed housekeeper in the past few days. It was obvious he had a soft spot for her baking, but she had a feeling there might be something deeper pulling him back to the kitchen at Beechwood Manor.

'Well, I really had better get going,' Amelia said, deciding to let the housekeeper and the estate manager have a bit of privacy.

'Good luck, my dear,' Goody called after her.

Amelia knocked quietly on Edward's study door, wondering if he would agree to her plan. She felt surprisingly nervous and wondered if it was because she wanted today to be a success or if it was down to her remembering the urge she'd had to kiss Edward the last time they'd been in the study together.

'Come in.'

Pushing open the door, Amelia summoned up her courage and stepped inside.

'Are you busy?' she asked.

'Yes.' His answer was curt and he immediately returned his attention to the papers in front of him.

'I've got something planned for today. Will you join me?'

'I've got a lot to do.'

Amelia felt her heart sink, but rallied. Over the past few weeks she had become an expert in drawing Edward out. He was a reticent and solitary man, but Amelia had learnt that perseverance and a sunny smile often won over his initial reluctance to engage with her.

'I won't take no for an answer,' Amelia said, wondering whether he was regretting asking her to stay for the foreseeable future.

'What have you planned?' he asked eventually.

Amelia suddenly felt a little nervous, but bit her lower lip and ploughed on. 'I thought we would go and see your tenants. You were only saying the other day they were well overdue a visit.'

He regarded her in silence for almost a minute.

'What about keeping your presence here a secret?'

'You said yourself McNair will have moved on by now and we can be suitably vague when introducing me. Just give my name as Amelia and tell people I'm your guest.' Amelia didn't say it, but she rather thought the tenants would be more interested in their landlord and his emergence from Beechwood Manor after all these years.

Edward frowned and looked down at his papers for a minute and Amelia thought he might decline, then he gave a short, sharp nod of his head.

'Good idea.'

'Mrs Henshaw has made hampers for us to take.'

'Hampers?'

'With food. As a gift.'

Edward grunted, but she could see he appreciated the thought she had put into their outing.

Half an hour later Amelia was dressed in a riding habit that was a few sizes too large, but certainly much more comfortable to ride in than an ordinary dress. She was waiting for Edward in the courtyard by the barn that was currently stabling the horses.

'Are you ready?' Edward asked as he strode from the house and gave his horse a hearty pat on its flank.

Amelia was just about to answer when Tom, the new groom, came rushing from the barn, a look of panic on his face.

'Sorry to bother you, sir,' he said, his words tumbling out of his mouth as though they were being chased.

'What is it, Tom?'

'It's Milly, sir.' Tom blushed and quickly corrected himself. 'The pregnant mare.'

'What's wrong?'

'I think it's her time and I've only ever birthed one foal, sir.'

Amelia peered over his shoulder into the darkness of the barn, but could not see anything.

'Come on.' Edward grabbed her hand and pulled her forward, then he paused. 'You're not squeamish, are you?' he asked.

Amelia gave him a scornful look and brushed past him, following Tom back into the barn.

Milly, the heavily pregnant mare, was in her stall lying down. On the floor there was a copious amount of liquid soaking into the otherwise fresh hay. As they entered the horse let out a small whinny and stood clumsily, tossing her head and tottering a little.

'Her waters went about ten minutes ago,' Tom said quietly.

'What should we do?' Amelia asked. Although the barn was quiet and peaceful Amelia felt an awful sense of panic welling up inside her.

'Nothing. Mares have been birthing foals for hundreds of years without man's intervention. Just stay quiet and watch, and we'll be ready to step in if there are any problems.' Edward was calm and cool and Amelia wondered how many times he'd done this before.

They watched silently as the mare settled back down on the hay, breathing heavily.

Edward stood right next to her, leaning on the wooden gate and watching the horse in front of him. Amelia felt his shoulder brush against hers and cast a quick glance at his profile. She felt as though she were getting a glimpse of the man Edward had been before tragedy had struck his life. She'd seen this side to him before, usually when a situation needed a cool head and quick thinking. Then Edward would emerge from his protective shell and take control calmly and authoritatively. Now was no different. He had instantly soothed the panic-stricken groom and inserted himself into the barn unobtrusively in case anything went wrong.

'How long will it take?' Amelia asked as the mare gave a whinny of pain.

Edward shrugged, never taking his eyes off the horse. 'It varies.'

The mare was back on her feet now, snorting and stomping her front left hoof. Amelia found she was holding her breath as the horse seemed to become more and more agitated.

'What's wrong?' she whispered, biting her lip. She prayed nothing would go wrong for the mare and a foal would soon emerge alive and well.

'She's in pain and distressed,' Edward said, still focused on Milly.

He gripped hold of the gate and watched the horse whinny and snort for another thirty seconds before seeming to make up his mind. Quickly he vaulted over the wooden partition and into the stall, murmuring soothing words to Milly under his breath as he approached her. Amelia felt her heart begin to pound as he got within touching distance. One wrong move and he could be trampled by the distressed animal.

'Be careful,' she whispered quietly. 'Please don't get hurt.'

She might not ever be able to have Edward's heart or his love, but Amelia knew she would be completely devastated if anything happened to him.

Carefully Edward reached out and began to stroke Milly on the nose, all the time talking to her in his soft voice. Even just his presence by her side seemed to calm the mare and slowly she relaxed. After a couple of minutes Edward helped to guide her back into the hay. He sank down with the horse, stroking her flank and talking to her softly.

'Nearly there,' Amelia heard him say as the mare tensed and snorted. 'You can do it, girl.'

Amelia didn't know a single other landowner who would sit in the hay coaxing a labouring mare through giving birth. Every new thing she learnt about him made her care more, to want something that could never happen between them more.

'Look,' Amelia whispered suddenly. 'I can see a hoof.'

Sure enough one hoof and then another came into view, followed shortly by a nose. Amelia found she was holding her breath, waiting for a little more of the foal to appear with each contraction. For a moment she forgot her troubles and instead focused all her attention on the mare, willing the foal to be born safely and wishing there was something she could do to help.

Edward remained where he was, stroking and talking, but Amelia could see the excitement and anticipation in his eyes. He looked more alive than she'd ever seen him and she felt as though she wanted to capture this version of him and keep it with her for ever.

Suddenly, with a rush, the foal was born. Immediately he was moving, uncoordinated and unsteady, but moving. Milly looked back, exhausted, at her baby, and allowed it to nuzzle in to her.

'Foal should be up and about in half an hour or so,' Tom said, smiling now the danger had passed.

'That was miraculous,' Amelia said, unable to take her eyes off the mother and baby. They were curled together, both sticky and wet, but both two halves of a whole.

Edward stood up slowly, careful not to disturb the mare and her foal. With a backwards glance at the two animals he vaulted back over the fence and took Amelia by the arm.

'Come, let's leave them to bond,' Edward said quietly, leading Amelia away. 'We can return and see how they're doing later.'

Out in the courtyard Edward helped Amelia to mount her horse, boosting her up and holding her steady whilst she rearranged the heavy material of the riding habit.

'I've never seen anything so wonderful,' Amelia said, still unable to think of anything else but the new life inside the barn.

She'd never really considered children before, but seeing the foal cuddle up to its mother had sparked some hidden maternal part of her. When she had been infatuated with

McNair Amelia had never been overly keen on the idea of a family of her own, it just hadn't really fit in to the idea of soirées and parties that McNair had painted for her, but maybe there was a part of her that would like to be a mother. Only if she found the right man to be a father to her children, of course.

Glancing quickly at Edward, Amelia tried to suppress the image of him as a father. From how he had talked of his son and the stories Goody had told her Amelia knew Edward had been a wonderful father. He'd been loving and involved, not distant like some. Just the sort of man she would want to be father to her own children.

Pushing the fantasy away, Amelia smiled brightly and urged her horse forward. Today was about Edward bonding with his tenants. She wouldn't make it about her. Nothing could distract her from her aim.

Edward was quiet as they rode over the green slopes and Amelia left him to his thoughts for a while. As they approached the cottages she reined in her horse and slowed.

'Tell me about your tenants,' she said, wanting to know just a little about the people they would be visiting.

'The estate owns twenty-four houses in total,' Edward said, allowing himself a smile at the surprised look on her face.

'I only brought three hampers.'

'Most of the houses are in the village itself. The cottages we saw the other day are rented out to the farmer labourers and their families.'

'The ones that work on Beechwood Farm?'

It was the farm surrounding the quaint farmhouse Edward had pointed out the other day.

'Exactly.'

'So who lives in each?'

Edward thought for a minute, his fingers tapping the leather of the reins gently as he stared off into the distance.

'The first cottage is rented to the Wilsons. They are a young couple without any children, or at least they didn't have any when I last saw them. In the second cottage are the Turners, Mr Turner has worked for the family for many years. They have seven children in total, but I think the eldest three have left home.'

'There's six of them living in that tiny cottage?'

'You have led a sheltered life. That's considered spacious for some families.'

Amelia bristled slightly. She'd probably seen more poverty than Edward could imagine. In India whole families often lived in one room with no access to clean water or sanitary facilities. Disease spread quickly in the heat and it wasn't uncommon to have whole villages wiped out in the course of a week.

The difference of course was the weather. Although whole families might only have one room, most of the living was done outside. Cooking, washing, sometimes even sleeping when the nights were clear and balmy. What she couldn't imagine was being cooped up in a gloomy cottage with so many other people in the dark, cold days of an English winter.

'And the third cottage?'

Edward grimaced and looked a little bashful.

'Mrs Locke and her three daughters live there.'

'I thought you said the cottages were for farm labourers.'

'They are. Mrs Locke's husband worked at Beechwood Farm until he died five years ago.'

'How awful.'

'I've never had the heart to turf them out, even though

it means some of the other farm labourers living further away in the village.'

'How do they pay their rent?' Amelia asked a little suspiciously.

Edward coughed and urged his horse forward.

'Mrs Locke takes in sewing and I think the eldest daughter has just got a job as a maid.'

'You don't make them pay, do you?'

'No.'

Amelia suppressed a smile. He'd been brought up to be a fair landlord, she was sure, but also to ensure his properties were profitable. She didn't think many men would take pity on a widow and her daughters for so many years.

They stopped outside the first cottage and Edward dismounted before helping Amelia down. Expertly he secured both horses to a fence and led Amelia carefully up the neat little stone path.

A woman in her late twenties opened the door with a baby in her arms and a toddler clinging on to her skirts. As she realised who was visiting her eyes widened with shock and she dipped into a nervous curtsy.

'Sir... Sir Edward,' she managed to stutter.

'Good morning, Mrs Wilson. I hope we haven't come at an inconvenient time.'

'Oh, no, of course not, my lord, it is a pleasure to welcome you into our home at any time.'

She stood aside and ushered them into a small kitchen with a few solid pieces of wooden furniture.

'May I introduce Miss Amelia? A friend who is currently staying with me at Beechwood Manor.'

'It's lovely to meet you, miss.' Mrs Wilson paused, switched the baby to her other hip and then ploughed on nervously. 'And may I say it is wonderful to see you out and about, my lord. I pray every week for your family.'

She blushed, wrung her hands and looked at Amelia beseechingly as if worried she had said too much.

Edward remained silent and Amelia could feel Mrs Wilson's concern building.

'That's very kind of you, Mrs Wilson. I know Sir Edward is grateful to everyone who has prayed or sent good wishes in these difficult times.'

'Would you like a cup of tea?'

'That would be wonderful, but you must let me make it. You have your hands full with these little darlings.'

Amelia and Mrs Wilson talked for twenty minutes about the children and by the time they were ready to leave the older woman had relaxed considerably.

'Is there anything you need, Mrs Wilson?' Edward asked on their way out the door.

Mrs Wilson glanced at Amelia, who smiled encouragingly.

'Well, the roof over our bedroom does leak a little. We've managed to patch it up for a while, but after the last storm it's got much worse. We never wanted to bother you, but it would be nice not to have a bucket in the middle of the room to catch the water.'

'I will send someone to look at it later this week,' Edward promised. 'And you must tell me if anything else ever needs doing. That is what I am here for.'

The second visit was just as successful, with Edward even relaxing enough to scoop one of the younger of the Turner children on to his shoulders whilst they were having a tour of the small garden.

Amelia watched him as the young boy gripped his hair and Edward laughed. He had picked the boy up so effortlessly, as if it were second nature to him. She could imagine him as a father, playing and laughing and loving his son. It made her heart constrict to realise just what he had lost.

'Will you be my horsey?' the little boy asked.

'Hush, Timothy, don't bother Sir Edward,' Mrs Turner said with an apologetic smile.

Edward tilted his head back, gave Timothy a mischievous smile and then began to trot around the garden, making the young boy squeal with delight.

'Faster, faster!' Timothy yelled.

Edward obliged, picking up speed and jiggling Timothy up and down until both man and boy collapsed panting and laughing.

Amelia realised it was the first time she'd seen Edward properly laugh. There had been a few self-deprecating chuckles, the odd smile and one or two twinkles of amusement in his eyes, but she'd never actually seen him let go and laugh like this.

'Sir Edward is a good man,' Mrs Turner said as they watched Edward and Timothy sit up, only to collapse back again on to the grass. 'And he's suffered so much.'

Amelia nodded wordlessly. Even when he'd told her about the loss of his wife and son Amelia hadn't realised quite how it must have destroyed his entire soul. Seeing him with the children showed her how he must have lived for his son.

After Edward had been completely exhausted by the Turner children and Amelia had eaten far too much of Mrs Turner's fruitcake they bid their farewells and moved on to their final visit of the day.

As they approached the last cottage the door opened before Edward could raise his fist to knock.

'Sir Edward,' the middle-aged woman said, with worry apparent in her voice.

'Mrs Locke, I hope you are well. This is Miss Amelia. She's a friend staying with me at Beechwood Manor at the moment.'

'Please come in.'

No sooner had the door closed than Mrs Locke was ushering them into the small kitchen and nervously tidying up around them. Two young girls peeked round the doorframe, both as anxious as their mother.

'You have a lovely home, Mrs Locke,' Amelia said, trying to put the older woman at ease.

'We're very grateful for all your generosity over the years, Sir Edward, and of course I understand the time has come for you to move one of the farm labourers into the cottage, but I beg you please let me find somewhere else for my girls first. I don't want them to end up in the workhouse.'

As she spoke the tears began running down her cheeks and her two youngest daughters rushed into the room to cling on to her.

'Mrs Locke,' Edward said, quietly but firmly, 'please don't worry. That is not why I am here.'

A glimmer of hope appeared in her eyes.

'It's not?'

'Your husband was a good man, a good worker, and it was a tragedy he lost his life so young. Believe me, I understand the suffering involved in losing one's spouse, one's life partner, and I have never had to worry about how I would provide for my family, too. I think you are an extremely brave and resourceful woman and I don't want you ever have to worry about losing your home, not whilst I am your landlord.'

'You don't want us to move out?'

'I don't want you to move out.'

'But we don't pay any rent.'

'Mrs Locke, if we can't show a little kindness to others in this world then what is the point of living? I don't want your money. I don't want you to leave.'

Mrs Locke threw herself at Edward and hugged him, encircling him with her skinny arms and sobbing like a child on his shoulder.

Amelia motioned for him to reciprocate and awkwardly he patted her softly on the back.

'Is there anything we can do to help, Mrs Locke?' Amelia asked.

The older woman released Edward and sniffled. 'You've been so kind. When I saw you coming up the path I thought...' She trailed off. 'I thought we were for the workhouse.'

'How old are your daughters?' Amelia asked, looking at the two skinny girls standing by their mother.

'Emily is fourteen and Ginny is ten. My eldest, Rebecca, is out at work. She's a maid over at Twittle House.'

Amelia glanced at Edward and tried to convey her idea with a flash of her eyes. He frowned at her.

'It won't be long until Emily is going out to work, too,' Amelia prompted.

'Oh, no, miss. As soon as we can find her a position she will be going into service.'

'I'm sure it would be a comfort to you if she could find a position locally.'

Understanding finally dawned on Edward's face.

'Mrs Henshaw, my esteemed housekeeper, is always telling me we need more staff at Beechwood Manor. I will have to check, but I can ask to see if she has a position for Emily.'

'Truly, Sir Edward?'

Edward retreated a little, as if expecting another hug, but managed a reassuring smile.

'Truly. I will talk to her later today.'

As they left the Lockes's cottage Amelia took Edward's arm and leaned in closer to him.

'What you said back there, to Mrs Locke, I think that's one of the kindest things I've ever heard.' Amelia could see the hint of colour in Edward's cheeks. 'You're a good man, Edward Gray.'

He opened his mouth to reply, but Amelia pressed a finger to his lips. She knew what sort of man he was and no amount of protestation on his behalf would change her mind.

Chapter Sixteen

'Stay right there,' Edward instructed, frowning as Amelia started to sit up. 'Don't move.'

'What…?' The question trailed off as Edward dashed from the room and disappeared down the hallway. He was back within a few minutes, sketchbook and set of pencils in hand.

'I want to draw you.'

'Like this? I look a state.'

'You look fine. Natural. Sit still.'

She was reclining on a *chaise longue* she had found in some distant part of the house and moved to the sitting room. It was a rainy Sunday afternoon and they'd been stuck in the house all day. Edward could see Amelia was getting restless; she kept running her hands through her hair and fiddling with her dress, all which gave her a natural and dishevelled look. A look Edward just had to catch on paper.

'Where should I look?' she asked, fidgeting.

'Just carry on reading your book and try to forget I'm even here.'

She was so easy to draw and as Edward let his pencil glide over the paper he felt all his tension and worries melt away. In this moment all that mattered was capturing Amelia's vitality, her sparkle, her aura of energy.

'Have you finished yet?'

'Be patient.' Edward smiled to himself. Patience wasn't one of Amelia's virtues. He was counting the minutes until she sprung up off the chair and declared she couldn't sit still for a moment longer.

A curl of hair slipped from its pin on top of her head and cascaded down over her shoulder. Edward closed his eyes for a moment before forcing himself to focus. He had felt unbalanced and restless ever since their trip to visit his tenants, and he'd hoped drawing would have its usual soothing effect on him.

'You've stopped drawing,' Amelia said accusingly.

'Just considering my next angle.'

In truth it had felt good to do something normal, something he had done for years before his self-imposed seclusion. Visiting his tenants, taking an interest in their lives… that was something he had been brought up to do and he found that he had missed it. He missed running the estate and getting out to talk to people, and for that one afternoon he caught a glimpse of how life could be.

In the moment he had thoroughly enjoyed himself, but ever since he'd been plagued by a nagging guilt. Before the fire he would have asked his wife to accompany him on tenant visits, or he would have taken Thomas out to explore the estate. Now he was taking enjoyment in the things they had done together when they would never get to do them again. Edward knew his entire life couldn't be governed by his guilt at surviving when his family had not, at allowing himself to smile and laugh when they weren't by his side, but he seemed unable to push through his regrets completely and leave them behind.

'Can I see?' Amelia asked, straining to catch a glimpse of her impromptu portrait.

'It's not finished. Sit still.'

Amelia flopped back into position, the neckline of her dress slipping a little with the movement and revealing a triangle of velvety skin underneath. Edward found himself not able to look away as she leisurely rearranged her dress, a hot wave of desire flooding through his body.

Forcing himself to return his attention to his sketch, Edward repeated the mantra that had become part of his daily ritual these past few days. *I do not desire Amelia,* he told himself, not risking another glance in her direction in case she could read his pained expression. *I will not desire Amelia.*

Every bone in his body wanted to cross over to the *chaise longue* and grip the hem of her dress that was currently carefully arranged to cover her legs. He wanted to gently lift her hem until the tops of her stockings were revealed, resting on those slender thighs. Now that would make a wonderful work of art.

I do not desire Amelia. I will not desire Amelia.

'I can't sit still for a moment longer,' Amelia declared, jumping up from her seat and gliding over to where Edward was still sketching. He liked her like this, animated and in motion. He wished there was some way to capture the essence of her movements on paper, but he had to make do with still portraits, not very realistic when you considered how much of the time Amelia spent moving about. Clearing his throat, Edward quickly made an effort to banish his inappropriate thoughts from his mind before she came into his personal space.

She leaned over the back of the chair and angled his sketch pad up towards her. Edward found himself holding his breath. He wanted her to like it. He hadn't shared his drawings with many people in his life and suddenly he felt nervous.

'Is that how you see me?' Amelia asked, her voice a little strained.

Edward glanced at the drawing. He couldn't quite tell if Amelia was upset or not, but something wasn't quite right.

Cautiously he nodded.

'You've made me beautiful.'

He mumbled something incomprehensible.

'Will you teach me?'

Edward blinked in surprise. He'd never expected her to ask that of him. Amelia was a restless, active person. Drawing took patience and serenity.

'What would you like to draw?'

'You.'

'Maybe we can start with something a little easier. That vase of flowers?'

Amelia shook her head. 'I've got no interest in those flowers. I want to draw you.'

Edward shrugged, laid out a pencil and paper for her and resumed his seat.

'No, no, no,' Amelia said, tapping the pencil on her lip. 'Something's not right.'

Edward raised an eyebrow, but shifted slightly.

'Maybe if you stand.'

He stood.

'Look out into the distance. Like a conquering hero.'

Edward looked, but kept his expression of mild irritation.

Amelia sketched, every so often pausing to pop the end of the pencil into her mouth and regard him for some minutes.

'This isn't going well,' she admitted eventually.

'Come here,' Edward instructed, pulling her to the floor to sit beside him.

He grimaced as he looked at her rudimentary pencil strokes and harsh lines. The perspective was all wrong, his body was out of proportion to his head and there were scribbles and dark lines where Amelia had obviously got frustrated.

'Let's go back to basics,' he said, picking up a clean sheet of paper and handing Amelia a fresh pencil. 'First of all, relax your grip. The pencil is an extension of your hand, allow the drawing to flow from you.'

Amelia giggled as she flopped her hand around a little, brandishing the pencil more like a weapon than an artistic instrument.

'Here.' Edward took her hand in his and adjusted her grip, his skin feeling rough against her satiny-smooth fingers. 'Press gently, allow yourself to relax and try long, smooth strokes.'

Carefully he guided her hand across the paper, showing her the ideal amount of pressure and control. She was sitting close to him, her body almost tucked into his chest, and Edward was acutely aware of her proximity. As Amelia tilted her head he felt his pulse quicken. A curl of her hair fell backwards and tickled Edward's neck and they were so close he could hear the soft intake of breath as she concentrated on her drawing.

After a long few minutes of torture Edward couldn't bear the anticipation any longer and reached out to trail a finger down the soft skin of the nape of her neck. Only at the last minute did he catch himself and stop, finger poised in mid-air.

He couldn't do that to her, she didn't deserve to be toyed with, subjected to a tormented man's uncontrolled desires and moods. It wouldn't be fair on her and it would only cause him further heartache.

Amelia turned and caught the haunted expression on his face.

'Do you think…?' Amelia began, but let the question trail off.

'What?'

She shook her head.

'Ask it.'

'Do you think you will ever be free?'

'Free?'

'From the guilt and the regret? Free to start building a normal life again?'

Edward saw the pity in her eyes and felt the squeeze in his chest as his heart constricted. Three years he had been in mourning, three years of pain and punishment and self-inflicted exile from the world. It would never be enough to make up for the guilt he felt at surviving when those he loved, those he should have protected, had perished.

'You wouldn't understand,' he said harshly.

He couldn't stand the sympathy and compassion in her eyes and suddenly he had the urge to push her away, to strike out with his words and wound her. Anything would be better than continuing to receive her pity. He didn't deserve it.

'Help me understand.'

'You'll never understand. How could you?' He hated the harsh tone of his voice and the hurt expression on Amelia's face as though he'd physically slapped her, but somewhere deep down Edward knew that was all he deserved.

'Maybe I couldn't,' Amelia said softly.

Sadly she reached up and placed a hand on Edward's cheek, tears springing to her eyes. She looked at him long and hard, as if committing his face to her memory, and then stood and left the room, leaving Edward wondering if he had lost the one thing which could bring him back to life.

Chapter Seventeen

'I do not know what you said or what you did, but for the love of everything that you hold dear, please make amends,' Goody was saying.

Amelia paused outside the door, intrigued by what was going on in the room. She heard Edward grunt and through the crack between the door and frame saw Goody level him with a look of despair.

'What makes you think *I've* done something?' Edward asked eventually.

'Sir Edward, I've known you since you were trawling the ponds for tadpoles. I know when you've done something wrong.'

Amelia knew she should leave, or at the very least make her presence known, but something held her in place. In the two weeks since she had pressed Edward about moving on with his life as they sat in the sitting room with him teaching her to draw, Amelia had barely laid eyes on him. Oh, they still dined together and occasionally passed each other on the stairs, and Edward still rescued her from her nightmares almost every night, but she hadn't properly talked to him. Not since she'd asked that question and ruined everything.

It was her impulsive nature that was to blame, of course. Most women would have just kept quiet and enjoyed his company, especially as Amelia suspected she was falling rather deeply in love with Edward, but of course she had to spoil everything. She'd pushed too hard, asked too much of him. Who was she to say when he should stop mourning his family? When he should move on and resume a more normal life? If only she'd kept quiet.

'You should do something nice to make up for it,' Goody suggested.

'Like what?'

'You're a grown man. I'm sure you don't need me to tell you what a young lady might enjoy by way of a treat. Maybe a little excursion, or a shopping trip. Miss Amelia strikes me as a young woman who follows fashion.'

Edward didn't answer and Amelia could see he was tracing patterns in some spilt flour on the kitchen table.

'Or maybe take her somewhere on those horses you two love so much. It doesn't really matter what you do, as long as you do something. Let her know you're sorry. Let her see you enjoy spending time with her.'

Amelia found she was holding her breath whilst waiting for Edward's response. Would he deny he wanted to spend time with her?

Goody's tone changed and her voice became much softer. 'I know it's hard, Sir Edward. I know these past three years have been the hardest challenge any person has to endure, but you have survived. I'm so proud of you.'

Goody's voice cracked and Amelia saw the older woman brushing tears from her cheeks.

'You've survived. Now it's time to start living.'

Amelia felt a lump form in her throat and quietly she turned and walked away. She shouldn't intrude on their private moment and if she entered the kitchen now she was likely to cry as soon as she saw Edward.

Flopping down into a chair, Amelia stared out the window morosely. It had been raining for the past four days, but today was dry at least. Every so often Amelia could even see a patch of blue in the sky. As she looked up she realised Goody was right; she would like a trip out. It wouldn't have to be anywhere special, but just to get out of the house, to see a bit more of the world than Beechwood Estate, would be wonderful. It might also stop her from worrying about the lack of news from Mr Guthry's man in London about her cousin. Lizzie should have received her letters by now and sent a reply, but there had been no word. Every day Amelia felt her levels of concern growing.

'Amelia,' Edward said as he entered the room, 'I have something to ask you.'

Amelia sat up quickly, rearranging her skirts and correcting her posture. She looked hopefully up at Edward.

'Do you fancy a trip to the seaside?'

The question threw her so completely Amelia sat with her mouth opening and closing like a fish out of water.

'The seaside?'

'Well, not Brighton, of course, and probably not anywhere too populated. I was thinking a quiet little cove not too far away.'

He was nervous, Amelia realised. Normally so blunt and to the point, Edward was nervous about asking her to accompany him on a trip out.

She hesitated, thinking of all the reasons she should refuse, make up an excuse and let Edward go back to avoiding her.

'I'd love to,' she said after a few seconds' pause.

Edward smiled then, a genuine smile of happiness and

relief, and Amelia saw the man he had once been, the carefree young man before his life had been destroyed by the fire.

'Mrs Henshaw is packing us a picnic. Shall we meet in the barn in an hour's time?' Edward suggested.

Amelia nodded and watched as Edward strode out, no doubt to gather his pencils and paper. She doubted he would go for such an excursion without them.

Two hours later and they were riding across the Downs in a bracing but warm breeze.

'Race you to the top of the hill,' Amelia shouted as she spurred her horse forward into a gallop. Behind her she heard Edward laugh and take up her challenge, hot on her heels as they mounted the top of the hill. 'Look at that view.'

They slowed for a minutes, regarding the rolling green hills before them with the sparkle of the sea in the distance.

'I love this part of the country,' Edward said. 'I couldn't imagine living anywhere else.'

'There's something captivating about it, isn't there?'

For a while they let the horses set the pace, plodding along whilst they enjoyed the scenery. It felt to Amelia that the further they got from Beechwood Manor the more Edward seemed to relax. It was as though out here he could become his own man again, not tied down by the painful memories of his past.

'Tell me about India,' he said as they started a gentle descent towards the chalky cliffs.

Amelia briefly closed her eyes and summoned a picture of home. When she felt scared or alone often she would picture she was sitting on the veranda of their house just outside Bombay, drinking a cool drink and fanning herself in the heat. From the veranda you could see the rolling green hills, thick with foliage, and the wonderfully blue sky above.

'I didn't realise England would be so completely different to India,' Amelia said eventually. 'Out there everything is bright and warm. There's no wind like this and when the rains come there's something almost magical about them. It's as though you're waiting for something to burst, a release, and suddenly the monsoon is there.'

Edward listened quietly and Amelia smiled as she remembered.

'I was so shocked when we disembarked our ship in London, I'd never seen anything like it before. The noise and the dirt and the sheer number of people.'

'But there are cities in India.'

'Father wasn't keen on me visiting the cities, or even the larger towns. He thought it was dangerous, even though I've never once felt threatened by anyone in India the way I have here. My world was made up of the sleepy little villages close to our home, the army base down the road and the small British community that lived nearby.'

'It sounds rather idyllic.'

'I didn't think so at the time. In fact, I couldn't wait to leave.'

'And now? Do you regret coming to England?'

Amelia considered the question. There was so much to regret: foolishly chasing after Captain McNair, losing control in his house, her need to live in fear now.

'No.' Quite simply if she hadn't come to England she wouldn't have met Edward and she wouldn't be here right now. 'I needed this,' she said. 'In India I was spoiled and bored. I caused havoc and I fear I was on a path to self-destruction.'

Amelia could see the problems with her behaviour now and she knew something had needed to change.

'I miss my home, and I miss my father, but I do not regret coming here.'

She glanced over at Edward, saw the small smile on his face and realised how much her answer meant to him. He didn't want her to be unhappy, even if it wasn't in his power to do much about it.

They had reached the cliff edge and Amelia gazed out to sea. Far from the brilliant blue waters she had seen during her voyage to England the sea here was moody and dark, a reflection of the clouds gathering above, but it was just as beautiful, just as striking, as the clear, calm waters of the Indian Ocean.

'It's rather dramatic,' Amelia commented, taking in the climbing white cliffs backed by rolling green hills and the crashing sea down below.

'Shall we go down?' Edward asked.

He helped Amelia to dismount, tied up the horses and led her down a narrow rocky path.

'You've been here before.'

'As a boy this was where my father would always bring me when we spent the day together. I know these paths as well as I know the hallways in Beechwood Manor.'

Amelia stumbled suddenly and Edward was immediately at her side. He took her hand to steady her, checking she was unhurt before leading her further down the path.

They reached the beach, a deep cove cut into the chalky rock face covered in large grey-and-brown pebbles. In front of them, close to the sea, was a narrow strip of sand leading round the cliffs in both directions.

'Where's the rest of the sand?' Amelia asked, frowning.

Edward laughed. 'This is a pretty generous amount of sand for beaches around here. Most just have pebbles and shingle. I'm sure it isn't anything as beautiful as the beaches in India.'

Amelia shook her head, 'It's more atmospheric.'

And she meant it. As she looked out to sea she could feel the salt on her face and the spray in the air. Here the coast was dramatic and almost alive. The sea looked powerful and even a little menacing, and Amelia knew nothing could entice her in for a swim.

'Shall we bathe?' Edward asked.

She realised he was joking just before he grinned, took her by the arm and pulled her closer to where the water was crashing into the sand.

'Can we head around the cliffs?'

Edward paused as if calculating something. 'You have to be careful not to be caught by the tide, but it's still on its way out so we should have an hour or two before it starts coming back in.'

With her hand tucked into the crook of Edward's elbow Amelia allowed him to lead her down the beach and round the base of the cliff. Here the strip of sand stretched along ahead of them for half a mile before disappearing as the cliff jutted out.

They walked until they reached a small cove bathed in the sunlight that was peeking through the clouds. Edward laid out the blanket he'd brought with them and set the basket Goody had prepared for them down in the middle.

Amelia watched as he sat down, pulled off his boots and socks and then sank his toes into the grainy sand. She giggled.

'Try it,' Edward said. 'It feels like freedom.'

Obligingly Amelia sat beside him and kicked off her boots, then paused.

'I won't peek.'

She looked at him with his eyes closed, face turned up to the sun, and wished he would.

Slowly Amelia peeled off her stockings, wriggled her toes and pressed them into the sand. He was right, it did feel like freedom.

As Edward lay with the sun warming his face he realised he felt content. For once everything felt good in the world. Mrs Henshaw had, of course, been right, he had needed to put things right with Amelia. These past two weeks had been uncomfortable and lonely, and he'd hated seeing her hopeful face fall every time he barely acknowledged her as they passed each other. The only time he had felt at least a little useful during the past fortnight was when he'd dashed in every night to hold Amelia as she sobbed in her sleep. She was still experiencing the nightmares about McNair. Edward had been hopeful they might dissipate once she knew the scoundrel was alive, but every night she was terrified by reliving the events in the Captain's house. Edward found himself anticipating the moment he got to wrap his arms around her sleepy body and comfort her whilst she calmed into a deep slumber. He didn't want to examine exactly what this meant, but for now it was enough to know his presence calmed her.

'Can we paddle?' Amelia asked.

Edward opened his eyes and looked up at her from his position reclined on the rug. As usual she was restless, eager to be moving about.

'It'll be cold.'

'Are you too much of a coward?'

'You injure me, Amelia.' Edward said, with mock indignation. He stood, pulled Amelia to her feet and without relinquishing her hand pulled her towards the sea. 'Mind you don't get your skirts wet, otherwise I've no doubt you'll moan the entire way home.'

Quickly he dodged as Amelia swatted him. As they neared the sea Amelia slowed.

'Are you regretting your challenge?'

'Of course not. How cold can it be?'

He wondered if she were imagining the beautiful warm waters of the Indian Ocean back home.

'Promise not to scream.'

She looked at him with defiance in her eyes, hitched up her skirts to reveal slender honey-coloured calves and dashed at the sea.

Edward laughed out loud as she uttered a string of expletives no young lady should even be aware of. She was out of the water in seconds, looking at him reproachfully. It felt good to laugh again. Out here, away from the memories of Beechwood Manor, Edward felt some of his lightheartedness returning after years of being locked away. Maybe once in a while it wasn't so bad to enjoy himself, to smile or feel pleasure in someone's company.

'I did warn you.'

'Not nearly well enough. That was really cold. My toes still hurt.'

'So you don't fancy a swim?'

'I'm not crazy, so, no.'

'I used to swim here all the time with my father, whatever the weather,' Edward said.

'Please don't let me stop you,' Amelia said, smiling sweetly.

'I think I'll just dip my toes,' Edward said, walking into the shallow water.

It was cold, so cold he felt his toes begin to go numb after about thirty seconds, but it was bracing and refreshing at the same time. The coldness gave him an unusual clarity, and, as he stood looking out into the grey foaming sea, he found himself wondering whether he'd judged things wrong over the past few years.

Turning back towards the cliffs, Edward returned to where the water just lapped on the sand and placed Amelia's hand in the crook of his elbow. For a while they just walked along together side by side, Edward allowing the small waves to surge over his feet whilst ensuring Amelia was always out of their reach.

As they got to the end of the cove they continued along the sand at the base of one of the high chalky cliffs. Edward realised he was wishing they could just carry on walking arm in arm for eternity, that way he wouldn't have this uncertainty about his decisions to face up to.

'Do you think Mr Guthry's man will return soon?' Amelia asked.

As Edward turned to look at her he realised how preoccupied with worry she was. He'd been so absorbed in his own concerns he hadn't even realised Amelia was thinking about her cousin so much.

'I'm sure he will. I do not know what has delayed him or any message from your cousin, but if there was bad news we would surely have heard by now.'

Amelia nodded and looked at least a little reassured by his words.

'I sent the letter to my father last week,' Amelia said as they strolled along. 'But I think it will be a while until he receives it and replies.'

Edward was just about to answer, to assure her nothing had changed and that she was welcome at Beechwood Manor for as long as she needed when there was a rumble from up above them. He looked up, frowning, but there was nothing to be seen.

'We should move away from the cliff,' he said, keeping his eyes fixed on the heavy rock above them. Rock-falls were common on this part of the coastline and he didn't want either of them to have their skulls caved in by a chunk of falling chalk.

'If you've changed your mind, I can find somewhere else to stay whilst I await his reply,' Amelia said.

Edward heard the anguish and uncertainty in her voice and momentarily took his eyes off the cliff above them to study her face.

'There's…' he began, but paused as there was another loud bang from over their heads. Edward looked up and his eyes widened as he saw the chunk of chalky cliff plummeting down towards them. Instinctively he pushed Amelia back against the cliff face, knowing she was unlikely to get hit there, then pushed his body against hers meaning to protect her from the worst of the falling rock.

He heard Amelia scream and then a bolt of pain shot through his head before the darkness descended.

Chapter Eighteen

Amelia screamed. She couldn't help herself. Then the scream was cut off as she watched Edward totter and collapse to the ground. There was a nasty gash in his forehead, and a steady stream of blood oozed from the wound and stained the sand.

'Edward,' Amelia whispered as she crouched down beside him.

He was dead, she was sure of it. His face was deathly pale and he wasn't moving at all. Amelia felt the despair and sorrow begin to overwhelm her and the sobs started to rack her body. She buried her head in Edward's chest and tried to will him back to life.

She couldn't lose him, even if he wasn't really hers to lose. Suddenly Amelia realised quite what Edward had come to mean to her over the past few weeks and felt an overwhelming sickness at the thought of never hearing his voice or seeing his smile again.

Just as she was about to become hysterical something made her sit up and pause for a moment. She'd already had a similar experience, convinced a man was dead when he was just badly injured. With a silent plea Amelia placed her ear to Edward's chest and listened. She almost cried with relief when she heard the steady beating of his heart and felt his chest gently rising and falling with each breath.

Open your eyes and I promise never to annoy you again, Amelia pleaded silently. *Just open your eyes, Edward, please.*

For some time she just sat beside him, stroking his hair and willing him to open his eyes and wake up. She wasn't sure how long he might be unconscious for, but she thought she'd heard somewhere people could remain unresponsive for days.

After what must have been almost an hour Amelia shifted slightly, stretching her legs out, but not relinquishing Edward's hand. With a shout of surprise Amelia turned to see the sea lapping at her feet. The bottom of her dress was soaking up the seawater and the icy water covering her toes. For a moment the implications of this didn't sink in, but slowly Amelia realised the tide had turned. The sea was on its way in.

'Edward!' Amelia shouted, shaking him by the shoulders. 'Wake up.'

No response.

'Edward, please wake up. The sea's coming in.'

He lay peacefully on the sand, his unconscious body not bothered by the approaching water.

Amelia stood, grabbed him under his arms and started to drag him across the wet sand back towards where they had left the picnic things. As she inched along she felt the first drops of rain splatter her and murmured a few uncomplimentary phrases about the English weather.

By the time they'd moved three steps Amelia's muscles were already screaming and her breath coming in laboured gasps.

Wake up, Edward, she begged, glancing back over her

shoulder to see just how far she had to drag him. It seemed an impossible distance and for a moment Amelia felt despair crashing down on her. If only she'd told him how she felt when he was still alive and well.

Gritting her teeth, Amelia tightened her grip and continued along the beach. She would not give up, not whilst there was still a chance of saving him.

After a further fifteen minutes Amelia had managed to pull Edward's body halfway back to the cove, but during that time the sea had advanced and now her every step was hampered by about three inches of water. Edward was soaked and Amelia could feel the wet material of her skirts dragging against her legs.

Despite all this, and despite her aching muscles, Amelia never gave up. She was under no illusion that if she didn't push on Edward would die. The tide would come in and the water would cover his supine form and Edward would drown just a couple of feet from the cliffs. On and on she pulled him, covering the ground inch by inch, minute by minute. Every time she paused to catch her breath Amelia was aware of time ticking away and the ever-rising water. Soon the water was above her ankles and then halfway up to her knees, slowing their progress even further.

With her breath coming in short gasps Amelia paused for just a moment and then with a loud roar born out of effort and fear Amelia dragged Edward's body up into the cove and out of reach of the sea, at least for now. Immediately she collapsed down on to the sand, one arm flopping across Edward's chest to check he was still breathing.

Amelia lay there whilst her heart stopped pounding and her muscles recovered. She didn't want to sit up, to have to examine Edward's pale face again and wonder if he would ever open those bewitching, kind eyes again.

All the time she had been dragging him along the beach she hadn't had any energy left to think, but now she could feel all the worry and the panic mounting up inside her.

He couldn't be dead, not Edward. Not the man who'd saved her and comforted her and allowed her to completely disrupt his entire life. Not before she told him how she truly felt about him.

Over the past few weeks as she had slowly got to know the man behind the grief and the gruff mask Amelia had often wondered if he would have preferred to have been taken in the fire with his family. She was sure on many occasions he probably thought he would, but recently she had glimpsed another side to him. Every so often she saw a glimmer of hope, a flicker of excitement about the future, something that told her that he would fight to stay on this earth.

'Fight for me,' she whispered.

Carefully Amelia leaned over and brushed his hair from his eyes, smiling as a wavy lock flopped back almost immediately. She lowered her head further before hesitating, knowing she should not kiss him, but already sure she would not be able to resist. Softly she pressed her lips against his, feeling the tears form in her eyes as she realised this might be the closest she ever got to a real kiss with the man she cared about so much. At first his mouth was cool and unresponsive, but as she began to pull away she felt just a flicker of movement.

'Edward?' Amelia whispered, sitting back and scrutinising his face.

Nothing. Amelia hesitated, knowing deep down that a kiss didn't make any difference to an unconscious man… that was just the stuff of fairytales.

What have you got to lose? she asked herself.

She kissed him again, squeezing her eyes shut, hoping and wishing for another flicker of a response.

This time there was no doubt. As she kissed him his lips began to move, drawing her in and taking some of her warmth.

Edward let out a prolonged groan and as Amelia sat back guiltily as his eyes flickered open. For a moment she could tell everything was unfocused and blurry, but after a few seconds his eyes locked on to hers and he frowned.

'What…?' he managed to murmur.

Amelia launched herself at him, reining herself in at the last moment so she embraced him gently. She felt Edward's hand on her back and had to choke back a cry of relief. He was alive, awake and he could move.

'What happened?'

'Part of the cliff collapsed. You were hit.'

Edward raised his hand to the cut on his forehead and grimaced.

'How long was I unconscious?' he asked, sitting up.

'About two hours. How are you feeling?'

'My head's pounding—' Edward broke off and looked around them. 'How did we get back here?'

'I dragged you.'

'You *dragged* me?'

'The sea was coming in, I didn't have a choice.'

'You managed to pull me all the way back here?'

Amelia nodded.

'Thank you,' Edward said, looking at her with renewed respect. 'You're stronger than I could have imagined.'

Amelia knew part of her success in pulling Edward to safety had been due to the knowledge that if she failed she would have to watch him die.

Slowly Edward sat up. He was still pale, but his eyes were focused and his expression determined.

'Did we...?' Edward started to say, looking at her thoughtfully, but then allowed the question to trail off with a shake of his head.

Amelia didn't press him, knowing he was probably remembering the kiss she had planted on his lips as he began to stir. He had never asked her to kiss him, never even indicated he ever would be interested in anyone romantically again.

'I see it started raining,' he observed drily after a minute.

Amelia laughed.

'I'm so glad you're awake,' she said, clutching on to his hand and hoping she'd never have to let go.

Edward was staring out to sea with a frown on his face. Suddenly he stood, stumbled a few steps before regaining his equilibrium and then ran forward.

'Edward,' Amelia shouted after him, wondering if the knock to the head had affected his brain.

He ran to the sea, wading into the shallow water for a few steps before stopping and turning to look to either side. The wind had picked up whilst Amelia was dragging him along the beach and now the waves were beginning to crash against the beach and the rain was pelting the sand. The clouds above had morphed into a menacing black blanket and Amelia knew another storm was on its way.

'What's wrong?' Amelia shouted from a few feet away, refusing to wade back out into the water without good reason.

'The tide's come in,' Edward said as he returned to her side.

'I know. That's why I had to pull you into the cove.'

'Look.'

Edward gestured back the way they had come, back towards where they'd left the horses and followed the narrow path down the cliff. As realisation dawned on Amelia she felt a wave of nausea and panic overcome her and she had to reach out and grip hold of Edward to steady herself.

'There's no way back,' she whispered.

Sure enough, the sea had already covered the narrow strip of sand they'd walked along to get to the cove.

Frantically Amelia ran up the beach towards the cliffs, looking for a path, a route up to the top. There was nothing. Down at beach level the cliff was smooth, all possible handholds and footholds eroded and flattened by the sea.

'Maybe it won't come in this far,' Amelia said as Edward joined her.

He didn't answer her and she followed his gaze to the very prominent water line about three feet above their heads.

'Amelia, I need you to keep calm,' Edward said, taking charge as usual.

'Keep calm? We're going to die. The sea's coming in and there's no way off the beach. Edward, we're going to die.' She could hear her voice rise in pitch with every word, but couldn't do anything to control it.

'No. We're not going to die. I will not let us.'

She wondered how he could remain so composed and assured in the face of certain death.

'Stop panicking and listen to me,' Edward said in his stern voice. 'We will survive this. I promise you.' Amelia felt him grip her by the arm and pull her to face him. When she was looking straight into his eyes he repeated himself. 'We will survive this, I promise.'

Slowly some of the panic seeped from her body and she nodded, wondering just how he meant to save them.

'I need you to take your dress off.'

Not quite what she'd had in mind.

'Why?'

Edward pointed to a spot in the cliff about eleven feet up from the ground. There, and leading up from it, were a series of grooves and ledges in the rock face that led up to the top of the chalky cliffs.

'I will boost you up and you will climb to the top of the cliffs. You can't do that with your bulky dress on.'

'What about you. Maybe I could pull you up.'

Edward shook his head. 'It's too far.'

'I'm not leaving you here,' Amelia protested.

He grabbed hold of her shoulders and held her tightly. 'When you get to the top run for the horses and then ride as fast as you can back to Beechwood Manor. Send a rescue party to fetch me, armed with ropes and horses, and I'll be back home with you in no time.'

'Is there time?' Amelia asked.

Edward glanced at the approaching sea and nodded. 'There's time.'

Quickly Amelia unfastened her dress and slipped out of it. Standing in just her long cotton chemise, she resisted the temptation to cover herself with her arms.

'I'll ride faster than I've ever ridden before,' she promised.

Amelia turned and faced the cliff, grimacing at the height and the thought of the long climb ahead of her. She felt Edward directly behind her and shivered as he placed a hand on her waist, turning her to face him.

A thousand unsaid words flowed between them and Amelia saw the concern and fear on Edward's face. She wanted to kiss him, to be enveloped in his arms and to draw her strength from him to sustain her on the long climb and journey home.

Gently Edward pushed the stray strands of hair that were whipping about her face in the wind behind her ears, not removing his hands from her face even once they were under control.

'Be careful, Amelia,' he said, gripping her tightly and for a moment Amelia knew he didn't want to let her go.

She watched as his eyes flickered over her face as if he were committing every detail to memory.

'Take your time on the climb, test each foothold before you transfer your weight,' he instructed, still not moving his hands from her face.

Amelia nodded, her heart pounding in her chest. Maybe he would kiss her, maybe he would hold her close and whisper that she was his hope, his reason for living.

Edward let his hands drop to his sides and nodded for her to begin the climb. Amelia's disappointment was almost overwhelming and she felt tears begin to form in her eyes as she turned and ran her hands over the cliff face. Of course he wouldn't kiss her and whisper what she wanted to hear in her ear—the idea was pure fantasy.

Just as she steadied herself for Edward to boost her up Amelia felt his strong hand on her waist, turning her back towards him. As they stood body to body Amelia saw the fire burning in his eyes and before she could dare to hope he pulled her close against him and covered her lips with his own.

He kissed her deeply and passionately, gripping her tightly as if he never wanted to let go. After her initial shock Amelia felt her heart soar and her body react to him as if she had been waiting her entire life for this moment.

Amelia was aware of his firm body against hers and wondered how she could have ever found any other man attractive. No one compared to Edward's wild appeal and sensuous charm.

Just as Amelia's lungs started burning and her brain started asking for air Edward broke away, his lips lingering gently on hers for a few seconds before he broke the contact completely.

'What...?' Amelia began to ask, all her hopes and dreams surging to the surface, chased closely by a very real fear of rejection.

Edward shook his head, 'There's no time,' he said quietly.

Amelia glanced over his shoulder and saw the sea creeping ever closer and decided not to argue. All her questions would be pointless if she didn't get help in time for Edward to be rescued.

'Goodbye, Amelia.'

His words sounded too final, too devoid of hope.

'I will be back,' Amelia said as she allowed him to boost her up the cliff face to grab hold of the first handhold.

At first it seemed too far for her to reach, but in the end, when she was standing on his shoulders, she could just about wrap her fingers round a jutting-out segment of the chalk. Slowly, with her muscles protesting, she pulled herself upwards until her other hand could reach above her.

Amelia's progress was painfully slow. She was already exhausted by the exertion involved in dragging Edward along the beach and the gusting wind and pelting rain weren't helping much either, but the memory of Edward's lips on her own, consuming her with a passion she'd never imagined possible, spurred her on. Inch by inch she hauled herself up the cliff face, trying to ignore the pain in her fingers as the skin was torn to shreds by the merciless rock face. Twice she slipped, her feet losing their precarious purchase on the ledges below her, and her body slammed against the chalk. Each time she had to wait for her heart to stop pounding and her vision to clear before she could continue the slow climb up.

Just as she wondered if she would ever make the top she

felt the grass under her fingers and let out a cry of relief. With shaking arms and burning lungs she was able to pull herself up on to the cliff top. She paused to glance back down to Edward's form below. He already looked despondent and for an awful few seconds Amelia wondered if he had given up, if this was the moment he'd decided to join his beloved late wife and son. Even the thought ripped at her heart. Surely his kiss had been more than a farewell, surely it had meant something more than that.

As she looked down Edward raised his head and waved. This small gesture pushed Amelia into action. It wouldn't matter if he had decided to live or die if she didn't return as quickly as possible with help. Later she could dissect exactly what their kiss had meant and exactly what Edward felt for her, but right now she had to run as fast as she'd ever run and ride faster than she ever had before. With a final glance at the man on the beach below Amelia turned and began her dash across the clifftop, praying she would make it back in time.

Edward had expected to feel at peace. As soon as he'd seen they were cut off from the route back along the beach he'd realised there was a possibility he wouldn't get out of this alive, but his panic had been largely for Amelia. He couldn't fail her now, not after all he'd done to protect her and keep her safe. Then he'd seen the route up the cliff, if only he could boost her high enough.

Although he'd told her she would have time to summon help, he doubted it was true. The sea was advancing quickly now and he'd only really said it to convince her to leave and get herself to safety.

He'd expected to feel a sense of relief. Many times over the past three years he'd contemplated taking his own life and joining his family, but something had tethered him to earth and a worldly existence. Now the decision was out of his hands he had thought he would welcome an escape from his grief, but he found his mind anything but peaceful.

Closing his eyes, Edward relived the kiss he'd just shared with Amelia. It had been spontaneous, totally unplanned and completely irresistible. As she'd stood in front of him just about to start up the cliff face Edward had known he couldn't let her leave without kissing her. The thought had taken over his entire body until there was no option but to spin her round and cover her lips with his own.

Now he had kissed her Edward could see the moment had been building for a long time, probably ever since they'd sat in the sitting room with him teaching her to draw. Deep down he'd been aware of his attraction for her, even been aware of the guilt that attraction had stirred up inside him. What was new was a curiosity of what might happen next. Visions of passionate kisses and tender embraces filled his mind and Edward was surprised not to be overcome with guilt. For the first time in three years he was considering his future and it did not look completely bleak.

He wanted to live, he realised. He wanted to escape from this cursed beach and return to his much-neglected home and fling open all the windows and doors, to let the light and the air into the darkest corners and whip off the dust sheets. Cautiously he wondered if maybe he wanted to start interacting with the world again, to embrace everything this life had to offer him and pull himself from the dark hole that had trapped him for the past few years.

Edward yelled in frustration. Why now? Why was it at the moment when he actually had something to live for and the urge to move forward with his life it was going to be cruelly taken away from him?

He ran at the cliff, launching himself up the smooth chalk, scrabbling for a handhold. Time and time again he slid back down, just to take another run at the towering white wall.

Eventually Edward sank to the floor with his back against the cliff and watched the approaching sea. It wouldn't be long now until it reached him, and then only a matter of time before the tide swept him out and pulled him under or dashed him against the cliffs.

Edward closed his eyes and thought about his life and about the past few weeks. What he regretted most was pushing Amelia away. He knew deep down he felt more for her than the friendship he pretended they shared. Every time he saw her his whole world lit up, every time she touched him his skin tingled and his heart pounded. Every time she smiled at him his heart squeezed. If only he'd seized his opportunity, if only he'd told her how he felt.

It wasn't fair. Any time in the past three years he would have welcomed the release from his guilt and sorrow, but now he finally could see a glimmer of hope in his life fate was going to give him what he had wished for.

Edward threw back his head and gave a primal roar, venting his frustration and his angst. He wanted to walk through his garden, to sketch and read, to hold Amelia in his arms and work out exactly what the future could hold. It was cruelly ironic that only now was he realising all that his life could be.

As the water rose to waist level Edward felt his hope fizzle and die so he focused on picturing his son and wondered if they would be reunited soon. He wanted to see his son's face, to kiss his hair and fold him in his arms, but still he wished he could have just a little longer on earth, a little longer to make up for all the time he'd wasted.

'Edward.' The voice floated down to him, and he for a moment he wondered if it were an angel from heaven. Then he recognised the tone and his eyes flew open. 'Edward.'

Quickly he stood, struggling to keep his balance as the waves pounded against him. Waving his arms above his head he opened his mouth and shouted as loudly as he could.

Amelia had managed it. She'd actually made it back in time. When he'd sent her up the cliff he'd never imagined she might return quickly enough to save him.

The rope fell just to his left and swung in to hit the cliff face a few times. Edward pushed through the seawater to reach it, grabbed hold with both hands and watched in amazement as slowly he rose from the sea.

Jerkily he was pulled higher and higher, inching away from the crashing waves below. As the distance between him and the sea increased Edward felt his heart soar. He was going to survive, he might be battered and bruised, but he would live. Now all of the things he had wished for more time to do would be within his grasp.

It took five minutes to pull him up on to the cliff. As Edward felt the strong hands grabbing his arms and swinging him on to firm ground his legs almost gave way beneath him. Amelia rushed forward, hesitating for just a minute before wrapping her arms around him and resting her forehead against his.

'You saved me,' Edward said quietly as he held her tightly.

Amelia didn't answer, instead burying her head in Edward's shoulder. He felt the shudder of her body before he heard the sobs and gently began to stroke her hair.

'I thought...' Amelia began, but couldn't finish the sentence.

'Shh,' Edward soothed. 'Don't think about it.'

He himself felt more than a little shaken by the experience and couldn't wait to get back to Beechwood Manor to get out of his wet clothes and warm up by a roaring fire. A good night's sleep would be very welcome and then maybe in the morning he might be able to start trying to work out exactly what he felt for the woman in his arms.

Chapter Nineteen

Edward paced backwards and forwards in the hallway, trying to stop himself looking at the clock every few seconds. Amelia was late, but that was her prerogative. He had rather sprung this surprise on her.

It had been a week since their disastrous trip to the beach and both Edward and Amelia had spent long periods in bed recovering from the cold and the physical exertion under doctor's orders. For Edward that had meant a lot of time to reflect on his realisations on the beach and a lot of time to plan.

He was very aware he needed to take things slowly. His growing desire to re-join the world of the living, his renewed excitement for the future, could just be a reaction to a near-death experience and he didn't want to rush into anything. What hadn't changed over the past week was his desire to spend more time with Amelia. He wasn't sure what his feelings for Amelia were and he couldn't quite put a name on them. He didn't feel that same comfortable feeling he had with Jane, but Amelia challenged him and riled him and lit a fire inside him.

Every day he still woke with a knot of guilt in his stomach and concerns that he should not be allowed to be happy, but instead of allowing these feelings to grow and fester Edward was taking a step back and distancing himself from them. Jane would never want him to be unhappy, so it was only he who had been holding himself back for the past three years. On the beach he had decided he'd wanted to live, so now he owed it to himself to give life a chance. And to give his feelings for Amelia a chance.

Whilst he'd been sitting in bed recuperating, filling his time with sketching and reading, Edward had decided he would approach Amelia as any man with an interest in a young woman would. He would attempt to court her. Not that he'd told her this yet, of course. Tonight he'd arranged for them to attend a small country dance, nothing too conspicuous, but an occasion where there would be dancing and high spirits and hopefully a few snatched moments alone. Maybe then he would be able to find the words to explain his cautious optimism about the future and gauge Amelia's reaction to his new level of interest in her.

Just as he glanced again at the clock he heard footsteps coming from the hallway above.

'Have I made you wait?' Amelia asked as she began to descend the stairs.

She looked beautiful. Dressed in a pale blue gown Edward had sent Mrs Henshaw to buy just for Amelia, she looked as though she belonged at the royal court, not accompanying him to a country dance. Her eyes sparkled with excitement and perhaps something more and she moved with such grace it looked as though she floated down the stairs.

'Yes.' He cursed his abruptness, but Amelia just smiled.

'Well, it's a good job I know you don't mind.'

'Oh, my goodness, don't you two look like royalty?' Mrs Henshaw said as she bustled out into the hallway and looked them both up and down.

Amelia twirled in her dress, letting Edward catch a glimpse of the bare skin of her upper back before placing her hand lightly on his forearm.

'You take care of her, Sir Edward,' Mrs Henshaw said. 'The young men will be flocking to her side.'

Edward didn't mean to let Amelia out of his sight. The young men of the village would not even get a chance to court Amelia. He had perfected his glare if any strayed too close or tarried too long.

'Goody, you look very lovely this evening,' Amelia said as she finished her twirl. 'Are you accompanying us to the dance?'

Edward looked his housekeeper up and down and realised Amelia was right, Mrs Henshaw was dressed in her finest. He wondered if she had taken it upon herself to chaperon them and his heart sank at the thought.

'Well, I *am* going to the dance,' Mrs Henshaw said, her ruddy cheeks colouring a little. 'But I wouldn't dream of inviting myself along with you two young things. Mr Guthry is calling for me in half an hour.'

'Mr Guthry?' Edward asked, bemused.

Amelia clapped her hands together in joy and Edward wondered if there was something he was missing.

'Well, you have a wonderful time, Goody, and give our regards to Mr Guthry. Perhaps you would be so kind as to ask him to visit tomorrow so we can discuss what his assistant found in London when he was seeking my cousin.'

'Of course, my dear.'

Edward could see the flicker of worry on Amelia's face at the thought of her cousin. They did not know the whole story yet, but Mr Guthry had sent a short note telling them his assistant had not been able to find Lizzie in London. There had been some sort of accident involving the house Lizzie had been staying in and Lizzie, along with

Amelia's aunt and other cousin, had travelled to Cambridgeshire whilst they recuperated. Amelia had been beside herself with worry, and Edward made a mental note to send someone to Cambridgeshire himself to track this errant cousin down.

Amelia placed her hand on his arm and together they walked outside.

'What was that all about?' Edward asked quietly, gesturing back towards Goody.

'I think Goody and Mr Guthry are courting.'

'Really?'

'Really. He's stopped by on a couple of occasions and always finds some excuse to head to the kitchens to seek Goody out.'

Edward supposed it made sense. Both had lost a spouse many years ago and now lived solitary lives, and both were kind and jolly people. When he thought about it they were a perfect match for each other.

'He'd better not steal my housekeeper,' Edward grumbled.

Amelia swatted him on the arm, 'I know you want them to be happy,' she said. 'Anyway, I don't think wild animals could drag Goody away from you and Beechwood Manor. No, if things go well I think you would be more likely to gain a live-in estate manager rather than lose a housekeeper.'

Edward grunted, but he rather liked the idea of Mrs Henshaw finding a bit of happiness of her own.

'Are you nervous?' he asked as he helped her up into the waiting carriage.

'I've never been to a country dance before,' Amelia answered.

'I'm sure it's not like the grand balls you're used to.'

Amelia shook her head. 'I've never been to a grand

ball. Sometimes my father would take my cousin and me to one of the regimental balls, but I've never been to anything special.'

Edward didn't say anything, wondering if she was regretting having to stay in the country with him rather than taking her rightful place in London society.

'I suppose if I hadn't run off to chase Captain McNair I'd be getting ready for some grand ball now,' Amelia said with a small smile.

'Do you wish you were?'

'There's nowhere I'd rather be,' she said, squeezing his arm.

Edward wondered if he should kiss her. Sitting next to her in the carriage with his thighs pushed up against hers and her hair occasionally tickling his neck, he felt almost intoxicated with desire. It would be so easy to lean over and kiss her. He knew she wouldn't object, he'd seen how she looked at him, how she shivered when he touched her. Amelia would welcome the kiss, but he knew he should hold back.

They both deserved more than a hurried kiss in a moving carriage. Edward deserved the time to work out what he was feeling for Amelia and Amelia deserved to be courted and wooed by a man who was sure of what he could offer. It would be the cruellest deed imaginable if he kissed her and led her on only to tell her he could never love her and they didn't have a future together. So with a gargantuan effort Edward sat back and listened to Amelia talk of the regimental balls in India and reminisce about the time before she'd met Captain McNair when she was happy.

As they pulled up to the village hall Edward jumped down from the carriage, turned and assisted Amelia out.

She looked nervous and quickly glanced right and left as if checking the coast was clear.

'He won't be here, Amelia,' Edward said softly. 'McNair will be far away by now.'

She nodded, relaxing a little as he led her into the hall. The dancing had already started. A group of lively musicians were playing a familiar tune on their assorted instruments and the hoard of people gathered in the village hall were twirling and stomping and sashaying in time. The room was hot from all the warm bodies crushed inside despite the large open windows and high barn-like ceiling.

As soon as they entered all eyes were on them and a murmur of surprise spread round the hall. He'd been a recluse for too long for his re-emergence into society to not cause a stir and now everyone would want a little piece of his story.

'Sir Edward,' a portly man called as he hustled over. Edward desperately tried to remember the man's name and summoned up a smile. 'What a pleasure to see you here. We are honoured you have graced our simple country dance with your presence.'

'May I introduce a dear friend, Miss Amelia?' Edward said, watching as Amelia curtsied.

'A pleasure to meet you. I hope you enjoy the dancing tonight, Miss Amelia.'

'I'm certain I shall. The music is so lively and the atmosphere wonderful.'

The portly man beamed at the compliment.

'Sir Edward, let me reintroduce you to some old faces who will be delighted to see you again.'

Edward was about to protest when the portly man beckoned over a rather handsome young man.

'This is my son, Mr Leonard Goone. Leonard, I'm sure

you remember Sir Edward? And this delightful young woman is Miss Amelia.'

Goone the Younger bowed over Amelia's hand. Edward felt his frown beginning to build as the younger man lingered just a few moments too long over her hand and flashed Amelia a charming smile.

'Maybe you could lead Miss Amelia in the next dance, Leonard, whilst I have a word with Sir Edward.'

'It would be my pleasure…if you would do me the honour, Miss Amelia?'

And just like that Amelia was whisked off in the company of an attractive young man whilst Edward could only watch. He wanted to run after them, snatch Amelia away and squirrel her back to Beechwood Manor where he didn't have to share her with anyone.

The next ten minutes dragged by, with reintroductions to all of the most important men of the area. Edward had known these men well before the fire and all were eager to renew their acquaintance, but he only had eyes for Amelia. Whilst the older men droned on about crop prices and finding a decent land agent, Edward nodded and agreed without paying much attention. His eyes were fixed on the dancing and in particular one very beautiful young woman in a light blue dress.

The young men were flocking to her and if he didn't step in soon she wouldn't have a single dance left for him.

'Please excuse me for a moment,' he murmured and stepped away.

Quickly he strode across the room, waited for the current dance to finish and then inserted himself in between Amelia and her partner.

'I say, old chap, I think it's my dance next,' a young man with a rather flamboyant taste in clothing said.

Edward restrained himself from growling at the man

and instead fixed him with a silent glare. The man backed away. Next to him Amelia giggled.

'There was no need for that,' she said as he took her into his arms for the next dance.

'There was every need.'

For the next five minutes it was as though they were the only two in the room. He held her close, probably closer than was socially appropriate, his hands pressing against the silky material of her dress. Amelia was light on her feet, a natural dancer, and she needed only the gentlest of guidance from him. For his part Edward actually enjoyed the dance. Never before could he remember wanting the music to continue for eternity, but tonight he didn't want the magical moment to end.

'Thank you,' Amelia said as the last note was played.

'Shall we step outside for a few minutes? It's rather warm.' Edward swept Amelia out of the path of an eager young man, glaring at the impromptu suitor until he cringed under the force of Edward's disapproval.

'That would be lovely.'

The doors to the hall had been thrown open in an attempt to cool the stifling room and many couples and groups had drifted outside. Edward guided Amelia to a spot under the great oak that stood in the village square a few hundred feet away. Here they were still visible to the rest of the guests in attendance, but they would have a modicum of privacy at least.

It was a clear night and for a few moments they stood looking up at the stars in the sky.

'When I was younger my father would spend hours pointing out constellations,' Amelia said. 'I never paid much attention, but I wish I had now.'

Edward smiled. He could imagine a younger Amelia restless and inattentive to her father's lessons.

'That one up there that looks a little like a plough, that's Ursa Minor. And this one over here that looks like a bear, that's Ursa Major.'

'You paid attention to your lessons.'

Edward smiled. 'My father was a bit of an enthusiast when it came to stargazing. Sometimes on clear nights he would take me up to the roof of Beechwood Manor and we would just lie back and spend hours looking at the stars.'

It made him feel peculiarly content to know that on one of those occasions somewhere half a world away Amelia might have been looking at the very same stars.

'Amelia, I've been wanting to talk to you ever since the incident on the beach,' Edward said, feeling as nervous as a schoolboy on his first day at school. 'That whole episode put a few things in perspective and…' He trailed off. Amelia wasn't listening.

He coughed, his heart sinking as he wondered if she just didn't want to hear what he had to say, then followed her gaze over his shoulder.

Strolling towards them down the village high street was Captain McNair. He had a cruel smile on his lips and twirled a walking cane as he approached.

Amelia was frozen in place and even as Edward grabbed hold of her arm she didn't respond. This wasn't the time or the place for a confrontation with McNair. If he could just get Amelia back to Beechwood Manor he would be able to protect her better.

Bodily he dragged Amelia a few steps before her head snapped round and her eyes met his. He'd never seen such an expression of despair or panic and he wished he could make her feel safe from this scoundrel and whatever else life had to throw at her for ever.

'Let's go,' Edward said quietly.

McNair was only two hundred feet away when Ame-

lia jerked out of her trance and responded. Hand in hand
they dashed down the high street and rounded the corner
to where the short row of coaches were waiting to take the
few people who lived outside the village home. Edward
spotted their coach and Tom the groom who was acting as
coachman for the evening in the middle of the row.

'Tom,' he roared, waking the slumbering man.

Tom sprang upright, rubbed the sleep from his eyes and
guided the coach into the middle of the road just as Edward and Amelia reached it. Edward near enough threw
Amelia inside and vaulted up after her. The coach was already moving by the time he'd settled on one of the seats,
but he was just in time to see McNair jump out of the way
of the moving carriage as they thundered past.

As the Captain disappeared into the distance Edward
saw him point after the carriage with the walking cane and
then slowly draw the handle across his neck. Next to him
he heard Amelia choke back a sob. Quickly he gathered
her in his arms and held her tight to his chest.

He would protect her, no matter what.

Chapter Twenty

Amelia was a nervous wreck. Every little sound made her jump and cower and every shadow made her heart beat just that little bit faster. She wasn't sure how McNair had traced her back to the village, but it didn't really matter. By now he would have worked out where she was staying and it was only a matter of time before he appeared to exact his revenge.

All night different scenarios had been charging through her mind. In one he arrived with an unforgiving magistrate who ruled she should hang for attacking a decorated Captain. In another he waited until she fell asleep and then slipped in and stabbed her whilst she slumbered. Needless to say Amelia hadn't slept at all.

Edward had stayed with her the entire night. On their return to Beechwood Manor he'd instructed a fire to be lit in his study, then he'd settled her down into one of the comfortable armchairs and taken up position in the other. All night he'd sat with her, talked to her in his calm, soothing voice, and when the first rays of light had filtered in through the window he'd escorted her to her room and promised to remain in a chair outside the door whilst she rested for a few hours.

A light tap at the door made Amelia sit up and a few seconds later Edward entered quietly.

'I heard you tossing and turning,' he said.

'I can't sleep, every time I close my eyes I think he's going to pounce on me.'

Edward approached the bed and after a moment's hesitation sat down next to her.

'I will protect you, Amelia. McNair won't get close to you.'

She looked up into his deep dark eyes and saw the sincerity burning there and felt herself relax a little.

'Why are you doing all this for me?' she asked quietly.

Edward frowned as if he didn't understand the question.

'All of this. I'm not your responsibility and I just keep bringing you trouble.'

Amelia found she was holding her breath whilst she waited for Edward's answer. She wanted him to declare his love for her, to tell her he would do anything for her, tell her she was his entire world. Deep down Amelia knew it couldn't be true, that it would be just too much to hope for, but she wished all the same.

'Come for a walk with me,' Edward said. 'It's a beautiful day and if we're outside then McNair truly won't know where to look. There's eight hundred acres of land out there for us to get lost in.'

She wondered if she should push him, repeat the question, but something told her he would answer in his own time. Maybe when they were away from the house and he'd had chance to clear his head a little.

Edward waited outside her door whilst she changed and escorted her downstairs to his study. Before leaving they picked up a blanket to lay on the grass if they fancied a rest and as usual Edward packed some paper and pencils into his bulging satchel.

Being in the fresh air did make Amelia feel better. All night she had tormented herself with McNair's face, but now with Edward's reassurance that he would protect her and a warm breeze clearing some of the cobwebs from her mind she felt a little more positive.

They walked in silence for a while, both lost in their own thoughts, and it was only as Amelia realised she didn't know where they were that she started to pay attention to their surroundings.

'Where are we?' she asked, looking around, trying to find some familiar landmark to orientate herself. In the time she had been at Beechwood Manor she had explored much of the estate, especially the parts close to the house, but she didn't recognise where they were now at all.

'I'm taking you somewhere very special,' Edward said with a small smile.

He led her down a grassy path, surrounded on both sides by overgrown, tangled bushes. Up ahead a mossy stone wall came into view, leading off in both directions for a few hundred yards.

'Come this way,' Edward said, pulling her off the path into a narrow gap between the bushes and into the long grass. Amelia could feel the skirts of her dress being dragged behind her by the undergrowth and at one point Edward had to stop to lift her over a particularly large fallen tree stump.

Eventually they met up with the mossy wall and Edward traced his hands along it as if searching for something. Amelia watched in amazement as he gripped an almost invisible knob, turned it and opened a concealed door.

Feeling as though she were stepping into some magical hidden kingdom, Amelia crossed the threshold into the secret garden and gasped in pleasure. Although it had obviously been neglected over the past few years the garden was beautiful, maybe even more so for the slightly wild air it had about it. The long grass was dotted with wild flowers, drawing the eye to a multi-coloured carpet stretching out before them. Tall trees were positioned around the edge of the garden and from one hung a wide rope swing. Amelia felt as though she wanted to sink into the long grass and never leave.

Edward closed the door behind them and caught up with her, taking her by the hand and leading her further into the garden.

'My grandfather built this for my grandmother,' he said quietly as he watched Amelia take in all the details.

A small white butterfly fluttered past and settled on a large daisy for a moment before continuing with its journey.

'How lovely.'

'They were very much in love. In a time when nearly all marriages were arranged they rebelled and married each other despite a big difference in social status.'

'Tell me their story,' Amelia said as they strolled arm in arm through the garden. She wanted to hear something positive now, something that would remind her of all the good in the world.

'My grandfather was titled and heir to the estate. When he was of an appropriate age his parents arranged a match with a local landowner's daughter. Their family were rich and her dowry would help to maintain the estate for years to come.'

'But your grandfather didn't agree to the marriage?'

'At first he protested quietly, refused to set a date for the wedding despite his parents' urging. And then he met my grandmother. She was a farmer's daughter, totally inappropriate for a man like him, of course, but they fell madly and irrevocably in love.'

Amelia felt herself smile at the thought of Edward's grandparents holding out for love despite societal pressures trying to force them apart. Maybe there was hope for everyone, if they were just strong enough.

'My grandfather informed his parents he was going to marry my grandmother. Of course they were livid, threatened to cut him off and disinherit him, but my grandfather stuck firm. For years he and my grandmother lived in exile from the family home. My grandfather worked as an estate manager for one of the local estates and they lived a simple but happy life.'

'What happened?'

'In the end his parents realised it was only them losing out. They wanted to see their son and their grandchildren and so they made an approach and slowly my grandparents were welcomed back into the family.'

'And your grandparents never regretted marrying for love?'

Edward shook his head.

'My grandfather built this garden for my grandmother when they were in their sixties, just a few years before they both passed away. I can remember being a small boy and watching them walk hand in hand as if they were courting. They loved each other for forty years.'

'That's a beautiful story,' Amelia said.

She wanted love like that. Amelia glanced at Edward and wondered if he was thinking of his late wife, wishing it were her he was bringing into the secret garden.

Edward laid out the blanket on the long grass in the sunshine and sat down beside Amelia.

'I need to tell you something,' he said in a serious tone.

Amelia turned her attention to him, pulling back from the self-pity she was wallowing in.

'You asked me why I was doing all this for you, protecting you and sheltering you,' he said quietly. 'You deserve an answer to that question, but I find it difficult to articulate sometimes.'

Amelia smiled encouragingly at him, her heart pounding in her chest. She could sense this was a monumental moment in their relationship and a small, excitable part of her dared to hope.

'Before you came into my life I was a husk of a man. I was overcome by grief, consumed by thoughts of the past. It wasn't healthy and it wasn't any way to live.' He looked at her as he spoke and Amelia could sense his sincerity and emotion. 'Many times in the past few years I've wondered if there was any point continuing with life, but last week on the beach when I was at a real risk of drowning I found myself desperate to be alive.'

He paused, staring off into the distance as if unsure how to continue. Amelia hesitantly reached out and placed her hand on top of his.

'I found myself wanting to restore the house and restore my life, to actually move forward instead of doing only the bare minimum to survive. I found myself wanting to spend more time with you.'

Amelia felt that small glimmer of hope start to swell and build inside her. She knew she cared for Edward, maybe more than she rightly should. He'd rescued her, kept her safe and welcomed her into his home and his life. In return Amelia had slowly and absolutely fallen in love with this gruff, gentle man, despite knowing she would never be the sort of woman he deserved. For weeks she'd been devastated by that realisation and the knowledge that he was still in mourning and might never love her back, but now maybe that was about to change.

'I miss my late wife and my son very much,' he said and Amelia saw the emotion on his face as he worked through the pain of remembering, 'And I don't think I will ever stop loving them.'

With those words Amelia felt all of her hopes crash to the ground. It must have shown on her face as Edward reached out for her hand and squeezed it tight.

'Listen to me, Amelia,' he said softly. 'Let me finish.'

She nodded, forcing herself to rein in all the negative thoughts and focus on what Edward was saying.

'I love my late wife and son just as I love my parents and my grandparents. They will always be part of my life, part of me. I will never forget and there will always be a place in my heart for them.'

Amelia nodded. In truth she couldn't expect anything less. Edward was a good man, of course he wouldn't abandon his love for his late wife and son just because someone new came along.

'For a long time I thought a man only got one chance in this life. One chance to live, one chance at caring for another.' He paused, looking deep into Amelia's eyes. 'I think now that I was wrong.'

She held her breath, hoping he would say the words, hoping he was going in the direction she thought he was.

'I care for you, Amelia, you've been the only person to stir me from my grief in the last three years and I find myself unable to stop thinking about you when you're not close. I think you were the reason I fought so hard on the beach to stay alive and I think you are the reason I have finally accepted I need to move forward with my life.'

It wasn't a declaration of love, but it was more than she had ever dreamed possible. He cared for her, the man she loved cared for her. Part of her cried out for love in return, but the sensible portion of her brain suppressed the thought. It shouldn't matter Edward hadn't declared his love, it was enough he wanted to see what might happen between them.

'I need you to know I can't forget my past,' he said, searching her face for a reaction.

'I wouldn't ever want you to,' Amelia said.

It was part of what she loved about him. He was a truly caring and loving man.

'I know I could never mean as much as Jane did to you, but—'

Edward shook his head, interrupting her as she spoke.

'Jane was a friend, a treasured friend, from childhood. We played together and grew up together and somewhere along the line the great regard I held her in turned into something more.'

'I think it is wonderful you grew to love each other,' Amelia said quietly.

Edward gripped her hand firmly, 'I'm not explaining myself very well,' he said. 'For a while I thought a man was only lucky enough to care for someone with every ounce of their being once, that I'd had my chance and I'd lost it. Now I see my thinking was completely wrong.'

Amelia felt her heart start hammering in her chest. Was this when he told her he loved her, that theirs would be an everlasting love?

'I cared for Jane the way I cared for my parents. She was kind and warm-hearted and had always been part of my life. But you, Amelia, you light this fire inside me. You make me want to shout and laugh all at the same time. I've never felt this depth of emotion before, this sort of connection.'

Amelia found herself grinning like a mad woman and threw her arms around Edward's neck. He might not have said the words, but Amelia could see the sincerity and emotion in his eyes. He loved her, even if he hadn't re-alised it himself yet.

'But I need you to remember I can't promise you any-thing right now, we need to take things slowly,' he said softly.

Amelia ran her fingers over his jawline and smiled. 'Just knowing you're giving us a chance is enough.'

She knew he was trying to temper the excitement that he must be able to see burning in her eyes. Edward was a good man, he wouldn't ever dream of building her hopes only to dash them on purpose, but he would be worried about his grief and guilt returning and sabotaging anything they built between them. All the more reason to take things slowly and allow him time to adjust, but already Amelia could feel herself getting carried away with dreams of a happy ending for herself and Edward.

Slowly he shifted position, sitting up so his body was close to hers. Amelia felt herself shudder with anticipation, knowing it was only a matter of time before he kissed her and losing herself in the desire she could see in his eyes.

'I think we should see if we're compatible,' Edward murmured, inching closer.

Amelia couldn't answer, but eventually managed a small, jerky, nod. Already her heart was racing and her body begging to be touched.

'Our kiss on the beach was very enjoyable,' Edward said, his voice low and seductive, 'but I think we need to repeat it to ensure nothing has changed.'

Slowly he raised a hand and traced his fingers over her cheek, before lacing them through her hair. Gently but firmly he pulled her towards him, claiming her lips with his own. Amelia felt herself lose control of her body as Edward expertly teased and tickled her with his lips and tongue.

She couldn't suppress a groan as he pulled away, but the loss of contact was for a mere few seconds as he regarded her with lust-filled eyes. It was almost inconceivable for Amelia that she was the source of such desire from the man she loved, but had never even dreamed could want her back, and she felt truly happy for the first time in years.

He whispered her name into her ear as he caught the lobe between his teeth and nibbled gently. Amelia gasped as he darted his tongue out to taste her skin, murmuring how sweet she was, how he wanted to kiss her all over. Amelia had been kissed before, but never like this. Never had her body responded so instinctively, never had she felt so out of control, so overwhelmed.

Something inside her was swelling and building, an uncontrollable desire for the man in front of her. She wanted him to lay her down and kiss every inch of her skin, she wanted to touch every part of him, to explore his body for hours on end.

Slowly, Edward pulled away.

'We're compatible,' he said gruffly, shifting a little uncomfortably.

Amelia immediately tensed, wondering if she had done something wrong. Edward must have caught her worried expression and reached out to pull her closer to him.

'You deserve more than a hurried fumble in the grass,' Edward said with a pained smile. 'If I kiss you for another second then I may not be able to control myself.'

With her heart soaring Amelia dipped her head and kissed the man she loved, giggling as he groaned as she pressed her body against his.

Chapter Twenty-One

Edward felt the warm glow of contentment as he lay in the long grass with Amelia in his arms. Lazily he traced a pattern on her back, stopping to pepper the silky skin with kisses every now and then.

After a few minutes Amelia rolled over so they were face to face. He couldn't help but smile. In this moment everything felt right in the world. He couldn't believe just two months ago he'd never wanted to see another human again. He'd been shut away in Beechwood Manor, spiralling into a never-ending whirlpool of grief and sadness and guilt.

'Lay right there,' he instructed Amelia as he sat up. The sunlight was bathing her in a warm glow and, with her hair cascading over her shoulders and her skin still pink and warm from their intimacy, Edward knew he had to draw her.

She looked at him questioningly as he took out his pencils and paper, but he gave her a smile of reassurance.

'Edward?'

'You've never looked more beautiful than you do right now,' he said. 'Let me draw you. I want to capture this moment for ever.'

He wondered if she might protest. Most women would laugh nervously and then refuse, but after a moment's contemplation Amelia rested her head back on her hand and relaxed.

'I just need to alter one or two things,' Edward said.

Gently he gripped the neckline of her dress and tugged until the material was off her shoulders, leaving the caramel-coloured skin exposed. She looked irresistible.

With long pencil strokes he sketched, tracing her contours and capturing her essence. As he drew he found his eyes roaming over her body, taking in her gentle curves and her perfectly proportioned features. He couldn't quite believe a woman like Amelia could want to be with him. She was young and beautiful, and if she were introduced into society she would surely be the belle of the debutantes, but here she was with him, a man with a complicated past and more unresolved emotion than most of her possible suitors would have put together.

'What happens now, Edward?' Amelia asked as he began to add the finer details to his drawing.

'Now? Now I think I need to kiss you again.'

She giggled as he pounced on top of her, kissing her long and hard. Leisurely they explored each other with hands and lips, and Edward felt as though they had all the time in the world. He wanted this afternoon never to end. Here in the secret garden it felt like a little slice of paradise just for them.

'You never answered my question,' Amelia said, resting her head on his chest.

'For now we need to focus on keeping you safe,' Edward said, brushing her hair back from her face and tucking it behind an ear. 'I will not let McNair harm a single hair on your head or inch of your skin.'

Amelia nodded, but Edward could see already the fear was back in her eyes.

'I don't know what he wants,' she said eventually.

'He wants revenge. You've hurt his pride.'

'Will he report me to the magistrate? Is that how he will punish me?'

Edward wished it might be as simple as all that. Given McNair's less-than-pure reputation he had no doubt he could convince a magistrate to drop any charges against Amelia. No, he thought McNair would want to exact a more personal revenge on her.

'From what you have said, and from Mr Guthry's report, I think he will prefer to take matters into his own hands,' Edward said slowly. He didn't want to scare Amelia, but he knew she had been through every option, every outcome, a hundred times in her head.

'He wants to hurt me.'

Edward nodded.

'I can't see how this will end. What will make him stop?'

It had been a question Edward had been asking himself over the past twenty-four hours. He wondered if maybe he could pay the scoundrel off, bribe him to forget the whole matter. It seemed McNair was pretty money-orientated and maybe a large enough amount would convince the man to leave Amelia alone. The only downside to the plan was they could never be sure he wouldn't come back once he'd spent the payoff and demand more.

That left a show of strength. Edward wasn't a violent man, but some people only seemed to understand power and violence. He rather feared the only way to make McNair leave Amelia alone would be to make the man see she was protected by someone stronger than he was. Edward might not have had the army training that the Captain had benefitted from, but he had something worth fighting for, and that was why he was sure he would beat McNair if it came to that.

'We'll figure it out,' Edward said, 'but for now just remember he can't get anywhere near you, not whilst you're here with me.'

Amelia leaned across and kissed him, squeezing her eyes shut as she did so.

Amelia felt as though she were walking through the air, bouncing easily from fluffy cloud to fluffy cloud. The memory of Edward's kisses were imprinted in her mind and she could see by the look in his eye that he cared for her. Amelia couldn't quite believe it was true. Ever since discovering McNair's betrayal she knew her confidence had been dented. Nevertheless, all of her worries and insecurities seemed to melt away when Edward was by her side and even if the future was a little uncertain, she knew that as long as she was with Edward everything would work out just fine.

Still, there was that occasional hesitation in his eyes, the fleeting expressions of guilt that Amelia thought might always be there in the background. His near-death encounter had shown him he wanted to live, but that didn't mean he would be able to leave his guilt and memories behind him easily. And of course he'd never said that he loved her. Having Edward care for her should be enough, but already Amelia was craving more.

They walked back to the house in the late afternoon sunshine hand in hand, stopping before they entered the courtyard to straighten their clothes and brush the last pieces of grass from their bodies.

'Can we check on Milly?' Amelia asked as they passed the barn.

Inside it took a few moments for their eyes to adjust to the gloom before they could make outMilly and her foal curled together in the hay. For a long while they stood side by side, watching mother and baby, and Amelia felt an unfamiliar maternal tug on her heart. She realised that she wanted this, this instinctive and natural bond between mother and baby. She wanted to cradle her and Edward's child in her arms and know she would love the baby she held for eternity. With a small smile she warned herself not to get too carried away. They'd shared a few kisses, nothing more at present, and there had been no mention of marriage.

Glancing sideways at Edward's profile, Amelia felt a surge of hope. There had been no mention of love or marriage, but perhaps one day there might be. A girl was allowed to dream.

'Tom,' Edward called out to the groom as they crossed the courtyard. 'Gather the servants. I want to speak to everyone in my study in ten minutes.'

They went inside and straight to Edward's study. Amelia recognised the determined look on his face as he sat her down in one of the chairs and began pacing up and down, murmuring to himself as he did so.

'Thank you for coming,' he said to the assembled servants ten minutes later. 'We have a problem and we need your help.'

Amelia thought she saw the servants standing slightly taller as Edward called them to action.

'Miss Amelia is in trouble. A dangerous man from her past has tracked her down and is intent on causing her harm. He knows where she is and he is determined to find a way to hurt her.'

The servants glanced at her, but nobody said anything, turning their attention back to Edward as he continued speaking.

'Now I know there are not many of us and I don't pro-pose this is a job for such a small band, but I wanted you to know exactly what was going on. Tom, once we've fin-ished here I want you to ride into the village and round up as many young men as you can. Tell them what's going on and tell them I will pay the first eight men who turn up to help guard the house.'

Tom nodded, looking eager to set off on his mission.

'Everyone else, I need you to be vigilant at all times. If you notice a window open that wasn't open before, raise the alarm. If you hear a noise in a room that should be empty, raise the alarm. Anything out of the ordinary, raise the alarm. This man is dangerous and we need to apprehend him.'

All the servants nodded seriously and Mrs Henshaw moved closer to Amelia and squeezed her arm.

'Don't you worry, ducky, we'll find this scoundrel and keep you safe. I will send a message to Mr Guthry, I'm sure he will want to be on hand to help.'

Amelia nodded. She just wanted this to be over. For weeks she had lived in purgatory, at first convinced she was a murderer and then scared beyond belief about what McNair might do to her if he found her. She still wasn't sleeping properly, and whenever she did close her eyes she imagined the letter opener slipping into McNair's soft flesh and the blood seeping through his clothing. Now the images had evolved and often it was Amelia's abdomen the small blade was plunged into and her blood oozing from the wound.

Edward waited for the servants to leave and then gave her a reassuring squeeze on the shoulder. 'We'll find him,' he said softly. 'And then we can get on with our lives.'

Chapter Twenty-Two

For three days men from the village had been positioned around the outside of the house and Mr Guthry had more or less moved in to one of the larger servants' rooms up in the attic, adding his calming presence to the household. Edward had accompanied Amelia nearly everywhere. Even when she had asked to take a bath he'd sat dutifully on the other side of the screen, much to Mrs Henshaw's absolute indignation. Amelia had caught his frown of displeasure as the housekeeper had taken up position firmly between him and the screen and couldn't help but giggle.

She had never been very good at being alone and spending time with Edward was never tedious, but Amelia was beginning to feel as though there were eyes watching her everywhere she went. Part of her wished McNair would just appear now so they could have their confrontation and the men of the village could see him off.

Edward seemed strangely calm. He was sitting across from her in his comfortable armchair, happily reading a thick book. Every so often he'd glance up, check the room and smile. She wished she could be so content to sit and read.

A light tap on the door made Amelia and Edward look

up in unison and Amelia felt her heart racing, but it was just Betty one of the maids who slipped into the room.

'There's a Mr Pollard here to see you, sir,' Betty said with a deferential curtsy.

Amelia immediately sat up straighter. Mr Pollard was the young man Mr Guthry had sent to London to warn Lizzie about McNair.

'Good afternoon,' Edward said as the tall young man entered the room.

'Good afternoon, Sir Edward… Miss Amelia.'

Edward motioned for him to sit down and Pollard awkwardly manoeuvred his lanky form into one of the free armchairs.

'Tell us,' Edward said simply. 'What did you find out?'

'Well, sir, I travelled to London as instructed and headed straight to the address Miss Amelia had provided. I could see as soon as I arrived that there had been a fire and the building looked to be damaged beyond repair.'

Amelia held her breath as he continued, wondering if McNair had decided to target Lizzie, to injure the woman Amelia thought of as a sister.

'I talked to some of the servants and it seems as though the fire was started by a candle being left burning by the curtains in one of the bedrooms. Luckily no one was hurt and there was no question of there being an intruder involved. What's more there had been no sightings of anyone fitting Captain McNair's description.'

Amelia felt herself begin to relax a little, 'And Lizzie, did you find her?'

Mr Pollard shook his head. 'The servants informed me she, along with the two women she had been staying with, had been taken to the countryside to recuperate from mild smoke inhalation by a gentleman, the Earl of Burwell.'

'Do you know him, Amelia?' Edward asked.

She shook her head. 'Maybe he is a friend of Aunt Mathilda.'

'I travelled to Cambridgeshire after satisfying myself Captain McNair was not involved in the house fire and approached a member of Lord Burwell's household. By the time I got there it seemed Miss Lizzie had left.'

Amelia frowned, wondering where Lizzie would have gone to next. Her cousin didn't know anyone else in England so she didn't have many choices.

'I bought one of the grooms a few cups of ale and he told me he thought there had been a lovers' row between Miss Eastway and Lord Burwell.'

'Lizzie, involved with an earl?' Amelia found herself smiling. If anyone deserved to find love it was her cousin, but she just hoped this Lord Burwell was good enough for her kind and generous cousin.

'I could not pick up her trail after that, miss, but I got the impression Lord Burwell is not the sort of man to leave your cousin stranded without anyone to turn to.'

Amelia felt some of the worry she had been carrying over the last few weeks begin to dissipate. At least it looked as though McNair hadn't decided to target her cousin, but she would feel much better if she could just lay eyes on Lizzie and reassure herself she was well.

'Thank you, Mr Pollard,' Edward said, standing and shaking the young man's hand. 'I am sure you understand what a matter for concern this is for Miss Amelia and you have done a wonderful job in reassuring us so far. I wonder if you would be against returning to Cambridgeshire and approaching Lord Burwell on our behalf.'

The young man's eyes widened and he looked from Edward and Amelia and back again.

'I would give you a letter explaining our predicament

and I feel confident you will be able to impress the importance of our queries on this Lord Burwell.'

Amelia held her breath, hoping Mr Pollard would agree.

'I am sure you understand how important it is that we find Miss Eastway. And you will be remunerated for your time and effort, of course.'

'I am honoured that you trust me with a matter of such importance, Sir Edward,' Mr Pollard said.

'Go to the kitchens and ask Mrs Henshaw for some refreshment and I will write the letter for Lord Burwell whilst you wait.'

'Thank you,' Amelia said as Mr Pollard left the room.

'We'll find your cousin, Amelia, even if we have to scour the whole of Cambridgeshire ourselves.'

He sounded so sincere, so concerned for the safety of a woman he hadn't ever met, that Amelia wanted to wrap her arms around him and kiss him. She took a step towards him, and then another, but before she could turn her face up to meet his the door burst open and Tom the groom came rushing in.

'We've caught him, sir,' he said, bending forward slightly and resting his hands on his thighs as he caught his breath.

Edward stiffened and immediately put a protective arm around Amelia.

'Where?'

'Sneaking through the gardens by the old gazebo.'

'Have you restrained him?'

'William and Big Peter are holding him, and I sent some of the other men to join them on my way over here. What do you want us to do?'

'I'll come at once.'

Amelia made to follow, but Edward placed a firm hand on her shoulder, pressing her back into the chair.

'I should be there,' she said quietly, knowing she needed to face her tormentor, but not really wanting to.

'There's no need. I'll have a quiet word with him and send him on his way,' Edward said with a stony expression on his face.

Amelia doubted it would be just 'a quiet word', but she saw the determination behind Edward's eyes and stopped fighting to stand up. Maybe it would be better if she never had to see McNair ever again.

'I'll be back soon.' He kissed the top of her head and strode out of the room, closely followed by Tom.

Amelia stood up and stretched, feeling suddenly free. In no time at all Edward would be back by her side and they would no longer have the threat of McNair hanging over them. They would be able to plan for the future and enjoy a proper life, not one just confined to the walls of Beechwood Manor.

'Hello, Amelia, my sweet.'

Amelia screamed, but the sound was cut off by a firm hand being clamped over her nose and mouth.

'There's no need for that. I thought you'd be pleased to see me.'

Amelia felt herself being dragged backwards towards the middle of the room, her feet tangling in the heavy rug on the floor.

'Now, if I release my hand, do you promise to be a good girl and stay nice and quiet?'

She nodded her head. At this precise moment in time she would agree to anything to get the oxygen her lungs were screaming out for.

McNair slowly released his hand and Amelia sucked in a few deep breaths.

'How lovely for us to be together again,' McNair murmured into her hair. 'Now, let me be very clear. I have a pistol and I'm holding it against your back. If you make any sudden moves, or if you do anything to displease me, then I will shoot you.' There was a cold, dead tone to his voice and Amelia wondered how she had ever fancied herself in love with this man. He might be conventionally handsome, but there was no warmth inside him, no capacity to love.

'You sent in a decoy,' Amelia said flatly, realising how McNair had outsmarted them.

'Of course. Your new beau had the house guarded round the clock, I needed some way to get you alone.'

Amelia wondered just how long they had before Edward reached the gazebo and realised the man they had captured was not McNair.

'I assumed your gentleman would have given a description of me, but it's not too difficult to find someone who looks vaguely similar in need of a little money.'

'What do you want?' Amelia asked, not sure she wanted to know the answer.

'What do I want?' McNair mused. 'Well, my sweet, I want you to realise quite how much you hurt me.'

'I'm sorry,' Amelia whispered.

'I'm sure you are, but that doesn't change the fact you stabbed me and left me for dead. That broke my heart, Amelia, and so soon after our reunion.'

Suddenly Amelia felt a flare of anger inside. 'You *used* me. I fell for you and you used me. If you hadn't been sent back to England, I would have run away with you and been ruined for ever.'

'That doesn't give you the right to stab me.'

He had a point, but that hadn't been why she'd stabbed him.

'I thought you were going to kill me,' Amelia said quietly. 'That was why I stabbed you.'

'How did that work out for you? Feel any safer for it now?'

'What do you plan to do?'

McNair chuckled. 'Do you know, I've no idea? I've thought of a thousand different things, of course. Maybe scar your pretty face, or plunge a knife into you at random and give you the same chance you did me. Or maybe I'll take you away with me and get your father to pay for your return, just as I'd planned all that time ago.'

Amelia wondered if he was a little deranged. She understood he was cruel and she understood he was angry that she'd bested him and left him bleeding, but there was a slight note of hysteria in his voice as he talked through the options.

'Amelia!' Edward shouted as the door burst open.

'Ah, your knight in shining armour. Keep back, Sir Edward, or I might have to harm Amelia.'

Edward froze and took a moment to assess the scene. Amelia could see the second he noticed the pistol. Carefully he stepped into the room, giving both Amelia and McNair a wide berth.

'What do you want?' Edward asked bluntly.

'No niceties? No formal introductions?'

'No. What do you want?'

'Has Amelia told you what she did to me?'

'She stabbed you.'

Amelia felt McNair stiffen a little behind her at Edward's bluntness, but the Captain soon rallied and continued.

'We had been involved, of course, which was why her actions were the ultimate betrayal.'

'You seduced her, planned to ruin her and blackmail her father to avoid any scandal. Then your commanding officer found out and sent you back to England quietly to pre-empt any trouble. When Amelia followed you here you hit her and she stabbed you in self-defence. Have I left anything out?' Edward asked.

He spoke slowly, and seemed cool and detached, but Amelia could see what was going on under the surface and realised Edward was petrified for her.

McNair shook his head. 'Quite accurate. At least we can't accuse Amelia of holding anything back.'

'What do you want?' Edward asked again.

'Why are you here, Amelia?' McNair asked, completely ignoring Edward's question again.

'Hiding from you,' Amelia mumbled.

'But why here? Tell me the truth. I'll know if you're lying.'

'I took shelter here from the storm when I was fleeing Brighton.'

'So you didn't know Sir Edward beforehand? Don't take another step, Sir Edward, or we'll find out just what shade of red Amelia's blood is.'

Edward had been edging forward, step by tiny step, but it seemed McNair still had his sharp powers of observation, even when distracted by the person he was holding at gunpoint.

'No, I met him two months ago for the first time.'

'So why did you stay here?'

'It was safe and I didn't have anywhere else to go.' She didn't see any point in lying to McNair. Besides, he'd known her for so long he'd probably be able to tell if she was speaking the truth or not.

'Why did you let Amelia stay, Sir Edward?'

'To protect her from you.'

'She was a complete stranger, yet you welcomed her into your home and have gone to a lot of trouble to protect her. Do I detect some deeper feelings here? Have you fallen for Amelia's considerable charms?'

Edward remained silent, but behind her Amelia heard McNair chuckle.

'Of course! Two little love birds cooped up in this dusty old house.'

'I suggest you tell us what you want and then leave,' Edward said. 'This is beginning to feel like the ramblings of a senile old man.'

McNair pulled Amelia a little closer to him.

'Careful, Sir Edward, or you might lose someone you care for. I hear it wouldn't be the first time.'

Amelia watched the flicker of pain cross Edward's face before his expression turned inscrutable again.

'But you're right, we haven't got all day. I have decided how we should settle this.' McNair sounded positively cheerful. 'Amelia injured me greatly and I demand recompense.'

For a moment Amelia's heart soared as she thought he was about to ask for money.

'I propose a duel. Tomorrow morning. Me and you, Sir Edward. Pistols. And only one of us will leave alive.'

Amelia felt her heart skip a beat and then another. An acute pain ripped through her chest as she saw Edward consider the proposal and nod slowly.

'That seems fair,' he said eventually.

'No!' she screamed.

'Shh, Amelia, everything is settled,' McNair said, releasing her and pushing her into Edward's arms. 'I'll see you at dawn tomorrow, Sir Edward, past the lake and on the rise near the northern edge of your estate.'

'Tomorrow.' Edward nodded.

McNair walked calmly out of the room without looking back.

Chapter Twenty-Three

'You can't go,' Amelia said, a note of hysteria in her voice. 'He'll kill you.'

Edward grimaced. It was quite possible. McNair had served in the army for a long time and had no doubt been trained to fire a pistol accurately. Whilst Edward owned a gun, and had learnt to shoot as a boy, he hadn't picked up his pistol for many years.

'It's settled, Amelia.'

'It's not settled. We can find another way.'

She reached out to him and Edward hated the look of pain and confusion that crossed her face as he let her hand hang in the air. He couldn't touch her, not now. He'd sworn to protect her, to keep her safe no matter what, and he'd failed at the very first test.

'Edward?' Amelia said, trying to catch his eye.

'I need to go and prepare. I'll see you later,' he said shortly.

Quickly, before she could react, he strode out the door and made for his rooms in the West Wing. He needed to think, to puzzle things through, and that wasn't possible with Amelia right there distracting him.

He closed the door to his bedchamber behind him and

sank down on to the bed. Edward couldn't believe he'd let himself be fooled by McNair's trick. The wily scoundrel had paid a man to sneak into the grounds and be caught in his place, then used the distraction to get to Amelia. He should have seen it coming, should have stayed with her no matter what. Instead he'd rushed off to confront McNair and left Amelia vulnerable. When he'd burst into the room and found her with a gun to her back he'd almost expired on the spot.

'You can't just run away from me,' Amelia said, flinging open the door to his bedroom and stepping inside. She was fired up, recovered from her ordeal only minutes earlier, and ready to do battle.

'Amelia, I need some peace.'

'What for? What's going on, Edward? You need to talk to me. You can't keep trying to solve everything by yourself.'

Edward remained silent. Amelia sighed dramatically and flopped down on the bed next to him.

'Do you know I've just been held at gunpoint by a man who would like to hurt me very much?'

'Of course I do, Amelia.' And he felt like such a cur for not being more supportive.

'I thought I might die. He threatened to cut me, you know. And to shoot me.'

Edward felt the nausea rise inside him as he pictured all the awful things McNair would likely want to do to Amelia. It was his job to protect her and so far he'd failed miserably.

'I was scared—in fact, I was petrified—but nothing scared me as much as hearing you accept his challenge to a duel.'

He was just about to open his mouth to reply when

her words hit him and he stopped to consider them for a moment.

'I don't know what I'd do if you were harmed...' She paused for a moment and took his hand. 'Please don't push me away.'

Her plea was so heartfelt and so sincere Edward knew that for once in his life he would have to share his innermost thoughts.

'I promised to protect you, Amelia,' he said quietly. 'And I failed.'

He watched as she opened her mouth and then closed it again as she digested his words.

'I swore I wouldn't let anything happen to you and three days later a man is holding a pistol to your back.'

'You couldn't have done any more,' Amelia protested quietly.

'You deserve someone who can take care of you, Amelia, a man who will protect and shelter you.'

'I deserve a man who cares for me,' Amelia said, 'Nothing more and nothing less. Everyone deserves to be cared for, but I can't ask someone else to be responsible for the consequences of my actions.'

He studied her face, saw her earnest expression and knew she believed what she was saying. She'd changed so much in the couple of months she'd been staying with him. The energetic, mischievous little minx was still there, but Amelia was more thoughtful, more considerate now. He supposed she'd had to do a lot of growing up in the last few months.

Amelia leaned forward and kissed him softly, conveying all of her compassion and understanding through the meeting of their lips. Edward wanted to give in, to let himself accept her forgiveness, but some small part of him held back.

'Kiss me, Edward,' Amelia whispered. 'Kiss me and show me you care for me.'

With a groan he surrendered and kissed her, pulling her body close against his and running his hands down her back. He wanted to stay in this moment for ever, just the two of them with no McNair and no duel and no threats.

His position hadn't changed. Tomorrow he was still going to ride out and meet McNair in a duel. Edward had no doubts that by early morning he would either be dead or a killer, but maybe that was all the more reason to enjoy today.

Amelia let her head drop back and felt her hair tickle her skin as it fell down her back. Edward was kissing her neck, making her shudder with anticipation as he slowly moved his lips across her skin. Alongside the almost overwhelming desire she felt elated. For once in her life she'd made a difference. Edward had come up to his room withdrawn and brooding, but she'd managed to coax the truth from him, and make him see he wasn't responsible for every little consequence when something went wrong.

True, they still had the dilemma of what to do about McNair, but Amelia was sure together they could come up with a solution. As long as Edward agreed not to go and face him in a duel, especially with pistols. McNair had years of army training and a familiarity with the weapon he'd chosen. Although Edward was more powerful than McNair, and surprising agile for a man of his size, Amelia knew he wouldn't have a chance in this sort of duel.

She knew Edward was just trying to protect her, trying to take McNair's wrath towards Amelia and direct it towards him instead, but in a way McNair had chosen the right way to wound Amelia when suggesting the duel. Right now physical pain would not be worse than the thought of losing Edward. For so long she'd felt alone and now she had someone who cared for her, all her faults and quirks included. And she rather thought she loved him more than she'd ever imagined was possible. If McNair killed Edward, then Amelia would be destroyed.

Pausing for a moment and pulling back, Edward looked at her face as if to check she really wanted him to go further. Amelia felt light-headed, swept away, but she knew if Edward pulled away now she would be devastated.

Amelia gasped as Edward pushed the neckline of her dress down to expose the skin of her chest. She shivered as the cool air hit her sensitive skin, but immediately Edward's hands were on her, warming and teasing. Never had she been touched like this before, never had she imagined a fingertip could cause such a delicious sensitivity.

Suddenly she wanted to see him as he saw her and with agile fingers Amelia lifted Edward's shirt up over his head and threw it on to the bed behind them, placing her own hands on his chest. For a moment they both paused, looking into each other's eyes and just enjoying the feel of the other's hands on their bodies. Then Edward was on his feet, lifting Amelia and pushing her dress down past her waist and over her hips so it fell and pooled around her ankles.

Amelia felt his eyes on her, roaming over her body under the thin chemise. She'd always imagined she would be self-conscious when a man saw her naked, but with Edward it just felt right.

Slowly he stripped her of the rest of her clothes, allowing her to savour the feel of the cotton chemise as it glided over her skin, baring her body as he pulled it up over her head. Five seconds passed, and then ten, with Edward's eyes darting over her body. Amelia felt a delicious anticipation as slowly he kicked off his boots and divested himself of his trousers. For a moment they both just stood there, then Edward took her in his arms and they tumbled back on to the bed.

There was something frenzied, almost wild, about their movements, as if both of them knew something had changed. Amelia told herself it was the brush with death, the residual feelings of danger and relief to be alive, but as Edward pushed against her she lost all coherent thought.

Amelia felt her body tense, but instead of the pain she'd been told to expect she just felt Edward's fingers stroking her gently. Rhythmically he teased and tantalised until Amelia felt as though her entire body was going to melt into the bedsheets. A warm sensation began building deep inside her and she felt her hips begin to rise to meet Edward's touch.

As he withdrew his fingers and positioned himself on top of her he searched her face as if checking she wanted to continue. Amelia moved her body up towards him, drawing him in, and groaned as he pressed into her.

Faster and faster he moved until Amelia felt something burst inside her and a warm wave of pleasure washed over her. Above her Edward stiffened and groaned before collapsing on to the bed beside her.

Afterwards she lay with her head resting on Edward's shoulder, his arm looped around her body and holding her close. She felt contented and safe, despite the events of earlier that day. As she traced her fingers over Edward's chest she wondered what this meant for them, whether it meant Edward would ask her to marry him. Of course she knew plenty of people were intimate and didn't marry, but she could dare to hope this might mean he definitely wanted a future with her.

They were no closer to finding a solution to their problem, no closer to working out what to do about McNair and his thirst for revenge, but Amelia felt strangely calm. Throughout this entire episode she had felt as if events had been taken out of her control. At first, when she'd been convinced she was a murderer she had been petrified and unstable. Then when she'd discovered McNair was alive and seeking her out she had been scared of what he might want and what he would do. Now, even though the threat was very real, even though he'd held a gun to her back earlier that day, Amelia felt as if for the first time in ages she had some say in what happened next.

Of course Edward couldn't go to meet McNair in the duel, so instead they would have to decide whether to involve the local magistrate or deal with him in another way themselves. Whatever they decided, Amelia was determined they would do it together. Edward might want to protect her from McNair and she was never going to discourage him from looking out for her, but this was her mess and for once she was going to face the consequences of her actions and help come up with the solution.

With this firmly resolved in her mind Amelia allowed her mind and body to relax into Edward. He held her close against him, every so often bending down to plant kisses on the top of her head.

The late evening sun was streaming through the bedroom window, warming up Amelia's naked body making her eyes droop. Edward's hand stroking her upper arm was lulling her off to sleep and Amelia felt her entire body relax. Right here, right now she felt safe. Later they could talk some more and decide what path they would take, but now she was going to enjoy resting in the arms of the man she loved.

Chapter Twenty-Four

Edward felt like a cur as he slipped out of the bed an hour before dawn. Amelia had slept soundly since their intimacy the evening before and hadn't stirred when he had gently rolled her off his arm. He knew he should wake her, he should give her the option of accompanying him to the duel site, but he just couldn't bring himself to do it. As she'd fallen asleep in his arms he'd watched her contented smile and peaceful expression and he felt awful for misleading her.

Edward knew Amelia had taken their intimacy the night before as a sign he wouldn't go and meet McNair and he hadn't disillusioned her. In a way it would be much easier to walk out with a pistol in his hand, facing down the seasoned army Captain, without Amelia watching.

Quickly he dressed, throwing on a clean shirt and breeches, and grabbed his boots to put on outside the bedroom. Before he left he bent over and kissed Amelia on the forehead, smoothing away her hair and taking a moment to take in her serene expression, how her eyelashes rested on her rosy cheeks and the gentle curve of her lips. He knew he might never see her again and he wanted to imprint her face on his memory to have something to hold on to if he was shot and his life blood was ebbing away.

Forcing himself out of the room, Edward strode down the stairs and out into the fresh pre-dawn air, pausing only to pull on his boots and pick up his pistol from the study. He didn't have a second. Over the years of his seclusion he'd lost contact with his friends and he had no desire to pull any of them into this mess anyway. No, if he was shot then he would just have to accept his fate without anyone to fuss over him.

As he began the process of readying his horse, securing the saddle and talking softly to the restless beast, he wondered if he was being a little self-indulgent going off to meet McNair in this manner. He knew the guilt he felt over his late wife and son's death had nearly consumed him, nearly destroyed him. He'd promised to love and protect them, and whilst he'd fulfilled the first part of his vow, he'd failed miserably on the second. Now, with Amelia filling his thoughts and his heart, he had someone else to protect. And this was the only way he could think about doing it.

Pushing all doubts aside, Edward mounted his horse. The fact remained that if he didn't go and meet McNair then Amelia would be at risk and he couldn't have any harm to her on his conscience.

It was peaceful riding out over the estate as the first rays of sunlight filtered up over the horizon. It was going to be a beautiful day and already the birds were chirping and singing.

He arrived at the duel site first, dismounted and secured his horse. Quietly he sat down with his back against a tree and waited for McNair to arrive.

'I see you honoured our agreement,' McNair sneered as he approached about ten minutes later.

'Of course.'

'You didn't bring a second.'

'Nor did you.'

The two men looked at each other warily.

'There's nothing to stop me shooting you where you sit,' McNair said eventually.

'Nothing but honour.'

'You think I'm an honourable man?'

Edward snorted. 'No. But I think you have some sense of justice, even if it is a little twisted. You won't shoot me until the duel is under way.'

McNair looked at him curiously and for a moment Edward wondered if he'd read the man wrong. Eventually the Captain threw his head back and laughed.

'So you left the little lady at home?' McNair asked, looking around as if checking Amelia wasn't hiding behind a tree or under a bush.

It was Edward's turn to laugh. He'd never heard such an inaccurate description of Amelia. She might be petite in size, but she was large in spirit and courage and soul. McNair would never understand just what he'd missed out on by not embracing Amelia.

'That is none of your concern. Shall we stop gossiping like old women and get this over with?'

Edward stood, drawing his pistol. McNair nodded, took two tarnished swords from where they were sticking out of a saddlebag and began to mark out the parameters.

When the two swords were a good distance apart McNair made his way back to Edward.

'Seeing as there's no independent witness we'll start at the swords. I'll shout advance and we shall begin walking towards each other. You may fire at any point.'

Edward had never been in a duel before, but it sounded fair enough. Of course McNair might decide to shoot him as he was walking out to the starting point, but he didn't think so. The army officer might be a scoundrel, but he seemed to have his own warped sense of honour.

Checking his pistol one last time, Edward began walking out towards the sword, occasionally glancing over his shoulder to check McNair's progress. Just before he reached the starting point he heard a faint thundering of hooves and turned sharply. Galloping up the gentle slope was Amelia, her hair flying out behind her and her expression frenzied.

Amelia had woken slowly, revelling in the warmth of the bed and the glow of the memory of the night before. As she allowed her eyes to flutter open she expected to see Edward's form lying beside her, but instead there was an empty bed.

Immediately she was wide awake, her eyes roaming the room for possible clues as to where he'd gone. The inevitable realisation that he'd sneaked out to meet McNair kept trying to push its way into her mind, but Amelia desperately sought for more pleasant alternatives. Maybe he'd gone to bring her breakfast in bed, or maybe he'd just woken early and had decided to go for a morning stroll.

Jumping out of bed, Amelia knew none of these things were true. Last night she'd been foolish thinking Edward had agreed to stay clear of McNair and the ridiculous duel. She had wanted him to see sense and accept her point of view on the matter and she had fooled herself into thinking that he had.

The anger she felt at him slipping out to meet McNair was overshadowed by a much greater feeling of worry. There was no way Edward could win this duel. She had seen McNair shoot—in fact, he'd been the one to teach her and her cousin to fire a pistol, setting up targets for them to practise on. McNair was good, better than good. She'd never seen him miss. And she doubted he would fire wide to preserve Edward's life.

It felt as though an icy hand of dread was gripping her heart, the pain shooting all through her chest. She couldn't lose Edward, not so soon after she'd realised how much he meant to her. Not when he had finally allowed himself to move on from his grief and start living again.

Amelia pulled on her dress, not bothering to do up all the fastenings, just ensuring it wouldn't fall down as she rode. Her hair was still loose from the night before and she probably looked a fright, but for once she didn't care. If she didn't get to the duel site before the men began pacing, then she would lose Edward for ever. She wasn't sure if McNair would then come after her also, but that point was moot. If she lost Edward, she would be destroyed.

Running out to the barn, Amelia began the time-consuming process of saddling her horse. Eventually everything was secure and she used a wooden crate to climb up and mount the restless animal, before urging it forward. Before she was even out of the courtyard she'd pushed the horse into a gallop, leaning low over its neck. Her eyes darted backwards and forward, trying to pick up a clue as to where Edward and McNair were. She knew she was heading in the right general direction, but the estate was vast and she could easily miss them. Right now every second counted and she knew just a few moments' delay might be the difference between life and death for Edward.

Finally she caught sight of the two men, standing a little way apart. As she watched, getting closer by the second, Edward and McNair began to walk away from each other. Amelia screamed as loud as she could.

'Stop,' she shouted. 'Stop.'

Both men paused and looked around. Amelia could see neither had reached the swords that were sticking out of the ground as markers for the start of the duel. Maybe she wasn't too late.

'Please, stop!' she shouted as she pulled on the reins and drew to a halt in between the two men.

'Get out of here, Amelia,' Edward said and Amelia could see the fear for her safety written all over his face.

'No.'

'Oh, no, Sir Edward, let Amelia stay. This way will be much more fun.'

'Come back with me, Edward,' Amelia begged, ignoring McNair behind her.

'I don't think so, Amelia, we have a deal,' McNair said. 'Get out of the way and let us get on with our duel.'

'Please.' She looked deep into Edward's eyes and saw the look of resignation. Quickly she slipped from the horse, letting go of the reins and allowing the animal to walk over to where Edward's horse was munching on the grass under a tree. 'Please don't do this. I can't risk losing you.'

'I have no choice, Amelia.'

'Of course you have a choice. Stop punishing yourself.'

'Hurry up. I've got a lunch engagement,' McNair called.

'I was meant to protect you. This is the only way McNair will leave you alone.'

'And what about when you're gone?' Amelia asked, the tears running down her cheeks. 'Then who will protect me? What's to stop McNair from coming after me when he's killed you?'

'He wouldn't do that.'

'You really think McNair is a man of his word? A man of honour?'

Edward glanced doubtfully over Amelia's shoulder and she felt a surge of hope. She was actually getting through to Edward.

'He will shoot you and then he will come for me.'

Edward shook his head slowly, but she could see the worry in his eyes.

'I'm getting impatient,' McNair called. 'If you don't hurry up, I'll just shoot the two of you.'

'What will happen when the duel is over?' Edward shouted.

'You mean once you're dead? Then the debt of honour is satisfied and I will leave Amelia alone.'

Taking Amelia firmly by the upper arms, he kissed her, pulling her body close to his.

'I love you,' she whispered as he stepped away.

Edward froze for a moment, a look of panic in his eyes at her declaration, then steadied himself before gently pushing her away from him. She stumbled backwards, only just managing to remain upright, the tears filling her eyes and blurring her vision. She felt paralysed, rooted to the spot, as she watched the man she loved slowly approaching the sword sticking out of the ground.

At the other end of the duelling ground McNair had reached his start point and was tapping his pistol impatiently against his thigh. Amelia knew the Captain was a good shot even at a long distance, but she calculated the two men would have to come a little closer together before they stood a good chance of hitting one another.

'Advance!' McNair shouted.

Both men began walking towards each other. For Amelia it was as if the entire world had slowed. Each step seemed to take an eternity, each movement was drawn out over long seconds. Her eyes darted backwards and forward between the man she loved and the man she'd thought she had killed. The pain in her chest was acute and almost overwhelming and her breathing had become shallow and ineffective.

Amelia saw the moment McNair decided he was close enough to fire, saw him begin to raise his pistol. Edward was still moving forward, his gun at his side. McNair paused, aimed and fired.

In that moment Amelia knew she couldn't lose Edward. He was her entire world and if he died her life wouldn't be worth living. She loved him with an all-consuming passion and wanted to spend the rest of her life helping him to heal and find happiness again.

Without thinking of the consequences, Amelia leapt forward, throwing herself between the two men. For a moment, as she hit the ground, she thought she must have been too late, that the bullet must have sailed past her before she had jumped, but then a strange burning pain just below her collarbone flared and all conscious thought fled her mind.

Chapter Twenty-Five

Edward saw McNair raise the pistol and knew he wasn't close enough to return the fire yet. He just had to hope the Captain was firing prematurely and would waste his shot.

The second the crack of the pistol sounded Edward saw the movement from the corner of his eye. Amelia was diving forward, right into the path of danger.

Edward sprang into action, running towards her, hoping to push her back. As he reached her side and saw her collapse to the ground he knew he was too late, even before the blossom of blood began seeping through her dress.

'Amelia,' he whispered, gathering her up into his arms.

A bubble of blood came out between her lips and Edward knew there was no hope. She'd been hit in the chest—people didn't survive wounds like that. He felt his entire world collapsing and his heart ripping in two.

'Stupid woman!' he heard McNair exclaim from somewhere beside him. 'Why did she jump?'

Edward didn't have time for McNair's callous remarks. The woman he loved was dying in front of him and there was nothing he could do about it.

Quickly he ripped the sleeve from his shirt and pressed the balled-up material against her wound, trying to stem the blood flow. As he knelt beside her he realised what he had just thought. *The woman he loved.* Pushing it aside, he focused on the oozing wound and gently pulled Amelia into his lap.

'I didn't think she would jump,' McNair mumbled.

Edward glanced at him and realised he was in shock. Far from the confident, callous scoundrel he had seen before, McNair looked genuinely worried.

'Get help,' Edward ordered.

'I'll be arrested.'

'If you don't get help then Amelia will die. If that happens, I will kill you myself. Slowly.'

Edward knew there probably wasn't much a doctor could do, but he had to try. He would move heaven and earth to give Amelia even the smallest chance of surviving this.

'Go!' he bellowed, and watched as McNair scrambled to his feet and ran to his horse. 'Send the doctor to the house,' he shouted after McNair.

There was no guarantee McNair would fetch a doctor. He might well just flee the county, probably even the country, but there was a small chance his conscience might stop him. Edward had to hope that was the case.

'Edward,' Amelia whispered, her eyes flickering open.

'Shh,' he said, leaning down and planting a kiss on her forehead. 'I'm here.'

'I love you, Edward.'

It sounded too much like a final farewell and Edward felt the tears rolling down his cheeks. He couldn't lose her, he loved her too much. She had helped him to heal, helped him to realise his life was worth living and now she was saying goodbye.

'Hang on for me, Amelia,' he whispered in her ear, 'Everything will be all right. I promise.'

It was a promise he shouldn't make, but as he scooped her up into his arms he knew it was one he had to keep. If Amelia died then his life would be over. He knew he wasn't strong enough to withstand the grief of losing the woman he loved for a second time.

Carefully he stood, then picked her up and draped her unconscious body over the front of his horse before mounting it. He was aware the movement of the horse could hasten her death, cause the bullet to dislodge or the blood to flow more quickly, but he also knew he didn't have a choice. Amelia was bleeding and struggling to breathe, that wasn't something he was going to be able to sort out in the middle of nowhere on his own. If he could just get her home and find the doctor, then maybe she might have a chance.

'Hang on for me, my love,' he said as he pushed his horse into a gallop, cradling her body in his lap.

The ride home had been the longest ten minutes of his life and as Edward thundered into the courtyard he felt a great sense of relief. Amelia was still breathing, he could see the rise and fall of her chest, but there were more bloodstained bubbles appearing between her lips. As he slid from the horse, lifting Amelia carefully down after him, he shouted for help, loud enough to wake the entire household. Before he had entered the front door Mrs Henshaw was hurrying out of the kitchen, the other servants trailing behind her.

'Amelia's hurt. Send someone to fetch the doctor immediately,' Edward ordered, knowing he couldn't rely on McNair to do as he had asked.

For a moment all the servants froze as they took in Amelia's deathly pale face, the bloodstained dress and her shallow, noisy breathing. Then Mrs Henshaw rallied and began issuing orders.

'Tom, ride and get Dr Bolton from the village. Daniel, ride and get Dr Peacewell from South Heighton. Girls, we need fresh water and clean sheets.'

Edward didn't hear any more as he was already half-way up the stairs, but he felt some relief that Mrs Henshaw was in charge of the practical matters. Now he just had to focus on Amelia.

He carried her straight to his bedroom, laying her down on the bed they had shared the night before. Carefully he peeled away the blood-soaked material of his shirt sleeve, pulled down the neckline of her dress and ripped open her chemise underneath.

With the wound exposed Edward felt himself sway slightly at the shock of how serious her injury was. A large circular hole gaped just below her collarbone, the edges ragged and seeping blood. As Mrs Henshaw entered with the water and sheets he took some of the clean material and pressed it firmly against the wound.

He felt an immense relief when Amelia grimaced. Of course he didn't want her to be in pain, but pain meant she was still alive and whilst she was still alive there was hope.

'Please don't die,' he whispered as he sat down next to her.

There was no response, just the shallow, raspy breaths that told him she was still holding on for now.

A commotion outside the doorway roused him from his vigil and he was relieved when the tall, thin frame of Dr Bolton walked into the room.

'Thank you for coming, Doctor.'

'I didn't have much choice,' Dr Bolton said. 'A young man raised such a fuss I couldn't exactly refuse.'

So McNair *had* gone to fetch the doctor. There was no

way Tom would have been back with the elderly physician yet, so McNair must have felt some remorse.

'What happened here?'

'She was shot, at a range of about twenty feet. She's lost a lot of blood.'

The doctor moved close to Amelia's side and carefully removed the wadding Edward had used to try to stem the blood from her wound. He drew a sharp intake of breath as he examined the damage.

'Can you do anything for her?' Edward asked, hearing the faint pleading note to his voice.

'The bullet has penetrated through to her chest cavity and hit part of her lung...' The doctor paused, frowning.

'What is it?'

'I can't quite work out why she isn't dead yet.'

Edward felt his whole world start to collapse.

'If the bullet penetrates the lung then normally the damaged tissue bleeds profusely into the rest of the lung, effectively drowning the patient. Or sometimes the lung itself will collapse. Either way the patient normally dies within a matter of minutes.'

Edward glanced at Amelia's pale face and the laboured rise and fall of her chest. He hated the detached, clinical way Dr Bolton was talking about Amelia. She was a beautiful, caring, vibrant woman, not some dead flesh on a slab.

'Can you help her?'

'Well, she's unconscious so she's not in any pain...' The doctor trailed off as he saw Edward's expression.

'This woman means everything to me,' he said quietly. 'You will do everything in your power to try to save her life.'

'I don't know...'

'Everything in your power, Doctor.'

Edward spoke softly, but the force of his emotion was obvious in his tone.

'Ah, I see you arrived before me,' a friendly voice came from the doorway.

'Dr Peacewell,' Edward greeted the young man dressed all in black.

'Everything is under control, Dr Peacewell, there is no need for *your* breed of medicine,' Dr Bolton said icily.

Dr Peacewell breezed into the room as if he hadn't heard the older doctor. Gently he pushed his way to Amelia's bedside, his eyes darting across her body, assessing the damage. Edward watched as the younger doctor felt for Amelia's pulse, laid a hand on her chest to check her breathing and then carefully examined the wound.

'She's been very lucky,' he said finally.

'Yes, thank you, Dr Peacewell. I established that almost ten minutes ago.'

Dr Peacewell ignored his colleague and turned to Edward. 'If she is to have any chance of surviving we need to remove the bullet, but that is not without risks—'

'I disagree,' Dr Bolton interrupted.

'Let the man speak,' Edward warned firmly.

'As we remove the bullet the lung could collapse, or there could be further bleeding.'

'And if we don't remove the bullet?' Edward asked.

'Then she will die.'

It wasn't as though there was much of a decision to make. Amelia was a fighter and she deserved the chance to fight for her life. Doing nothing would be cruel and stupid.

'Do it,' Edward said, grasping Amelia's hand to give him strength.

'I object,' Dr Bolton said.

'Do you have an alternative plan?' Edward asked.

'This is cruel and unnecessary. We should ensure the young lady's passing is as peaceful as possible.'

'Either you help or you get out,' Edward said.

Dr Peacewell was already rolling up his sleeves and unpacking row after row of surgical instruments from his bag.

Edward watched as Dr Bolton hesitated, but then pushed up his own sleeves and began to prepare the wound.

'The bullet looks as though it has gone in at an angle and chipped against the clavicle,' Dr Bolton said as Dr Peacewell stretched open the already gaping hole. 'It will be difficult to grab hold of, especially as there might be bone fragments loose in there, too.'

'I propose you stabilise the area externally. I will try and hook the bullet forward and then, once it is visible, you grasp hold of it with the forceps.'

Both doctors set to work and Edward watched with a worried fascination. Dr Bolton held the skin back for his colleague and waited whilst Dr Peacewell fished around in the wound with a long, thin instrument. Edward grimaced as he struck bone and a dull scraping sound followed. Amelia's breathing was shallow but steady throughout and Edward was just beginning to wonder if maybe she might survive when she uttered a low, animalistic groan. It was a primal sound, like that of a wounded animal, and it made both doctors stop momentarily.

'She's in pain,' Edward said, grasping her hand even tighter.

'We need to continue,' Dr Peacewell said, his expression worried.

Edward wanted to stop them, wanted to ease Amelia's discomfort, but he knew if he did then she would certainly die. Hearing her moan in pain and doing nothing was the hardest thing that he'd ever had to do, but he didn't interfere any more.

'I've got it,' Dr Peacewell said five minutes later.

Dr Bolton reached into the wound with the forceps and plucked out the small bullet Dr Peacewell was pushing forward. Once the bullet was out all three men watched Amelia carefully. If she was going to bleed or her lung was going to collapse, it would be now.

'I'll dress the wound,' Dr Peacewell said. 'It is too soon to say if she will survive or not, but there's not much more we can do.'

Edward nodded, his eyes fixed on the rise and fall of Amelia's chest. For now, at least, she was still breathing.

Chapter Twenty-Six

'Why don't you go and get some rest, Master Edward?' Mrs Henshaw suggested, addressing him as she used to when he was a boy.

'I can't leave her.'

'I'll sit with her a while. You must be exhausted.'

He was exhausted. It had been nearly two days since the duel, two excruciating, tortuous days. In that time the doctors had been to check Amelia over four times, but not much had changed. Still she was breathing, still her heart beat, but her eyes never flickered open and there was no sign Amelia was behind her closed lids. A few hours after the impromptu surgery to remove the bullet Amelia had grown hot with fever, and over the past two days both doctors hadn't dared speculate whether she would survive this latest development, but were clear she would only wake once the fever was under control.

'I can't leave her,' Edward repeated. If he left her then he had this peculiar fear that she might die whilst he was away. If he could just sit it out, remain by her side, then maybe everything would work out.

'Then let me sit with you for a few minutes.'

It was comforting to have Mrs Henshaw's presence by

his side. For a while he could imagine they were just waiting for Amelia to wake from a normal sleep, ready to jump up and enjoy the new day.

'What happened?' Mrs Henshaw asked softly.

'I was a stupid fool,' Edward replied, keeping his voice low. 'I didn't realise what I had until I lost it.'

'You pushed her away?'

Edward nodded, for in a way he had. Oh, he had held Amelia tenderly, whispered he cared for her, even made love to her, but he hadn't given himself to her fully, that he could see now. If only he'd let go of that final piece of himself, if only he'd shared the decision about McNair with her, then maybe it would be him lying in her place as it should have been.

He regretted not telling her he loved her. He hadn't realised it before the duel, he'd been too afraid he wasn't good enough, wasn't the man to protect her and cherish her. He'd been too preoccupied with regrets about failing to keep her safe from McNair that he hadn't realised what she truly had needed from him. Now he'd give anything to see her face light up as he whispered a declaration of love into her ear.

'I thought it was my duty to protect her,' he said eventually, 'but I didn't realise the thing that would hurt her the most would be pushing her away.'

Mrs Henshaw remained silent by his side, stroking the back of Amelia's hand.

'I wish I could tell her I'm sorry,' he said. 'I wish I could tell her how much I regret my actions.'

'You can, dear,' Mrs Henshaw said. 'She's listening, even if her eyes aren't open. Talk to her, let her know you're here and let her know she's got something to wake up for.'

The older woman stood and kissed him lovingly on the top of his head, then made her way from the room.

Edward sat in silence for a few minutes, wondering if Mrs Henshaw was right or if he would be stupid to sit here talking to an unconscious Amelia. Realising he had nothing to lose, he took a deep breath and gathered his thoughts.

'I'm sorry, Amelia,' he whispered quietly, holding on to her hand as though it were an unbreakable connection between them. 'I got so caught up in my own head…so caught up in the idea that I had to protect you I didn't even think about what you really needed.' He paused and then pushed on, knowing the words had to be said. 'I thought I'd failed you. I promised to keep you safe and protect you from McNair. When I couldn't do that I felt an absolute failure. I thought that you deserved better.'

Gently he shook his head. If only he hadn't tried to punish himself by agreeing to the duel. It had been self-indulgent and selfish, and if he'd just thought things through a little better then Amelia might never have got hurt.

'I know you saw that, I know you saw I was going to meet McNair for the duel to punish myself, but I was too caught up in the moment to realise it.'

He wished he could turn back the clock…that he was still in bed with Amelia tucked into the crook of his arm and instead of misleading her he had actually discussed the situation and came up with a better solution than meeting McNair with pistols at dawn.

'Please don't leave me, Amelia. I need your strength, your resolve. I love you.'

He watched her eyes, hoping for some flicker of acknowledgement, some sign that she might have heard what he was saying. Edward knew there was a good chance she might never wake up. Both doctors had been pretty clear on the subject. Right now Edward couldn't think about how he would survive if she died. At first he had wondered if he would shrivel and die, too, but as he had spent the hours by her side he knew no matter what he would keep on fighting his demons for Amelia.

Another thing that scared him was the thought of her walking away from him. He knew if she ever did wake up there was a good chance he had ruined any possibility of having a future together. He'd misled her and even if he hadn't lied to her outright, he'd certainly lied by omission.

Edward stood, stretched and carefully got on to the bed beside Amelia. Gently he wrapped an arm around her and held her as he had the first night they'd met.

Amelia struggled to open her eyes. She'd never been a morning person, but today it felt particularly difficult to lift her lids. As she became more aware of her body she realised there was a dull ache in her shoulder and a sharp, shooting pain every time she breathed in. The events on the duelling field came rushing back and Amelia felt her pulse quicken as she remembered the searing pain as she'd dived in front of Edward.

'Edward,' she murmured, her voice coming out as a dry croak and her lips cracking painfully.

She felt his warm presence beside her, his arm draped over her midsection protectively. He looked exhausted, even in sleep, with deep dark circles around his eyes and a few days' growth on his jawline.

As she tried to sit up in bed the pain ripped through her chest and she let out a loud squeal. Immediately Edward was awake, looking at her with a mixture of disbelief and hope.

'Amelia,' he said, gently taking hold of her and propping the pillows behind her so she was comfortable. 'I thought I'd lost you.'

'Water,' she managed to croak and sipped gratefully at the glass he held to her lips. The water was warm, but as it soothed her parched throat she thought it was the most delicious drink in the world.

'Are you in pain?' Edward asked. 'The doctor left some laudanum.'

Amelia shook her head. Maybe soon the pain would get too much, but for now she wanted to think without the heavy haze laudanum brought on.

'What happened?' she asked.

'What do you remember?'

Amelia closed her eyes for a moment. Trying to think was like putting together a puzzle where half the pieces were missing.

'I remember waking up and finding you gone and dashing out to the stables.' She paused, frowning, 'And I remember reaching you just as you were walking out to the markers to start the duel.'

'Do you remember what happened next?'

Amelia bit her lip, trying to focus. The memories were all there, but they were fragmented and distorted, as if she were looking at them through curved glass. Then all of a sudden things came into focus and she remembered the sound of the shot being fired and her jumping out in front of Edward, followed by nothing but pain.

'You saved my life,' Edward said softly. 'You jumped into the path of a bullet for me.'

'How silly of me,' Amelia said, trying to keep her voice light.

'Downright reckless,' Edward agreed. 'The bullet hit you in the chest, just below your collarbone.'

Amelia glanced down at the bulky white bandage covering her entire shoulder.

'It penetrated your lung and glanced off the bone. The doctors said you're very lucky to be alive.' Edward's voice held just a hint of a tremble. 'We weren't sure if you would ever wake up.'

'Is the bullet still in there?' Amelia asked, running her fingers over the bandage gently.

'No, they fished it out. Apparently you are more likely to die of the wound putrefying if the bullet is left in.'

'It sounds as though you've become quite an expert.'

'I've never been so worried in my entire life.'

'Edward, we need to talk,' Amelia said softly.

She saw the panic in his eyes and wanted to reach out and soothe him, but quickly he stood up, distancing himself from her.

'I know,' he said. 'But first you must rest. We'll talk later, I promise.'

Gently he leaned over and kissed her on the forehead, brushing his lips against her skin as though she were made of porcelain.

Amelia didn't protest as he left the room. In truth, she did feel exhausted and to manage the emotional intensity of the talk they needed to have she wanted to be in a better condition. Closing her eyes, she listened to Edward's retreating footsteps and wondered just what the future held for them.

Chapter Twenty-Seven

A week and a half later Amelia was feeling much stronger and now she was beginning to get restless. She'd never been good at sitting still and now she'd spent the longest time ever confined to her bedroom. Edward had sat with her most of the time, reading passages from his book aloud, or discussing the renovations he planned on the house, and that had helped to pass the time, but now Amelia was desperate to get out of this room and feel the sun on her face.

'You have to be very careful,' Dr Peacewell warned. 'The wound could still open up and your lung needs time to heal.'

'But maybe I could just take a short trip outside,' Amelia suggested.

She'd even settle for sitting in a different room for an hour or two.

Dr Peacewell looked at her appraisingly. 'Very well,' he said, 'but just a short trip. And then it's back to bed to recuperate.'

'Yes, Doctor,' Amelia said meekly, catching Edward's eye and grinning once the doctor had turned his back.

'A short trip,' Edward reinforced after the doctor had

left, 'And if you begin to look tired I'll bring you straight back to bed.'

Amelia nodded, not bothering to argue. She'd got what she wanted. Soon she would be sitting with the sun warming her face and the breeze in her hair.

'And then maybe we should have that talk.'

Amelia looked at Edward in surprise. Every time she had brought up their need to discuss the future since she'd woken up he'd shaken his head and said she wasn't strong enough. Now he was agreeing to talk Amelia felt nervous about what he might say. She was very conscious that she had declared her love just before the duel had started and not received any words of love in return. Edward cared for her, he looked after her more than anyone had in her entire life, but she craved another sign that would tell her he felt something deeper.

An hour later Edward reappeared and looked her over carefully.

'Are you sure you want to do this?' he asked, concern etched on his features.

'Edward, if you don't take me outside now I might scream.'

Carefully he scooped her up into his arms and ensured she was comfortable before making his way through the house.

'Be careful, ducky,' Goody called after them as Edward pushed out through the front door and into the sunshine.

Amelia sighed with contentment. Finally she had escaped her sick chamber. Even just a few minutes out here in the daylight would do her the world of good.

'I heard from Mr Pollard,' Edward said as he carried her carefully across the lawn.

Amelia stiffened and found herself struggling to breathe.

'There's no need to worry,' he soothed her. 'Your cousin is back with the Earl of Burwell. Mr Pollard has delivered your letters and I am sure you will hear from Lizzie soon.'

Amelia let go of the breath she had been holding and smiled. Finally she could stop worrying about Lizzie and instead await the news on what was happening between her beloved cousin and this Earl. Maybe Lizzie had found the man she wanted to spend her life with, too.

'Can you bear to be carried a bit longer?' Edward asked.

'If you're not tiring,' Amelia said, 'I could spend all day up here.'

He carried her through the gardens, treading carefully so as not to disturb her wound. After a few minutes Amelia realised where they were going and couldn't help but smile. He was taking her to the secret walled garden, the first place they had allowed themselves a long, leisurely kiss. It was very apt for the serious conversation they were going to have to have.

Once inside the garden Edward set her down in a chair he must have brought over from the house earlier and spent a moment ensuring she was quite comfortable.

'Stop fussing,' Amelia said, swatting him away, 'I'm not an old invalid.'

'You were shot in the chest less than a fortnight ago. I'm allowed to fuss.'

Amelia smiled, closing her eyes and lifting her face to the sun. For a few minutes she just sat there, enjoying the feeling of being alive, listening to the buzzing of the bees and the hum of the insects.

'What has happened to McNair?' Amelia asked as the thought popped into her head.

She heard Edward grimace and opened her eyes.

'He's fled the country. I should imagine he was scared of retribution for shooting you.'

'He's actually left the country?'

Edward nodded. 'I think he realised I would have killed him if you died.'

'Do you think he'll come back?'

'Maybe once he's heard you're alive, but I don't think he will bother us again.'

'I suppose he exacted his revenge. I was injured just as he was.'

'Let's not talk of McNair any longer,' Edward said and Amelia sensed the conversation was about to get serious.

'We need to talk about the future,' she said after a minute.

Edward looked nervous, she realised, as if he had been dreading this conversation. Her heart began to sink as she wondered if he wanted to pull away from her, whether this brush with death had been enough to make him realise he didn't love her.

'Before we make any decisions I need to apologise,' Edward said, 'for many things.'

Amelia frowned. Yes, he had been a bit stubborn racing off to the duel with McNair, but his heart had been in the right place.

'I wanted to protect you.'

'There's no need to apologise for that.'

'Let me finish. I wanted to protect you and when I failed I felt as though I didn't deserve you. That clouded my judgement'

Amelia leant forward, grimacing as the pain shot through her shoulder, and took hold of Edward's hand. She didn't interrupt, sensing he needed to get whatever he wanted to say off his chest.

'After the incident on the beach I felt as though I'd been

given another chance at happiness. Even with the threat of McNair's revenge hanging over us I thought if I could protect the woman that I loved then all would be well.'

Amelia felt her heart leap in her chest and struggled to concentrate on what Edward said next.

'When McNair broke in and I wasn't there to protect you, it felt as though I'd failed all over again. I didn't think I deserved you, not if I couldn't protect you from a man who wished you harm.' Edward paused, looking into Amelia's eyes. 'But I shouldn't have deceived you. I should have told you I was going to meet McNair, not let you wake to an empty bed. For that I am truly sorry.'

'I know you acted out of consideration for my well-being,' Amelia said quietly. 'It might have been the wrong thing to do, but I can't question your motives.

'I think there was also a little bit of me that wanted to punish myself for not protecting you.'

Amelia shrugged. 'We're all human, we're all flawed.'

'I should have realised we needed to make that decision together. It was wrong of me to push you out and I know it was what got you shot.'

She studied his expression, trying to read his thoughts. For a while she had wondered if Edward blamed himself for her injury. It had been McNair who had aimed the pistol, McNair who had pulled the trigger, but it would be just like Edward to blame himself.

'You need to let go of this guilt and this sense of responsibility for everything. I made my own decision when I followed you to the duel site, I made my own decision when I jumped in between you and McNair. That wasn't you.'

'I know,' Edward said quietly.

'We both made mistakes, but you can't live your life in a perpetual cycle of guilt and regret.'

'You're right,' Edward said. 'But I refuse to give up my sense of responsibility for you,' he added with a smile.

Amelia leant forward, ignoring the pain shooting through her chest, and pulled Edward towards her until his lips rested on hers.

'You saved me, Edward,' she said after a long, deep kiss. 'You saved my life.'

Amelia felt her heart soar as he kissed her back. For ten long days, ever since waking up after being shot, she had wondered what the future might hold, but sitting here kissing Edward she was in no doubt. His kiss contained love and hope and passion. He couldn't kiss her like that and then tell her they couldn't be together.

'What's next?' she asked as she pulled away, looking up into Edward's dark eyes.

'Well, I thought I'd kiss you again,' Edward said, a teasing note to his voice.

Amelia swatted him on the arm, but before she could exert herself any further Edward slipped from his chair and knelt in front of her.

'Before you came bursting into my home I thought my life was over,' he said. 'I couldn't see a way through the grief and the guilt. I'd built this cocoon of solitude and I was slowly suffocating in it.'

Amelia thought back to the man she'd first encountered on that stormy night when she had stumbled into Beechwood Manor. He *had* been slowly suffocating in his self-imposed solitary confinement.

'It's not just your life that's changed,' Amelia said, her heart beginning to beat faster as she realised what Edward was building up to.

'Well, you're no longer a murderer,' Edward said with a grin.

'I'm no longer a lot of things.'

She'd been bored and lonely before coming to England, a spoiled young woman who was acting outrageously to try to relieve the tedium. No wonder her father had been eager for her to find a husband and settle down.

'I know exactly what you are, Amelia.' Edward paused, looking into her eyes before continuing, 'The woman I love.'

Amelia felt the tears spring to her eyes. He loved her. There was nothing more that she desired in the world.

'And I love you, too.'

'I would very much like you to be my wife.'

Amelia grasped Edward by the shoulders and pulled him in for a passionate kiss. His wife. That would mean they would spend every blissful day together for years and years to come.

'And I would very much like for you to be my husband,' she said as they broke apart.

'I can't promise it will be easy. I know I have a lot of issues to work through.'

'Stop trying to put me off.' Amelia laughed, kissing him again. 'You won't succeed.'

'But I will promise to love you for eternity.'

'Eternity is a very long time.'

'You'd better behave yourself then,' Edward said, dodging Amelia's hand as she swatted at him.

Amelia took his hand and squeezed her eyes closed. When she had first stumbled on Beechwood Manor in the middle of the storm she'd never imagined things would end like this. Fear and regret had been turned into love and compassion and it was all thanks to the man she would spend the rest of her life with.

Epilogue

~~~~~~~~

Amelia darted forward and dabbed a blob of paint on Edward's nose. For a moment he looked disapproving and stern, making Amelia pause, before he grinned and caught her by surprise with a paint attack of his own.

'So this is why you wanted to help decorate,' Edward said as he drew Amelia in closer to him.

The workmen from Turnball and Son, the decorating company who had transformed much of Beechwood Manor over the past few months, largely ignored Edward and Amelia now. Although it wasn't normal for clients to want to pick up a paintbrush, Sir and Lady Gray seemed to live in their own little world, one where they didn't much care for the customs of normal society.

'What do you think of the colour?' Amelia asked, standing back and admiring the progress.

'I think it looks very fetching on you,' Edward said, daubing another blob of paint on her cheek. 'Although it does clash with your dress a little.' He came in closer and whispered in her ear, 'Maybe we should take the dress off.'

Amelia felt the familiar surge of desire as Edward's breath tickled her neck and she knew it wouldn't be long

until he scooped her up into his arms and carried her up
to the bedroom.

'Focus, Sir Edward,' Amelia said, trying out her best
strict voice.

'Yes, darling, now what was the question?'

Amelia struggled to maintain her composure as Edward moved in closer and peppered kisses across the back
of her neck.

'What do you think of the colour?' she managed to
stutter.

'It's grey.'

Amelia sighed. It wasn't grey—well, not exactly. Mr
Turnball the younger had explained it was called celestial
blue and was a calming, delicate shade that worked perfectly for a nursery.

'It's a very nice grey,' Edward added as he caught her
sigh. 'I'm sure young Mistress Gray will appreciate it.'

Amelia felt her hands move instinctively to her round
belly, her fingers trailing over the hard bump that held
their first son or daughter. Edward was convinced she
was carrying a girl, a daughter for him to dote on and
indulge. Amelia secretly thought the child inside her was
a boy, but she was content to wait another month to find
out.

'Do you think they'll be finished in time?' she asked,
smiling as she felt a kick from inside her.

'As long as little Mistress Gray stays put for another
few weeks, the nursery will be perfect.'

Rather than rebuild the nursery in the East Wing they
had decided to transform one of the rooms in the main section of the house into a space for their children. Edward
had suggested the idea, stating he wanted a fresh start for
their growing family. The East Wing had been largely de-
molished and in its place they had planted a rose garden

together, somewhere Edward could go and sit, surrounded by the beautiful flowers, and remember his son and his late wife if ever he needed to. Often of an evening they would walk through the rose garden together, hand in hand, talking of the past and planning for the future.

'I think she's perfectly comfortable where she is,' Amelia said, placing Edward's hand on her belly so he could feel their child's kick. 'I doubt whether she's going to grace us with her presence any time soon.'

Edward smiled as he felt the strong kick of their baby and after a few moments he took the paintbrush from Amelia's hand.

'She'd better wait for your father to arrive,' Edward grumbled. 'He is adamant he wants to be here for the birth of his first grandchild.'

It was the first time Amelia would have seen her father since leaving India almost eighteen months ago, and although she knew he would reprimand her for all that had happened with Captain McNair, Amelia couldn't wait to see him.

'That's enough exertion for one day,' Edward said, taking hold of her paintbrush, 'Now you must rest.'

Amelia pulled a face. Even at eight months pregnant she wasn't good at sitting still.

'Your cousin will be here later this afternoon and I'm sure you'll want to have some energy to greet her properly.'

Amelia let Edward lead her from the nursery, but when he tried to guide her upstairs she pulled gently on his arm and directed him outside. They walked through the garden in the crisp mid-morning air and Amelia enjoyed the crunch of the lingering frost under her feet.

She couldn't wait to see her cousin Lizzie later and show her all the changes they'd made on the house. Lizzie was coming to stay, with her husband Daniel, the Earl of Bur-

well, and their six-month-old baby, Oliver, for the foreseeable future. She'd promised to be there for the birth of
Amelia's baby even though she had a little one of her own.
When Amelia had protested Lizzie had laughed her off,
saying it was unthinkable that she could miss the birth.
It was typical of her cousin, always putting everyone else
before herself, but Amelia wanted her there so much that
she hadn't protested too much.

'Do you think everything will change once the baby is
born?' Amelia asked.

'Are you worried?'

She shook her head. Ever since their wedding just over
a year ago Amelia had known she'd wanted to be a mother.
Before Edward she hadn't really thought of having a family of her own, but as soon as they'd said their marriage
vows Amelia had known she wanted to make a family with
the man she loved. He would be a brilliant father and she
couldn't wait to hold their baby in her arms and share some
of the love she already felt for the little person inside of her.

'I think a lot will change, but much will stay the same.
I will still love you.'

'I can't imagine having someone completely reliant on
me, someone who needs to be cared for every minute of
the day.'

'You'll be a brilliant mother, Amelia, you've got nothing to worry about.'

She supposed maybe she was a little worried if she was
honest. She loved the baby inside her already, but she just
hoped she was good enough to be its mother.

'And I'll be by your side every moment of every day.'

Amelia felt some of her worries melt away as Edward
squeezed her hand and then pulled her along the path that
led to their secret garden. Once they were inside he di-

rected her to the rope swing and ensured she was comfortable.

'Are you sure this will take my weight?' Amelia asked, testing it carefully.

'You're still tiny,' Edward said. 'And remember in the summer it took the weight of both of us.'

Amelia felt the blood rushing to her cheeks as she remembered the balmy evening they had spent entwined on the swing. Of course she wasn't still tiny. Her pregnant belly was huge compared to many women in the same stage as her, but Edward always brushed it off, saying she would just have a healthy, bonny baby.

'Sit back and relax, my lady,' Edward instructed. Gently he began pushing her backwards and forwards, every so often darting in to place a kiss on the nape of her neck.

Amelia was just starting to relax back when she felt something warm and wet soaking through her skirts. For a moment she was paralysed, unable to speak, unable to comprehend what was happening.

'Edward,' she managed to whisper eventually, 'I think my waters have just broken.'

Edward paced up and down the corridor, growling at anyone who came near him.

'Relax, old chap,' said Daniel, Lizzie's husband, as he prowled past him. 'Women have been giving birth successfully for thousands of years.'

He knew it was true, but surely it shouldn't take this long. She had been labouring for nearly twenty hours and the cries of pain coming from the room were no less intense, even if Edward could hear the exhaustion in Amelia's voice.

'Don't fret, Sir Edward,' Mr Guthry said in his perpetually cheerful voice. 'I've never known a stronger or more determined young woman than Miss Amelia.'

All three men were positioned in the corridor outside Amelia's bedchamber, with Mrs Henshaw dashing backwards and forwards with cups of tea and plates of biscuits to sustain them as they waited. Every so often she would stop and let Mr Guthry squeeze her hand in reassurance, before busying herself again.

The muffled voice of Lizzie came through the door. 'Come on, Amelia darling, push!'

Edward couldn't bear it any longer. He threw open the door to their bedroom and dashed inside. The midwife turned to him with indignation, but Edward pushed past her to Amelia's side.

'You can do it, my sweet,' he said, grasping her hand.

For a second their eyes met, then Amelia squeezed her eyelids shut and put every ounce of her being into pushing. Edward couldn't see what was happening down below, but he heard a slippery little gush and Lizzie's intake of breath.

After a couple of seconds an insistent tiny cry started and Edward found himself holding his breath as the midwife carefully wrapped their child in a bundle and handed it to Amelia.

'Your son,' she said.

Edward felt himself stumble a little and had to sit down on the edge of the bed. He had a son…another son to dote on and cherish. Throughout Amelia's pregnancy he hadn't known how he would feel if their child was a son. He knew no one could replace Thomas in his heart, but now, looking down at the small, perfect little baby boy in Amelia's arms, Edward knew he had been silly to worry. This was his child, his son, and he would love him with all his heart, just as he loved Amelia.

He watched as Amelia kissed their son on the tip of his tiny nose and then grimaced.

'It hurts,' she said, groaning again.

Quickly Edward took the baby from her as she clutched at the bedsheets and moaned in pain.

'It's just the afterbirth, Amelia,' Lizzie said, coming to her cousin's side.

'It hurts,' Amelia repeated, her face pale.

The midwife fussed around for a few minutes whilst Amelia grew increasingly agitated, placing her hands on Amelia's belly and then disappearing to the foot of the bed.

'I'm not quite sure,' the midwife said eventually, 'but I think there's another baby in there.'

Edward and Amelia froze and looked at each other, before another spasm of pain took all of Amelia's attention.

'We need the doctor,' the midwife said.

Immediately Lizzie left the room, returning a couple of minutes later.

'One of the servants will ride to fetch Dr Peacewell,' she said, coming back to her cousin's side.

'I can't wait,' Amelia groaned.

Edward saw all the tension and pain on her face as she focused on pushing. He wished he could take some of the agony and suffer it for her. She was so brave, his wonderful wife, and he vowed to cherish her every single day of their lives, just as long as she made it through the next little while. He couldn't bear the prospect of a future without her. Together they were strong, but as Edward looked down at the baby in his arms he knew no matter what he would survive for his son.

Thirty agonising minutes later a second cry filled the room and Edward watched as the midwife handed his wife their daughter.

'One of each,' she said, looking up at him, 'We were both right.'

Edward perched on the bed next to her, helping her hold both their children in her arms, and found himself wondering at how close he had come to giving up on life. If he had given in to his grief and his guilt then he would never be sitting here right now, holding the woman that he loved and his two children. Two years ago Edward would have dismissed this sort of happy family scenario, but now it was his reality.

He smiled as Amelia tried to push herself up in the bed, wriggling her backside and kicking off some of the bedsheets.

'For once in your life sit still, woman,' he said gruffly. 'You've just given birth twice.'

Amelia flashed him a tired but mischievous grin. 'You'll have three of us to run after now.'

'What have I let myself in for?' Edward murmured, bending forward and kissing Amelia gently on the forehead.

* * * * *